CJ WARRANT
AWARD WINNING AUTHOR

FORGETTING
JANE

FORGETTING JANE

CJ WARRANT

Forgetting Jane
by CJ Warrant © 2019

Cover Design by Anne Berkeley

Dedication

I want to dedicate this book to some special people in my life. First, to my husband David. You are, and always will be my steady rock, my home when I feel lost and the center of my universe. I love you. To my children, for all of their patience when dinner isn't ready.
Love you three!
To my parents. You've given me life, but also taught me that no matter what life hands out—good or bad, I have to push back or pull with all my might to achieve what I want. Through happiness and loss, I learned by example; to be strong, persevere and strive to be the best I can be. I love you both!

PROLOGUE

October 6th
Edge of Beaver Lake, Wisconsin

'm alive.

The first drag of cold air into her lungs burned like acid. Her fingers stung deep under their nail beds as she clawed to get free from the hard ground.

She tried moving her legs, but her energy waned fast. No matter how hard she wrestled to get out of the hole, the lower half of her body was bound in the heavy, compacted earth.

She wanted to lift her head, but her neck seemed craned the wrong way and her right cheek was stuck to the putrid dirt.

The sharp wind layered over her like an icy blanket. A prickly sensation skated across her bare back—like hundreds of razor blades, making her shiver in pain.

An owl screeching in the distance gave her pause. Where was she? Murky darkness surrounded her.

Although a sliver of morning light skimmed the horizon, the day hadn't warmed yet. God, she wished for that heat now.

Still too exhausted to move, she closed her left eye —her right one didn't seem to be working, then listened to what was around her.

With each breath she took into her sore lungs, jumbled images she didn't understand began to drift in and out of her consciousness.

In the distance, hollow reeds and cattails rustled as they were stirred by the wind. She jerked fully awake and pain instantly lashed throughout her body like a bull-whip, unbearable, and tears blurred her vision.

Remaining as still as possible, the pain finally dissipated from her body... or was she becoming numb from the cold? Maybe so, since the sharp whacking at the back of her skull had subsided to a continual dull ache.

Her joints were rigid; her brain screamed out orders to get up, but her muscles refused. She was too cold and too tired to move, though she suspected she had no choice. Even with no memory of how she came to be in this wretched state, her instincts told her that whoever did this to her might come back and finish the job.

If only her body would cooperate. Her left eyelid was the only body part that moved semi-normally. It opened, drifted closed, and opened again; she used whatever energy she could muster to keep it from closing for good.

But no matter how hard she tried to focus on her surroundings, she wasn't able to see anything specific.

Then a filmy splash of yellow drew her good eye. Was that a girl? She stood at a distance—what, to watch her die?

I need your help! She wanted to call out but her tongue

was stuck to the roof of her parched mouth. She attempted to draw out some saliva, but without success.

Keeping her focus on the girl, she noticed that the yellow sundress rippled softly with the wind but the girl's long, golden hair did not, which sent a jolt of unease down her spine.

Despite that, she needed help. Between her injuries and still being half buried, she wasn't going to last much longer out here.

With every ounce of energy she could scrape together, she attempted to call out, but with the cold, her jaw felt wired shut.

Why won't she help me out of this hole?

Frustrated and with pain coursing through her, more tears blurred her vision. As she blinked to clear the haze, the girl vanished as though she was never there.

Where did she go?

A scream lodged in the back of her throat for the girl to come back. But it was no use, and now she was alone again.

Fear scurried down her spine like a fast-moving millipede. She closed her eye to ward off the sickening knowledge that she was going to die.

Nothing made sense anymore. Between the icy chill and the pain crawling into every cell of her body, the lure of sleep dragged her into the dark, wanting to take over her dreams.

Let this be a nightmare, and I'm in my bed, safe and warm. And when I wake up, I'll be safe—

Pop! Pop—pop!

She jerked awake again. This time the pain lanced through her body as though it carved out a permanent space right in her core.

Pop!

That was a gun. Could it be *the one* who did this to

her? Did he come back to finish her off? Terror flooded her like she was drowning. No hope for her at all.

No, damn it. Don't give up. Fight.

She compelled herself to move again, but her muscles had no strength left—no viable power in them.

Clinking sounds of metal resonated in the air, and her lungs seized.

The noise was getting louder. Her gut ratcheted tight. She swallowed was difficulty, taking the grit and copper on her swollen tongue to the back of her dry throat.

Whoever this was stood so close that the frozen sprigs of grass next to her head crackled. She didn't dare move, but waited to see what *they* would do.

She waited. And waited, until her lungs burned from holding her breath.

She wished this nightmare was over, and asked Death to finish her. As tears slipped from the corners of her eyes, she prayed it would be quick.

Please—

A soft yap halted her plea. A coyote? Her fear intensified. Being eaten alive wasn't how she saw her life ending.

The animal sniffed about. So close now. She took a quick bleary glance. *A wolf?* No. He yapped and nudged her arm. Needles shot from her elbow to her fingertips. With every rough caress of the animal's tongue, electricity zapped her limb.

Another hazy look, and relief flooded her. It was a dog.

The dog barked feverishly. Then muted voices carried on the wind, and she stifled her budding hope of a rescue. Instead, dread coiled tighter inside her chest like wrestling pythons.

But what if the dog belongs to... him?

It doesn't matter. So tired now. Her eyelid became heavier, and without fighting it, she let it close. She didn't care anymore.

Don't sleep, her conscious told her, but she wanted to ignore it.

Those muted voices became clearer. Men... bickering?

"Skill, brother. That's what I got."

"What the..."

Silence.

Pushing away the pain and sleepiness, she tried once more to move. Her index finger twitched, which gave her a shot of hope. If she could jump for joy, she would have right then.

The sound of clomping boots echoed through the ear not stuck to the ground. The vibrations of their movement reverberated off her body like a tuning fork. Her skin seared with heat as a pair of hot hands clasped around her wrists.

"She's alive! Call Eli..." one man shouted, though she didn't care who.

Someone's found me.

CHAPTER ONE

"Slow down, Harold, and tell me what you found." Elias McAvoy kept his tone even. First time anyone had called him before dawn on a Sunday morning since he'd taken over the chief position four months ago, and it had to be one of his childhood friends.

"A naked woman, dammit," Harold repeated through haggard breaths.

"Try to stay calm—"

"Calm? She's a fucking popsicle! She's covered in blood—and she's dying," Harold's screech resonated like the phone was a bullhorn.

Elias yanked the cell phone away from his ear, hating that he was being yelled at, but understood his friend was freaking out.

He needed to calm Harold down before the man did something stupid. "Got blankets?" Elias's voice raised an octave, but retained a level of calm.

There was a whoosh of breath. "Yeah. W-why?"

"I want you to cover her, but don't move her in case her injuries are severe. Where are you guys?"

"West side of Beaver Lake, just by the buckthorn cover, where we used to go duck hunting." Harold's voice shook.

"Stay put, I'll be right there." Elias jabbed the off button on his cell, got out of bed and grabbed his radio.

Once Elias got a hold of his second in command, Officer Tom Faber, who patrolled the west side of the county, and Officer Tyson Ryan for back up to the scene, he then called for an ambulance.

Elias rushed out of his family farmhouse and drove to the outer edge of Beaver Lake. Thankful he knew the area well. He had the lights flashing and sped all the way there.

He jammed on his brakes, the vehicle screeched to a halt, and he threw the shift into park just at the edge of a gravel trail.

As he jumped out of the truck, the ambulance pulled up right behind him. Elias waited until the EMTs got out, and they raced together toward the direction of the lake.

They rounded a small thicket of skeletal buckthorns, arriving at the location as the sun was peeking over the horizon. But it was still hard to see the ground clearly.

He shivered as the heavy breath of early morning cold seeped into his bones. He zipped his jacket up, adjusted his ball cap, and gave a cynical thanks that he hadn't had a recent haircut. The added length kept his neck warm.

Just past a small grove of pines, Elias quickly scanned the surroundings. The large, round lake was an eerie scene. No geese flew overhead, but the icy wind gently stirred the cattails at the edge of the water. Something unsettled inside Elias. He felt it in his gut, but shook off the odd feeling and focused on his friend, Raymond, who cradled the woman like a child.

His brother, Harold, stayed a good distance away with their dog Traitor at his side, watching.

"You okay?" Elias squatted next to Raymond, whose brown eyes were hooded with weariness.

"She's so cold, Eli." His teeth chattered as he spoke. "The blankets weren't doing anything, so I decided to hold her. I don't want her to die."

Raymond's teeth clacked. His face was paler than his normal light pink skin tone. Elias assumed that was from the cold and seeing the blood. The man never could stomach the sight of it.

"Good thinking, Ray. Just hold on a little longer while the techs look at her." Elias stood and stepped back, giving the EMTs more room to work.

While they examined and assessed the victim, Elias carefully walked around the hole from which Raymond and Harold had pulled her. How fucking awful to be buried alive.

A soft groan caught Elias's attention. He looked down at the woman, and saw she was somewhat conscious. "How bad?" he asked the EMTs.

"We need to get her to the hospital now. Her temperature is dangerously low." One of the EMTs wrapped a brace around her neck before he and the other tech gently turned her and pointed to the gash on the back of the woman's skull. "There's a large laceration on the back of her head, and she's suffered a good amount of blood loss."

The deep wound made Elias's stomach churn. Her long black hair, mixed with the blood and the dirt, gave the appearance of dark red clay. The smell of iron fused with the decomposed soil would make anyone's weak stomach revolt. But add in the odor of cow manure, and even the strongest of constitutions would lurch.

"Get going then," Elias said and let the EMTs continue their work.

After they wrapped her head, they carefully lifted her out of Raymond's arms and put her on the body board they'd carried over, then strapped her down.

Elias took another long look at the woman's face, hoping he'd recognized her. Her skin was smeared with dirt, and marred with purple and black bruises. With her swollen face, especially the right side, her profile no longer looked normal, but almost Quasimodo-like.

He hadn't seen this much brutality since he'd served overseas in Afghanistan where some women were brutally raped, then beaten to death and discarded like trash. She also reminded him of Elise...

Don't. Elias closed his eyes for a second, trying to shake the image of the battered woman that constantly haunted his dreams.

He dragged in breaths to center himself, but each inhale was like glass shards imbedding into his lungs.

He opened his eyes, and focused on the present, the unknown woman.

Who could have done this?

As he watched the EMTs cover her with a thermal blanket, the woman's good eye popped open and looked right at Elias. Fear and pain reflected from its depths.

Elias lost his composure for a second, but regained it before he gently conveyed, "You're going to be okay. You're safe now."

The woman opened her mouth, like she wanted to say something, but passed out.

"We have to go," one of the techs urged.

"Go. I'll be there as soon as I can." The gnawing in Elias's gut grew as he watched the EMTs carry her off toward the ambulance.

Not a minute later, Officer Tyson Ryan rushed up.

"Sorry, Chief," he sputtered, all flushed and breathing heavily.

"About damn time, Tyson. What took so long?" Elias bit out.

"I had to drop Beth off at the station," Tyson said with trepidation.

Elias rubbed the back of his neck and eyed the officer. He never remembered just how tall Tyson was until he stood next to the man. His six-foot four frame towered over Elias's six.

Anytime the officer got into trouble, particularly dealing with his wife, Beth, who was also a Beaver Ridge officer, he slouched in defeat and his reddened face became marred by a frown. It was a sure-fire tell that they were doing things they shouldn't be doing on the clock.

"We'll deal with this later," Elias said with a grimace. "Right now, I want you to head to the hospital and report everything you see and hear about the victim. Stay close. Once Tom gets here, we'll secure the scene and I'll get over to the hospital."

"Will do, Chief." The lanky officer nodded and hustled back to his patrol car, ready to follow the ambulance.

Jesus, how he hated being called chief, but that was his title.

Harold's dog, Traitor, barked, which pulled Elias's attention to his friend.

Elias walked over to Harold, who stood stiffly at the edge of the lake, scanning the area as though he was looking for something.

Elias also studied the area. As a young boy, he used to fish and swim in this lake with these two friends. It was ironic that the lake had been his only safe haven from his brutal home was now tarnished by an attempted murder.

Harold, who was three years younger than Elias, had a dejected glower on his face. He kept glancing at the edge of the lake closest to the crime scene, and then back to Traitor, who was showing teeth and quietly growling.

"Shut up, Traitor." With a sharp tug of the collar, the dog quieted down.

"What is it, Harold?" Elias studied the moving reeds along the lake's edge before looking back at his friend. "Do you see something?"

Harold peered at him. "Nothing. I didn't see nothing," he clipped. His eyes were bloodshot and glazed over as though he hadn't slept in a week. Or was he on a bender? He'd worry about Harold's drinking later.

Elias bent over and examined the tufts of long yellow grass floating like blonde hair in the murky water. Unease cinched at his nerves. He wasn't sure if the feeling resonated from the scene, the victim, or something else entirely. Maybe all three.

He straightened and took in a long, silent breath. This situation was just too fucked up. Everyone, including the dog, was on edge.

If the gnawing in Elias's gut was a foreshadowing of how this case was going to go, his plans to leave Beaver Lake by March would need to be postponed until he caught the son of a bitch who had committed this atrocity.

He hoped the woman survive, for her own sake, but also because from the appearance of the crime scene, she might be the only one who could describe her attacker.

As dawn brightened the horizon, the gray-dusted clouds outlined the burnt orange against the coming blue sky. The calming colors had always reminded him of his place off the beach in California. Elias wished he were there now, but cast off the yearning.

He knew he wouldn't get anything out of Harold, so he walked over to the other Kantor brother.

Wrapped in a camo blanket, Raymond looked like hell. His eyes wide and full of disbelief. His shoulders shook inside the woolen blanket as shivers racked through his body.

"Are you alright?" Elias asked, as Harold strode over with Traitor's leash still tight in his grip.

"Once I get a pot of coffee in me, I will be." Raymond shivered.

Elias took out his notepad and began questioning Raymond. "How did you find her?"

"Harold got off a lucky shot and the goose fell near where she was buried," Raymond explained with a tremor.

"Not luck. Skill." Harold shot his brother a sneer. "You're just jealous." Harold's indignation was somewhat diminished by his chattering teeth.

Elias covered his amusement with a cough and cleared his throat. That was so typical of these two brothers. Always arguing about stupid shit.

Raymond huffed. "I'm far from—"

"Hey!" Elias shouted. "The victim?"

Harold wiped his nose with his sleeve. "I sent Traitor to retrieve my goose, but he started barking like a rabid dog. So, we ran over to see what he was yapping about and that's when we found her." He shrugged, as his eyes focused on the ground where they had dug her up.

"She was stuck halfway out of the ground. We dug around her and pulled her out," Raymond clarified. "Will she die?"

"Don't know. Was there anything else? Did you see

something or someone?" Elias looked up from his notes and saw both men shaking their heads. "All right, head home. I'll call you two later with more questions."

The Kantor brothers took off. They didn't have to be told twice.

Elias walked over to the four-foot hole again. Multiple footprints obliterated the crime scene. It was going to be hard to distinguish whose footprints belonged to whom.

Officer Faber pulled up and hurried out of the squad. The balding man stumbled up with police tape under his arm and an evidence kit in his hand. Elias met him at the edge of the small dirt mound.

"Where the hell were you?" Elias asked, a bite in his tone. "I needed you here sooner."

"I was near Stockbridge when I got your call. And I had to get the evidence kit from the station." Tom lifted the black case up. "How's the woman?"

"She's barely alive," Elias said, silently hoping for good news when he got to the hospital.

Tom eyed the area and whistled. "What a damn mess. I'll cordon off the perimeter of the crime scene." He placed the evidence kit down next to Elias and opened it.

"Yeah." Elias expelled a breath. "I know."

He was grateful that Tom had stayed on as his second in command. However, the officer's constant tardiness rubbed Elias the wrong way, like he did it on purpose because it did bother Elias.

As Tom staked posts in the ground, Elias cordoned off the area with the crime scene tape to protect any viable prints and possible evidence.

Tom ducked under the yellow tape and cautiously approached the four-foot hole. "Damn," he said, studying the trampled ground. "I have some solid shoe prints here."

"Most likely they're from the EMTs, me and the Kantors," Elias pointed out.

"We have to get their shoe prints before the day's gone." Tom tilted his head to look up at the brightening sky. "It's going to be a clear, crisp Monday." Then he handed Elias a pair of latex gloves.

"It's going to be a long one as well. Once I'm done here, I'm heading to the hospital. I'll contact the EMTs on what we need." Elias examined the edge of the hole again, where blood from the victim's head had pooled.

Tom bent down, grabbed a digital camera from the kit and began taking pictures. "Fine by me. You know, my granddaddy used to say, 'A cold, long day of work cleanses the soul.'"

"I've heard you say that before. You were close to your grandfather?" Elias asked, as he grabbed the small slender shovel out of the kit and scooped up the clumps of bloody dirt and studied them.

Tom chuckled while he grabbed the small evidence bag and handed it to Elias. "I guess you can say that," Tom said evenly, his attention on the hole.

"If it gets any colder, my ass will freeze off," Elias confessed as he glanced at his second, then back at the red-black dirt in his tiny shovel, before he put the soil in the evidence bag and sealed it.

"Well, cold or not, we have to scour through every part of this area." Elias looked back toward the lake. "Maybe we should check around the lake too."

"Why?" Tom paused and glimpsed in the direction Elias was studying.

"My gut is telling me to." Elias turned back to Tom. "I don't know why, but I think we should."

"We should leave that part up to CLS. It's too big an

area for us to work. Trust me, they have more man power than us," Tom suggested.

Criminal Laboratory Services handled all forensic services throughout Wisconsin. A small town like Beaver Lake wasn't able to manage evidence of this magnitude. Elias had realized it immediately when his predecessor killed himself six months ago.

Elias wanted to argue that they could look, but Tom made sense. It was too big of a region and he wasn't sure what to look for anyway.

"You're right," Elias relented.

It took nearly an hour to comb through the crime scene, leaving the hole for last.

At the bottom, Tom pulled out a partial ripped, button-up shirt. He placed it inside the evidence bag and sealed it. The fabric was the only thing they were able to find—at least with the naked eye.

"What do we have so far?" Elias asked, moving his right shoulder around. Slight jabs of pain came from the bullet wound he'd gotten four years earlier.

Tom clicked his tongue. "Your shoulder okay?"

"Yeah. Fine. What do you have?" Elias wasn't in the mood to discuss his health issues.

The officer got the hint. "More soil samples. One full shoe print—of what I could find. Hair and partial ripped shirt—Maybe you need a cigarette?"

"Jesus Christ, Tom." Elias couldn't contain his agitation toward Tom's insubordination. Or the small amount of evidence they'd collected.

"You're jonesing hard, aren't you? I can tell. My granddaddy was the same way." Tom's mouth quirked.

Elias snapped his gloves off, dropped them in the kit and pulled out a pack of nicotine gum. He popped a piece into his mouth and chewed it quickly. The taste reminded him of a hot-boxed cigarette filter.

Nasty, but it did the trick when he needed that boost of nicotine.

"Not anymore." Elias exposed the chewed piece of gum between his teeth.

Tom nodded, then turned his attention back to the shallow grave. "Jesus, Eli. How in the hell did they find her? Alive, no less."

"Raymond said Harold got off a damn lucky shot. Traitor went to retrieve the bird and found her."

"That is lucky."

"I guess." Elias's heart sank in his chest. "If you'd seen the way she looked—that bastard..." He clamped his teeth tight and tried to still his emotions.

"That bad?" Tom's eyes widened and a grim frown settled on his face.

The image of her beaten face was plastered in the forefront of Elias's mind. He would never forget the way she'd stared up at him with one fright-filled eye while the other was swollen shut.

"Let's just say, I hope she lives because with her help, I want to catch the son of a bitch who hurt her."

"I wonder how she's doing." Tom snapped at his gloves, which snapped Elias out of his red haze.

Elias cleared his throat. "I'm not sure. I sent Tyson to the hospital. I told him to call me if there was any change in her condition."

"Should we call Waldon County? I'm sure Chief Bartoz could assist us with a few men."

"No. We'll wait for CLS. No more contamination," Elias insisted. "Besides, he has his own crap to worry about with that Jolie girl and the few others that have gone missing in that county."

"Yeah, you're right." Tom sighed. "You think this was random? Or do you think this is connected to their cases?"

Elias blew out a breath. "I don't know, but I'm sure we'll find out."

Tom nodded once. He grabbed the evidence bags of dirt, fabric, hair, and blood, and carried them back to his squad car.

"Do me a favor and call CLS. Tell them to notify the station when they arrive. I'm heading to the hospital. Call me if you find anything else," Elias said as he turned toward his truck.

"Will do." Tom saluted. "Hey."

"What?" Elias turned around.

"You look like shit," Tom said with all seriousness.

Elias rubbed the back of his neck. "Just as shitty as you."

"When was the last time you had a good night's sleep?"

Three years ago. "Yesterday." Elias lied. It had been three years since he stepped back into this town and sobered his ass up. He hadn't expected he would stay this long.

"A few hours of rest aren't going to kill you." Tom opened his trunk and placed the evidence inside.

"What, now you're my mother?" Elias glared at the man. He trudged his way around to his truck. "I'm heading to the hospital. Call me when CLS arrives."

"One last thing." Tom hesitated. "I got a call from Adams County yesterday. I didn't want to tell you, but now with what's happened, you need to know."

"What?" Elias growled out. Sometimes, Tom grated him the wrong way. This was one of those moments.

"One of their officers found a guy squatting in an abandoned farmhouse in Amery. He said the guy looked like your father." Tom closed the trunk and leaned against the vehicle.

"And you tell me this now?" Elias stepped toward the officer.

"I figured James wouldn't dare come around here after what he did last time." Tom shrugged.

"It's not your decision to make," Elias countered. He squared his shoulders and asked, "What did they do?"

"They ran the bastard off," Tom said with chuckle. "James is too stupid to come back. But with this woman, we have to check every possible lead."

"Yes, we do. Put the word out for him."

"What if—"

"Let's just hope for everyone's sake that he has nothing to do with this and stays away from here." Elias took one more look around before he got into his truck. He put his father out of his thoughts and focused on getting to the hospital.

He shifted the truck into reverse and looked in the rearview mirror while he backed into the trail to turn around. Halfway down the path, a flash of black rushed across it, and then vanished out of sight. He jammed on the brakes and twisted to look out the back window. Nothing stood in the distance, except trees.

Fucking losing it.

Damn, he still needed a cigarette. He licked the dry corner of his mouth. "Fuck it," he uttered under his breath. Bad time to quit smoking. His jaw hurt from chewing on his gum too long. He spat out the gum into a discarded wrapper and tossed it into the ashtray.

He threw the gear in drive and drove straight to the hospital.

CHAPTER TWO

E lias stepped out of the elevator into a hallway and noticed Tyson leaning against the wall outside the door of the victim's room.

Tyson shifted his slender frame away from the wall as Elias approached. "Hey, Chief," the officer quickly said.

"Tyson. I'm not Chief Henley, you can call me Elias or Eli."

The officer's brows furrowed and he nodded. "Okay... Eli." Tyson's face scrunched up as though he had sucked on a lemon.

Elias gave in. "Call me whatever you're comfortable with."

"All right, Chief," the young officer quickly said, relaxing his shoulders.

"How is she?" Elias thumbed toward the doorway.

"Jane is stable now, but she's in bad shape. She actually died, but Dr. Rollins brought her back." Tyson fidgeted with his belt buckle as he kept glancing at the wall clock by the nurses' station.

"Why are you calling her Jane?" Elias asked in a rigid tone, ignoring the anxiousness rolling off the officer.

"The hospital listed her as a Jane Doe, since she had no identification." He wrung his hands.

"What's wrong, Tyson?" Elias stepped closer, his voice lowered to an angry growl.

Tyson gulped before he took a deep breath. "Beth texted me ten minutes ago. She's ovulating," he whispered.

Elias shook his head and raised his hand. "TMI, Officer Ryan. TMI." He rubbed at his face, trying to wipe clear any imagery Tyson's confession brought. Elias straightened and narrowed his eyes on the man. "That's not my problem. You're on the clock and this situation is far more important than your wife's time of the month. Do you understand me, Officer Ryan?" Elias's voice had just enough punch that the officer nodded like a bobble head.

"Yes. I'll text her back and tell her I can't."

"You do that. Now head out and finish your patrol. And Tyson, keep an eye out," Elias said levelly.

Life was a hell of a lot better when he was in the dark about his officers' personal lives.

"Got it, Chief." Tyson bolted straight for the elevator.

As Elias headed into Jane's room, he saw Mayor Daniels exited the elevator.

"Damn. That's all I need right now." Elias muttered, and adjusted his cap. He was in no mood to deal with the meddlesome old man. Yes, he was the mayor, but he was also a nosy son of a bitch who got into everyone's business.

The vulture stared straight at him. There were no pleasantries on his face or in his bearing. Especially not in the way the end of his cane hit the linoleum floor with every step. His usual sloth-like gait shifted to a swift stride.

"Chief McAvoy, I want a word with you," Mayor Daniels called out. He pointed at Elias with a rigid, thin finger and signaled him to come.

"Mayor. What's the honor?" Elias folded his arms across his chest.

"I heard a naked, beaten woman was found on the outskirts of town. How are you going to handle this?" Daniels tapped the end of the cane to the floor with each word.

"I'll handle it by the book." Elias stared straight at the man's face. This was bullshit. Who was in charge?

"Is she local? Does she know who did this to her? I need answers, quick. People in this town have the right to know, especially if we need to protect ourselves." Mayor Daniels kept on with his inquisition but Elias turned his back to him.

"There is nothing yet to report. But if anyone is in immediate danger, I will let you know right away. Now excuse me, Mayor. I have a job to do." Elias said as cordially as possible as he scrutinized the old man.

The mayor's nostrils curled, and he grunted. "Wait—"

Elias stepped into Jane Doe's room and closed the door. That man had been a pain in his ass since he took on the chief's position.

With another deep, cleansing breath, he pushed the mayor out of his thoughts. Elias took off his Giants cap and slowly walked to the bed.

Jane was hooked up to IVs and an EKG monitor. Her tangled bloody hair had been cleaned and cut short. It poked through the gauze wrapped around her head like tiny spikes.

The rawness around her wrists and ankles wasn't as bad as her face. Jane's black and blue skin had an appearance of dark purple charcoal smudges.

Elias knew better. Flashes of Elise and of his mother penetrated—no, more like barreled, their way through his mind. His stomach tightened and twisted up tight into his ribcage.

Will the terrible memories of their deaths ever cease? Probably not. It was *his* penance for not saving their lives.

The oxygen tube that aided Jane's breathing reminded him of Elise's first day in the hospital. He stepped closer. His lungs constricted, but he forced himself to calm down. This was not the woman he had tried to save from her abusive husband.

He took a slight step back and attempted to wipe that horrific day away from his mind. Elias had to keep his head clear and focus on Jane's case.

Once he was centered, Elias studied Jane in a whole new light. Judging from the barbarity of the assault, the bastard had meant to kill, but not before he wanted her to suffer.

Elias couldn't imagine how much Jane had endured, and survived. Her jagged fingernails were proof of her will to stay alive. He admired the woman for her strength.

Leaning in, Elias hoped his words cut through even in her comatose state.

"I promise to keep you safe. I'll find the bastard who did this," Elias whispered his quiet oath. He had failed in his attempt to save Elise's life four years ago. Or his mother's many years before that. But he wasn't about to fail again.

CHAPTER THREE

One week later
11:57 p.m.

Where am I? Jane peered through slitted lids into the murky blackness of the room.

When she turned her head, dizziness and nausea slammed into her, making Jane shake.

The back of her skull felt bludgeoned. *Oh, the pain.* Jane squeezed her eyes shut, until the pressure ebbed into a light headache. Tears welled up and slid down her face.

Jane's arms were like lead weights as she lifted her hands to her face. She touched the IV taped along her left arm.

A soft beeping sound to her left increased. Jane looked over and noticed she was hooked up to a machine. She was in the hospital.

What happened to me?

She framed her face with both hands. Pain needled each fingertip as she pressed them against her skin. The bandage on her forehead stretched from temple to temple.

Jane tried moistening her lips, but they stung sharply, like paper cuts, as her rough dry tongue slid over them. She attempted to sit up, but her body felt like a punching bag, bruised and beaten to hell.

Her heart banged like a kettle drum, matching the beats from the machine next to her. The rush of blood pulsing in her ears made her lightheaded. The sound seemed to echo off the quiet walls of the room. Panic took root.

Breathe. Her esophagus tightened and an acrid taste burned the back of her throat. She took a few gulping breaths and closed her eyes.

The spinning stopped and the nausea finally eased. She opened her eyes and let the panic dissipate. She had to think. What had happened to put her in the hospital?

Once her nerves settled, she made a slow sweep of the space. Aside from her bed, a rolling table, and the machine she was hooked up to, there was nothing strange in the room.

What time is it? She tried finding a clock on the walls, but the room was too dark.

Although visible through the gaps of the vertical blinds, the fingernail moon cast no light. She assumed it had to be around midnight.

The howl of the loud wind caught her off guard. The fir tree near the building knocked and scratched against the windowpane, like nails on a chalkboard. Jane shuddered. Jumpy, and cold too; the thin sheet that covered her wasn't enough to keep her warm.

She wanted a nurse. Jane needed answers. Her right hand touched the slender bed remote. Several times, she tried to pull it closer, but the cord snagged around the metal bed rail. Finally, the damn thing loosened.

Jane's eyes focused in and out. The pictorials on the remote blurred. She pushed all the buttons at once. Her bed shifted up, then back. The TV flashed on, then off. A chirp echoed out, from where, she had no clue. She gave up and dropped it.

Closing her eyes, Jane concentrated on the noise around her. The beeping from the EKG broke the silence, and she was comforted by the continual sound. A sudden chill blew against her skin and startled her. Jane clutched at the thin sheet as her exhaled breath turned into a veil of white. The room turned frigid.

Instant pressure from inside Jane's head made her nauseous. Vomit rose fast—she gagged it back, but the slimy liquid came up too quickly. She turned her head to one side, expelling the bile from her mouth onto her pillow. She wiped the foulness with her sheet.

She focused on the ceiling. The roiling in her stomach subsided, but her temples drummed hard and the back of her head burned deep into her skull. Shifting to the right for relief didn't help.

The honed pain suddenly stopped, but the residue of hurt lingered. Jane threw up again.

Please don't throw up. Jane gulped in air while trying to regain some control of her bodily functions.

The pain in her head intensified; she couldn't focus on anything. She closed her eyes for a few minutes to concentrate on pushing back the pain. When she opened her eyes, a black figure hovered over her and swung something at her head. She screamed and instinctively blocked it with her arms.

With every hit, she recoiled into a ball. Tears welled in her eyes as the spasms in her skull intensified.

Jane screamed again and the dark figure suddenly vanished. But in its place were images of the young girl in the yellow dress. Each picture bulleted through her mind like the rapid fire of a machine gun—one right after another, pictures of smiles and laughter, then of a blood-covered face, then finally silence.

Jane convulsed with each gasping breath. She had no control of her body. Terror flooded every part of her. Without thought, she yanked the IV out of her arm and tried to sit up, but the room spun faster and faster, out of control. She wanted the hell out of there.

Her legs were tangled up in the sheets. Once freed, she dangled them off the side and planted her feet on the cold floor.

Her stomach cramped tight, more vomit escaped her mouth; the bile spewed down her gown and splattered on the floor. Jane slipped off the bed and collapsed onto the linoleum like a broken doll.

A spike of light blinded her. Blurred gray figures hovered over her like ghosts with no faces. She tried pushing them away. Her body floated up in mid-air. She was dead, and Death and his crew had come to claim her.

Jane wasn't leaving without a fight. She swung her fists, hitting anything in her reach, putting everything behind her punches.

"Damn it, stop!" Death ordered.

Jane froze when she heard his voice. Gruff and hard. Almost human.

Everything went quiet. Jane tried to focus on Death's face. She blinked, but all she saw was a distorted monster. Her hysteria crested. Her arms flailed, she kicked, and then a sharp pain on her right arm made her lose what strength she had. She tried fighting back, but it was too late. Death had her.

CHAPTER FOUR

Elias's heart stopped when Jane's screams pierced the air. With each long stride down the hall, his anxiety spiked higher. He opened the door to her room, turned on the light and rushed inside. On the floor, Jane lay in a crumpled heap.

As Elias picked her up, he slipped on slimy liquid, almost falling on top of her.

He quickly got his balance and swept her up into his arms. She screamed like a banshee and swung her fists.

"Get the hell away from me, you bastard!" she shouted.

Magda Burstone, the head charge nurse, rushed in. "Who is Jane talking to?" she asked, while Elias tried to keep a tight hold on her.

"Maybe her attacker," Elias said with a grunt. Surprised by her physical strength, he struggled to not drop her.

He braced his legs apart and stood there, partially coated in what he now realized was her vomit, and held her until she calmed down.

Damn. Jane's vigorous fight was unexpected. Her

small fist landed on the left side of his face with purpose. It didn't hurt, but made him stagger back a step.

Elias yelled, which spurred Jane to punch at him again.

Relief filled him to see her awake and with fire. He had hope for her, and this case. She had lain comatose for a full week and he'd feared she might never wake up. For the first time since she had been brought in, tension eased out of his shoulders.

A nurse rushed over and planted a shot in Jane's right arm. Within a few seconds, Jane's body turned limp, and she passed out.

Elias put Jane down on the bed and retreated to the door. He watched as the medical team tended to her.

Magda pulled him out of the room. "Follow me, Elias," she said gently.

"I need to stay," Elias countered. He shrugged her hand away.

"No. You don't." For a tiny woman in her late sixties, Magda had a commanding presence and strength in her grip. Her Southern stubborn streak gave no room for backtalk. "Follow me."

Magda's beautiful silvery gray hair gleamed under the fluorescents as he dutifully trailed behind her.

Elias held her in the utmost respect. Her handsome gray-blue eyes met everyone with kindness, and he remembered the way she'd looked at his mother, Barbara.

This woman was the only person who'd helped his mother during her short bout with breast cancer seven years ago, before it took her life. Magda had stayed by her side to the very end. Something he couldn't do himself.

Magda silently led him to a bathroom down the hall. When she turned and focused her attention on Elias, he smiled at her, but her frown remained in place. She handed him a few washcloths and walked away.

Elias watched her disappear around the corner before walking into the bathroom. Looking down at the washcloth and then sniffing at his hand, he realized just how awful he smelled. Though, who cared how he reeked? His concern was only for Jane.

Ignoring the growing anxiety heavy in his chest, he washed off the rancid puke as fast as he could. Eli sniffed at his jacket and winced from the odor. He doused the other washcloth with hot water and soap, and wiped his jacket and pants the best he could. The mix of puke and sterile soap curled his nostrils. He washed his hands for the second time, and then dried them off quickly.

Elias stepped out of the washroom. The adrenalin rush had eased, flooding his body with nervousness. He popped a piece of gum in his mouth and hurried back to Jane's room.

As he walked around the corner, Elias saw Harold outside Jane's doorway.

Why the fuck was he here, in the middle of the night, with an armful of weeds? And how ironic—the one night he was here, Jane woke up.

The second Elias locked eyes with his friend, Harold hid the sad bouquet behind his back.

Grabbing Harold's arm, Eli pulled him away from the room. "What's with the flowers, Harold? And why are you here?"

"Will you stop yanking me! I wanted to see how she's... Damn boy, you stink." Harold waved his hand across his crinkled nostrils.

"Why?" Elias repeated with a growl.

Harold squinted up at him. "Why-what?" His voice squeaked like a child's.

"Don't play stupid, Kantor," Elias pushed.

"I wanted to make sure Jane is safe. That's all." Petals from the daisies drifted down from behind him.

"So why the flowers?"

He brought the sad bouquet back to his chest. "These will cheer her up." Harold smiled, then looked at Elias and frowned. "I'm doing nothing wrong, McAvoy."

Elias glowered. He regarded his comment. "I'm sure she'll appreciate it. But for now, you can't visit her. She's my only witness, and I don't want tainted information."

Harold's mouth dropped open. "What does that mean?" His yellowed teeth clenched tight and his scalp turned bright pink.

Elias leaned and lowered his voice. "I want to make sure she tells me what happened to her from her point of view. Got it?"

"I don't want her to get hurt. I'm here to protect her too," Harold claimed.

"Harold, it's *my* job to protect her. In order to do *my* job correctly, I can't have anyone impeding this investigation. That includes unsolicited visits, and flowers." *She deserves better.*

"Come on, McAvoy."

"So, no more flowers and no more visits. Not until we find out who did this to her and only when I give you the okay."

"Whatever... Asshole." Harold walked off, but not before, he dumped the crushed flowers at Elias's feet.

"Dickhead," Elias said under his breath. He gathered up the battered flowers and threw them in the garbage.

A single daisy fell at his feet. Elias picked it up and stared at the saggy white petals. Sounds of laughter caught his attention. He looked over and saw his deputy flirting with a red head at the nurses' station. He tucked the flower inside his coat pocket and walked over.

"So, what were you and your girlfriend talking about

—Damn." Tom took a step back, and sniffed, as he waved his hand in front of his face. "You need to change your cologne."

"Don't you have something important to do besides chasing tail?" Elias retorted in a whisper while sniffing at his arm.

"Always do, Chief." Tom wasn't deterred. He gave Elias a wide smile before he continued to say, "So what's with Harold and the flowers? And what's that god awful smell?" Tom wrinkled his nose and pinched the nostrils.

"Jane finally woke up. She screamed. I ran in and slipped on her puke," Elias explained as he took off his coat, turned it inside out, but didn't put it back on.

"And you had to be a hero. And the flowers?"

"Harold came to see Jane. He said they would cheer her up. I told him to stop." Elias took another sniff at his hand. "Why are you here, Tom?"

"I had an hour for dinner, so I decided to check up on the Jane Doe before grabbing a bite to eat." Tom turned to the nurse and smiled. "And to say hi to Dorothy here. Why are you here? Aren't you supposed to be sleeping?"

Tom leaned down, whispered something to the nurse, chuckled and then straightened up. He looked at Elias and shook his head.

"Just checking in on Jane." Elias eyed the man before walking away. He didn't want to admit to Tom that he was losing even more sleep since Jane had been found.

"Well, that's ironic how Harold happened to be here when Jane Doe woke up. He usually doesn't give a shit about anyone but himself," Tom said.

"I told him that he can't visit her during this investigation until I say it's okay."

"What did he say?"

"He's pissed and called me an asshole." Elias smiled.

He panned a look around the hall. "We need to keep a steady eye on that guy, he's bound to do something stupid. I know him too well."

Tom agreed. "By the way, we got the results back of the blood and soil samples. They rushed it. They're on your desk."

"And?"

"The blood, hair and fabric piece from the shirt confirms that all of it belongs to Jane Doe. They put her picture and prints through the WIMEC database for missing persons and came up with nothing. Now they are being sent through the national system. Hopefully if she is in the database, we will get a hit on who Jane really is." Tom sounded somewhat hopeful, but Elias wasn't.

"I hope we didn't miss anything." Elias raked his fingers through his hair.

"It's been a week, Chief. Any evidence not found is probably gone now. CLS and I went through every dirt granule out there. I assure you, there's nothing left." Tom folded his arms across his chest.

"I hope you're right, but I'll keep checking the lake, just in case. I swear, that day, Harold was acting funny. And Traitor was jumping out of his collar."

"Funny, how?"

"Almost paranoid."

Tom looked at his watch. "Well, he is a freak. It's nearly one and almost past my dinner," the deputy countered. "Right now, I'm hungry," he said, looking back over his shoulder, checking out the nurse.

Elias eyed Tom with a smirk. "I'll see you later."

"10-4." Tom saluted. He cast a Cheshire grin, then walked off without another word.

Elias entered Jane Doe's room and almost bumped into Magda, who stood just inside.

He cleared his throat, and took off his hat. "Miss Magda." His eyes stayed trained on Jane.

Magda placed her hand on his arm. "She's resting now. Amy and Mary cleaned her up and redressed her. Dr. Rollins said she is settled. There is nothing to worry about for now." She patted his forearm. "You need to wash your stuff as soon as you get home."

"I know." Elias rubbed his jaw and continued. "I have to say that for a woman who went through hell and back, she has a powerful right hook. I wouldn't have believed it if I hadn't felt it myself."

Magda wasn't smiling when she ushered Elias back out the door. He knew something serious was about to be said and braced for it.

"Dr. Rollins wants to restrain her," she said quietly. Her Southern tone was slightly off rhythm. There was worry in her words.

"Why?" Elias's teeth ground together. Yelling wasn't the answer. "What's the reason?"

"What if this happens again? He feels that she might hurt herself and the nurses. Elias, you know he's right. Look what happened tonight. What if she'd punched me? I for one couldn't take a hit like that."

He raked his fingers through his hair. "I don't like it —Damn it."

"Elias James McAvoy." She glared at him and her lip pursed together.

Her look spoke volumes and Elias got the hint. She hated swearing of any kind.

"She isn't stable, not yet. It's for her protection, and ours," Magda finally said earnestly.

A flood of mixed emotions filled him. It brought out a terrible image of his mother beaten and tied to the bed. Damn, he hadn't thought of that in years. He'd only been six at the time, but that memory still choked him.

He wasn't ready to relive his tragic past and shook that image out of his head.

Elias stepped back from the senior nurse. He barely contained his outrage. "She's the victim, not some rabid dog ready to be put down."

"Calm down, Elias... I'll see what I can do. But no promises. Now, why don't you go home, and get some sleep? You could use it. I'll call you if something happens."

"I'll wait for a bit." Elias stood rigid, legs apart, and eyes unwavering. He was in no mood to argue.

"You are so stubborn, just like your mother. Now what would she say for not listening to reason?"

"Nothing. She never did." He knew the truth of that statement well, and so did Magda.

"Only for a few minutes, Elias." Magda walked away shaking her head.

Elias waited only seconds before walking back into the room. He took a slow deep breath, blew it out and headed to Jane's bed.

Pain tightened his chest when he saw Jane shake in her sleep.

He had a hard time being objective about the leather straps too. Those damned things brought out more bad memories of his past—his mother and the fucked-up father that was now roaming the Wisconsin countryside.

The room was quiet except for the monitors and the peaceful sound of her breathing. What a peaceful noise. His shoulder relaxed as he saw her chest rise and fall evenly. She was okay.

Elias stared down at her battered features, which had been ingrained in his mind from the first time he saw her. They had changed even from his last visit. Her skin had turned more yellow, less purple. The black and blue marks were fading. The swelling had almost gone completely around her eyes. Her features were somewhat normal.

Her chestnut brown hair sprung out through the clean white bandage around her head. Her arms were almost as thin as the rails of the bed, but strong. He knew it to be true as he rubbed his jaw again and grinned.

His gaze returned to the leather bands connecting her wrists to the metal railings. The indignity suddenly drove his ire high again. He had to leave.

Jane's restraints weren't the only root of his anger. What pulled him out of his own skin was Jane, herself. Her face reminded him of Elise Hathaway. The one he accidentally killed four years ago, which had driven him straight to the bottom of the bottle.

Elias grabbed his coat and rushed past the nurses' desk, right into a closing elevator. He stabbed at the button for the ground floor, then leaned against the wall, his mind racing back to that day. Her death would burn in his soul forever.

He wished he had talked Elise into staying with family. But not listening to reason, the stubborn woman wanted to go home. She had assured him that she was safe.

He'd ignored all the alarms that went off in his head and drove her home, to her death. Her husband had waited for her to come home. The men squared off, gun to gun, and Elise's husband shot first. The bullet caught deep in Elias's shoulder while his bullet was trained on the man's arm. But Elise stepped in front of her husband and the bullet hit her dead in the chest. She died almost instantly.

Knocking his head back against the hard wall, he hoped the pain would bring him back to the present. He reminded himself of the vow to not cry and then wiped the wetness from his cheeks.

As the elevator door opened, he rushed out of the confining box and then the hospital. The cold wind slapped against his face, sharp and precise. His head cleared some, but the familiar, gripping thirst scratched his throat. His angst goaded him.

"Fuck!" He let out a loud shout in the parking lot. The longing for a drink was more powerful than before. He wanted a cigarette too, dammit.

The second he reached his truck, he opened the door and grabbed the pack of cigarettes he had been saving for an emergency. He pulled one out, sniffed deep, pulling the sweet scent of tobacco into his lungs, then placed the filtered end between his teeth.

The urge to light it had his fingers twitching. Instead, he stroked the tip of his tongue to the end of the filter. The taste placated some of his craving, but it didn't quell the need for nicotine. Or for a bottle of scotch—a fifth would do.

He rubbed at his right shoulder and ignored the pinch of pain that shot through to his collarbone. He leaned against his truck and took in a deep, shuddering breath. The thirty-degree wind chill started to settle his taut nerves. He unbuttoned his shirt, leaving his chest covered in only a white T-shirt.

"Why am I here?" he questioned as he leaned against the truck, with both arms crossed over his chest, looking up at the black, clear sky. The only response was the twinkle of the stars above.

Ever since he was appointed chief, he'd felt out of step. The Jane Doe case had him even more off balance. He hadn't picked up a drink in three years or a cigarette for a week. Now he was craving both. *Desperately*.

He pulled a Bic lighter from his pocket and contemplated firing up the cigarette. Instead, he threw the lighter inside the truck.

"Get your head out of your ass, McAvoy," he said to himself. His job was to serve and protect the people of this town. He needed to keep a level head at all times. It didn't matter if he was a simple officer or a chief of police. There were no allowances for past mistakes or emotions getting in the way of doing what was important, and right.

Then why did this case, or Jane for that matter, get under his skin? He knew deep down, if there was a chance to redeem himself...No. There was no room for redemption.

Self-doubt covered him like Jane's puke.

The wind shifted suddenly to the north. It felt colder, harsher than before, then stilled. An eerie lull filled the night. A tingle ran across his skin. He rolled his broad shoulders back and shifted his head from side to side. The sudden tightness in his neck felt like a warning.

He was being watched. Elias could sense it. It was the same feeling he'd had when he and his unit almost stumbled into a trap in Bagram, Afghanistan. And the same as when he'd stood by the lake a week ago.

Looking around, Eli saw nothing unusual. He blew out a breath, ignored his instincts and slid into the truck.

Chalk it up to no sleep. He shook his head, returned the cigarette into the pack and threw it into the glove compartment. Then he started the truck, put the shift in gear and headed home.

CHAPTER FIVE

A drenaline ran high in his bloodstream. He'd waited two long days before going to see Jane again. The anticipation ramped up his mood to play.

Now he slithered through the hospital like a snake, hiding in the shadows, avoiding the night staff. He was good at it—had been working unseen for years.

He stepped into Jane's room and quietly closed the door. He strolled up to the bed and tamped down the rage burning in the pit of his stomach.

How in the hell did you survive? Who would have guessed you'd make it through? Stubborn little bitch.

He lightly touched her puffy cheek; the heat from her skin seared the pads of his cold fingertips.

The small overhead light cast a soft glow around her, almost ethereal. But she was no angel. Only a whore. Just like all of them before her.

He grabbed the chart that hung on the wall and read it. *Jane Doe. Ha. Wouldn't they like to know your real name?*

After returning the chart back to its place, he walked to the foot of the bed with great satisfaction in knowing what others didn't. He reached out and touched her left foot, shaking it gently back and forth. He wanted her to wake up and see him. That first reaction was critical, it set his heart pounding while he waited for her to move.

She didn't move. Didn't even a moan. *How fucking disappointing.*

He walked to her side and studied her face. "You should have stayed dead and buried. You are nothing but a complication to me," he whispered, shaking his head.

The chloroform had never fully worked on her when he'd snatched her from her car. He should have smacked her a few more times then with the shovel—that would have done the trick.

She'd given him such a thrill when he'd yanked her hair and dragged her down to the basement—she'd fought like a stray wild cat. Remembering her screams sent a rush of adrenaline right down to his dick.

When she'd kicked free and ran out of the house, it had stopped being fun. He'd had no choice but to kill her. Granted, smacking the metal shovel against the back of her head before she escaped wasn't the brightest idea. He'd never thought she would dig herself out of the ground.

Eyeing the gauze on Jane's head, he thought it was a shame her head was covered. He wanted to see what it looked like. He trailed his finger along the edge of the white cotton dressing across her forehead, almost tempted to cut it open and take a peek inside.

The nurse had cut her hair. That really pissed him off. That redheaded bitch chopped it too fucking short. It wasn't pretty and long the way he liked it.

He'd loved the way it had tangled in his fingers, especially when he pulled Jane down the stairs. It had been a special moment for him. For both of them.

The still-raw markings around her wrists and ankles made him shiver with joy. His branding from the old rope he'd had since he was a child would leave a permanent scar. That thought made his cock even harder. The need to stroke it made keeping his hands away from his crotch a challenge.

Not yet.

He refocused, and studied her torn, blackened fingernails. The damage showed him just how much of a fighter she was. A thin smile sliced across his face as he imagined her frantically digging herself out of the hole. A soft chuckle escaped his lips while he squeezed her fingertip.

A slight groan came from the bitch, like a feminine purr. He sucked in a breath and smiled wider. "You do strange things to me, Jane."

He clutched the bedrail, his knuckles turning white. The urge to drag her off the bed consumed him. He took a deep breath, tilted his head to the left, and then cracked his neck side to side.

He closed his eyes for a second to enjoy the pleasure spiraling in the pit of his stomach. Once he got his feverish urge under control, he lowered the metal bed railing.

Could this be a second chance to have her? Maybe keep her longer than the rest...

Smother her! Clean this up before anyone finds out! The imposing words roared through his brain.

No loose ends. Leaving her alive to play with was too risky. Loose ends would lead back to him.

He reached down and grabbed the pillow off the chair with both hands, paused and hovered over her face. He regretted that he'd never gotten to properly play with this one.

"*C'est la vie,*" he whispered. He slipped the oxygen tube out of her nose and pressed the pillow down on her face. As he compressed it, muted satisfaction settled over him as her body jerked lightly. No real struggle. How disappointing.

The sound of footsteps from the hall broke his concentration.

Shit, someone's coming.

With gritted teeth, he threw the pillow back on the chair and slipped behind the curtain crushed against the wall.

The door opened, and... *Fuck.* It was the tall, redheaded slut again. *One of these days...*

The EKG monitor's beeps were erratic for a few seconds and then they slowed to an even rhythm again.

"Dang you, Jane. Touching the oxygen tube is a no-no." After slipping the tube back into Jane's nose, the nurse checked her vitals.

She picked up the chart and wrote something down, all the while she chattering away like Jane was listening. Then she tucked Jane's sheets in, hung the chart where it belonged and left.

Glued to the wall, he listened for retreating foot-steps. Once the door closed, he stepped out from behind the curtains and watched the succession of beeps from Jane's heart monitor.

It had been a long time since he'd had a challenge such as this. He wouldn't waste it this time around. He was much more creative, much too smart for that, or he would've been caught years ago.

She was a thrill *he* was willing to risk everything for. His dick continued to throb. The zipper rubbed his sensitive foreskin. It added to the pleasurable pain he desperately needed to quench.

A heady rush flooded his senses as the intricacies of a

new game formed in his head. Adrenaline and excitement almost made him come in his pants.

As he reached Jane's bed, he bent to whisper in her ear, and the fine hairs on the back of his neck stood straight out. Goose flesh rose tight along his skin, like a thousand ants, biting his body.

He spun toward the door. No one was there.

A shadow fluttered outside the window. He moved to peer out through the open blinds. A branch from a fir tree tapped against the pane. He spread the blinds farther apart and his hand splayed against the glass. Flashes of yellow near the base of the tree caught his eyes—*was that a dress?*

His heart hammered in his chest. Sweat beaded on his forehead and slipped down his reddened temples. He wasn't going to get caught by some nosy little bitch. Little girls needed to learn lessons of obedience, too. If he caught whoever was watching him, he'd make sure she learned a valuable lesson about spying on others.

He wanted to bang on the window, but that would have caused attention on the room.

He glanced at Jane for a second and then turned back to the window. *Nothing but the fucking wind and a lone fir tree.* Looking down, he realized it was impossible for anyone to peer inside the window. They were on the second floor. It must have been a plastic bag blown and hung up on one of the branches. There was nothing there now.

Pinching his eyes closed for a second, he opened them again, and noticed a solid handprint marked on the window. *His* handprint. Without hesitation, he grabbed a towel from the bathroom, and wiped his presence away.

Right after he dropped the towel in the small hamper, sounds from the hall drew his attention. The chief's voice streamed in loud and clear. *Fucker.*

He slid back against the wall and pushed the curtain closed.

* * *

Elias walked into the room, his attention solely on Jane. He sat down next to her and leaned his head back against the chair. Every night he woke up and drove to the hospital. And every night, he sat by her side and waited, watching her sleep.

Exhausted and tired. Unable to sleep himself, his mind spun a whirlwind of images from his past, and of Jane. If he couldn't sleep at home, the hospital was the next best place.

It had been ten days and nothing else had been pulled from the crime scenes—nothing new to work with.

Jane hadn't awakened again yet. Until that time, Elias had to be patient. All the answers were in her head. Who was she? Who did this to her? And why?

Those questions were like nails pounding into his skull.

Elias took a deep breath and let his body give in to the fatigue. He adjusted the shoulder holster, so his Beretta wasn't digging into his side.

Dropping the bill of his hat over his eyes, his eyelids fluttered shut. The sounds of Jane's heart monitor lulled him into a light sleep.

As he sank deeper, an icy chill blew across the nape of his neck. Eli's scalp tightened in response. He jumped out of the chair, knocking his hat off. Eli swung around the room, gun drawn, ready for what waited there.

They were alone.

Damn. He could have sworn...

Elias checked out the bathroom. Empty. He swiped

at the swaying privacy curtain, pushing it away from the wall. Stepping out into the hallway, no one was in sight. Not even an echo of shoes hitting the linoleum.

Rubbing the back of his neck, Eli thought that maybe he'd gone crazy.

He headed back into Jane's room and sat down. Taking a deep breath, he kept his eyes wide open.

CHAPTER SIX

Six a.m. came too soon, especially when his nightmares had kept him up for most of the night. It didn't help that he'd finally gone home and gotten into bed after three.

Elias slammed his hand down when the clock radio screamed out. "Uhh. Fifteen more minutes," he yawned.

He drifted back to sleep, but his cell phone vibrated on his nightstand.

He flipped it open with force. "What." His voice was razor sharp.

"Is that how you answer the phone, Elias?" Magda charged.

"I'm sorry. But is there a reason why you're calling me this early, Miss Magda?" He became more contrite.

"Bad dreams again?"

"Yeah," he said, rubbing his eyes.

"I called because Jane's fully awake now."

It was about damn time. He wanted—needed answers. Three days had passed since Jane had awoken with a shriek, and nothing since.

"I'll be right there." Elias snapped his cell phone shut and threw it on the bed next to him.

His back ached from tossing and turning on the old spring mattress. The weariness had caught up to and overtaken him.

Elias sat up, draping his legs over the edge of the bed and raked his hands through his sweat-dampened hair. It was cold in his room, which was partially his fault for not getting the furnace's thermostat fixed.

He pulled at his right shoulder where the old bullet wound throbbed. Just another memento of his past.

Elias grunted as he stood. His body begged for more sleep, a luxury he hadn't given into for a long while.

He stumbled his way to the bathroom, nearly breaking an ankle when he tripped over his dirt-encrusted boots. Elias kicked them to the side and lumbered into the bathroom.

Looking into the oval mirror, a zombie stared back at him. Eyes were red and glazed over from lack of sleep. It'd been a month since he'd taken a razor to his face. Elias was always too tired to shave.

Instead of a shower, he splashed cold water on his face and did a once over with the toothbrush. He dragged yesterday clothes off the floor and put them on as he trudged downstairs.

He stalked out of the white farmhouse he had grown up in, zipping up his jacket and heading to his truck. He glanced over at the swinging real estate sign that had been posted in the front yard for almost two years.

The hundred acres were broken into two huge lots, one for farming and the other half, woods. Elias wasn't sure if it would ever sell. A few prospective buyers had come looking, but when they saw what the land needed, they dropped it like a hot frying pan.

His father claimed, since he had never divorced

Elias's mother, the property rightfully belonged to him. But Barbara McAvoy's bequest stipulated the land and everything on it belonged to her son, and no other. It was her revenge against James, and that fucker deserved it.

He ignored the uneasiness the sign gave him and got in the truck. Elias radioed in to the station and then headed straight to the hospital.

Still foggy from lack of sleep, he detoured down Becker Street to the Coffee Barn at the edge of town.

The small red building resembled a barn. It had a drive-up window Elias loved because he never had to get out of his truck. The owner, Penny May, added that feature a year after she bought the small building.

He lowered his window, and the aroma of the dark liquid dancing on the cold air called to him like a siren. He ordered his usual, black with four sugars.

"Here you go, Chief." Penny reached out and handed him a large paper cup.

"Smells great, Penny." He cupped it with both hands and sipped it as though his life depended on it.

He took a moment to let the caffeine filter into his system. "Aah. That's more like it. Great as usual, Penny." He smiled at her and handed her a five, double what the coffee cost. It was worth it. "See you tomorrow." And he drove off toward the hospital.

Elias drank the rest in slow gulps as he pulled into a parking spot.

He entered the three-story brick building and went straight to the elevator. He avoided eye contact with any of the nurses at the welcome desk, especially Caroline Weaver. He wasn't in the mood for her cat and mouse games.

At Magda's insistence, he'd taken Caroline out once. She'd been nothing but a pain in his ass from the moment they had their one and only date a year ago. He learned that night, she'd go to any lengths to get him in her bed and a ring on her finger.

Caroline had chattered throughout the entire dinner about how cute a couple they were. She had idealized the thought of being married and having children. But her shallowness and rude behavior were as obvious as the huge diamond she craved would be on her finger. She was trouble and he'd had to break clean from her fast.

Marriage wasn't a consideration in his life, or children, for that matter. He thought both symbolized the loss of freedom and thinking for oneself. He and his family were proof of that.

Elias had seen firsthand what happened when a man didn't give two shits about his wife or his son. James McAvoy was the epitome of a lowlife alcoholic father and abusive husband, and he did them a favor when he took off.

Elias promised himself he would never pass that disease down to children. His life wasn't worth the sacrifice. And relationships only caused misery.

Sex? Well, that was a beast he'd rather tackle with someone besides Caroline. "*No strings attached*" had always been his motto, and she was a gnarled skein of yarn.

Crap! She'd seen him. He turned to the opening elevator door, but he was too late. The tall voluptuous blonde rushed to block his way. She stood nearly eye to eye with him. One of her brows was arched high and her pouting lips wore a fresh coat of glowing red lipstick. Caroline wasn't about to be ignored.

"Hey, Chief. When are you going to ask me out on that second date? I'm still waiting, you know." Her lips went into a tighter pout, as her left hand planted on her hip and her right pressed against his chest. "Why are you making me wait?"

He removed her roaming fingers and shook his head with an unwelcoming smile. "Caroline, I'm not interested. Never will be."

She smiled. "Well, a girl's gotta try."

Any normal red-blooded American male would jump at what Caroline offered. But Eli knew better and was disgusted. He hated the dumb blonde act and the tits and ass charm never interested him.

Elias stood there quietly, eyes fixed on the lipstick on her front teeth. Silence was golden at that point.

She stepped closer, to where he smelled her mint gum and her large breasts brushed lightly against his chest. "I'll see you around, Chief." She took a step back, which gave him room to escape.

Under his breath, as the elevator door closed, he muttered, "Let's hope not."

The ten seconds of peace in the enclosed space gave him time to adjust his soured mood. Elias slipped a piece of gum in his mouth before the doors opened to the second floor.

As he stepped out, he noticed Magda at the end of the hallway, talking with a tall, reed-thin nurse who couldn't stand still. They stood six inches apart and the contrast between the two women in appearance and affect was startling.

The fidgety nurse walked way, and Magda slowly turned in his direction. She smiled while she smoothed back the perfectly set silver hair that framed her smooth porcelain face.

Oh, no. He knew that look. He was in trouble for something.

Normally, her Georgian charm was apparent in the grace, patience, and civility she typically exuded, but not at that moment. Even the stroke she'd had a year and a half ago hadn't dismissed the intensity of her stare. Her skin was drawn slightly down, which emphasized her frown even more.

"Is everything all right?" Elias asked, as he met her half way. "And why are you here? I thought your shift ended at seven last night."

"We are short staffed today, so I came in early to help. Gloria will be here in a half hour to replace me. But that's not the point. What's chafing me right now, Chief, is that your phone manners could improve."

"I'm sor—"

"I'm not finished." Elias snapped his mouth shut when she interrupted him. "Whenever you come around here, some of the nurses are more preoccupied with your presence than their patients. Why is that?" She looked up at him with a frown but Elias saw the twinkle in her eyes. She knew the answer but loved to poke fun at him.

"I'm sorry about the phone. No excuses. But I don't have an answer to your nurses' problems. If you want, I could arrest them?" Elias gave her a wide grin and took out his handcuffs from his belt and let them dangle off his forefinger.

Her frown changed to a smile. She grabbed his forearm and led him down the hall. "Thank you, but I don't think that will be necessary. It would cause more chaos in my hospital. Nurses would be lined up, waiting for you to arrest them and nothing would get done." Magda chuckled. Her laughter always softened his heart. He often felt like a little boy around her.

"I'm glad you have your sense of humor back." Elias enveloped her hand with his. "How is she?"

"Jane woke up around midnight, screaming again. She tried to get up and out of bed, but luckily, we were there with another syringe. It stopped her before she seriously hurt herself."

"And now?"

"She's calm. But Elias, she was yelling that a man was here to kill her."

Elias's jaw was rigid, his temples aching from the strain of grinding his teeth together. Of all the things... he needed to calm his shit down. He took a breath before he spoke. "Did she say a name?"

"No, she didn't." Magda admitted. Her shoulders slumped, and he knew she was exhausted.

He nodded. "All right. Why don't you rest a bit while I go talk to her. I'll try to get a quick statement and then drive you home."

"I don't need to be coddled. I'm fine. Really. I'll sit a bit when I finish this round, which will be shortly. I want to wait for Gloria to get in. Elias." Magda patted his arm, a serious note to her voice. "Jane's teetering on the edge already and she doesn't need a push from you." They stopped outside the doorway. "Please, take care what you say to her."

"I'll do my best not to push." Elias laid a hand on her shoulder and squeezed it as reassurance, then walked inside Jane Doe's room.

She was propped up, face turned toward the window.

The early morning sun sieved through the vertical blinds, casting shadows across her face. It hid the faint bruising around her jaw line. Aside from the bandage that wrapped around her head, she looked normal.

From her pert nose to her oval face, Elias admired the way she sat in a regal manner in the bed.

Elias cleared his throat to get her attention. "Excuse me for the interrupting, but I'm Chief Elias McAvoy. Are you feeling well enough to answer a few questions?" He walked over to the side of the bed.

Her relaxed hands turned into fists at her sides. Her body stiffened. When she tilted her head toward him, fear shone in her light brown eyes.

He caught himself staring and turned his attention to the window. He found her simple appeal attractive.

What the fuck is wrong with me?

Elias ignored his brainless libido, swiped his sweaty palms down his jeans and looked at her again.

Jane eyed him like he had three heads. Her close scrutiny made him uncomfortable.

"Are you well enough to talk?" Elias dragged the light blue vinyl chair by the door to the side of her bed and sat down. "Sorry. I know you probably have a lot of questions of your own. I will answer them the best I can. But right now, I need a few answers cleared up about what happened and who did this to you."

Jane stayed silent, but her lips quivered as if she wanted to say something. Was she afraid?

He'd been warned to tread lightly with her, but he didn't realize he had to tiptoe on paper-thin glass.

"We can start off simple. What is your name?" Elias sat back and waited. But he was met with silence. "Where are you from?" Again, nothing. "Do you know what happened, or who did this to you?" His voice strained from controlling his agitation.

She shook her head slightly, then looked down at her lap. "No. What... happened to me?" Her voice was a little hoarse.

Elias scratched at his jaw, hesitant about how she'd react. In the past, he'd sugarcoated the truth and, in the end, it got a person killed. He wasn't about to do it again this time.

He blew out a quick breath and explained without the bloody details. "You were found by a couple of hunters and their dog. Someone buried you, and we're guessing you dug yourself halfway out before they found you."

She took in a shuddering breath. "Okay... Who did this to me?" Jane touched her cheek, winced, and dropped her hand.

"I don't know yet who tried to kill you, or why. Do you remember anything that can lead us to your attacker?" Elias stood, but quickly paused when Jane's body went rigid. Damn, he was scaring her. He sat back down, but he softened his voice. "You had no identification, and your prints aren't in the local or national database. We have no clues to who you are."

Tears welled in her eyes, overflowed and slid down Jane's cheeks.

Women with tears made Elias extremely uneasy. His stomach ached from watching her weep. And his throat hurt from the strain of holding back his anger. He wanted to shout on Jane's behalf, for the atrocity she had endured.

Out of nowhere came a sudden urge to hold her until she stopped crying and calmed down, but he shut that shit down. He knew all too well that crossed the line. No matter what, he had to maintain his professional distance.

"Do you remember any detail of that night or something about your attacker?" Elias kept his voice level.

Jane shook her head no. She carefully cupped her knees to her chest and placed her face in her hands. "I don't remember anything." More tears flowed.

"Are you kidding me?" The words slipped out in a low hiss before Elias was able to wrangle them back.

Jane shot a sparked glare at him. "Really?" Her tears ceased, and anger replaced her sorrow.

Elias quickly recognized her steely temper. Maybe being gentle with her wasn't what she needed after all.

Only hard facts and truths could bring out her memory. She was a fighter, just like him.

"I'm sorry the truth hurts, but at this point we don't have any leads. I need you to remember something, anything, no matter how small in detail. It will help." His brash tone bothered him, but he suspected Jane would stay strong through this crazy nightmare. To hell with what the doctor said.

"Like I said, I don't remember anything." Her lips became thin. She shifted her face back to the window and remained quiet.

Her silence irked the hell out of him, but what more could he say?

"This is unbelievable." Elias's words came out soft, but they grated between his teeth. His eyes never wavered from her face. "Do you at least remember your name?"

Jane turned back. Wetness threaded through her lashes, making her light brown eyes more intense. "Everyone here calls me Jane." Her voice came out hard and fast. Her body shuddered and she turned away, dismissing him. Was it his cue to leave?

Elias got up and walked around to the other side of the bed. He wanted to be sure she was going to be okay. "Jane," he uttered with sincerity this time. "Look at me, please."

The moment she looked up at him, he saw dejection on Jane's face. He was being a total jackass for pushing her too much, but it was for her own good.

"Look, I'm sorry," Elias said as he raked through his hair. "But you're the only one who has the answers. There might be another victim out there who this son of a bitch is trolling for or caught. They might not be as lucky as you."

She reached over and grabbed the last tissue from

the box. Tears flooded her face again. She took a breath before answering. "I wish I could help you. I don't remember anything other than bits and pieces of when I woke up in the hospital."

"That's okay." His gut twisted tight from her admission. His attempt to reawaken her memory had been futile.

"I'm sorry." Jane wiped her tears with the now saturated tissue. "Though I have these dreams...they're killing me," she admitted. "They're constantly running through my head and I..." Jane shook her head and leaned back into the bed. She closed her eyes, cupping her hands to her chest. "Forget it."

"No. Dreams?" Elias said softly. He wished he never had one himself. "Maybe Dr. Rollins will have some insight. You rest." He didn't wait for her reply and walked out of the room, rubbing the back of his neck in frustration.

With Jane's inability to give him any information, Elias realized that he had nothing on this case. Not only did he lose his only witness to what he assumed was amnesia, but the only proof of a crime committed was the hole in the ground she came out of, the blood from the victim and the shredded clothes. Nothing else.

With so little evidence, no proof of who did it, and no viable witness, he was literally screwed. He couldn't see this case having a successful conclusion. Unless Jane remembered.

He might never find out who did this to Jane. But one thing was for sure: he had a victim who wanted answers, and so did he.

CHAPTER SEVEN

J ane swiped the wetness with the back of her hand as tears trickled down her face. Her nose stuffed up and she couldn't breathe.

Damn you, Chief. Is it hard to show some compassion?

Her calm mood had flipped to anger the second he walked in. Jane didn't like him from the moment he opened his mouth. Actually, she didn't like anything about the man. His demeanor was deplorable, not to mention the way he looked. His face wasn't shaved. His clothes were so disheveled, Jane assumed he'd rolled out of bed with them on. She wondered if he had even showered. What kind of man was he who was supposed to help her but couldn't even take care of himself?

As much as the chief's appearance irritated her, his penetrating green eyes unnerved her and she couldn't keep eye contact for long. Too intense.

She'd had to turn away before she really broke down and wailed like a baby. And lately, that was all she had been doing.

She wanted the truth, yet he didn't have to be so

blunt about it. He made her feel incapable, and she didn't need his help with that either.

Jane had questions. However, instead of asking them, she ended up tight-lipped because of his harsh attitude. His nose flared when she told him that she couldn't remember anything. He had even gnashed his teeth.

Why hadn't she just answered his question about the girl? Jane hadn't remembered much, but she did recall seeing the child's yellow dress the morning she was found. A few blips of memory—flashes of images of things and people, but nothing that drew her memory out.

Looking down at the last bit of tissue in her hand, she wiped her nose with it and stared at it again. That tissue represented her nearly shredded emotions; she was falling apart, and fast. No hint of her name shadowed her thoughts, nor did she have a clue as to where she was from. Who were her family and friends? She concentrated on those questions but the black veil over her memory stopped her, and the effort left her with a pounding headache.

Who had tried to kill her? *What if the bastard came back? What if I never regain my memories?*

Jane shook off the fear while she stared out the window and watched the fir tree sway in the wind.

She felt so alone.

The idea that she might never get her memory back made her stomach lurch. She closed her eyes to let her frustration and self-pity run their course.

Get over it. Life's too short to dwell. Actions speak louder words. Somebody once told her that. But who? She was drawing a blank.

Jane took a deep breath and sat up very carefully. She placed her feet onto the cold floor and moved to the edge of the bed. Using her IV stand as support, she toddled her way to the bathroom.

The nurses insisted that she needed assistance, but Jane didn't want anyone's help. If she'd survived a vicious attack and lived, then she could walk on her own and go to the bathroom unaided.

The white porcelain sink was an arm's length away. Jane reached out with both hands, grabbed it and leaned against it. She looked into the rectangular mirror. The person reflected back was a frail, beat-up woman. There wasn't a spark of recognition as she studied her own features.

This was the first time she'd had the courage to look at herself. The sight of her battered face struck her hard. Jane didn't realize that she'd been beaten so badly. She had some idea from the way the nurses talked, but not to that extent. Even her cheekbones were sore to her touch.

She touched her fingers at the back of her head where stapled ridge-line of the gash was and shuddered. She didn't want to think about how that injury happened.

Jane gently ran her palm over the sprigs of hair that poked out of the white gauze. She looked like she wore a choppy short wig. From her multi-colored skin and bloodshot eyes, to her head, where some of the gauze wrapping was coming loose, she definitely wasn't a prize. She looked scarier than the walking dead.

She closed her eyes and shifted her stance for a moment to regain some calmness, but moved too fast and the room started to spin. She wanted to puke from the dizziness. Jane's pulse quickened as the room spun faster. A burning migraine seared the back of her head like a branding iron to flesh. The pain became unbearable.

Jane clutched her head with one hand from the pressure, but it wasn't helping. She almost collapsed onto the floor, but she held onto the sink with her other hand and tried breathing out the pain.

Just keep breathing, she told herself as she focused on the water dripping from the faucet. The pain couldn't get any worse. She squeezed her eyes shut, and hoped that would help, but it didn't.

She refocused on the drops of water and counted. *One. Two. Three...* Jane gulped in a lungful of air and thankfully, the hard spasms subsided.

Then the room turned ice cold in an instant. Jane glanced at her arms and watched her skin tighten into goose flesh. The hairs stood to attention. She shivered from the chill, and dread seeped into her body.

She slowly straightened, looked up, and saw that frost iced the edges of the mirror. It climbed inward, toward her reflection.

Her breathing see-sawed in and out of her lungs, and it painted the air with white plumes of smoke with every exhale. She froze, and watched in horrified fascination as the ice completely covered the mirror. Terror filled her, but she couldn't look away.

Jane hastily tried to wipe the ice off the mirror. The moment her reflection was uncovered, she realized it wasn't her face she was seeing.

Jane let out a blood curdling scream that pierced the small room. She collapsed onto the tiled floor, her IV stand toppling on top of her as she curled up to protect herself. She assumed death came in many forms but never would she have thought something so cold and horrific would come for her.

CHAPTER EIGHT

J ane's scream echoed at the other end of the hallway.
"Not again," Elias spat out. He bolted to the room.
He rushed in and found her crumpled on the bath-
room floor.

She shook uncontrollably. Jane covered her face with
her arms and kept repeating, "No..."

Elias dropped to the floor and gently pulled her into
his arms. His heart was racing as he held Jane tight to his
chest. Her scream had scared the crap out of him.

With Jane in his arms now, Elias knew she was safe...
But that scream.

Jane wrapped her arms around his neck like a vise.
Elias had to turn his head to breathe.

Magda, Dr. Rollins, and another nurse rushed in.

After Magda disconnected the tangled IV line from
Jane's arm, Elias managed to stand while holding her
close. Dr. Rollins encouraged him to put her down on
the bed, but Jane wouldn't let go of him.

"Please, don't let go," Jane whispered in a weepy
whisper in his ear.

Elias's heart stuttered at her plea. Jane's tears soaked

his collar. "I won't," he whispered back and held her tighter. "You're safe, Jane."

Her cold cheek against his warm skin sent chills down his back. Elias's instinct was to take her and run, but he stayed cemented. He'd hold her for as long as she needed him.

The fear he saw on Jane's face—in her watery eyes, sent rage flashing through his body like an electrical storm. "What happened, Jane?" he whispered so only she could hear him.

Jane loosened her grip enough to lean back and look straight into his eyes. She held his full attention.

She shook her head. "It's not safe." She put her face back in the crook of his neck. "He's after me."

"Who, Jane?"

"I don't know," she sobbed. "I can't see his face,"

Elias tightened his hold on her, but his anger was breaking down fast.

"Jane, look at me." Elias's tone came out harsher than he wanted, but he needed to know who she was talking about. "Look. At. Me."

She complied but didn't release her tight grip around his neck. Their lips were an inch apart; her stuttered breath caressed his jaw. Elias had a hard time thinking straight. The sudden urge to lean in and kiss her shocked him. Where did that irrational inclination come from?

He clamped his lips tight and leaned farther back until his face was a safe distance away from her mouth.

"Please," she uttered.

"I won't let anything happen to you. I promise. Do you trust me?" Asking her to trust him was a lot, but that was the only way he could cut through some of her fear.

"I... trust you," Jane gulped out.

"Then let me put you down. Magda and Dr. Rollins

are here to take care of you." She looked over at them, then back at Elias and she nodded.

With reluctance, Elias laid Jane on the bed. The second he released her, both nurse and doctor came forward and nudged him out of the way.

As the medical team checked her out, Elias cautiously entered the bathroom. He found nothing in the small space. No girl. Not even a bug. However, the air had an odd odor that he wasn't able to place, almost... rotten. No cleaning solution smelled that way. Not even the soap by the sink.

Aside from the unidentified scent of cleaner, nothing seemed out of place. Then a single drop of water slid down the side of the mirror and plopped into the sink. With his finger, he touched the droplet and brought it to his nose. No smell. He stuck out his tongue and tasted it. Water. He touched the edge of the glass and moisture rimmed it.

How odd.

His hand came back wet. Elias couldn't imagine what had caused the condensation. The sink was dry, except for the slow drip of the faucet.

Elias scratched his head, bewildered by what he saw. He gave the room one last look before he left it. Nothing there.

Magda pulled him off to the side. "So? What scared her?"

"I don't know, but there is nothing in there." Elias kept the condensation to himself. "How is she?"

"She's calm, but she needs to rest, Chief," Dr. Rollins interrupted.

Elias pulled the doctor out into the hallway, out of earshot of Jane. "Can her head injury cause delusions?"

"That's a good possibility. Her occipital lobe has a severe sub-hematoma. The type of trauma she experienced, especially to the brain, can cause numerous effects."

"Simple English, Doc." Elias folded his arms to the chest, his patience wearing thin.

"Swelling to the brain. Such trauma to the brain will cause memory loss in various degrees and affect the healing process. How much? Every case is different. She could be seeing or hearing things too. That could be what she was experiencing in the bathroom. Her past. Or like the girl in the yellow dress."

"A girl in a yellow dress?" Elias asked, uncertain of this information.

"Yes. The morning Jane was brought in, she was rambling about a girl in a yellow dress and how we needed to help her," Dr. Rollins explained, writing notes on Jane's chart.

"Why didn't anyone bring this piece of information to me? It could be a witness." Elias was pissed. If this girl had seen Jane, she might have seen the killer too. "Doc."

"I'm sorry. I didn't think it was pertinent. And, at that point she flatlined."

"I would like to ask her a few questions." Elias began to walk back in, but the doctor stopped him.

"Chief, Jane needs more time. You pressing her with more questions might delay her recovery. Give her a few more days."

"I've waited long enough. I have her trust now. Maybe there is something she's remembering, like more details about the girl in the yellow dress."

"Pushing Jane might do more harm. Remember that."

Elias's body stiffened. He looked down at the doctor. Between gritted teeth, he said, "I understand." He raked both hands through his hair as doubt settled in the pit of his stomach. This elusive girl in the yellow dress might be the only clue to solving the case. He wasn't going to wait, especially if it could help him capture the bastard who'd tried to kill Jane.

"A few more days will help." Dr. Rollins walked away.

Elias walked back into the room and instantly locked eyes with Jane. Her tense body relaxed and she gave him a small smile as he approached.

Magda cleared her throat as she fixed Jane's sheet and blanket. She walked past Elias and glared at him, which could only be understood as a warning.

He proceeded with his questioning. "Jane, tell me about the girl in the yellow dress," he said gently.

Jane lost her smile. She bit her lower lip and looked away. "I don't know who she is."

"Tell me the truth. Where did you see her?" He wasn't going to leave until she opened up.

Jane wrung her hands and looked back at him with watery eyes. "The morning I was found—I only remember bits and pieces of that time."

"Did she say anything to you?"

She pressed her hands together to her chest. "No. But like I said, she was there and then disappeared."

"Disappeared? Like walked away?" Elias couldn't hide his agitation.

"No. Like she just vanished," Jane said with worry.

Elias cocked a brow at her. "Like a ghost or something?" He couldn't help but let out a single chuckle.

Jane scowled at him. "Something like that." Her eyes cut away to her lap, but Elias saw them glaze with tears. Shit.

"Jane." He had no one to blame but himself. "I'm... sorry for..." That apology was half-assed and not very contrite.

Her silence didn't deter him from pushing her. "So, you saw a ghost."

She blew out a heavy breath before she spoke. "Yes, I think so. Now get out of my room. I'm tired." Jane grabbed her bed remote and reclined the bed back. She pulled up the white sheet and blanket to her chin and turned away.

Elias hated the way she had dismissed him. Maybe the doctor was right, and Jane was delusional. Waiting a few more days couldn't hurt.

He pulled his card out from his back pocket and placed it on the tray next to her. "Here. In case you remember anything else, you can reach me at this number. And Jane..." he waited until she looked at him. "I am here to protect you. I will find out who tried to kill you, that's a promise." He strode out of the room. Ghost or not, he needed to find out who this girl in the yellow dress was.

CHAPTER NINE

E lias left the hospital in a rush. He drove straight to the lake, to where they'd found Jane, to clear his head, and refocus his body.

What a fucking idiot.

He'd actually gotten a hard-on when her brown eyes went wide and sparked with anger. His dick had sprang tight against his jeans and he'd had a hard time walking. This wasn't what Elias thought he'd be doing on this late Friday night. But here he was, making a sweep of the area.

Somehow, even in the cold weather, the smell of cow manure filled the air and stifled the sweet scent of the coming winter. Not finding a damn thing, he finally drove back to town with a clearer conscience.

Heading down Main Street, the eight-block radius of the town center had a quiet heaviness to it. The same feeling he'd gotten when he was a child before walking into his house. Elias never understood it, until he was older. It was that fear of the unknown. The weary antici-pation of what was next to come. The same drudgery day in and day out, with a side slap across the face every other day, when he used to find his mother beaten.

That was another reason why he escaped into the military.

Breaking free from all that was around him, good and bad, had been the best thing. That change had made him a better person, or so he'd thought until Elise was killed. Truth was, it hadn't made a damn bit of difference. He was still fucked with nightmares of the past plaguing him.

With his sleeping schedule messed up, and since he was on the books for Saturday's rotation, he decided to head to the station, four hours early.

When he pulled up to the small brick building, he noticed Harold's red pickup truck parked two spaces down. A bad feeling came over him. Elias walked into the station and expected chaos.

To his surprise, no one was at the front desk. He called out a hello, but there was no answer. Then Cindy Lee peeked around the corner from the dispatch room and thumbed toward the back office.

A clank from the storage area got his attention right away. Elias headed back, and stepped into the eight-by-ten square room. His three officers, Tom, Tyson, and Tyson's wife Beth, stood in the corner, oblivious to him, whispering something.

Tom seemed to be doing all the talking while Tyson and Beth stood there in silence, regretful frowns on their faces.

"What's going on?" Elias spoke loudly, and startled all three. He eyed each of them, and quickly guessed the beef of the situation. "Why are you here, Tom?"

"No reason. Just giving these two a little pep talk," Tom replied with a smirk and walked toward Elias with a big fat grin on his face.

"Do I want to know?" Elias asked under his breath.

His second in command shook his head no.

Elias scowled at Beth and Tyson. The two stood in the room like statues. He wasn't in the mood to deal with them. "We'll talk later." They cast their down to the floor while they nodded.

Right now, Elias was worried more for his friend. "I saw Harold's truck outside. Where is he?"

"I did my usual patrol around the hospital and found Harold's truck in the back. I called in and Magda confirmed that Harold was visiting Jane Doe. And he brought Traitor with him. Would you believe he brought in that dog?"

"He brought Traitor into the hospital?"

"Yep."

"I must have just missed him." Elias shook his head. "What did Magda do?" That woman wouldn't tolerate a fly in the hospital.

"Nothing. She said Jane was ecstatic to see who had saved her life. So, she held her tongue."

Elias wanted to wring Harold's neck, but at least he'd had the right idea about the dog. The animal made Jane happy, and that mattered, especially after he had left her in an agitated state. "Then what?"

"So, I waited for him to come out and I made him follow me here, and then I put him in the green room." Tom flicked his thumb back toward the holding cell.

"Did he put up a fight?" Elias knew the answer to that. Harold hated confined spaces.

"What do you think? He was about to cry when I closed the cell door behind him." Tom laughed. Actually, it wasn't funny but Elias had to stay impartial.

"What about Traitor?" Elias asked as he pulled off his coat and threw it on a chair.

"I drove the dog home and came back."

Elias gave him a nod. "Do me a favor and stick around. I want a word with you."

"Sure." Tom walked to his desk and sat. "I have a bit of paperwork to finish."

Elias opened the door to the holding area. The jail cells were located in the back. He stuck his head inside and saw Harold pacing like a caged cat.

Harold and his older brother Raymond were the only friends Elias had growing up. The three had stuck together like glue until Elias joined the military at eighteen.

Harold enlisted three years later, went to Iraq, and got a dishonorable discharge two years later, for punching his sergeant. He hadn't been his normal self since he got back. Ever since, his temper was on a short fuse. And Elias learned to never underestimate Harold's short skinny stature, which reminded him of an anorexic with muscles.

Harold looked up at the groan of the steel door. "It's about damn time, McAvoy. I didn't do anything wrong. Your Deputy Fife threw me in here for no good reason. I want the fuck out of here."

"Harold, you were told to not visit Jane until this investigation is over. I wasn't saying it for my health." Elias unlocked the cell door and opened it wide but stood in the doorway. "But what you did for Jane was good. However, don't do it again."

"I thought Jane would want to meet Traitor. He was the one who found her. And I thought it would make her feel better and heal faster."

"Like I said, that was thoughtful but don't do it again. I mean it, Harold. Next time we catch you, I'll let you rot in here."

"Fuck you, Elias. I didn't do anything wrong," Harold

shouted but his voice cracked as he plopped down on the cot.

Elias's jaw went rigid, his teeth ground together. He took a deep breath and exhaled hard, grabbed the metal doorway and squeezed tight. "I told you, Kantor, I don't want anything or anyone to impede this investigation and that includes you. I'm assuming our conversation at the hospital didn't get past your thick skull. You cannot see her. She is now in protective custody until all this is over."

Harold stood and said, "You are acting like I'm a suspect."

"For right now, everyone is, until we get more details on who tried to kill Jane." Elias didn't want to discuss it any longer. He left Harold's cell door open and walked away. He stood in the doorway to the main part of the station and watched his friend ponder what he needed to do.

"Are you coming?"

Harold rushed out of the cell, followed Elias halfway across the station, then abruptly stopped. He spun, with a look of anger on his flushed face and pointed his finger at Elias. "What's the real reason you don't want me near her... Wait. *You* have a thing for her, don't you? I see it."

Elias had never seen anyone's skin shift from pale pink to red in a matter of seconds.

"And you." Harold pointed at Tom. Bits of spittle sprayed out of his mouth when he shouted. "If you ever come near me again..."

Tom's smile changed to a vicious frown. He took a couple of long strides toward Harold while pulling back his sleeves. Harold's mouth snapped shut and he shuffled backwards as the officer rushed forward.

Elias stepped in front of Tom and grabbed his arm. "Tom," he warned.

"I know. It's not worth it." Tom pulled his arm away and walked off toward the back room.

Elias walked up to Harold, looked straight into his friend's eyes. "I think it's best you leave."

"Answer my question first. Why?"

"Why what?" Those two words came clipped and hard, which made Harold wince a bit.

"What is the real reason you want me to stay away from Jane? Eli, you've known me since we were kids. I would never harm a person, especially a woman, especially Jane."

It was taking everything Elias had to not grab Harold by the throat and throw his ass back in the cell. The stubborn bastard was assuming shit. "I'm doing my job, Harold. And my job is to protect the people in this town, and that includes you and Jane. Especially Jane. I want to catch the asshole that tried to bury her—who tried to kill her. So, I suggest you occupy your time doing something else instead of seeing Jane and riling up my officers."

Harold's face turned a darker crimson. Sweat beaded across his brow. "This is bullshit. I found her! If it weren't for my shot, she wouldn't be alive! I have no choice but to look out for her!" Harold was waving his arms like a lunatic.

Leaving only a slice of space between them, Elias leaned in and grabbed his neck. Harold stopped his protest when his back came up against the brick wall.

"She isn't a wounded dog you found, asshole." He wanted to knock some sense into his friend. "Jane is very lucky to be alive, but it does not give you the right to do as you please." Elias's voice dropped into a low menacing whisper. "Listen to me and listen good, you son of a bitch, because I'm only saying this once more. I want you to stay away from her. Or your ass will be in jail until this case is closed. I don't care how long it takes. You can rot." He released his grip.

Harold's face paled and he nodded his head.

Elias stepped to the side, which gave Harold space to escape. He took it without any encouragement and fled the station.

Silence blanketed the room. Elias turned around and headed to his office. "What is everyone staring at?" he barked. "Officer Tyson, why the hell are you still here?" He narrowed his eyes on the tall, lanky man, before turning to his second. "Tom, head out. I'll talk to you later."

They all stood there, gawking at him as though he had three heads. "Go, or get back to work." Elias slammed his office door shut, which knocked down a pile of magazines from the top of a filing cabinet.

He waved off the mess and threw himself into the chair. *What the hell is wrong with me?*

What he needed to do was calm down and focus. This case, Jane—and now Harold, grated at him. He blew out a slow breath and looked around the room. He couldn't concentrate on what he needed to do next.

Why would Harold assume that he, Elias, had ulterior motives regarding Jane? He was only doing his job. And what was with Harold's obligations to her? He said he had to look out for her. What the hell did that mean? He should have pulled him back into the cell and interrogated him.

Everything about the Jane Doe case was strange. From the way she was found to the lack of evidence. And with her ghost sighting, he wasn't sure if she needed to be committed.

He rubbed at his aching shoulder and neck. The strain of the last two weeks wore on him. A craving for nicotine and a beer formed on his tongue. He needed to redirect his energy toward something other than his current aggravation and gnawing addictions. It didn't help that the office smelled of cherry wood smoke. And sweat.

Elias stared at the pile of missing person reports Tyson had put on his desk, then picked up the DNA reports from Jane's case. It was his fifth time looking through the information.

Nothing had changed from the first time he'd looked through it. He took the fax, placed it in his Jane Doe folder. Elias's stomach ached every time he saw the results. This case was nowhere near its end.

He slipped the file in his side drawer and shoved it closed. Then the thought of the girl in the yellow dress had him considering driving around the neighboring farms and houses around the lake to find that elusive girl.

Oh hell, ghosts. He couldn't believe he actually regarded what Jane was saying. Talking with her was disappointing, since he'd gotten nowhere with her.

Elias tried concentrating on the mass of paperwork and items strewn in front of him but wasn't in the mood. Instead, he scanned the small space. It'd been four months since he'd taken over Henley's mess and the place had turned into an even bigger pigsty.

When it came down to this office, the old chief of police had everything where he wanted. No one touched any of Henley's things. He knew right away when something was out of place. Elias figured the old man had a compulsive disorder of some sort.

He'd never cleaned up after Henley's death. His magazines were still piled up neatly on one of the filing cabinets—well, most of them were, as he eyed the few that had slid to the floor when he'd slammed the door. Stacks of folders were heaped on top of the other. Small trophies adorned the few shelves, and medals and other citations for valor were hung on the walls.

Elias hadn't had a chance to go through the old man's things and weed out what he didn't need. As he picked up the old chief's nameplate on the edge of the desk, the same question arose. Why? After years of commendable service, why would he kill himself?

Elias had worked with Henley almost two years, and the man had never missed a day of work. When he didn't show up for duty and hadn't called in, Tom had driven over to his house. After breaking in the front door, he'd found the old man dead on his recliner. He had shot himself in the mouth with a forty-four.

Even after all this time, Henley's suicide still bothered Elias.

A knock on the door disrupted Elias's thoughts. He looked up at the clock and saw it was nearing eight in the morning. "Come in."

Tom popped his head in. "Mayor Daniels is here."

The mayor gave Tom a dirty look, pushed past him, and walked in. "Chief McAvoy, I want a word with you." He sat down and turned toward Tom. "Alone."

Tom closed the door but not before he gave the man a look that could have melted the back of the mayor's head.

"What do you need, Mayor? I have tons of work to do." Elias knew what the nosy bastard wanted.

Daniels leaned his cane on the edge of the desk and pointed a bony finger at Elias. "I want to know what you are doing about the Jane Doe case. It's been weeks. What's the progress?"

"Well, nothing right now. Until we have further evidence, we have to wait."

"Wait? I put you in charge, McAvoy, to get things done efficiently. I thought you were capable of handling things in a quick manner. Our town isn't used to terrible crimes. Maybe I *should* have had Tom take over." Daniels shallow threat didn't go far.

He stood up and leaned toward the mayor. "What's stopping you? I'll step down right now." Elias was too damned tired for the mayor's bullshit, but he got the right reaction.

The mayor tried getting up but he stumbled back in the seat. "Wait. Maybe I was hasty saying that. Chief, I am only looking out for this town."

"I know you want to get information about this case as quickly as you can, but it doesn't work that way. Please, let me do my job. The moment I know, you'll know. All right?"

Daniels stood, grabbed his cane, and walked to the door. "I knew I made the right decision listening to Henley. He always said if anything happened to him, I should appoint you in his place." He rubbed his nose, and continued. "Hopefully soon." Daniels walked out.

Elias was speechless. *What the hell did he mean about what Henley had said?*

He'd never understood why the mayor appointed him chief, until now. Elias assumed Henley would have picked Tom as his successor because they were close. Apparently, not close enough.

Tom walked in soon after, and sat in the chair. "That man is something."

Elias shook his head.

Nearly twenty years Elias's senior, Tom had been a part of the Beaver Ridge Police Department for a long time. Elias was relieved that the officer hadn't walked off the job after he took over. If it weren't for Tom at his back, he wasn't sure who to trust as his second in command. Tom was a good man, a good officer, and a good friend.

"Want a drink? What about a cigarette? God, that man can drive anyone crazy."

"Not funny." Elias shot him a dirty look. "I'm not in the mood today."

"Okay," Tom conceded, holding his hands up. He propped his feet up on the desk and leaned back as though it was his own. "So, what did the ass want?"

Elias looked up from his paperwork and eyed Tom's feet. He didn't mind. Tom should have gotten this position. "He wanted to know what we're doing with the Jane Doe case."

"Hmm. Well, speaking of Jane Doe. What about Harold?"

"Harold is so pigheaded. It's not going to matter what I say to him, he's going to do what he wants." Elias also leaned back in his chair and stared up at the ceiling. "I don't want him near Jane."

"I know, but...what is the big deal? Why are you so worked up about this? You know Kantor is harmless. Or was he speaking the truth?" The officer angled his head, wiggled his brows and smiled.

Elias grumbled. "This is purely professional, nothing more." He dropped his fist on the desktop. "Sorry. But this damn case is getting to me. We have no leads, no real evidence against the person who did this to her. And worse, Jane has amnesia."

Tom's mouth dropped open. "Are you sure?"

"She can't remember a single thing about who took her and tried to kill her. I think she has some delusional issues too. Dr. Rollins thinks it's caused by the damage done to the back of her head."

"Delusional?"

Elias scratched at the stubbles on his face and chuckled. "Yeah. She thinks she saw a ghost. I don't know what to make of it. Walking into that hospital today, I thought I was getting answers. I was dead wrong."

"What did Dr. Rollins say about getting her memory back?" Tom dropped his feet and sat up.

"It can come back at any time, or never. Sometimes objects or certain events can trigger a memory, but I'm not holding my breath."

"What of the ghost? Do you have any leads on it?" Tom let out a hearty laugh.

"You're funny... Hey, I got an idea. I will leave that part to you. You can find out who this ghost is, or was," he said, without cracking a smile.

Tom almost fell off the chair. He grabbed the edge of the desk and righted himself. He smoothed back his thinning hair and let out another chuckle. "Thanks. But I like to deal with the living and the dead. Not the in-between."

Elias's silence and somber stare made the deputy turn ashen.

"You're not serious?"

Elias couldn't help but laugh at his deputy's expense. Since day one they'd always had a great rapport with each other.

Tom stood up and walked over to the door. "Well, if we're done here, I have Rafferty's cows on Biggers's property to tend to. And if I don't get there soon, there will be dead cows on the property." Tom tilted his head to one side, clicked his tongue and continued. "I don't want to get caught for slacking off on the job, so I'm off... Hold on... Do you think cows come back as ghosts too?"

"Get the hell out of here." Elias threw a wadded-up paper at his deputy.

Tom scooted out, but glanced back at Elias, laughing. "Ghosts."

"Wait," Elias called out. "Before you go, tell me why you and the love birds were in the back room?"

Tom stuttered in his steps. "I was hoping you forgot that."

He narrowed his eyes at the deputy. "Do I want to know?"

"Give the kids a break. They're in love," Tom said. "You'll be in love one day, too."

"Right," Elias said with resolve. "Head out."

Tom saluted before he closed the door.

Elias took a minute before he called Officers Beth and Tyson Ryan into his office. Beth's head hung low and Tyson's shoulders were slumped. Both faces were flushed pink from ear to ear.

Without Tom's explanation, Elias knew exactly what the two had been doing in the back room. He'd caught them once before, right after they returned from their honeymoon. They'd been mauling each other like two teenagers since they got married.

He tried to enforce the rule about married officers and had split their shifts. Beth took the first and Tyson had the second, but an hour overlap gave way to quick liaisons.

He stared at the two as they stood side by side. He realized what an odd couple they made. In looks, they were polar opposites. Beth barely reached to Tyson's shoulders. Where he was thin and lanky, with short, straight blonde hair, she was short in stature, with meatiness to her build, and shoulder length, dark brown curly hair.

"Do I need to separate you two by giving Tyson the third shift? Or should I be firing one of you?"

In sync, both popped their heads up and looked at him. Beth had watery eyes, while Tyson went from pink skin to pale. They shook their heads no in unison.

"I don't want to lose either one of you, but your actions need to stop now. You two need to fi—"

The radio chirped. "Dispatch. There's an accident on Route U5, near marker 9. A hit and run, two victims. Request an ambulance and backup." Tom's voice came over with urgency.

Before the dispatcher, Cindy Lee, answered back, Elias responded on his hand held. "10-4. En route now. Cindy Lee get on—"

"Already on it," the short blonde shouted out as she passed the doorway of his office.

"Tyson, stay here and man the station. Beth, you're with me," Elias ordered as he shot up from his chair, grabbed his jacket, and then headed out the door.

CHAPTER TEN

Elias and Beth arrived on the scene within ten minutes. A Volvo had crashed into a large balsam fir that grew out of the side of the deep ditch. The way the car sat, the front end was smashed against the tree and the back end sat wedged on the rim of the ditch.

As Elias pulled to the side of the road, Tom rushed over to the driver's side of the Elias's truck.

"Both victims are breathing. The man's out, but the woman's awake. Eli, I think it was Harold who ran them off the road. From the way the woman rambled on about a red truck, it has to be him."

Elias got out of the vehicle. "We got this. Go bring him in."

"Wouldn't it be better if you went?" Tom asked.

"No," Elias snapped.

"Okay, Chief." Tom got in his squad and raced off.

Elias ignored Tom's barb, got out of the truck and focused his energy on the vehicle. "Beth, grab the blankets in the back and the med kit."

He looked down at the ditch. The slope pitched in an almost ninety-degree angle with a few crags jutting out. The small patches of ice and snow made it difficult to find footing. If he wasn't careful, Elias could easily slip under the car.

Afraid the car would tip sideways and slide into the ditch, Elias dug his feet into shallow divots and slowly opened the driver side door.

The front end started to creak as he opened the door wider. Without wanting to test the stability, Eli left the door ajar. It was wide enough in case he needed to pull the driver out.

Elias touched the man's neck; his pulse was strong. Since Tom had seen her, the woman had passed out. He unlatched the man's seatbelt and waited for Beth to reach the passenger side.

The female came awake and turned her head toward him. Her eyes were glazed over with fear. She mumbled about a red truck and then a girl in a yellow dress.

Girl in a yellow dress? Elias paused. Too coincidental to ignore. "Ma'am, can you tell me what happened?"

Beth eased open the passenger side door with caution. The car creaked again and jerked forward slightly. The officer jumped back and let out a small yelp. Elias looked over and gave a silent *don't move.*

Once the car stopped, Beth finished opening the passenger side door.

"Careful," he warned with a whisper. "I don't want the front end to give out."

With sloth-slow movements, Beth checked the female's pulse. She gave a nod of okay. "Her pulse is strong."

The woman began to get agitated. "Why was the girl in the middle of the road?" She frantically yanked at her seat belt, and the car shook, which made both women scream. She tried to get out of the seat, but Beth placed a hand on the lady's shoulder to keep her still.

"Please, I need you to stay still for me, ma'am—Your head is bleeding. What is your name?"

The woman calmed down. "Brenda... James."

"Brenda, can you tell me what happened?" Beth asked while she placed a gauze square on the victim's forehead.

The woman stopped talking. The blood drained from her face. Her eyes turned wide with terror. She pointed straight ahead and screamed again. "Do you see her?" the woman shouted.

Elias shifted his footing to see all around him. "Beth, do you see anything?"

Beth bent over to look out the front window. "No, Chief. I don't see anything, or anyone."

The woman grabbed at Beth's jacket, which caught the officer off guard. She lost her footing and slipped down to the bottom of the ditch. She landed face up, under the vehicle.

"Get out from under the car," Elias shouted. He wasn't sure if the woman would try to move again, but he needed his officer safe.

The woman yanked at her seatbelt, which made the car shudder. The tree shook and the car groaned.

"Move your ass, Beth!" he yelled. Elias hurried to the passenger side and grabbed the woman's shoulders. "Brenda." His voice turned hard as steel. Just as fast as her screams began, the woman collapsed into her seat and passed out.

Beth emerged on the driver's side with mud on her face, the right side of her jacket and her hands.

"Are you all right?" Elias asked. He was finally able to take an even breath.

"Yeah. I'm good." Beth looked at her hands, then at the chief. "She kept repeating 'the girl'. I didn't see anyone."

"Neither did I," he admitted, scanning the area around them.

They stood by the victims until the fire truck and ambulance showed up. Not wanting to push their luck, they waited for the fire department to remove the victims. They were taken to Beaver Ridge Hospital. The officers followed.

The moment he entered the building, he thought of Jane. The sudden urgency to see her seemed unnatural. His pulse quickened and a knot formed in his gut. Almost anxious.

That's ridiculous.

Elias had visited every day since she was found and hadn't once gotten the need to rush to her room. Why now?

He instructed Beth to get statements when the victims regained consciousness, then turned and rushed through the white metal door that led to the staircase and ran up to the second floor. Elias stopped within the threshold of Jane's room and watched her.

Elias stood there like a stalker, which annoyed the hell out of him. So, he stepped inside, staying quiet.

Jane was sound asleep, and he couldn't help but take in the serenity of her face, even in its battered state.

The late afternoon sun ribboned through the blinds and masked the discoloration on her skin. The swelling of her yellow bruised cheeks was nearly gone. Her natural beauty was more apparent.

Her body showed frailty, but it didn't camouflage the strength she had hidden within her. He still admired her, despite her claim of seeing ghosts. Maybe, more than admired.

The way Elias had treated her before wasn't right. That had to be the reason he felt so uneasy. He had acted like an ass.

As Elias stepped closer, Jane's breathing stopped and her eyes popped open. They were cold and focused on him. The fury in her gaze stalled his breathing.

Jane's vulnerability had vanished. The serenity was gone and replaced with something ugly. Her brows furrowed deep and her unwavering eyes were dark, almost black. She didn't utter a single word. Just glared at him with a snarl across her face.

He didn't move—didn't dare. Elias exhaled and saw his breath crystallize. The room became ice cold. It made no sense. Frost coated around the edges of the window. He moved to the window and grazed his hand around the pane, but found nothing to let in the cold. He turned his attention to the thermostat. It blinked seventy-two degrees, then shot down to sixty-five and then lower. *What the hell is going on?*

Elias looked back at Jane. Her eyes were closed and the sound of her breathing evened out again. Peace returned to her features. The room wasn't cold any longer and the frost evaporated from the panes. Was this what had happened in the bathroom?

He knew he wasn't going nuts. Or was he? Lack of sleep could do that to a person, but this—this was real. He'd seen Jane's face, the way the temperature dropped and how the window frosted up. Could it be something supernatural?

The events that led up to this point were making him rethink his non-belief in the supernatural—because this was fucking crazy. Demented. Questioning his own mental stability seemed like a daily occurrence, ever since Jane had entered his life.

One thing was for certain; he had to check out if a girl lived in the area of the accident. It was the only logical explanation. The yellow dress she wore had to be purely coincidental and not connected to Jane.

Looking at her, he remembered the way he'd found Jane in the bathroom. A very small part of him wanted to believe in her ghost remark.

The crackle of Tom's voice on the radio pulled him out of his thoughts instantly. He shook off any remnant of the chill and walked out into the hallway.

"Go ahead, Tom."

"I got Harold at the station. He is full of piss and Scotch right now. He's ranting that a girl caused the accident. He keeps saying it isn't his fault. I think he's lost it."

Haven't we all? "10-4. I'll be right there." He glanced at the doorway of Jane's room before he headed back downstairs.

He found Beth talking to one of the ER doctors. He called her over.

She flipped through her notepad. "The male is still unconscious, but the woman, Brenda, said that a girl in a yellow dress appeared out of nowhere and stood in the middle of the road. She said that the oncoming red truck swerved into their lane and ran them off the road.

"I tried to get more from her but she became hysterical when the doctor checked her pupils. They had to give her something to calm her down. The man was patched up and taken upstairs."

Has everyone gone crazy? The same details from three different people were too coincidental. The acknowledgement of a ghost clawed at his sense of factuality, but he couldn't ignore it any longer.

"I need you to stick around and get more information about this girl she saw. I have to get back to the station. Tom has Harold locked up. Radio Tyson to come and get you when you are finished here."

"All right, Chief."

"Beth?"

"Yes, Chief?"

"You did good." He gave her a slight smile and headed out.

Elias passed through the sliding doors into the parking lot, where he saw Caroline leaning against his driver's side door.

"I don't have time for your shit, Caroline. I have an emergency and you need to get out of my way," he said as he tried to open his door. She blocked the handle with her rear end.

"Come on, Elias. I'm your emergency. I need to be taken care of, right now." She tried to sweep her arm around his neck but he took a step back from her. "You've been ignoring me for way too long. I can't take it anymore. I want you, and I know you want me," she said with a pout.

He glared down at her as though she'd spat in his face. "Caroline, I don't know what drugs you're on, but get sober. I don't like you. Never did. Now get over it or you'll be taking a ride in the back of my truck and I'll book you for harassment. Your call."

Caroline's eyes turned wide and her mouth gaped open. She puffed out her chest. "Fine." She took a step away from the vehicle.

Elias glanced down at her chest and then back at her scowling face. It didn't impress him how large her breasts had become since last year.

He reached for his door handle, dismissing her.

"You'll pay for this, Elias. Mark my words, one day you're goin' to want me and I won't be around for you."

"Don't make me any promises." He got in the truck and started it without giving further thought to her threat. He slammed the shift into drive and headed for the station.

With the lights flashing, but the siren off, Elias made

it in less than five minutes. He didn't want to leave Tom and Harold together too long.

"Where's Tom?" he asked Tyson.

"The deputy headed back out for patrol. He's pissed."

Elias went straight back to the cells. To his surprise he found Harold curled up in one corner on the cement floor. He rocked back and forth, mumbling, "Not my fault. Not my fault."

Elias grabbed hold of the bars that separated them. "What happened, Harold?"

Harold's right eye was red and swollen. "Did Tom do that?" Elias unlocked the door and stepped into the cell.

"I swung at him first," Harold confessed. His head fell forward, and he broke down into tears. "I didn't see that car until it was too late. I swerved to get out of the way but I killed them, didn't I?" His body shook. It was hard to see his friend cry.

The fear etched on Harold's pale face softened Elias's anger. He sat on the cot, pushed back his hair and rubbed at his neck. "What should I do with you, Harold?"

Regret and sadness swirled inside Elias. Having Harold behind bars didn't seem right. He wanted to believe his friend, but the law held him accountable for the accident.

Thin as a rail, Harold's pale sallow skin was a drastic contrast to the dark smudges under his blue eyes. He had problems, some dating back many years. Always doing stupid crap, but never to the point of taking someone's life.

Reeking of scotch, Elias's own addictive call for a drink choked his throat like strangling hands.

"Tell me, Harold. Were you drinking and driving?" Elias asked sternly.

"I only took a small swig." Harold wiped his eyes with his hands.

Elias's shoulder relaxed a bit. "What happened then?"

"I left here to go straight home. I saw a girl standing in the middle of the road. I slowed down and veered out of the way but she disappeared. Then next I saw a white car coming straight for me. I tried to avoid them. I don't know what happened next but... I kept on going."

"Why?"

"I didn't want to see the girl again. She scares the shit out of me, Eli!" Harold cried out.

Elias blew out a heavy breath. Jail wasn't the place to talk about ghosts. He already regretted his decision, but out of loyalty, he decided to temporarily let Harold go. "Come on, I'll drive you home. We'll talk in the truck."

"What about the accident?" Harold sat up and wiped his hands across his face. "I killed those people."

"They aren't dead. Shaken and scratched up pretty good, but alive." Elias stood by the door. "I don't want to stand here all day, Harold. Get your ass up and let's go."

Harold swallowed hard and rose to his feet. He wiped his eyes again with the heels of his palms and followed Elias out of the holding cell.

"Don't ask," Elias told Tyson, who'd gotten up from his desk. "Call Raymond for me. Tell him I'm bringing Harold home. And tell Tom I want a word with him later."

The ride through town was quiet. As dusk shadowed the night, the small neon sign on Betty's Diner glowed. Main Street in the middle of town looked deserted. Sunday night, everyone hunkered down, but him. His job was twenty-four seven.

As they drove past the town center, next to the

mayor's office, the small gazebo was decorated for Halloween.

"Nice orange lights. Great for Halloween." Elias broke the silence. He wanted Harold to calm down before they talked about the girl.

"Yeah, I guess." Harold sniffled and wiped his nose on his jacket sleeve.

He glanced over at Harold then back to the street. "I want to know what really happened."

Harold stared out the window. "I told you everything already."

"I want to know about the girl."

Harold shivered as he spoke. "I first saw her on the side of the road the day after we found Jane. I thought it was a—"

"A hallucination?"

"Yeah. And now, I see her everywhere." He took a gulp of air and continued. "After I left the station today, I headed down County F. That strip is always deserted, so I took a drink, and that's when I saw her. She was standing at every mile marker I passed—I'm going fucking bat shit, Eli. You know I haven't been able to sleep?" He clutched his arms tight to his stomach.

"No, I didn't know that. Why aren't you sleeping?" Elias knew exactly what his friend was going through. Anyone could turn a little crazy.

"It's because of that girl. She gives me nightmares. That's the reason why I go see Jane. And..."

Elias shook his head slightly. "What?" A cold chill like icy fingers ran throughout his body. The hair on the back of his neck stood on end. He wasn't going to like what his friend had to say.

Harold huffed out a breath. "Eli, I see this girl in my dreams." He raked his fingers across his scalp and shook his head. "I'm so confused and... I'm scared."

"Why are you scared of a little girl?" Elias asked as he turned down Bonner Street.

"She's no little girl," he blurted out. "Her face. It's not the same all the time. It changes, and not in a good way."

Elias pulled up to the stop sign before he proceeded left onto County H. "What do you mean her face changes?"

Harold gave out a snort and laughed. "Sometimes... she's smiling, but mostly... her face melts off her bones."

He tried hard to understand what Harold had described, but it seemed too fucked up to believe. "All right. Then how did the accident happen?" Elias had to ask again.

"I told you, she stood in the middle of the road. I slowed down and swerved out of the way to avoid hitting her and that is when I saw the white car coming. I swerved again."

Elias remained quiet. He needed to digest the information his friend explained.

"I'm sorry," Harold choked out.

"No one was seriously hurt. That's all that matters," Elias said as he pulled up to Raymond's house.

Raymond charged out of the house like fire was on his heels. "Is he okay?" Raymond opened the passenger side door. "What the hell happened to his eye?"

Elias shook his head. "Don't know. But he's exhausted, Raymond. He's not to leave your sight."

"Are the people pressing charges?" Raymond asked while pulling his brother out of the truck.

"What do you think?" Elias replied.

"I don't know, but keep me in the loop," Raymond called over his shoulder as he lugged Harold back to the house.

Elias called out, "Raymond, make sure he doesn't leave town either."

"Got it," Raymond shot back and then pulled his brother inside the house.

Elias waited for the front door to close before putting the truck into drive and heading home. He wanted to head back to the hospital to see Jane but he needed some sleep first.

He radioed in. "Cindy Lee, I'm heading home. Call me if anything happens."

"10-4, Chief."

Elias pulled up to the farmhouse and got out of the truck. The whisper of the cold wind was a soft brush across his face, like a caress.

Another day gone, and thankful for it but nothing came about on Jane's case. One thing was for certain, this girl in the yellow dress was tied to Jane and Harold. Finding her was the key.

Tomorrow.

Dreamless sleep was what he needed now, but it was the last thing he got. The usual nightmares came to him as predicted.

CHAPTER ELEVEN

J ane had a good night. No dreams of ghosts or
nightmares of unfamiliar faces had hovered over
her. There weren't bodies stuck out of the ground,
calling to her for help. No hands reached out of the
murky soil, trying to pull her in.

It was a new day, and Jane was thankful and lucky to
be alive.

She stretched onto her side as she looked out the
window to see a snowy world outside. Dawn had peeked
over the horizon and the morning colors of orange and
yellow welcomed the day.

She closed her eyes and made an oath to stay strong
and not break down into tears every time she thought of
her sad dilemma. Rediscovering her identity wasn't going
to be easy, but she had to think positive. And she had to
be able to laugh at herself.

At the mess she was in.

The pain in her muscles hurt like hell and the back
of her skull still had a dull, heavy ache. The bandage
around her head moved when she turned, which caused

some of the staples to snag on the cotton binding. She couldn't wait for remove the wrapping to be removed.

Even though her body was healing, Jane still felt broken, and old. Twenty-six wasn't old by any means but... "Wait. I'm twenty-six." Jane had to say it out loud as a confirmation. "I'm twenty-six."

Her eyes watered at the small accomplishment. *Don't cry!*

The sound of footsteps from the hall drew Jane's attention. Leaning against the doorway stood a large breasted, tall blonde in fuchsia-colored scrubs.

"Can I help you?" Jane had never seen this nurse before.

"Yes, you can help me. And no, I'm not here to wipe your back side." The nurse's clipped tone was the last thing Jane needed to hear. Her good mood vanished the moment the blonde opened her mouth.

"Apparently, you're not here to do your job. So, what do you want?" Jane folded her arms and countered.

The nurse walked inside the room but kept her distance. She mashed her red lips together and looked around the room before she spoke. "I'm Caroline. I came here to see what all the fuss is about. I know Elias is doing his job, and he does it quite well by the way. But I don't get the reason why everyone is in a tizzy over you. It's not like you have any looks. There is no comparison between me and you. I win hands down."

"Nurse—"

"Caroline," she interrupted.

"Caroline, I don't know what you are talking about." Jane glared back at the blonde.

"Everyone is saying that you and Eli are together. I knew the rumors weren't true. But I came to hear it from the horse's mouth." Caroline snickered then continued. "There is no way he would be into you." She pointed one of her pink polished nails at Jane.

"You mean like, dating?" Jane shook her head no. This Caroline was off her rocker.

"Dating. Very good. Oh, I forgot you lost your memory—let me make it simple for you." Caroline leaned toward Jane and lowered her voice. "You're not ever to sleep with Eli. He's mine. Got that?"

Jane almost choked on her spit. She couldn't believe what she had just heard.

"I don't know where you're getting your information, but I want you to understand something. The chief and I are not, nor will we ever be, sleeping together. He is only helping me reclaim my memory and find the person who did this to me. Got that?"

Caroline's lips turned into a wide toothy grin. "I knew that. But I wanted you to understand there is another woman. And if you have any ideas floating around in your battered head about hooking up with my man, you will find yourself six feet under, again." She walked out without giving Jane time to digest her threat.

Jane let out a loud huff. She almost lost it and wanted to run after the nurse and yank all the bottle blonde hair out of her head. Instead, she tightened her grip on the bed rails and tried to ignore the stupidity of what the nurse had said.

She was still fuming when Magda came walking in with elation pasted on her face. "Good morning. I'm surprised you're awake this early." Magda stopped at the foot of the bed and wrinkled her nose at Jane.

"It's too early to be that cheerful, Magda." After Caroline's visit, Jane wasn't in the mood to be happy anymore.

"What's wrong?"

Jane wasn't sure if she should tell her what happened. "I couldn't sleep. Bad dreams."

"You want to talk about it?"

"No."

"Are you sure? I'm a great listener."

"I'm fine, thanks."

"If you change your mind." Magda patted her heart and gave Jane a gentle smile. "Since you don't want to talk, let's check your vitals."

With one end of the stethoscope in her ears and the other over Jane's heart, the elderly woman watched her with a careful eye. "The darkness under your eyes is much lighter and most of the bruises are barely noticeable now. A good sign of a healthy recovery. But you are going to have a heck of a bruise on your arm, if you keep messing with your IV."

"I can't help it. It itches like crazy."

"I understand. I'm a mover too. I have to sit you up to fix it." Magda gave a soft chuckle as she elevated Jane's bed and repositioned the line and taped it.

"I don't think it's funny." Jane frowned and looked away.

"Aww, honey, I didn't laugh at your discomfort. I'm so happy that you are finally doing better. For a while there... Let's not talk about what if."

Jane checked out the secured tape. "I'm sorry for sounding bitchy. I had a rough morning."

"No need to apologize," Magda said. She kept moving. Right after she filled a small pitcher of water and put it on the table, she grabbed her chart and jotted things down.

Jane watched in fascination as the silver-haired woman walked around her with grace. Compared to the other nurses who wouldn't utter a single word to her, she found the older woman refreshing and calming.

"How long was I in a coma?" Jane asked with hesitation.

Magda sat down next to the bed. "Twelve days."

"Really?" Jane absently touched her IV. "Was I that bad—I must have been."

"You were unconscious when you arrived here and in very bad shape. At one point you almost died, but thankfully Dr. Rollins revived you." Magda gave her a gentle smile. She patted Jane's shoulder. "You can't touch this IV or you're going to get an infection and your arm is going to hurt something fierce," she said while putting on another strip of tape.

"I almost died," Jane whispered to herself.

"Don't dwell on that, honey. Everything is going to be all right. I believe that, and so should you."

"What actually happened to me?"

Magda paused and looked at her. "Didn't Elias explain everything to you?"

"Yes, and no. When I met Harold and Traitor yesterday, he evaded my question. I want to know how my body got so broken." Jane's chest tightened with each word that passed her lips. Her throat constricted but she knew she had to get past this fear. Just from the state she was in now, it had to have been bad. But just how bad was it?

She swallowed down the hard lump while she remained calm. "Please."

"You want details?"

"All of it." Jane pleaded with the woman. "I need to know the truth, no matter how bad."

"Okay." Magda took in a breath and began. "You came in frozen, beaten black and blue and barely alive. The back of your head had a four-inch gash. You barely clung to life. Two fractured ribs on your right side and a sprained wrist."

Jane shivered. Her jaw hurt from clamping it tight. She wasn't sure if she wanted to remember any of those parts. Pressure formed at the back of her throat. The truth was hard to swallow. It overwhelmed her to the point that she wanted to rewind the past hour and forget what she'd been told. Actually, she wanted to rewind the last month to reclaim her life.

But life wasn't a fairy tale.

She couldn't dwell on what had already happened. But she could take charge of her future.

"You know I have no memory of what happened or who I am."

"I know that, dear."

"I don't know anyone here or anywhere else for that matter." Jane wiped the wetness from her cheeks. "I just want to say that I trust you, Magda."

Magda's eyes glazed with tears as she reached out and held Jane's hand. "I'm here for you, Jane."

"Thank you. I might need someone to talk to," she said, relieved.

"We do have a wonderful psychologist in residence. I'm sure he could help too. That is a part of healing, inside and out." Magda stood up and patted her shoulder. "You know I'm not the only person you can trust around here."

Jane knew who the woman was talking about. "The chief."

"Very perceptive. Yes, Elias is a wonderful person. He may be gruff and very rough around the edges, but he can be sweet and he is here to help you. You only need to trust him."

"Maybe at times. In your eyes, Magda, everyone is wonderful. I don't think he cares one way or the other about me, except to clear this case up and be done, which is fine by me. I want answers to who I am and who did this... And rough doesn't begin to describe his attitude. Rude, insensitive and a stubborn ass is more like it."

"Is that gumption I hear? I like that. You are much stronger than I gave you credit for. And no, not everyone around here is wonderful. I'm only telling you to trust him. He will help you."

The nurse leaned in and looked straight at Jane with no hint of a smile. "Do you know from the moment you were brought here, Elias visited you every day. Every day, even on his off nights. Do you think he doesn't care?"

That information surprised Jane. She had no clue the chief had watched over her that much.

"Why?" Jane's voice cracked. Though, it gave her some sense of relief that he'd sat by her side the whole time. Strange, but at the same time comforting.

"Because Elias does care."

"It's weird for me to hear that. He doesn't know me. So why take the time? I know his job is to protect but—"

"Because, Jane, he does care for you. He's not the ogre you see him as, or how he portrays himself," Magda interrupted.

Jane's heart pounded a little harder. "Thanks."

"For what?"

"For everything. I guess I needed that talk after all." Jane tilted her head toward the window, then back to her nurse. "Magda, did the chief mention anything about what I saw yesterday?"

"No. What did you see?"

She shook her head. "Nothing."

"Come on now. You started this. I have a few more minutes to spare."

Jane swallowed hard and looked down at her hands. "I think I saw a ghost."

"And?" she asked nonchalantly.

"Crazy, huh? Either I'm losing it or I'm really seeing a ghost."

Magda sat on the edge of the bed. "Jane, you have a major head injury. There are many explanations for why you might be seeing things. What did Elias say?"

"He laughed at me. He didn't believe me."

"Maybe you caught him off guard. Not everyone believes in ghosts, especially Elias. He only believes in hard facts."

"Maybe I am delusional."

"I will let the doctor know. He will probably want to run some tests. Don't be disheartened, Jane. We will get to the bottom of this. In the meantime, I've taken too much time visiting. I have to make my rounds. I'll see you later. Breakfast is in an hour. Rest and please try to be careful of your IV." Magda gave her a sincere smile. She grabbed the controller and leaned the bed back.

"Thank you." Jane gave the woman a small grin back. "Can you call the chief for me? I'd like to talk to him again."

"Yes, I'll call him," Magda agreed, then left the room.

Exhausted by her roller coaster of emotions, Jane leaned her bed back and closed her eyes. She couldn't wrap her mind around the truth about Chief McAvoy. Jane couldn't imagine him sitting there and watching over her. That would take heart and respect. Where was that compassion when he had grilled her with questions? With his condescending attitude and his abrupt demeanor, he still protected her like some guardian angel. She had to chuckle at the image of him standing over her. Wings spanned out and a lance in his hand. Or was that a surfboard?

A sudden rush of warmth flooded her body. Jane sighed. For a moment, she found herself wondering what

Elias McAvoy really looked like under all that scruff and tried to shake off her curiosity.

She even tried to think of something else. Anything other than the chief. Magda. But every time she focused on the woman's face, Eli's intense green eyes kept intruding. She gave up and let her imagination take over.

An image of the tawny-haired policeman arose, causing flutters in her stomach. His was shirtless and his was a skin golden bronze from the sun, with sinewy muscles in all the right places. The sun and a beach hung in the backdrop with his gleaming smile as the focus. She wasn't sure why she saw him happy, but he looked damn good with it on.

Then a flash of a blonde with big boobs stood next to him. The freaky nurse, Caroline. Jane wanted to rip the woman right out of her mind. *Bitch*. She can even ruin a good daydream.

Jane let out a yawn and tried to relax. Pressure like lead weights clamped down on her skull. She shifted her body slightly to one side and pressed at her temples. It wasn't helping. Her eyes watered from the hurt.

With her lids closed, Jane focused on the chief's face, hoping that would lighten the pain. Instead, his image smeared into black. Another picture replaced it, like a slow-motion movie projector playing in her head. She tried to turn it off, but nothing helped. The images played out anyway.

A young girl stood in the middle of a golden field. In the distance were others, but she couldn't see their faces clearly. A small marshy lake was to her right. She was a pretty little thing. Her long blonde hair was carried by the playful wind. Her bright yellow sundress rippled with every spin she took. The warm and innocent smile on her face made Jane smile.

Jane asked for the girl's name.

"You know my name, silly. It's Janey."

The spinning stopped and the girl's smile faded into an ugly sneer. Her body contorted and hair melted into a hideous green slimy mess. The yellow dress changed to dark faded green and black hues, like wet mold.

The warm sun disappeared—replaced by shadows and cold. The smell of spoiled earth suffocated Jane.

Jane kept repeating. *It's only a dream. Open your eyes, dammit*. She tried to open her eyes but they stayed glued shut. Her heart raced so fast that she hyperventilated. Strangled breaths caught at her sore throat. A scream lodged in Jane's throat but wouldn't come out.

The grotesque figure moved forward—arms out, calling for help. Jane stared down into her sunken eyes and saw death.

With all the strength Jane could muster, she forced open her eyes and bolted upright in the bed.

Tears trailed down her face. She sucked in deep ragged breaths to calm her pounding heart. Both her arms shook as she held onto the rails in a death grip, while she attempted to erase the haunting image from her thoughts.

She laid back down and yelled out, "Why me? Why are you doing this to me?"

Jane covered her head with the sheet. She didn't want to see the colors of morning anymore. She'd thought she had woken up to a new and brighter day. She was horribly wrong.

CHAPTER TWELVE

Dressed in his regular clothes, he slipped into Jane's room. If he got caught—which he wouldn't—he would use the excuse that he was checking up on her. He'd waited all Sunday to see her.

He was desperate for this release.

He jammed the chair under the door handle and sauntered over to her bed. Jane's chest rose and fell in an even rhythm—the opposite of his adrenaline-swamped body.

Coming into the hospital in the middle of the night wasn't a big risk, but still a risk. The price of playing this game was worth it. It took pleasure to a whole new level. And with Jane, euphoria was his to gain. Besides the pleasure for himself, the satisfaction of revenge encouraged him to steal her away sooner rather than later.

Aww. When he buried her body again, he'd make sure she was posed like how she had been found the first time. That would fuel the fire in the chief's ass. He wanted to enjoy the aftermath her death caused.

There was a thrill with all his victims, but Jane doubled his pleasure.

The image of Jane naked and spread-eagled gave him an endorphin rush. Like a flu virus, it spread through his system. He became dizzy. He wanted to bite her, but that would leave defined marks. He clamped his teeth shut and waited for the shivers to end.

He loomed over Jane and studied the gentle play of her long lashes against her smooth cheeks. Her lips were full and biteable. He wanted to lick the scar from a scabbed tear at the corner of her mouth.

If he had taken his time before, he would have enjoyed her to the fullest and then discarded her properly. *Fool.* But he realized he had a second chance to finish what he had started.

The way she had screamed and clawed had brought him to a new level of ecstasy. He hoped to capture that rush again. The only obstacle that stood in his way was the damn chief. Elias wasn't much of a cop. Fooling him was easy. Taking Jane from under his nose would be like stealing candy from a baby.

Jane whimpered—her hands balled into fists on her chest. Even in her dreams, she fought. He loved that about her. Was she dreaming of him? He hoped she thought of him often.

The wrist and ankle restraints had been left loose on the bed. His smile grew wide as he touched the sprigs of hair that popped out of her bandage. "Oh, there is a God."

He pulled clear rubber gloves out of his pocket and put them on. Leaving fingerprints would only lead to his identity and that would be bad.

Carefully, he took a capped syringe out of his other pocket. He'd stolen it off of a tray in the dispensary.

After taking off the cap, he poked the needle into the IV outlet in her arm. *A little morphine will do the trick.*

Jane's breathing slowed and her body turned limp.

Her hands fell loosely to her sides. He'd given her enough to slow her reaction down if she woke, but not enough to kill her.

As the drug coursed through her system, he took each of her limbs and strapped them into the tightest loophole of the restraints. Her hands and feet turned red from the constriction.

Next, he yanked out the IV and placed it between her legs. The liquid and blood from her arm saturated the thin blanket and sheets. He stripped them away and proceeded to tear her blue gown down the middle, exposing her bruised flesh. The small sharp knife he used tore through the garment easily. His mother had given it to him when he was a boy. It was the first tool he learned to use.

With each exhaled breath, his nipples perked tight. To touch her without gloves would have driven him over the edge. To feel her pale skin on his and taste the fear on her sweet lips would have made him come right there —but he was there to play, tease, not kill or get caught.

Jane's small breasts drew into tight peaks. He couldn't resist and pulled at her nipples. They turned red from his abuse. "Oh, what fun I want to have with you," he said in a sweet whisper.

Just for me. He licked at the corner of his mouth. Rapture gripped his cock like a fisted hand. With every caress of her skin, the tighter the pull on his ball sac. He felt the compulsion to jack off all over her. Leaving his DNA, though, was a big no-no. He had no worries about his pubic hair; he'd shaved clean every single hair on his body.

He pulled a wrapped condom out of his back pocket and placed it on Jane's leg. The rigidness in his pants made him hurry.

It wasn't his intention to pleasure himself, but he

couldn't resist. He pulled the front of his pants down and freed his dick. He yanked at his shaft from its scarred head to the tight balls—the gloves gave him more friction. He shivered from the single jerk.

As his right hand hammered, he trailed his index finger down to Jane's triangle of hair. He stopped at the folds of her opening. He wished she felt the power of him entering her. Stretching out her dry hole like the whore she was made his cock harder.

If the chief walked in and saw how he had Jane... The shock and outrage on Eli's face would be worth the risk of being caught.

He gave his cock another jack before he slid his fingers hard into her. Dry, tight, the way he liked his women. Jane turned her head and let out a slight moan. He yanked his fingers out immediately. He wasn't there to pleasure her.

He picked up the condom and ripped it open with his teeth. After shoving the purple foil back into his pocket, he covered his dick with even pressure placed on every inch of his flesh.

The zipper of his pants rode up against his sac, cutting into his thin skin.

Looking down at his dick, he yanked the rubber off and placed it on her stomach. It was dangerous without protection. He'd been told this many times. Like a repeating parrot, but he took care of that problem months ago. The risk of exposure definitely added to his excitement. He'd been trapped in a rut for a while. He needed this. Needed Jane.

As he squeezed his scarred shaft, a drop of essence pearled on top. He wiped it off with his finger and licked it. The rapture of the moment quickly rose high. He gripped his dick tighter and jerked until he nearly came. With each hard yank, he felt less and less in control.

He wrenched his hand away right before he ejaculated. He threw his head back, closed his eyes and took deep breaths. He hated losing control. He would punish himself later for it.

As he tried to regain his composure, his dick pulsed for relief. He took in another breath when he noticed Eli's card in Jane's hand. Why hadn't he seen it before? Jane clutched the card as though it was her lifeline. *I don't think so.*

Rage coursed through him. He wanted to plunge his knife into her chest. The need to punish her clawed at his senses. Instead, he bit hard on the inside of his cheek to stop himself from using his knife.

He sucked in a breath through his clenched teeth. He pulled his pants up, took out a clear snack bag from his back pocket. He grabbed the condom off her stomach and dropped it in the bag. He shoved it back into his pants.

Still seething about the card, he wrenched it out of her hand. He looked at it for a quick second—then ripped it into small pieces and scattered them over her. *I wonder what that bastard's going to think about this?*

Jane's eyes fluttered open. He paused and watched. Her movements were slow and lethargic. The haze of the morphine still coursed through her system. He knew he didn't have much time left.

Right after he zipped his fly, he grabbed Jane's jaw firmly and whispered, "You belong to me. Remember that." Her eyes fluttered open. He let go of her face and took a small old knife out of his pocket.

With precision, he sliced thin lines onto her limbs. Twice on the left arm and once on the right and a couple on each leg. He did it the way he'd been taught—not too deep. His mother had made him repeat it over and over until he got it right. She would be proud.

Like a gentle lover, he kissed Jane's lips. He reclaimed her, just as before.

After placing the chair back against the wall, he was satisfied at how his message would be conveyed. He chuckled. His edict was clear and easily read. If he timed it right, the nurse should arrive at any moment.

After stepping into the empty room next to Jane's, he stood behind the curtain and waited.

The clop of shoes signaled him to still. The night nurse walked past. *Right on time.*

He wouldn't have minded a bite of that cherry pie.

The redheaded nurse went into Jane's room. A loud cry of horror echoed off the walls. The nurse raced out of the room yelling for help. He leaned his head against the wall and smiled with gratification.

Immediately after, the sound of Jane's screams filtered out to the hall. Laughter filled him as he imagined her struggle with the straps.

As medical personnel charged into Jane's room, it was his cue to leave. He slipped out unnoticed, down the hall toward the back stairwell and out of sight.

CHAPTER THIRTEEN

When Elias got the call from Jane's nurse, he scrambled out of bed so fast he almost fell on his face.

He called Tom right away. "I don't give a shit what time it is, Deputy!" Elias yelled into the cell phone. "Get your ass to the hospital now." He slapped the phone closed, shoved his clothes on, and grabbed his ball cap.

Elias barreled out of the house, and raced down the road with lights and siren blaring. When he passed the station, he saw one of his officer's squad cars, and radioed Tyson to meet him at the main entry of the hospital.

Once he arrived, Elias met with two security guards by the main doors. He instructed the men to guard the front and emergency entrances. "I don't want anyone leaving without my permission."

The second Tyson showed, Elias had the officer secure the first floor while he headed to the second.

Elias ignored the elevator and took the back stairwell two steps at a time until he reached the second floor. As he opened the metal door, he ripped off his baseball cap and wiped the sweat off his forehead with his forearm. The heat in the stairwell was suffocating, even in the middle of winter.

To his surprise, Magda was at the end of the hallway. She stood outside of Jane's room, worry etched on her face as plain as day.

"What are you doing here?" He hurried past her, into the room and rushed back out. "Where's Jane?"

"We had to move her. This way," Magda said as she led him down the hall. "I told Mary to call me if something happened. They moved her to room 211. She's placid now. The doctor had to give her a sedative to calm her down. No one touched her without gloves. They also swabbed for DNA too."

"Okay, that's good." He shook his head. "Why don't you head back home. There's no sense in you being here."

He took another step before he heard the crackle in Magda's voice. "Elias, I promised Jane that if she needs me, I'll be here. I'm here for her and I'm staying until I know she's all right."

"I can't tell you what to do—I never could," Elias said looking back at the woman. "But *I* will *not* allow *you* to risk your life. This guy might still be around here and I won't take that chance," he implored. He had to turn away from her before he grabbed her arm and dragged her out of that hospital.

He'd never shown any aggression toward Magda. But he needed her to understand; her life could be in danger too. He'd shout at her from the rooftops of the hospital if it made her realize how dangerous the situation really was.

She stood her ground and said nothing to him.

Elias caved. "Okay, stay with her. I'm doing a complete sweep of the hospital and I'll talk to the third-floor personnel, too. Don't let anyone else come into the room."

"All right. But do you really think this person is still here?" Magda's brows knit in worry. She rubbed at her upper arms. "What about the staff?"

"I don't want anyone in here, unless they have to be. Everyone is a suspect." Elias walked away, Magda trailing him.

"Elias." She pulled him to a stop. "Be careful." Her voice cracked.

"I will," he said, then strode down the hall.

It took Elias a while to scour each floor, commandeering the help of a few orderlies. He even checked the morgue, down in the basement. He wanted to know where all the exits and cameras were located.

Elias radioed Tyson. "Gather what information you have and meet me in Jane's old room."

"10-4," his officer chirped.

The bloody sheets on the bed stood out in the white room. Aside from the bed and the privacy curtain, the room was sparse. All the machinery had been pulled out; nothing was visible on the floor or in the garbage can.

The room felt strange. The walls, curtains and vertical blinds were so sterile white. Even the air in the room smelled off. It made his adrenaline rise, and his stomach ached as though it was churning barbed wire.

Elias circled the room slowly. Nothing was out of place but Jane's blood. The color pushed his urgency almost over the edge. He contemplated calling in the state police but reined in his compulsion. He had to handle this.

He blamed himself for not protecting Jane. Assuming Jane was safe there was a shallow belief, even naive. She could have been killed. What bothered Elias the most as he stared down at the blood was that the son of a bitch had had the opportunity to kill her. Why didn't he?

Elias had to walk away. He entered Jane's new room, his heart pounding hard against his ribcage as he watched her chest hitch up and down in stuttered breaths.

Magda and another nurse stood on the other side of Jane's bed, quietly observing her.

"Is it safe?" Magda's face showed fear in every wrinkle.

"I believe so."

"Okay then. I need to use the lady's room. I'll be right back." Magda walked out, which left him with the nurse.

Stress and anxiety brimmed to the top as he stepped closer to Jane. He hadn't been able to take a normal breath since his cell phone had gone off.

Elias saw Jane's face and exhaled with relief. Everything seemed the same, but it wasn't. That bastard had snuck into her room and pretty much violated her.

After the nurse adjusted Jane's IV, she turned around and walked over to him. She was about to say something, but Elias pointed toward the hall and the redheaded nurse agreed and followed him out.

"I'm Bridget," she said, introducing herself with an arc of a brow. "I'm the one who found her." She handed him a small bag with ripped-up paper inside.

"What's this?" he asked while he examined the contents of the bag.

"I found the pieces scattered across her body," Bridget replied, then totally changed the topic. "Are you and Caroline really dating? She's telling—"

Elias cut her off. "Did you see anything before or after you found Jane?" he asked, ignoring the loaded question. He took out his notepad from the front pocket of his coat and replaced it with the baggie.

Bridget hesitated for a second before answering. "Nothing strange beforehand. I went about my usual rounds. Jane's the last patient I looked in on. I came into the room and found her strapped in with cut marks on her arms and legs," the nurse said. "I called the staff and then called you."

"Anything else?"

"No."

"Please don't leave. I might have further questions for you."

The nurse nodded, "I have an hour before my shift ends if you need to talk to me." Bridget half smiled at him, then left the room.

Of all the crap that was going on—maybe he should wear a sign that read "NOT AVAILABLE," then maybe... But Magda always said, *it doesn't matter to these nurses*, so he believed his efforts would be for nothing.

Now, where in the hell is Tom? Let him wrangle in all the nurses.

Elias pulled out the baggie and took a better look at the bits of paper. He knew immediately that it was his card. *Son of a bitch.* Hands down, this bastard was playing some sick game and Jane was his pawn. Simply, this was a message—but to whom, Jane or him?

He crammed the bag back into his coat pocket, and headed back to Jane's room.

The wrenching discomfort in his gut hadn't subsided and his temples ached. Elias rubbed one side in a circular pattern to ease the tension. But as he walked into the room, all his focus was on *her*.

Watching the subtle twitch of Jane's eyelids, Elias couldn't help the unease coursing through his blood. She was safe, but for how long?

Jane's tranquil state turned fitful. The way her hands balled into fists, it was as though she was fighting demons. He wished he could help banish her nightmares. All he could do was sit down next to her and touch her clenched hand.

"I won't let that bastard get near you again. I promise," he choked out, his head forward as if in a prayer.

Magda surprised him by touching his shoulder. In a flash, he grabbed her by the arm and cocked back his right hand.

She let out a yelp and he instantly released her. "Magda, don't surprise me like that," he said. "Sorry."

She rubbed her arm and stood back from him. "It's all right. I didn't mean to scare you."

"Did I hurt you?" He got up.

"I'm good." She walked around to the other side of the bed. "Jane's strong. She'll be fine."

"I know. It's just—I'm angry at myself for not having someone here watching her." He sat back down and touched the bandages on her arm. "How are the cuts— were they deep?"

"The ones on her arms are deeper than those on her legs," Magda explained.

"I want to see them."

"Are you sure?"

He nodded.

Magda undressed the IV arm and lifted the patch of gauze that covered the wounds.

Elias's jaw hurt from clenching his teeth. "That son of a bitch—these are for me."

"Are you sure?" Magda's brow furrowed deep.

"I'm positive." Eli's gut twisted even tighter at that acknowledgement. "He's telling me that he can get to Jane anytime. That is why he didn't kill her. He wants to make this a game."

"Who is this crazy person?"

"I don't know, but it has to be somebody local—someone who could slip in and out without notice and would know all the exits. And someone who would be least likely to be a killer—that would be the only way to come inside this hospital unnoticed." Drunk or sober, Elias's instincts were never wrong.

The hospital was no longer safe. Elias's only solution was to move Jane. And there was only one place he could take her, where no one would ever think to look.

"What do you want me to do?" Magda asked.

"Stay with her. I'm going back to the old room and wait for Tom. If she wakes and remembers anything, get me."

Magda nodded in agreement.

Elias walked into Jane's room with a fresh perspective. Nothing jumped out at him, except for the blood. He stared out the window for a second and noticed the dawn lining the horizon.

In the reflection of the glass, he saw Tom stumble in. The deputy's pajama shirt was partially tucked into his unzipped jeans. The hair on the side of his balding head was flattened to on one side and porcupined out on the other.

The smell of beer and something slightly harder filled Elias's nostrils. He wrinkled his nose and gave Tom a severe frown. "It's about damn time you showed up. What the hell took you so long?"

"It's supposed to be my night off, remember? I had to sober up a bit before I drove here. Do you want me to get a ticket?" Tom said with a grin.

"You're not funny." Elias shook his head. "Got your gear?"

Tom lifted the black case and looked around the room. "Where should I start?" He placed the case down on the tray table and scratched the back of his neck.

"The bed," Elias said.

"I'll cut out some blood samples from Jane's sheets." Tom bent over and popped open the case. He grabbed a couple of gloves and snapped them on. "Then I'll go over the room for fingerprints. How's she doing?"

"They have her secured." He rubbed at his jaw in agitation. "Dammit."

"Relax. You aren't helping anyone by losing it," Tom conveyed with conviction.

"I've already lost it, Tom. To know the bastard was so close. He could have killed her. Instead, he slashed her up—just to prove a point," Elias spat out. He pulled the bag from his pocket and handed it to his deputy.

"What's this?" Tom took the bag and examined the contents.

"My card. One of the nurses found the pieces scattered over Jane's body," Elias said and then pointed to the baggie. "This was a message to me, I know it."

"This guy is playing some sick, twisted mind game," Tom said, handing the bag back to Elias.

"Twisted or not, I know the next time, Jane's dead."

Tom shook his head. "Don't think that. It might be a fluke he slipped in." He took out a plastic bag and scissors. He pulled at the bloodied sheets and began cutting pieces out.

Elias paced the room, stopping every few seconds and staring at the deputy. "I don't think so."

"Eli, will you stop. You're making me dizzy watching you," Tom said, wiping his forehead.

"We've got to move her."

Tom stopped in mid-cut. "Where? We don't have a safe house around here. Unless you want to bring in state cops. They take over this case and Jane will definitely be moved. And you'll be out of it. Is that what you want? I know we can catch this S.O.B. without those yahoos interfering," Tom expelled a breath. He scratched at his head and shrugged. "But, it's your call."

"We have to finish it. It's our case," Elias said with surety. Moving Jane was his first priority. There was no other choice. But how to do it without anyone's knowledge—that was his challenge.

Tom returned his focus to collecting evidence and finished cutting pieces of the bloodied sheet. He placed the cut material in the bag and marked it. "I'm done with the blood samples. I'll do a sweep for fingerprints and anything else that might be viable as a clue."

"After you're done here, check the security feeds. You have a better eye than Tyson. Maybe the cameras caught him coming in or out of the hospital."

"Okay," Tom said as he put away the samples.

Elias wanted to tell Tom more about his plan to move Jane, but he changed his mind. The deputy's conviction to find the bastard gave him renewed assurance but he kept silent about moving her. Why? He wasn't sure himself, but he stayed tight-lipped.

The lack of evidence in the room really bothered him. It was too clean. Jane's attacker had been meticulous in covering his tracks. Another reason Elias wanted to keep quiet was his assumption of where the killer was from.

Besides, the fewer people who knew her whereabouts the better. In order to keep Jane safe and alive, only three could know: Jane, Dr. Rollins and himself. And to keep up with appearances, with the help of the doctor... *Yes*—a lie would be spread through the hospital that she was moved to the psych ward for better protection. And it gave a false path for the attacker.

As Elias strode toward the door, out of the corner of

his eye he caught a glimpse of a small purple object under the drapes against the wall. "Tom. Check this out."

The deputy stepped up and squatted down in front of the curtains. He lifted the fabric off the floor and picked the purple foil up with his long tweezers.

"Is that what I think it is?" Tom said as he examined the wrapper.

Excitement surged inside Elias like a bolt of lightning. "I can't believe it. That is our break."

"I'll be whipped. The man upstairs answered your prayers. Out of all things, a condom wrapper."

"Bag it and send it out right away. The bastard finally fucked up and maybe left us a fingerprint or DNA."

"That would be—"

"I want you to find out who was in here. Nurses, interns, I don't care if candy stripers stuck their heads inside this room. I want names and reasons for them being here."

"Okay, but..."

"But what?" Elias shot out.

"Nothing. Just that I want to sweep the room further. Let Tyson get that information."

"Good idea." Elias left the room in haste. To know there was a possible break in the case made him hope. Before he saw Jane, he searched for Tyson and found him on the first floor. He told him to get everyone who went into Jane's room in the last six hours.

Once he finished his explanation, he headed to the elevator. As he approached the door, Caroline called out to him, but he ignored her with satisfaction.

The door opened on the second floor and he almost careened into Dr. Rollins.

"Sorry, Doc." Elias grabbed hold of Rollins' arm to steady the man. "Any changes in Jane's condition?"

"She's as well as anyone who finds themselves bound, naked and lacerated. For the moment, she's sedated and calm." His voice cut lower. "Chief, who could be doing this? This is a hospital. How did they get in here without being seen?"

Elias's tone matched the doctor's. "I don't know, but I wanted to talk to you about moving Jane out of here."

"Jane needs our care for at least a few more days. Especially after what just happened to her. She is in a fragile state. I can't risk her health and life. Can you have one of your deputies stand guard? She should be protected."

"Don't you get it, Doc?" Elias's voice turned sharp. "She's not safe here, period. This proved it. Whoever did this, will do it again. Next time he'll kill her, and I can't chance it. No. I'm not asking for your permission. I'm moving Jane out of here tonight." His last remark had enough bite; the doctor took a step back.

"Okay. But only on the condition that you take a nurse to watch over her," Rollins insisted. "And I need to know where you're moving her to."

"You aren't privy to that information, Doc. The fewer people who know where Jane is, the better. I'll ask Magda which nurse to bring. And Doc?" Elias scanned around them and made sure no one was around. "I need this information about Jane's whereabouts kept tight-lipped. Tell whoever is inquiring about her that she was moved to the psych wing. Tell them she is better protected there."

The doctor gave a slight nod. "I understand. When exactly are you planning on moving her?

"Now."

"Okay. Then I'll get a small med bag ready for her." The doctor sounded slightly defeated. He strode down the hall and disappeared around the corner.

Elias rubbed the back of his neck with relief. He hadn't been sure if the doctor would go along with his plan and was glad he'd agreed. There was no choice—Jane had to be moved.

In order for his plan to work, he must slip Jane out of the hospital without anyone seeing her. Not as easy as it looked, especially with everyone on high alert. With dawn fast approaching, the daylight would surely highlight his actions.

As Elias entered the room, Magda came out of the bathroom. He took her arm gently and nudged her back into the washroom.

"Elias, what are you doing?" Magda demanded as she backpedaled.

"I'm moving Jane out of here tonight. She isn't safe here anymore," he whispered in her ear.

"Where are you taking her?" Magda's voice shook. "She isn't a hundred percent."

"A safe house," he lied.

"A safe house? Where?"

He ignored her question. "Doc insists that a nurse go with her. I don't like it. The fewer people who know, the better. So, I'll be taking care of her needs."

"No, you can't," Magda said with conviction. "For now, she needs professional care. You can't give that."

"I can't risk someone else's life."

Magda looked up at him, "You can take me."

"No."

"Yes," she countered. Her frown made him hitch a breath.

"No, Magda. I don't want you to be involved. This guy—he is a sick, twisted person. I don't want to take any chances with your life."

"I'm already involved, Elias." Magda's face softened into a gentle smile. Her gray eyes glistened with tears.

She reached up and touched his cheek. "My boy, I can handle this, I know I can. Yes, I might be age-challenged but I can hold my own. I am going with Jane. You can't tell me anything different. Besides, I don't know a single nurse I trust to give this duty to."

Elias wanted to shake some sense into the stubborn old woman. But he knew it wouldn't do any good to argue.

"Dr. Rollins is making a med bag right now," he said between his teeth.

"I'll go get it, along with some clothes for her. I'll be back soon." She shot out of the bathroom before he could answer. Elias swore he had never seen Magda move so fast.

He wiped his palms on his jeans, already regretting his decision to take the old nurse with him.

Elias stepped out of the bathroom and walked over to where Jane lay.

The first thing he noticed was the dark shadowing under her eyes. The redness around her wrists and ankles looked raw again. She had been through so much. To know how close the bastard came to either raping or killing her made his rage flare high and if possible, it could have scorched the dark sky.

Elias's anger settled deep into his bones; his throat tightened and his hands shook. He shoved them in his pockets and swallowed down his ire.

Feelings of helplessness had him remembering his terrible childhood when his father used to beat his mother, and Elias would hide—because his mother told him to.

He hadn't been able to help her. Tears escaped his eyes at the memory of the sheer desperation and pain in his mother's cries.

He quickly wiped the wetness away and took a few

deep breaths to push those images out of his head. Then another face rose in his mind.

Elise. She should have never gone back home. She'd be alive right now if only she had listened to him. Her screams echoed in the back of his head. He tried to push those memories away too, but they caged him in every time he thought of Elise and the day he killed her.

As though on cue, pain from his old shoulder wound seared him. The bullet had gone straight through—but what ratcheted up his agony was knowing that *his* bullet, intended for her abusive husband, hit Elise's chest, killing her.

Elias sat down on the edge of the chair next to the bed. He bent his head down and covered his face with both hands. A flood of emotions drowned him. The yearning for whiskey coated his mouth and his parched throat—tugging hard on his three years of sobriety. He desperately wanted a drink. He deserved it. It was the only remedy he knew that worked to obliterate the nightmares of his past.

"Why?" Head bent; remorse was a bitter taste on Elias's tongue.

"I don't know," Jane answered.

Elias jerked his head up and stared into a pair of frightened brown eyes. He wiped the wetness off his face. "I'm sorry." He cleared his throat.

"For what?" she asked, groggy.

"Waking you. And for not being here to protect you. I didn't—"

"It's not your fault, Chief." She reached out to touch his hand but Elias pulled back from her reach. "Who would have guessed." She tried to smile but failed miserably.

Uncertainty and fear lined corners of her mouth and

the corners of her eyes. He'd seen this look many times before.

Elias's face turned stoney. "It won't happen again. I promise."

"I know—I trust you."

His stomach lurched at what Jane said. He'd said the same thing to Elise. Though he failed in his attempt to keep her safe.

"Who's Elise?"

He ignored her question and the churning nausea in his gut, gulped down the past and focused on Jane's face. "Never mind—I'm moving you tonight. You're not safe here anymore."

"What did Dr. Rollins say?"

"Doc agrees. And against my better judgment, Magda will be coming with us. Jane, do you understand, once I move you out of here, you have to stay in hiding until your memory comes back and/or we capture the person who did this, whichever comes first?"

She nodded. Jane looked down at her wrists, her eyes filled with tears. She bit her lower lip and closed her eyes.

"What?" He could tell something was bothering her.

"Nothing," she said. "When do we leave?"

"You're lying. If you trust me, tell me the truth."

Jane's lips pressed tightly together for a second, then eased into a frown. "He could have killed me. So why didn't he?"

"I don't know."

Jane gripped the bed sheet at her side. "I remembered a few things."

"All right, tell me."

"I'm twenty-six years old. Don't ask me how I remembered that, but I did. I also remember a man. He had an odd smell about him. Can't figure what it was.

And I couldn't really see his face. The image was blurry." She wiped away a tear. "That's it."

He exhaled—just realizing that the whole time he'd been holding his breath. "Okay. Hopefully more will come out soon. Is that it?" He spoke evenly so as not to sound disappointed. At least she remembered her age. It was one step closer to knowing anything about her.

"Yes."

"It's a good start. I will have Tyson add that to your file and check out all missing women in that age group. I'm sure we will find you." He took a step closer but still kept an arm's length from her reach. "Jane. I won't let anything happen to you." His solemn promise was the only thing he could give her.

CHAPTER FOURTEEN

His oath made her breathe easier and feel safe. But the intensity in his green eyes unnerved her. Just like before, she wasn't able to hold his stare. And some of her words seemed to be lost.

Jane swallowed down the tightness at the back of her throat and nodded again. She couldn't help wanting to cry, and tried to keep the tears at bay. But, one right after another, drops escaped and trailed down her cheek.

"Please don't cry. I can't handle women crying." Elias stepped closer and tenderly erased the tears with his thumb.

His simple touch soothed her and gave her hope and strength. It also brought a flutter to her stomach. Jane wasn't quite sure how to handle the odd reaction to his gentleness.

"I don't generally get emotional like this, I think," she blurted out. Jane could barely remember a few days ago, let alone the rest of her life. It sounded so absurd that she chuckled.

He looked at her as though she had lost her mind. But he cracked a smile and said, "Me either."

Jane teared up and her stomach ached, but she felt good for a change. The laughter helped her to forget the nightmarish way she'd woken up. She almost sounded normal.

When Magda walked in with a wheelchair, Elias's smile disappeared like the elusive girl in the yellow dress. The switch in his disposition caught Jane by surprise.

If only I can turn off my emotions like that.

Magda wheeled the chair next to the bed and placed the small pile of clothes on the bed.

Elias cleared his throat. "Is everything ready?" he turned and asked Magda.

"I had to make sure my duties are covered during my absence." Magda then turned to Jane. "How are you feeling, Jane?"

"A little dizzy. What's ready?" She glanced at Elias for the answer.

"You'll be fine," Magda said, patting her arm. "Whatever was in your system is almost out."

"What's ready?" Jane repeated but neither of them answered her.

Elias took out his card, wrote something on the back and handed it to Magda.

Jane's anxiety rose. "Don't ignore me. I have every right to know what you are planning."

The nurse looked at the card, her mouth gaping open. "Are you sure?"

"What is it?" Jane asked, trying to look at the card, but Magda shoved it in her pocket. "I've had enough of this. It's bad enough I don't know who I am—I'm so confused—even my own hair is coming out a different color—I don't need you two keeping secrets from me." She put her hands over her face to stop from screaming.

Elias touched her hands. Jane yanked away and put

her hands in her lap. She didn't want to look at him, but couldn't help it.

"Jane, listen to me. I have to keep everything tight lipped. It's for your safety. Magda will tell you once you are on the road. Okay?" His eyes softened—his tone of voice eased some of the stress pulsing through her.

Jane took a stuttered breath. "All right."

Elias turned to Magda, "I'm positive about the location. I'm counting on you to get her out of here, unnoticed. Can you handle it?"

"Can *we* handle it?" Frustration laced Jane's word.

"Yes." Magda smiled at Jane. "But I assumed you were coming with us."

"That was my original plan but with so many eyes, it would be better that you take her by yourself. It looks less suspicious."

"I agree," Magda said with a nod. "If anyone stops me, I'll say that I'm taking her down for x-rays."

"Good. I'll have Tyson study the security footage for the last few hours while you sneak away. He's so distracted by Beth, he won't pay attention to the screen."

"So why aren't you coming with me?" Jane's voice cracked. Her chest hurt with each breath. She wanted to cry, again.

"It's better this way. I'll see you later. You are in good hands with Magda. Remember, stay away from the windows and doors. Okay?" Elias didn't wait for her to agree. He gave Magda a gentle squeeze of her shoulder before walking out.

Jane wanted to yell for him to come back but bit her tongue instead. She suddenly felt alone, which was foolish with Magda next to her.

For the first time since she had woken up from her coma, Elias's coarse attitude had given her a sense of security. But now, she felt abandoned. Strange how her own feelings contradicted everything she assumed about the chief.

His absence made Jane's heart race and she wasn't able to breathe. Her stomach pulled tight and her temples ached. Jane tried to shake off her anxiousness but it rose anyway.

Focus. No crying!

Jane turned to the clothes in her lap. She furrowed her brows as she lifted the tie-dyed T-shirt three times her size to her chest. "Whose are these?"

"Lost and found."

"Really?" Jane examined the white Keds with no laces and a pair of gray sweat pants with holes at the knees. "Someone actually wore this stuff?"

"They are good enough for now." Magda waved off Jane's scrutiny.

Jane swung her legs off the bed to slip on the baggy sweat pants. "Whoa, I feel sick." She clutched Magda's arm for stability.

"It's the sedative. It'll wear off soon. Breathe through it. You can rest in the car."

With help from Magda, Jane got dressed and slipped on the shoes. As she slid herself into the wheelchair, bile rose—she wanted to throw up. Jane swallowed down the nasty bile, and shivered as it burned her throat.

Magda covered her up with a blanket so as not to show her clothing. Jane snagged the cover tight around her, to protect herself from the cold.

Magda went out to the hall and made sure it was empty. She rushed back in, "All clear," and quickly pushed Jane out into the empty hallway.

As they headed to the back elevator, Jane's vision teetered in and out of focus. A nauseated stomach was the worst thing to have when one was in a rush. Magda tried to push the wheelchair at a steady pace but failed miserably.

Rounding the corner, she spotted Elias with Tom at the end of the hall, at the nurses' station. Magda jerked the wheelchair to a halt. "Sorry." And spun Jane around and wheeled her in the other direction.

Vomit rose again, but she managed to swallowed it down again.

Whoever said roller coaster rides were fun was fucked in the head, Jane thought as she slowly breathed in and out, to ease away the dizziness.

"I guess we're taking the service elevator instead," Magda leaned in and whispered.

As they approached the wide double doors, one of the night nurses passed them. "Miss Magda, why are you still here and where are you off to with Jane?"

"I'm taking her to x-rays, then I'm heading home."

"Would you like me to take her so you can go?"

"No—thank you, Abby. It won't take long. You go about your rounds."

"Have a good night, Miss Magda. Or good morning." The nurse chuckled and walked away.

"Bye," Magda called over her shoulder. "That was close," she lowered and whispered in Jane's ear. She then patted Jane on the shoulders and pushed her faster.

Jane remained quiet while they made it to the service elevator—taking them down the back corridor toward the double metal doors that led to the outside.

The cold wind chafed Jane's face right away, though her dizziness began to subside. She took a deep breath in and let the chill clear her head.

Down the wide ramp, Jane finally felt a sense of ease settle over her. Of course, it didn't help that the old woman behind her pushed her like she had chronic shakes. Jane just held onto the armrest and prayed Magda's car was close.

The vehicle was at the back end of the parking lot. By the time they reached the gray Corolla, Jane's dizziness and nausea had dissipated. She was able to breathe a lot better with the icy air in her lungs.

Jane had to smile as she watched another day being born. Just like her life, with each new day, she was one step closer to her identity and that was all she could hope for.

Magda helped Jane into the passenger side, slipped the seatbelt over her shoulder and clipped it. She closed the door and pushed the wheelchair out of the way, then went around and slid into the driver's seat. She started the car without trouble and let it run for a few minutes to warm up. Neither of them said a word. Silence was good.

It was light enough that Magda didn't need the headlights. She shifted into drive and slowly drove out of the parking lot, passing the hospital's main entrance.

Jane hoped that no one was watching. That's all they needed—to attract attention.

As they passed a single fir tree, the back of Jane's head began to pulsate and she swore her temples was pressed in a vise. Jane folded forward and took deep breaths to push the pain away. *Just ignore it.*

"Jane, are you all right?" Magda asked, slowing the car. "What's wrong?"

Jane glanced back at the tree, and saw the girl in the yellow dress. She rubbed at her watery eyes and looked again. But she was gone, and so was the pain. "Nothing. Just dizzy and my stomach hurts," Jane lied.

"It won't take long. Can you hold on a little longer?"

Jane nodded. "Yes." She leaned her forehead against the window as though it was a cold compress. The coolness was more of a relief than the heat blowing from the vents.

But she kept her mouth shut because Magda was shivering.

With one final glance back at the tree, Jane wondered why she kept seeing this girl. Not wanting to think about the child anymore, Jane blanked her mind and turned her attention to the road ahead.

CHAPTER FIFTEEN

"How's Jane doing?" Tom asked.

"She's scared, but she's doing better now. Dr. Rollins cleared a room in the psych wing. I think it will be the safest part of the hospital for her," Elias said. He tapped on the evidence kit Tom had laid on the nurses' station. "Did Tyson check the security cameras? Was there anything on the video? What about the staff—did they see anything?"

"Whoa. One question at a time, please. My head is still spinning." Tom took out a pad from his pocket and released a breath. "Okay.

The staffing was minimal at that hour. I talked to the cleaning staff and they saw nothing out of the ordinary. Tyson got the statements from the few nurses that were on duty and they said the same thing. Nothing showed up on the security cameras either. I dusted for prints on the bed rails, but I have a feeling they're Jane's.

"I pulled a few partial prints, but I don't think they are enough to get a concise match. That's it."

"Not much." Elias grouched.

"Nope. Now, Eli, if there is nothing else, I'd like to head home. The sun is coming up and I need to get a few hours' shut-eye," Tom said firmly. "You should do the same."

Elias frowned. "I'll sleep when this case is closed. Besides, we need to rush the evidence to Madison. I know there's something on that wrapper; a fingerprint or DNA we can use. We can't sit on this, Tom. I'll call my friend, Mike. He owes me a huge favor. He should be able to process the wrapper and card right away."

"Last time, the labs took almost two weeks to get us back the results," Tom said as he stared down at both baggies.

"Not this time," Elias admitted, studying the purple foil. "This might be the only real chance to solve this case."

"We'll catch this asshole soon enough. But I need to get out of here or I'm going to fall over." Tom blew out a heavy breath and yawned. "How about this? Since you're needed here more than me, I'll take the evidence and make sure it gets into your friend's hands." He grasped Elias's shoulder. "But I got to get a few hours of shut-eye, man."

"Are you sure?"

"Yes. It's Monday now. The traffic down to Madison is going to be a bitch. By the time I leave, Mike will be at the lab. I'll drop the evidence off, then head back. I'll be gone maybe five hours, tops," Tom said in an expelled breath.

His deputy was right. Elias had no choice but to let Tom go. "All right, you go." Elias adjusted his cap. "When you get to Madison, ask for Mike Mansfield. I'll call him and let him know you're coming."

"How do you know this guy?" Tom asked as he picked up the kit and placed the baggies with the condom wrapper and torn up card in a bigger evidence bag.

"He's an army buddy of mine," Elias replied. He followed his deputy to the elevator.

"Are you sure he'll take care of this right away?" Tom raised the evidence bag.

"Oh, yeah."

The deputy slightly bowed his head. "Okay. Now that it's set, can I go home and sleep? My head is swimming."

"Head out."

Tom straightened, snapped his teeth together. "Thanks boss," he said in his usual smart-ass tone. "Seriously though, I'm glad Jane's safe."

Elias let out light huff. "Me too. She's in a secure location now and that bastard can't get to her."

"I think that bastard thinks he can get to her no matter where she's at."

"Trust me, Tom, she can't be touched where she is," Elias said. He rolled his shoulder to not let his strained muscles get to him, or the lie.

"I hope you're right," Tom voiced softly. "I'm out."

"As soon as you can." Seriousness coated Elias's voice.

"Will do." Tom saluted and quickly turned his attention to the redheaded nurse that passed them. He strode off toward her. "Just want to say hi, then I'll be off," he called out with a big grin.

Elias shook his head. He guessed no matter the urgency, booty call came first—even over sleep. The elevator doors opened and Tyson came out. "Chief."

"Tyson, I need you to go through the national database again and narrow the search to women matching the age of twenty-six. Oh, and change her hair color to light brown or dark blonde—maybe we can get a hit on that."

Tyson wrote down the information. "Is that all?"

"There's nothing else to be done here, so start your search. I'll see you later."

Elias went to Jane's room and found it empty. He hoped that Magda and Jane had gotten out without being seen.

He lingered around the hospital for about thirty minutes more, keeping watch for anything or anyone unusual. This bastard was sly—but not all that cautious, which was his mistake. The condom wrapper proved that.

Elias finally left the hospital. The cold morning air grazed his face like a crisp linen sheet—hard but welcoming. He sucked in the chill and let it filter through his system. *A Marlboro would be nice, and a coffee too.*

He went straight to the Barn, got his usual coffee and sipped the brew slowly. Once the caffeine filtered through his system, he took a turn around the town before driving to the station.

Down Main Street, Betty's Diner seemed to be filled with its usual Monday morning customers. From simple farm folk to churchgoers rehashing Sunday's sermon. Elias's views on religion were only for him and his maker.

An eight-block radius—end to end, nothing much happened in this town of Beaver Ridge. Except for the Coffee Barn, which Elias appreciated, Stanley's Hardware, and Porter's Grocer run by Mrs. Choy.

A slight grumble from his stomach brought him back to Betty's. Breakfast would be good, but ever since Jane was found, his appetite was next to nil.

Jane.

The trepidation and fear in Jane's eyes as he left her room dug down into his gut. Elias wasn't abandoning her —but it felt like he was.

He kept reminding himself he couldn't get close to her. The last time he got too involved, he got the victim killed. He wouldn't let that happen again.

Elias pulled up to the station and remembered to call his forensic buddy Mike. He took out his cell phone and dialed his number. After he left a quick message, he downed the last of the coffee before tossing the empty cup into the garbage.

The police station was quiet when Elias walked in. His plan was to do some paperwork, clean his office and then head home. The whole time, though, his thoughts were on Jane and Magda, hoping they'd made it to their destination.

Beth and Cindy Lee had already arrived for their morning shifts. Elias gathered the two officers and explained what had happened and the details of the evidence.

"We will have to cover Tom's shift while he's gone. We'll work the usual rotations. Cindy Lee, radio Tyson to cover the first half of Tom's shift. I'll handle the second half. Beth, you'll cover town and Cindy Lee, you handle the station as usual."

Both women acknowledged him and went on as ordered. Beth didn't look happy.

Right before Elias closed the door to his office, he overheard her telling Cindy Lee about babies. He quickly shut the door. He didn't want to hear the rest. Too up close and personal for his liking.

He let out a breath of relief. The wood paneled walls of his office were thick enough that he wouldn't hear the women's chatter.

After Elias hung his hat and coat on the coat rack, he took out his phone and dialed Magda's cell phone. She didn't answer, which made him nervous. He trusted Magda, so he left a message to call back.

The large clock on the wall read nine. He had an hour or so to kill before he headed out. He eyed the piles of magazines and old folders stacked on the cabinets and decided paperwork could wait. It was time to clear out Chief Henley's stuff. The ten-by-ten space needed a little more breathing room.

With a mélange of papers and folders amassed on the cabinets, Elias had his work cut out for him.

"Why in the hell did he keep all this crap?" He sifted through five inches of thick mangled old paperwork—dating back as far as the early nineties.

He used his foot to slide the rectangular garbage can over, grabbed the stack of old magazines on top of the taller cabinet and chucked them in one at a time. The next pile Elias grabbed slipped out of his hands, knocking into the pile on the shorter cabinet. Folders and magazines spilt like confetti onto the floor.

"Shit." As he bent over to pick up the mess, he stopped. "What the—"

A collection of photos of dead women had landed on top of the magazines. Stunned at what he was seeing, Elias bent over and counted forty lifeless faces. Some of the images were black and white, the rest in faded color.

Some of the victims' faces were beaten badly and some were left flawless. However, most had deep slash marks on their arms and legs. But there were a few that had deep gouges on their wrists and crisscross cuts on their cheeks, like they were marked.

The more he examined the pictures, Elias realized they all had one commonality. All the women had been buried. He assumed the same killer might have murdered all those women.

What were you working on, old man? The way Henley did things wasn't generally normal. The man had secrets. The old chief could have been working on a case without anyone else involved before he killed himself.

Elias's heart sped up. His gut twisted tight as he placed the pictures in a folder and sat at his desk to study them.

When he turned the photos over, all of them had two sets of numbers in the corners.

One could be dates, but the other number wasn't making sense. *Possible codes Henley gave in direct connection to something—but what?*

Some of the pictures dated back as far as forty-five years, and the most recent was about five years ago. Elias looked at the most recent victim and quickly recognized the officer in charge in the picture. The woman was discovered two counties over.

The similarities between the photo and Jane were uncanny. They were beaten, had black hair, and they had the same slash marks on their arms—only Jane's limbs had been slashed in the hospital. And she was alive.

He wouldn't speculate until he made a few calls to corroborate what his gut knew. But Elias would bet his life on the fact that it had to be the same person or a copycat.

"Now why would you hide these pictures between hunting mags?" Elias spoke out loud as though Henley was in the room.

If Henley was working on a case, why didn't he tell anyone about it? This was huge. With the number of victims in that file, he had to have had some help. The situation made no sense. But lately, a lot of things weren't making any sense. Including Henley.

He'd been a meticulous man. He'd crossed the T's and dotted the I's several times to make sure they were permanent—a bit of an over-compulsive guy.

Elias started a list of lead officers who were in charge

of those cases. Contacting them was his first priority, but not before he cleaned up the mess on the floor.

He put the folder off to the side and finished picking up. He was more careful, in case something else fell out. As he picked up the rest of the magazines from the floor, he noticed a small folded piece of paper under the filing cabinet.

Elias retrieved the paper and unfolded it. There were words, letters and key symbols, of which some were barely legible, on a hand drawn map. Right away, he recognized some of the markings. Beaver Ridge was scrawled in the center, with Beaver Lake to the left. Other towns were written in tinier print.

A simple legend was at one corner of the paper. There were dots scattered around Beaver Ridge. But some dots were as far out as five towns over. The marks were scattered into the adjoining counties too, into the back woods where only hunters go. There were lines that crisscrossed, but not all of them connected. Though Elias wasn't sure what it meant.

There were two different initials, one next to each dot. They were written so small that Elias wasn't sure on some of the letters.

He grabbed his magnifying glass from his drawer and took a closer look at the dots and lines on the diagram. There were a lot of dots around the lake.

Beth knocked and peeked her head in. "Chief?"

"What, Beth?" He quickly folded up the paper and shoved it in his shirt pocket.

"Tom radioed in. He's heading out. And I'm leaving in few minutes. I'll make my rounds, then head home." She looked down at the mess on the floor. "Do you need me to clean this up?"

"No." Elias checked his watch and noticed he had been in his office for over two hours. "Just leave it."

His cell phone rang.

"Ok." Beth closed the door.

Elias sat back down and clicked open his phone.

"Beaver Ridge Police, Chief McAvoy."

"Hey, it's Mike. Got your message. What's up?"

"I need a big favor. My deputy, Tom Faber, will be dropping off evidence later today that needs first priority. It's connected to the Jane Doe case."

"How urgent?"

"That evidence might be the only lead to finding out who's trying to kill Jane. Can you do it?" The silence lasted a breath or two, but it felt too long for Elias. "Mike."

"I owe you, bud. So, of course. Tell your deputy to ask for me when he gets here."

"Will do. Thanks, this makes us even."

"Yes."

Elias cracked a smile. He remembered the night he'd saved his friend from a bar fight in Seoul. Mike had drunk too much to fight back and Elias took on three Marine assholes himself. After a few broken ribs and busted up lips, he'd pummeled the men and gotten Mike out of the bar before they all were arrested.

"We're even, then," Elias said, feeling his left rib.

"It may take a week. But I'll call you when I have it done."

"Sounds good." After Elias hung up with his friend, he grabbed the unmarked folder with the dead women's photos and headed out.

He stepped out of the station and immediately saw Mayor Daniels heading his way up the sidewalk on the east side of the street. There was a small group of women around him—like pecking hens, chatting away. Daniels finally took notice of him the second he stepped off the steps.

Holy shit. Elias turned away, briskly walked to his truck and hopped in. He took off as Daniels tried to flag him down. He wasn't in the mood for any more confrontations with the man, especially with photos of dead women in his possession.

Before heading home, he got gas and stopped at Porter's Grocer for some supplies. His thoughts switched to Jane as he grabbed the last box of Ho Ho's on the shelf—his go-to when the nicotine withdrawal was greater than his will power. Something sweet always made him feel better—especially after a night of drinking too, but that was the past.

Though the Ho Ho's weren't for him—they were for Jane.

After he left the grocer, Elias decided to make a quick detour to the lake. As he passed the town limits, the images of the dead women rolled around in his head. The dates bothered him.

Elias couldn't get past the dates of the murders. Forty years. Could Henley have been working on a case for a while? Why start an investigation, then shoot himself in the head later? *Unless... You're grasping at straws, McAvoy.*

As Elias reached the lake, a headache was beating at his temples. His eyes yearned for sleep. He was way too tired to think anymore. He'd come back later, after a few hours of shut-eye.

Elias turned down Route 41. A mile down, he saw Harold on the side of the road. Broad daylight and this fool was walking around with only his thermals on and no shoes.

Harold stumbled along on the edge of the ditch. His feet dragged against the gravel and his head bobbed back and forth. It was as though a rope was pulling him.

Damn. Raymond was supposed to be watching him.

Elias pulled up next to him and rolled the window down. "Hey Harold," he called out, but his friend didn't respond. "Harold Kantor," he yelled loud enough that the next town could hear him.

Harold stopped in mid step, turned and gave Elias a blank stare.

"Harold," Elias shot out.

The man turned away and walked off again.

He stopped the truck and got out. Elias walked up to Harold and grabbed him by the arm before he blocked his friend's path and made him stop.

Elias didn't like the way Harold's breath reeked of whiskey, and his eyes were glazed over as though he'd downed a case of it. A slight itch formed in Elias's throat and his stomach flipped.

"Harold?" Elias snapped his fingers in front of his friend's face. He shook him by his shoulders. "Harold."

The man blinked and shook his head slightly before he came out of his stupor. "What the— McAvoy? What's going on?" Harold looked around him. "Where the hell am I?"

"I think you were sleepwalking again," Elias said.

"No fucking way, it's daytime." Harold shivered, rubbing at his arms.

"Then explain why you don't have any shoes or clothes on. The temperature is in the twenties." Elias let his friend go.

Harold looked down at his socked feet and wiggled his big toe out of a hole. "Can-can I have a ride home?"

He shook his head, but said, "Come on."

Harold put the grocery bag on the floor, got in and asked with trepidation, "How's the couple?"

"The man woke up and is doing fine—just a concussion. They aren't pressing charges. You're lucky, man."

Harold gave a slight nod. "I know," he said in a whisper.

Elias remained silent the rest of the way to his friend's trailer, which was situated next to Raymond's house. He dropped him off and called out, "Lock your door. And stay out of trouble."

"Thanks." Harold stumbled into his trailer and slammed the screen, then the metal door.

Elias backed the truck up and headed straight home.

Pulling up to the farmhouse, the For Sale sign on the side lot was gently swinging. He parked in the rear and got out. With no wind, but the sign swaying, the eerie quietness had the hairs at the back of his head standing on end.

Elias couldn't wait to sell this place, and get away from the many bad memories it held.

As he walked around to the passenger side to get the groceries, something caught his eye in the second-floor window.

A flash of a woman with long brown hair stared down at him from his mother's room. But that wasn't possible. That room had been empty since her death. It couldn't be Jane—her hair was short and her head was still bandaged. Elias rubbed at his tired eyes and looked up once more. There was no one standing there. It had to be his eyes playing tricks on him, even in broad daylight.

A sudden frigid wind had Elias shivering. He'd always hated the cold. Shrugging off the chill, he left the groceries and checked around the house, his usual routine.

After the incident with his father breaking into the place, Elias couldn't chance that encounter again. The cellar door was chained and all the windows were closed. He then headed for the dilapidated barn.

If James McAvoy stepped one foot on the property, Elias would put his drunken ass in jail for the rest of his miserable life. Even though that was too good for the man. He would rather kill the bastard for what he had done to Elias's mother. But death was too easy. If it weren't for his old man's boozing and womanizing, Elias's life would have been different. Or maybe not.

After his mother passed away, Elias drank himself into that dark and deep hole for a month. He eventually pulled himself out from the bottom of the bottle, but he wasn't quite the same.

With the death of Elise, he'd sunk right back into the bottle and his guilt kept him firmly in black hole of despair. The repeated nightmares of the last few seconds of her life, before his bullet killed her, were on constant. And the only way to numb the pain was by picking up the bottle again.

So, his father wasn't there holding the glass to his lips. Drinking was Elias's choice—his getaway from the hard pain of reality, it always had been—yet, never once had he raised a hand to a woman or child. Not the way his fucking father had.

Elias was *not* his father. He hoped, but one couldn't tell by the amount of drink he'd consumed during that dark period.

After his suspension from Half Moon Bay PD, he decided to head home. Three years of being sober, on his own—without AA—except for Magda. She was his rock. As much as he regretted coming back, this place was his only saving grace. He hoped it would be Jane's also.

He slid the barn door open and saw Magda's Corolla parked inside. He wasn't happy that she'd taken a chance parking in the rotting barn. With the unstable roof, the walls could cave in at any time. Her car had to be hidden, though, and he assumed this was her only solution. Elias would have done the same.

He closed the doors carefully and headed back to his truck. He grabbed the bag with the Ho Ho's, then dragged himself into the house.

Elias desperately needed sleep, but for his peace of mind he had to see Jane first to make sure she was all right.

CHAPTER SIXTEEN

Four painful, boring days.

It was Friday, and Jane had been cooped up in Elias's house, with nothing to do but rest. She couldn't lie in bed any longer, no matter how many times Magda told her she needed rest. She was beginning to hate that word, and winced every time the nurse came to check on her.

With Magda here, Jane had less freedom than at the hospital. Being stuck in the house, especially in her room, she was going insane with boredom.

Hiding out wouldn't be bad, if the cabinet style television had more than two channels. Like watching livestock on the farming channels could be the highlight of her day. Boring.

There was no internet in the house either, so she couldn't go on the computer... If Elias even had one. And the dust-covered magazines were at least ten years old.

Talking to Magda was great, but when she—Elias told her to rest, Jane wanted to pull her hair out in frustration... or what was left of it.

How much can one person rest?

She'd heard it all from Magda and the neurotic chief. Too many times to count. *Go rest, Jane. Don't do this. Don't to do that. Get away from the window, Jane.*

Elias was the worst. He drove her nuts as he spouted safety strategies, to the point that she wanted to run him over with his truck. Every time he got all high and mighty on her, she called him "Ass"—under her breath of course.

The chief was right about one thing. Her safety was important. And calling him "Ass" hadn't helped her cause. Yet, she couldn't help herself when he repeated his litany of rules.

The air of depression that permeated the room weighed heavy on her, which didn't help her frazzled, roller coaster of emotions. She might be the victim, but she felt more like a prisoner.

Restlessness urged her up from bed. The wrought iron squeaked as her weight shifted. She sat on the edge and looked around the room for the fifty millionth time. The green, scalloped, crocheted blanket was old and rough and the coarse wool scratched her palm.

Aged yellow and green curtains shaded the small window above the bed. She couldn't tell which color started out first. The odor that permeated the air was of old flowers and dust, mixed with a slight mildewy decay. Jane's nose tickled—she sneezed with a squeak.

The ivy-patterned wallpaper was yellowed and peeling at the corners. Jane's fingers itched to rip the edges down, but she didn't. Instead, she focused on placing her feet securely onto the dark hardwood floor.

As she straightened her twisted shirt, she stood and proceeded to pace the small attic room. She was on edge. Maybe cleaning the room would help her anxiety.

A small mirror was perched on top of the tall dresser. She'd start there.

Jane walked over to it and hesitated, studying the dust that coated the glass. She swiped the dust with her hand, coming away with a worm length of particles stuck to her palm—she shook it off, onto the floor.

She stared at herself for a moment then realized she was holding her breath. Relief gave way and so did her breathing when she saw her own reflection—sallow skin, furrowed brows and all. Jane smiled and the tension eased from her shoulders.

The bandages were annoying; Jane wanted to remove them right away. Almost a month being wrapped up like a mummy was enough. With delicacy, she unwrapped the dressing, exposing the rest of her forehead. She tilted the mirror, took a step back to see her entire head. *Not bad.*

Her cheekbones were defined—skin pale but not *dead*—no dark swollen bruises anymore. Her left eye had a few broken vessels but the right was clear. Her vision didn't blur, and there was no pain.

Her choppy boy hair needed a huge makeover. If she had a pair of scissors she could fix a few areas, but it wasn't terrible to look at. She spread her hair apart and saw the outgrowth at the roots. She couldn't imagine why she'd colored her hair black. She pulled the mirror closer to see the hair at the root. "Ha. Blonde."

She pushed back the longer, straggly pieces behind her ears and turned her face from side to side. Jane wished she could see the gash on the back of her head. It didn't hurt, but the healing incisions itched. "That's going to leave a scar," she uttered while tracing her fingertip along the ridge.

The bandages still on her arms and legs itched, too.

She wanted to rip them off and scratch until the itchiness was gone. Magda had made her promise to leave them on for a few more days. Instead, Jane rubbed her arms along her sides and her legs against each other like some demented dancer.

Physically, she was pretty much healed, except for her head and her memory. Jane's mind wouldn't relinquish its secrets. The biggest was... Who had tried to kill her?

She would rather tolerate a thousand bruises and lashes, if for a moment she could remember something more—anything—her name, where she lived or the make of brown car.

"Holy crap. I have a brown car." Tears came and slipped down her cheeks as she remembered the beat-up piece of crap she drove. As Jane grabbed a tissue from the dusty Kleenex box on the nightstand, the sound of a car door closing stifled her mini celebration.

She couldn't help but break the rule and shifted the curtain an inch to see out. She looked down at the familiar truck. "Elias." She whispered his name.

Her skin tingled and her breathing quickened. Warmth grew in her belly, spreading out across her body. It was silly to think one prickly man made her feel *safe*, but he did. Even with his asinine attitude, she still trusted him. Though, his attitude over the past few days, had gotten stranger.

Elias had been keeping his distance from her—acting odd whenever he was near her. He came home and went straight to his room—eating alone as well.

Once, Magda tried to involve him in a game of cards, but as soon as he looked at Jane, he said *no* and took off out the door.

His actions proved his dislike for her, and that was

fine with Jane. She didn't particularly like the man either. Though she had to admit, she was relieved to see him every time he walked through the door. And nervous, too.

Her stomach fluttered at the sight of him patrolling the back of the house. This was his routine. Elias did this safety check every time he came home. His strong gait showed assurance. His broad shoulders promised strength. Elias's hard features exposed his anger—or maybe it was pain, she wasn't sure which. Maybe a little bit of both.

What did he look like under his wrinkled uniform?

What the hell am I thinking? Jane couldn't be attracted to the man. Was she nuts? Being cooped up in the house had muddled her mind.

Jane shifted to get a better view when he looked up and saw her.

"Oh crap." She was caught. The severe frown on his face had her stepping back from the window. He was pissed. She was going to get another lecture about her disregard of his rules. All those fuzzy feelings went away in a flash the moment he strode toward the house.

Jane forgot all about her brown car too.

She released the curtains and sat back down on the bed in a slump. What if he hadn't been the chief? *What if- what if- what if?* She shook her head and tried to calm her erratic heartbeat.

The two rules were simple: stay away from windows and doors, and rest. She'd broken rule one, *again*. Did she always ignore what people said when it came down to her safety? Or was she just plain stubborn? She shook her head and tried to clear the angst that weighed her down. Jane pulled at her shirt while she waited for Elias to come up.

The house became quiet. Too quiet for Jane's liking.

That was when she heard faint crying. Her head was being knifed with sharp, painful stabs at the back of her skull. She fell sideways onto bed, curled into a ball, with her arms covering head.

"Please stop. Please stop," Jane cried out. A spasm sliced through her brain in one swift slash, then it eased up.

Heavy sorrow flooded her, the sound of the crying got louder—Jane cried too. She screamed for relief but the sound lodged in her throat. The pressure became too much.

Twisting herself, Jane jerked tighter into a ball and sobbed harder. "Why me, damn it? Leave me alone." Her plea came out in a whisper. Jane fisted her hair at the sides, pulling at her scalp to stop the electrical pulses that zapped down her spine. Sharp jabs at her stomach made her lose her breath but they faded fast.

The room turned prickly cold. Her skin drew tight into goose flesh. The tears that coated her cheeks turned frosty. Her exhaled breath was visibly white. Fear controlled Jane.

In the far corner of the room, a shadowy figure manifested. It hunched over, weeping as loudly as Jane was. The grief that emanated from the spirit tore through Jane like a hot jagged knife to her heart.

The girl—no. This time something was different. There was no malevolence like she had felt in the hospital. This was someone else, another woman, but Jane wasn't sure who.

The soul stopped crying, but didn't move from the corner. The aroma of baked apple pie replaced the staleness in the air. The sweet scent warmed Jane's soul, giving her a sense of peace. A contradiction to how she suffered moments before.

Jane wasn't afraid anymore. She slowly reached out

and tried to touch the dark form. As Jane extended her arm further, the shadow recoiled and faded away.

The crying returned, but the sound came from Jane. She turned around, grabbed the green blanket and wrapped it around herself while the room's temperature returned to normal. Even the apple pie smell was gone.

CHAPTER SEVENTEEN

Elias placed the bags of groceries on the beige laminate counter and dropped his hat and jacket on the kitchen chair. "Do you know what Jane just did again?" He took a seat at the light oak table.

"How was your day?" Magda asked, putting the last pan in the oven.

"A blatant disrespect for her safety—"

"Elias, she's bored. You can't shut her in totally," Magda interrupted. "I'm getting a little antsy myself. How was your day?"

He raked a hand through his hair. "I got a call back today about the wrapper. They weren't able to lift the partial print off the foil. And the fibers they found inside it is from a carpet. Mike said he'll keep searching, but it might be near impossible to match specifically."

"That's strange. How did carpet fibers get in the condom?" Magda asked.

"I don't know," he said, rubbing his eyes.

"Tired?"

"Yeah. And speaking of tired—I'm tired of seeing

Jane peeking out that window. She can't follow one
simple rule."

"Maybe she knew it was you," Magda said with a
small smile, then began drying the wet countertop.

"What the hell is she thinking? Is she thinking?" He
blew out a breath to calm his sudden spike of ire.

"Elias, I understand this is all for her safety. But you
can't shut her in this house like a prisoner. I'm sure she
was careful," Magda said as she folded the kitchen towel
and sat down across from him.

He bit his tongue. Yelling wouldn't do any good.
Magda's explanation was reasonable—but he still didn't
like it. Those rules were important for keeping Jane safe.
He didn't care about hurt feelings.

He grunted. "There is a sick, twisted person who
gets off killing women and burying them. Miss Magda,
I'm here to protect Jane, and I'll be damned if one small
mistake such as looking out the window gets her killed."

"I know," Jane agreed.

He glared at her. "No, you don't," Elias's voice rose
sharp like a slap.

"Sorry," Jane bit back. She stood in the threshold,
arms wrapped around her middle. She had dark smudges
etched under her eyes. "I'm sorry—What more do you
want me to say or do?"

"Sorry?" Elias shot her a look. "Stay away from the
window." The words came out like venom. He regretted
them the second they came out.

Tears welled fast. Jane looked at Magda, then fled
back upstairs.

Frustration jabbed him like a hot poker. He wanted
to apologize but not until he calmed down. He couldn't
think straight when his anger controlled his emotions.
His mouth became dry and the urge to reach for a bottle
punched him in the throat.

Elias swallowed the craving and stood there with his fist on the table. He wasn't sure what to do next.

Magda stayed quiet, but her eyes radiated disappointment. He had seen that look before. Many times.

"Damn it." He headed upstairs, taking each step slowly as he tried to calm the edginess coursing through his body. He walked to the end of the hall where his mother's—now Jane's, bedroom was located.

He knocked but there was no answer.

"Jane, can I talk to you?" He turned his head to listen. Not a single sound came from the room. "I'm here to... Apologize." That word tasted bitter on his tongue.

She didn't respond.

Elias turned the knob and found the door unlocked. As it swung open, he saw her sitting on the edge of the bed, facing the wall. She didn't turn around or address him.

An icy texture permeated the air—his exhaled breath crystallized. The hairs on his arms stood on end, as if electrified. Strange. He wasn't sure if he should step in.

Elias ignored the uneasiness swimming in his gut and walked in. "Jane?"

Her head was bowed—she didn't utter a word.

Elias figured she was upset, hence the silent treatment. It should be the other way around. *She* was the one who had broken the rule.

"I'm..." he said, not sure what to say. But Magda's words came to mind. *Be gentle.*

Elias took another step toward her but Jane shrank back from him. The way she sat hunched over, broken down and defeated, she reminded him of... His mother. "Are you okay?"

Jane didn't look at him. She curled her legs to her chest and wrapped her arms around them.

Elias sat next to her, leaving a foot-wide gap between them. "Jane, I can't imagine what you went through, but I'm trying to do my job the best way I know." He scratched at his cheek and continued. "I'm here to protect you, damn it, even if it's from yourself."

A soft whimper caught his attention, but he wasn't sure what she'd said.

"I know I'm an insensitive asshole. But you have to understand, your life is still in danger and I won't risk losing you."

Jane nervously turned her head toward him. Tears clung to her cheeks like thick clear syrup. Her eyes were big, filled with regret. Elias's chest ached as he remembered the same look on his mother's face after every beating she got from his father.

Sliding down to the floor, he knelt in front of Jane. Elias touched her hand and caressed her fragile, thin fingers, which were tightly wrapped together. His calloused hands seemed to loosened them into his gentle hold. Her eyes never wavered from his. He wasn't able to form a word or a thought in his head.

He was mesmerized. Jane's prettiness was more than he ever wanted to admit. Elias couldn't help himself and touched her cheek. Her skin was cool. She leaned into his big hand. He brushed away the wetness with his thumb.

The urge to hold her overpowered his sense of duty. He wanted to kiss her, but tried to push the yearning away. His job to protect and serve went right out the window as he inclined his head toward hers.

Staring into her golden-flaked chocolate brown eyes, Elias couldn't help but be spellbound. A slight stir of Nordic air chilled him straight through his shirt, bringing him out of his trance. Her eyes changed in a matter of seconds to a dark obsidian. He wasn't able to see the brown.

He released her hands and edged back, looking around the room. He saw nothing but the frost of his breaths. The atmosphere turned oppressive, which made his stomach lurch.

What the hell?

Jane's cold touch on his cheek brought Elias's eyes back to hers.

She leaned in, her black eyes sad, and lips formed in a soft frown. "I'm sorry too, baby," she said, cupping his face. "I love you." Her voice broke down. Jane closed her eyes and fell back against the bed.

Elias's breath hitched as he grabbed Jane. Did he hear her correctly? Her voice—sounded so much like his mother's. "What did you say?" he demanded as he arranged her on the bed.

Jane blinked a few times, eyes were wide with confusion. The blackness was gone and those beautiful gold flakes were back. The cold room regained its warmth and the old smell filled his nose.

"Elias?"

He pulled her to his body. She was trembling, and so was he. "Damn it, Jane, why did you say that to me?" His voice was above a whisper.

"Elias," Jane sobbed. "What is happening to me?"

He wrapped his arms around her and enveloped her with his heat. Elias wished he did know what was happening to her.

Jane tilted her head back and stared at him for a second before her eyes rolled back and she went limp.

"Jane!" Elias shouted. He scooped her up and rushed out of the room. He flew down the stairs, calling to Magda as he passed the kitchen.

"What happened?" Magda shadowed him to the couch, where he laid Jane down. She checked Jane's pulse and then covered her with a purple crocheted blanket.

"I'm not sure what happened. One second I was apologizing, next—she sounded like my—but that's impossible. Absolutely crazy," he rambled while pacing in front of the sofa. Elias rubbed the back of his neck, stopped in front of Magda and said, "I must be going nuts, because that shit doesn't happen—not to me."

"Elias, I don't understand what you're saying." Magda grabbed her stethoscope and checked Jane's heart. "Everything sounds normal, but you on the other hand..." She reached out to touch his wrist.

He jerked his hand away. "Don't worry about me— I'm fine. Please, take care of her," he said curtly. He went over to the window and stared out at the cold expanse. *This is fucking crazy. I'm going crazy.* "I just need to eat and get some sleep, that's all."

"Well, you don't sound fine. What happened upstairs?"

Elias turned and studied Jane's sleeping form for a second before a tinge of fear skipped down his spine. He ignored it. "She passed out," then walked off to the kitchen.

So frustrated of being tired all the time, short-fused from the case going nowhere, and now he was hallucinating. He wanted to forget the whole thing, but couldn't. What Jane said shook him deep down. No one other than his mother had ever called him "Baby." He wouldn't allow it.

"Elias." Magda trailed after him.

"Let it alone, Miss Magda. I'm fine." He sat down with a plateful of cold food and drew the spoon to his mouth. "Where did all this ham come from? I didn't buy any."

Magda's wry grin offered up guilt. He wasn't going to like what she had to say.

"Don't change the subject, Elias. I want to know what happened upstairs." She took out a cup, filled it with coffee and placed it in front of him.

Elias put down the spoon and folded his arms across his chest and waited.

"Okay. I'll tell you where the food came from but first, you need to tell me what happened to Jane," she said, wiping down the counter.

"I'm tired. That's what happened. After I eat, I'm heading to bed. Now, what's with all this food?"

"You are a stubborn man, Elias McAvoy. You never learned to compromise."

"Lady, you need to stop beating around the bush and tell me where this food came from."

Magda kept cleaning the counter. "We were running low on food..." she stopped explaining, while twisting the kitchen towel.

"I knew that. That's why *I* went shopping. But?"

"I saw no harm in leaving. I got some things from my house and quickly went to the store, but not in that order." She kept her back to him while she re-folded the towel numerous times.

Elias got up from the table. He walked over to her and turned her around. "Magda?" He glared down at her.

"Before you open your mouth, no one questioned me. I always do my shopping on Mondays, so I didn't see any harm in it. We needed the food. I went in, got what I needed and walked out before anyone said anything." Magda's southern twang drawled out. She scooted around him and sat down.

He rolled his eyes and sat back down across from her. Elias pushed the half full plate away—he'd lost his appetite. "I made it very clear that if you needed anything, call me. I don't want you to take any risks. You could have been followed. For all we know, the killer knows where Jane is now."

"I didn't attract any attention. For all you know, if I didn't show my face around, that could have raised suspicions. And it's not like Jane came with me."

Elias's jaw clenched tight. He kept reminding himself that yelling didn't work with these women.

He couldn't look at Magda. Instead, he focused on the scratches on the table, until he was able to talk. "Don't do it again. Please."

"All right." Magda sounded defeated. But the smile on her face showed that she'd won this battle.

Elias couldn't eat the rest of the meal. He got up and placed the plate in the sink. His hands gripped the edge of the old farmhouse sink and leaned in. As he stared out the small window, Magda touched his shoulder.

"Elias. What's going on? You've been on edge all week."

He turned around and faced her. "Everything."

"What does that mean?"

"I mean everything—You and Jane, taking risks with your lives. Maybe Jane should have stayed at the hospital."

"You're wrong. Jane is the safest here. She hasn't set foot out of the house. And for me, no one questioned my actions. What else is bothering you?" she asked softly.

Elias wasn't sure if he should share his opinion about the killer. "This case is driving me crazy." Elias lowered his voice. "I... I think the killer is local."

"Why do you assume it might be someone local?" She hugged her arms to her chest. "That can't be true. I know everyone here, and to imagine one of our own had tried to kill—" Magda shivered.

"Magda, Tom and CLS found nothing at the crime scene. The area was too clean. Only Jane's DNA was only found. The person covered his tracks well. But this is only my assumption. And—"

"I have to keep that to myself, too—I know." She placed her hand to her heart.

"I also found crime scene pictures of dead women in my office. I think they might be connected to Jane's case. Henley hid them in some magazines."

"You mean there are other victims this sick person has killed?"

"Not sure, but Henley was working on something before he killed himself."

"That simply doesn't make sense. How many?" She got up and put on the kettle. "I need some tea to ward off this chill."

"A lot. The murders date pretty far back."

"So, what's the connection with Jane's case?"

"There are a few variables I'm still waiting on, but they were all buried."

"Are *you* sure it's someone local?" Magda asked, getting cups and tea bags.

"I have to follow my gut," Elias said. He went to the refrigerator and grabbed a soda.

Magda rubbed at her arms and asked, "What happened upstairs with Jane? This time tell me the truth."

Elias looked down at the woman he'd known for all of his life and cracked a smile. He knew she wasn't going to let what happened with Jane go.

"I thought I heard my mother's voice. Crazy, huh?" He gave a chuckle before wiping away any remnant of pop on his lips.

Magda shook her head and walked up to him. She reached up and gently cupped his cheeks. "I know you miss her very much. She is a part of this house, in every room. That isn't crazy, Elias."

"When you hear a dead woman's voice, *crazy* is the only logical thing I can think of." Elias scrubbed at his face with both hands. He turned away from her touch. "I can't do this anymore. This job—this town—everything about this place has a hold on me.

"I came here to heal and sell this damn place once and for all. Do you know what I really want?" He flailed his arms out. "Come April, no matter what—I'm gone, Miss Magda. I don't care about this house anymore. If it doesn't sell, James can have it. This job—this town, it's not for me. And I don't care who knows about my past." Tears filled his eyes and blurred his vision. He cleared his scratchy throat from the stranglehold of emotions.

"You can't mean that," Magda said. "This place helped you to heal. You've been sober for over two years now. As for your job, you are a great leader. People listen to you, Elias. That's a good thing." Magda wiped her nose with a tissue she pulled from her sleeve, and then asked, "You want James McAvoy to get this house? You want him to win? Your mother is probably turning in her grave right now."

"If he wants it, he can have it. Why am I holding onto this place so tightly when all there is, is bad memories?" Elias shook his head and strode out of the room.

CHAPTER EIGHTEEN

J ane woke with the warmth of the sun on her face. The heat felt good, and safe. But her serenity vanished when the room shifted to gray and cold, and an overpowering scent of whiskey spiked the air. The heavy stench made her gag.

The shadow of a man, distorted and dark, hovered over her. Jane let out a gasp. Shouts filled her ears—she attempted to get up but couldn't move. She struggled to discern the words, but she understood "bitch" loud and clear.

With all her might, Jane used her arms and fists, and punched out toward the man. She shot up from the couch, ready to defend herself.

Between the gaps of her arms, she saw no one standing in front of her, nothing except the late afternoon sun shining in.

She lowered her arms and rubbed at her eyes to remove the blurriness.

"Damn it," she said under her breath. Jane scouted the room once more making sure she was alone. Was it a ghost—a dream? It sure didn't feel that way. Maybe a past memory—she hoped not. A dizzying rush hit her system. She wanted to lie back down to steady herself. Then it dawned on her that she was in the living room. How did she get downstairs?

Jane eased herself up, still woozy from what had happened, and headed into the kitchen. She found Magda reading the paper and sipping tea.

"Can I have some?"

Magda looked up from the Herald and smiled. "Sit. How are you feeling?" She grabbed a mug from the cupboard, dropped a chamomile teabag in it and placed the cup in front of Jane.

"I guess okay," I admitted, watching the steam rise from the hot water Magda poured into the cup. "How did I get downstairs?"

"Don't you remember?" Magda sat down. "Elias brought you down."

"Last thing I remember was looking out the window when the chief arrived. I came downstairs to apologize. Right after the ass opened his mouth, I went back to my room. I sat on the bed and I think I heard crying again, then nothing." Jane shrugged her shoulders and stared down at the scratched oak table. "That's it, I'm going crazy." She took the cup of hot tea in her hands, blew into it and sipped with caution.

Magda gave a slight laugh. "No crazier than Elias. Honey, you need to stop calling him an ass. For one, it isn't polite and two, he is doing the best he can."

Jane looked up from her cup. She knew the nurse was right. "I know—but sometimes I can't help it. He drives me nuts. I feel like I'm his prisoner."

"He is only trying to protect you. I know he can be a bit brash, but he is trying."

"Why does he ignore me when I ask about the case?"

"Maybe there's nothing to tell, I don't know. But I do

know he's trying his best. You should go talk to him, he's upstairs." She finished her cup and got up. "Now I know you're feeling better, I have some stuff to sort out down in the basement. If you need me, just call out."

The nurse was right. Jane took another sip of her tea, which calmed her raw nerves. She considered what Magda had said. There were kinder ways to get information. Calling him an ass wasn't one of them.

Jane stood up and pushed the kitchen chair in. "I can handle this, like an adult." She grinned. "And I won't call him an ass anymore," she added that shallow oath.

She took the stairs at a cumbersome pace. With each step, her bruised hips clicked with soreness. Not quite a hundred percent yet, Jane thought as she rubbed her thighs.

At the top step, she was about to knock on his bedroom door when it swung wide open. Her breath hitched. Elias stood in the doorway with only a towel around his waist. He'd shaved, and trickles of water slid down his bare chest.

Jane's imagination didn't need to go far. Under all that grunge hid a gorgeous man with a well-sculpted body. Her eyes trailed upward from the curve of his waist to broad shoulders that carried his height quite well. She took quick mental notes of his perfect V form. His abs ripped into a nice tight six. Elias's slicked-back hair, darkened from the water, hid the blonde streaks that gave him a surfer persona.

"Are you enjoying the view?" Elias frowned.

"Oh, um. Sorry. You caught me off guard." *Holy crap.* Her heart tripped. For some reason she couldn't take her eyes off of him. A burn ignited in her cheeks and abdomen. The sudden spark of lust made her shudder a little. Almost breathless, she wasn't sure what to say next.

"I hear you trudging up the stairs. Now what do you need?" Elias was curt.

Even with his rudeness, she thought him gorgeous. Her eyes wavered back to the edge of his towel, which sat loosely around his hips. He stood there, with his boxers in his hand, staring at her. The aroma of his soap wafted up, numbing her senses. But Jane wasn't going to be deterred. "Got a minute? I want to talk to you." She had to look away or she'd lose her dignity and kiss him.

"How do you feel?" His question came out more like a caress. Elias acted as though standing almost naked in front of a woman was an everyday occurrence. He wasn't affected by his lack of clothing the way she was.

Her cheeks bloomed even more crimson as she focused on the hallway floor. "Can you put something on? Please." Her mouth went dry. She had a sudden thirst for wet skin.

"I'm not naked," he said nonchalantly. "What do you want?"

Jane kept her head forward. "Please," she stressed. Then tried to change her focus from Elias's torso. "Cleaning isn't your strong suit."

"Is that what you came up here to tell me?"

"No, but just glancing at your room—you lack organization. Or is it cleanliness?"

"Being a slob is one of my good traits—now say what you wanted to say."

Out of the corner of her eye, Elias stood there, still not dressed. Heat grew in her stomach—lower. "Please get dressed."

"Okay. Come in while I throw some shorts on." Jane heard him laugh.

If it weren't for his coarse behavior, she could actually like the man. "You are not funny."

Don't look. Too late. She tilted her head slightly

toward his direction and caught him dropping his towel. *Ooh.* Everything about his body was simply beautiful. *What a gorgeous ass.* He left the door wide open for her viewing pleasure. Did he do that on purpose? Her chest hurt from her frantic heartbeats. She couldn't catch a full breath.

What the hell is wrong with me? A peeping Jane?

Sense and reason flooded back as coldness seeped into the hallway. The chill brought her out of her fascination with his backside. Jane reached in and partially closed the door, leaning her head forward and focusing on the other end of the hall.

The aroma of mildewy decay filled the hallway. A slight fear trickled through her, but she stood there with her feet fixed to the floor. The now-familiar burn returned, branding the back of her head, but it was nothing she couldn't handle. Until it got worse.

Her mind filled with such cruelty, then it went blank, before shifting again, changing into a medley of dark colors. Jane looked around and saw only dirty walls. Words etched in red appeared before her: *blood, rape, and death*. Their colors bled down to a cement floor. Chains clanked and the smell of decay suffocated her lungs. Was that her past or her future?

Bile rose fast, filling Jane's throat until she threw up, and then she crumbled into a heap.

CHAPTER NINETEEN

Elias slipped on his shorts, turned and noticed the door partially closed. As he opened it, Jane dropped to the floor.

"Not again. Magda," he shouted. He rushed to her side and picked her up. He carried her inside his bedroom, kicking clothes out of his way, and placed her on his bed.

"Jane, wake up." He touched her cheeks lightly. She didn't move.

Magda hurried in. "What happened this time?"

"I don't know what happened. I was changing, and when I turned around, she was on the floor. What the hell is wrong with her?"

Magda checked Jane's pulse. "All her vitals are good. Maybe we should take her back to the hospital, Elias."

"No. Let her rest for right now. If she doesn't wake up, then we take her back."

"All right."

Elias stepped out of his room and inspected the hallway. He swiped the wall with his fingers; moisture clung to his fingertips, then evaporated. He stilled for a heartbeat—this was no hallucination. There was wetness on the walls. Then poof, it was gone.

Unable to explain it, Elias walked back in, his worry centered on Jane. He tipped the rocking chair, dumping the clothes onto the floor and then sat down.

"We need to keep a close eye on her. Jane can't be left alone." He stared at Jane, confusion swirling in his head.

Magda's eyes creased in the corners with worry. "I don't know what's happening to her, but that's a sound plan."

"I'll watch over her right now," he said as he rocked back and forth.

Magda nodded, looked over at Jane once more and headed back downstairs.

"Damn," Elias hissed quietly.

He hated seeing Jane this way. And the way she was crumpled in a heap on the floor—she reminded him of when he'd found her in the hospital bathroom. His gut gnarled up like mangled barbed wire, again. He hated being completely helpless, like he had when he was a child. Truth was, she reminded him of his mother more and more. Wasn't sure if that was a good thing or not.

He regarded her, as she lie motionless in his bed. Elias hated the way she made him remember things from his past. It didn't matter where he was. Whenever she was around, he was reminded how much he detested the memories this house held.

He couldn't be near her.

With a migraine pounding at his temples, he needed something to drown the pain. A bottle of Jack would do it, but Magda had taken care of that on the very first day he'd arrived home. She threw out all the liquor his mother had hidden in the house. She went as far as to tell the grocer not to sell it to him. How he had despised her for the months of hell she put him through. Now, he was grudgingly thankful for it. Most of the time.

Elias leaned back against the rocker and blew out a slow breath.

He looked over at Jane. *At least one of us will sleep.* Elias got up from the chair and sat on the edge of the bed. As he drew the blanket halfway up her chest, his eyes memorized her face. She had a simple beauty.

Her eyelids harbored a thick forest of long lashes, which accentuated her slightly almond-shaped eyes. Jane's lips were smooth and full. Elias wanted to trace his thumb along her bottom lip, but didn't. He wondered what they tasted like.

A fan of freckles crossed the bridge of her nose. He hadn't noticed them before with all the bruising. They gave her a carefree, impish look, but she'd been far from playful. Jane's skin seemed smooth as velvet.

He pulled the blanket to her shoulders, hoping it would ease his sudden need to kiss her, but the urge became greater. Being near her made him want to break the rules.

Elias took a gulp of air and pulled the blanket to her chin. That didn't help.

He was so close, bare inches from her luscious lips. One kiss wouldn't hurt—to see what they felt like against his lips.

What am I doing? Get your head out of your ass and think.

Elias eased back. He had to rein in his burgeoning desire.

He released the blanket, which covered Jane's face, and woke her up.

Jane sat up, slightly glassy eyed and confused. She looked around the room then back at him. "Wait..." She sounded even more confused.

"You fainted again," he grumbled, sounding mad. But he was irritated more at himself than Jane.

"Oh, okay," she said. Jane rubbed her eyes and looked around the room again. "So...this is what your cave looks like."

"Really?" Elias stepped behind the chair, needing the distance. He extended his arms out and asked with a laugh, "You want to talk about my room?"

Jane's mouth quirked tight to one side, but she shrugged her shoulders. "I don't know."

Silence hung between them lasted for a few seconds until Elias asked, "Why did you faint?"

Jane let out a soft exhale before she answered. "I don't remember." She got off the bed and stood there, arms folded, and tapping her foot.

He stepped around the chair and faced her. "What do you mean, you don't remember?"

"That's exactly what I mean." Jane let out a huff and continued. "Every time you want an explanation, and I can't give you the answer, you get all pissy. I'm sick and tired of your shitty attitude, Chief McAvoy. I'm the victim, remember? You've had me cooped up in this house. I can't deal with this, and you anymore. I want to go back to the hospital. At least there, I have other people to talk to. And, don't ever try to kiss me."

His anger spiked with hers, wondering how she knew what he'd nearly attempted. "Don't you worry about that —I'm far from that inclination. As for cooping you up, you're here for your safety. So, don't ask to go back to the hospital. Deal with it."

"That's my point. You treat me as though all this is my fault."

"Not true."

"True! Especially when I can't give you the answers you want. I don't remember what happened," she yelled right in his face. "This place—you, it's driving me bat-shit crazy."

"How do you expect me to act? A killer's after you—of course I'm going to keep you safe. Then you pass out cold on the floor, twice. Both times you've given me a fucking heart attack." Elias threw up both hands. "Damn this case, it's going to drive me to drink again." He let it slip. The pain in his stomach returned, then rose to his chest in a flood, drowning him.

Jane shot forward. Her feet got snared in the clothes on the floor and she almost fell face first onto the hardwood.

"Easy." Elias caught her around her waist. He didn't want to let her go. Her breath quickened as he tightened his hold, pulling her closer to his body. "I got you."

Elias could feel her breath on his neck. It tickled. Their eyes met at the same time—their lips were centimeters apart. He wanted to close the gap, but his ethics tripped up his desire to taste her.

Instead of sitting next to Jane, Elias squatted in front of her, but leaving several feet open between them. "I'm sorry for shouting." He shook his head. "I have no right to talk to or treat you that way. I know I have issues, which don't involve you. But you are passing out, and *that* worries me."

Jane nodded, a few tears slipping down her cheeks. "I can't help what's happening to me, Elias. I don't know why I'm passing out. I get a bit of flashes here and there but it's not clear or complete images. Not sure if I'm remembering something or if they're just dreams."

Elias reached up and wiped the tears. Maybe he shouldn't have touched her but he couldn't help himself. He sat next to her, their arms touching, but neither moved.

"Jane, I don't know why you keep passing out either.

But no matter what, it's going to be okay." Elias nudged her.

Jane leaned her head onto his shoulder. "I feel like I'm losing my mind, Elias."

His breath caught in his throat from her personal gesture. And he liked the way she called him by his first name. Warmth pulsed through him with every beat of his sore heart.

Elias had to touch her, and gave in to his desire. He wrapped one arm around Jane and gently squeezed. "I'm here to protect you."

"Even from me?" Her face tilted up; her lips wet from her tongue. Elias had to rein in his impulse to kiss her—again. He cleared his throat and got up to, once again, distance himself.

"Even from you," he chuckled.

"I am sorry for looking out the window."

"What happened earlier?"

Jane's face was blank. "What do you mean?"

"I went up to talk earlier." The word "apologize" stuck like a burr in his mouth. But it seemed like that was all he was doing. "I opened the door and you were sitting on the bed, pale as a ghost. Your... your voice changed."

Jane bit at her lower lip before she spoke. "Who was the woman that lived here?"

"Why?" A familiar pang knocked around in his chest.

"She has long, almost brown hair. She's a little shorter than me and very, very thin. She looked like she had been beaten pretty badly. She told me to beware of James? Who is he? Why would she warn me about him?"

"Whoa." He grabbed her arms tight and yanked her up to stand. "Where did this come from and how do you know about James?"

"Please let go, you're hurting my arms." Jane tried to pull away but her strength couldn't match his.

He tightened his grip. "What game are you playing, Jane?" His face was a mere inch from hers.

"Elias, let me go!" Jane shouted. She shook with fear.

He realized what he was doing and released her immediately. Jane bolted to the other side of the bed, her back plastered to the wall.

"The only women in this house are you and Magda. How did you find out about James?"

"I didn't say she *still* lives here. I said she *did*. And she told me about him."

"No more lies, Jane," Elias growled.

"You think I'm lying to you?" she shouted, her hands fisted at her hips.

He knew he was frightening her but Elias didn't let up. "I don't believe you," he said through his teeth.

"I am telling you the truth, you stubborn jackass. That woman told me to beware of this man. Who's James?" The conviction in her voice faded when he stepped closer to her.

"I don't know who told you, but this better not be another bullshit ghost story you've made up."

"You think I made up the story about the girl?" She shifted toward the door.

"I went along with the idea for your benefit. But not here—not in my home. I want the truth."

"I'm done. I can't deal with you anymore. I want to go back to the hospital. I'd rather face the killer than one more day here with you." Jane tried to get to the door but Elias moved much faster and blocked it with his body. She tried pushing him out of the way but he wouldn't budge.

"You can't go back. That son of a bitch is still out there. I will not let you leave." He reached out for her but she moved away. He dropped his hand. "I want the truth, Jane."

"I am telling you the truth." Her voice cracked in a low but firm whisper.

Elias glanced at the redness on her arms that he'd caused. "I'm so sorry." He walked past her with his shoulders slumped.

"That's all you can say?" Jane raked him with a glare.

Elias dropped onto the bed and covered his face. "I am sorry for grabbing you that way. I don't want to be like my father."

CHAPTER TWENTY

J ane wasn't sure what to do next. His apology
provoked some empathy, but was he sincere?

She could leave, but instead, she nervously
walked over to Elias and sat adjacent to him on the bed.

"I wouldn't lie to you, Elias. I'm telling you the
truth." She had to tell him everything she'd seen, no
matter how crazy it sounded. "I have seen other things."
Jane twined her fingers together. "It might be nothing,
but I'm tired of keeping it to myself."

His watery eyes slowly met hers. "What things?" His
voice sounded a little lost.

"Not sure if they were ghosts, or memories. But I've
seen two men. Not clear on the faces, but both were
very angry. One smelled of liquor and the other smelled
of blood."

"Blood?" Elias's eyes widened. "And the woman—
what did she smell like?"

"Apple pie. Elias, this woman..." Jane swallowed hard.
"...she was heartbroken. I felt it down to my soul." Jane
rubbed the chill from her arms.

Elias's eyes turned wide with surprise. A small tear

escaped past his long tawny lashes. Jane's heart broke when she looked at his face. She hated to see a man cry. She couldn't help but cry herself.

Jane wiped the wetness away. "She told me to take her baby and run. Are you her baby, Elias?" She hitched in a breath.

"How can this be?" he asked, shaking his head.

"Who is she—and why did she warn me about James?" Jane hiccupped again.

Elias rubbed at his jaw. "This can't be possible—she's been dead for years." He spoke more to himself than to Jane.

Jane swallowed down the ache in her throat before she spoke. "Please tell me who she was, then?"

Elias leaned back and folded his arms across his chest. His eyes were so intense a green that they could match the emerald hue of Ireland's countryside.

"If we're telling truths... she was my mother. Barbara was her name. She died seven years ago from breast cancer," he choked out. "James is my father. He made our lives a living hell until he left with a waitress when I was ten." His voice lost all emotion when he talked about his father. "No one had lived here until I came back three years ago, after my..."

"After what?" Jane asked.

He wouldn't answer. Jane wasn't going to push. She took a calming breath before she spoke again. "I don't know if I'm seeing things because I'm going crazy, or because of my head injury. But the truth is, I saw her. She was in a lot of pain. I *felt* her sorrow."

Elias stood up and looked down at her. "What do you want from me, Jane?"

He was less than a foot away from her. She wanted to hold him, console his pain. Instead, Jane stayed seated. "Just your help," her voice almost a whisper.

The room filled with silence for a long minute. She wasn't sure what to say next. "Elias," Jane whispered his name. She wanted to reach out to him but restrained herself by folding her arms around her middle.

Elias walked over to the window and stared out. "For most of my life, I regretted never really helping my mother. I was too small and young to fight the bastard. He beat her almost every day. My mother protected me, especially when he drank way too much, which was mostly every day. She took the brunt of his abuse so I wouldn't get hurt."

"I'm sorry."

He turned his attention back to her. "Why?"

"I feel like I've caused you more pain by asking, and I don't want that."

"Too late." He gave a laugh, but it never reached his pain-filled eyes. "You know, he used to beat my mother to the point that she couldn't walk. At times, she'd be passed out for days and I couldn't do anything about it."

"Elias." She was crying again, but for him. "I don't know—" Jane stood, wiping the tears from her face, trying to stay strong.

"Don't. I don't need your pity tears. You can't choose your family. I learned that a long time ago." The hollowness of his words and the blankness in his eyes had Jane's heart lurching.

"Where is he now?" she asked.

"I don't know and don't care," He growled vehemently.

Jane couldn't resist anymore and went to him. "Look at me," she insisted.

He stood fixed. Elias wouldn't look at her.

She turned him so they were face to face.

Don't get close. Her thoughts were a contradiction to what her heart wanted.

A single tear escaped his eye and it ran down his cheek. Seeing him vulnerable, destroyed her willpower to restrain herself. She wiped away the evidence of his sadness.

Without a word, she wrapped her arms around his middle and hugged him tight. Her head lay against his chest, she listened to his heart race.

* * *

Elias kept his arms down at his sides. What was he supposed to do, hug her? She was consoling him. He didn't expect kindness when he'd treated her like crap. His knees nearly buckled under him.

He put his arms around her and held her tight. Her arms cradled him with loving care. The heat from her body warmed him with... Need. Admitting his hidden feelings for her gave Elias some sense of release.

The freshness of her scent filled his senses and calmed his angst. Elias kissed the top of her head. For a moment, she made him forget all the hurt in his life.

What he wanted to do was kiss her. He needed her. To forget himself and the past that haunted him almost every night.

She turned her face toward his and whispered, "Sorry." Her voice was heartfelt and genuine. He couldn't resist and leaned in and kissed her cheek. Satin soft against his lips, just as he imagined it. Warmth sizzled down his spine. He ached for more.

Jane hugged tighter. She tilted her head back slightly and kissed his collar bone.

A surge of longing pushed past his morality. Elias kissed her with all the need that had been trapped in his heart. Soft, smooth and gentle, like rose petals at first— simple and tender. He pulled back but she tightened her arms. She lifted her head and kissed him back, more assertive, which he liked.

Elias pulled back a bit and looked down at her face, staring at her full, reddened lips—slightly parted, wanting him back.

This wasn't right. He was there to defend—had made an oath to protect—not to taste her sweet mouth or have sex.

"Elias, please." Her plea was his undoing.

He came down hard. His tongue delved deep into the heat of her mouth. Her moan encouraged him as his hands touched, coveting her body. Heat rose fast, from spark to flame.

The fire raged hot as his kiss left her lips and trailed down her neck, then back to the hunger of her mouth. As his tongue played with hers, Elias attempted to pull off her flannel shirt. Jane helped and yanked it open. Buttons flew.

"Beautiful," he said as he appreciated every creamy curve of her body. From her well-defined breasts to her slender hips, his need to be inside her had been almost incessant from the moment she stepped into his home. His grew impatient.

He gently framed his hands around her silken mounds. His thumbs grazed against her hardened nipples. She took in a sharp inhale. "Don't stop," she moaned, tilting her head, eyes on him.

Without hesitation, Elias dipped his head down to taste her taunting buds. She pulled at his hair, encouraging him while he licked and suckled, savoring her breasts. He pulled away, but only to get rid of her shirt. Then Jane surprised him.

She pulled him to the bed, trailing her hands down his body. First his shoulders, down his arms and then along his chest as though Jane was tracing his body for a memory. His skin felt electrified by her touch.

Jane traced along the ridges of his abs, stopping at the edge of his shorts. A tease.

Elias hardened even more as the tips of her fingers dipped below his elastic waistband, a hair away from touching his dick.

She kissed his chest, then using her tongue, circled one nipple in a slow lazy lap, then the other. She grazed her teeth against them. Elias trembled—almost losing his control.

The heavy ache turned into a desperate need. Elias couldn't ignore his desires, or hers, any longer.

His hands worked quickly to pull her sweatpants down. He grabbed her around her waist—the only barrier between them now was his shorts and her underwear.

Without pause, Jane pulled his shorts down to his ankles. A twinkle in her eye made her look like a sex nymph. And just like that, she ran her palm against the ridge of his cock. Elias swallowed hard as she touched him with a slow stroke. He couldn't endure the torture any longer. He lifted her up and she wrapped her legs around his waist.

He seared her with a kiss that meant more pleasures were to come.

Her thin panties were the only obstacle between them now. His hands palmed her ass and ground her against his hard shaft. He wanted to be sure she wanted him as much as he wanted her.

Eyes level, Jane leaned in and kissed him with such ardent need, Elias had no remaining doubt and turned her back to the bed. Right before he laid her down, he stopped. His conscience slapped him across his face.

He tore his lips from hers and took in a deep hard

breath. His forehead met hers. "I'm sorry. We can't do this."

"What?" Jane's voice came out like a ragged whisper.

"We can't do this. This isn't right." He slid her down to the bed and took a step back to pull up his shorts. "I can't take advantage of you, Jane. No matter how bad I want you. Not like this. Not this way." He walked out of the room. "I'm sorry."

CHAPTER TWENTY-ONE

E lias had to gather his composure before he faced Jane again. He knew he'd cave in to his desires if he looked at her. Her vulnerability and compassion were his weakness.

He could taste her on his tongue—tried to swallow her down, but it was hard to erase the sweetness from his mouth. His skin had tingled under her touch. Every nerve ending was charged.

With his cock rock hard, he got into the shower and turned on the ice-cold water. Leaning into the icy stream, the heat coursing through his body wouldn't ease. His skin was tight to his bones, cold, but he was still achingly hot.

The image of her lying on his bed intensified his hunger. There was only way to clear his mind of this lust, and Jane.

Elias gripped his cock, closed his eyes and stroked. Slow at first, remembering how Jane's legs wrapped perfectly around his hips. His fingers tightened around his shaft like an iron band, jacking faster and faster. That familiar charge at the base of his balls surged and he fell over the edge with a grunt. With a final twist and yank of his tip, he slowly descended back down to reality.

As he stood there, watching his seed swirl down the drain, Elias realized his hand didn't do jack shit, and Jane was the only cure for what he had.

Draped with only a towel—his second shower of the day, he looked into the mirror with shame. If he didn't control his impulses, it wouldn't be his last.

The deep need to be with her unsettled him. How could this have happened? He could barely stand being in the same room with her. She annoyed the hell out of him. Especially when she called him *ass* to his face. He admired Jane for her survival, but he didn't have to like her—*shit*! Who was he fooling? He liked all of her. So much so that he could fall in love with her... *No!* Elias would not let that happen.

Instead, he ignored the burn in his groin and stomach and got dressed.

After Elias loosened the gray T-shirt that clung to his still-damp body, he made his way down the hall. He peeked into his room and noticed she wasn't in there. He went downstairs where he saw Magda heading into the basement.

"What are you doing?" he asked. He pushed back his bangs.

"Going downstairs. There's a lot of your mother's clothing still down below. Jane could easily fit into them. You should get a haircut." Magda reached up to touch his hair but Elias evaded her hand.

"Uh, no." He gave her a big grin. "Um, where is she?" His throat tightened up when he spoke. The idea of Jane wearing his mother's clothes sparked fire in him. Though, what was the use of getting mad? At least they were being used.

"In the kitchen." Magda tilted her head and stared up at him. "You aren't giving her a hard time, are you?"

"No ma'am." *Almost.* He wished.

"Okay, then please go talk to her." She took the creaky steps slowly down. "She needs rest," she threw over her shoulder.

After watching Magda make her way downstairs, Elias walked into the kitchen and found Jane sitting at the table. She was dressed in a purple terry robe—his mother's favorite robe. She'd worn it all the time.

He remembered when his mother used to sit at the table right beside him, enjoying breakfast together, waiting for the school bus to come. Elias's chest hurt from the flash of memory. Those were the moments he cherished. Unmarred by James McAvoy's brutal hand.

He took a deep breath, cleared his mind of his past and stepped up to the table.

The second Elias saw the file he had brought home, he knew there was going to be a shit storm of questions. All the pictures were face up and spread across the flat surface.

He gathered the photos into a pile and reached for the two still in Jane's hands. "You aren't supposed to look at these."

Jane pulled away. "What are these?" Her voice shook.

"Possible links to your case, but I don't want you to worry about it."

"They're staring up at me, calling for help." Tears welled up in her eyes. Jane wiped them away with her sleeve. "Who are they?"

He wished he could wrap his arms around her and take her away from all the pain. Instead, he gathered all the photos in a neat pile and placed them in the folder.

"I'm not sure yet, but don't look at them, Jane." Elias

put the file folder at the far end of the counter. "Give me the rest."

She ignored him. "How are these women connected to my case?"

He cleared his throat before he answered. "I'm not sure, yet."

Jane's brows furrowed tight but her eyes filled with sorrow. "You're holding something back. Tell me, Elias."

He had to look away. His strength waned. "Jane, you need your rest. Magda told you to go lay down, I suggest you listen."

She shook her head, ignoring his orders. "What about these numbers, are they dates? They go back twenty years."

"This has nothing to do with you," he lied. Stress and worry still shadowed under her eyes. He didn't want to add to it.

Jane's eyes bored into him. "I want to know," she said, the intensity of her voice giving no quarter.

Elias sat down across from her. "Actually, the dates go back even further. Almost forty years."

Jane dropped the pictures like white-hot pokers. "Forty? So, you're thinking that I'm not the first victim." The last sentence came out in a whisper. "Jane could be."

"What are you talking about? You're Jane."

"No, the girl I see. Her name is Jane too."

Elias remained quiet. He still questioned if Jane—this Jane—was delusional.

"Do you know what this means?" Jane said, slightly perked up.

"What?"

"I'm not going crazy." But Elias wasn't too sure about that.

"I will have the names of these victims by tomorrow. In the meantime, you need rest."

Sadness etched the corners of her eyes. "How can I rest when there are clues in these photos that might lead to who tried to kill me? And he's still out there." Tears slipped down. She looked at him as though he was guilty of something. At that point, he'd do anything to make her smile.

He came around to her chair, knelt, and took her hand. "Jane, nothing is going to happen to you. You're safe here, as long as you stay hidden," he said, squeezing her hand.

She pulled away. "All this time, this bastard has been mutilating and killing all these women and no one has caught him yet? How can I feel safe knowing that?"

"Jane, you need to rest. I really don't want you—"

"Don't you see?" she interrupted. "I know these women. I dream about them every time I close my eyes. They call to me for help," Jane cried out. "I can't sleep without seeing them trying to pull me into the ground. I can taste the dirt and wet mold. I can feel their pain." Her voice seized. Tears flooded down. She cried harder. "I... need to know... Who I am." She folded her body up in the chair and covered her face with her hands.

Jane made no sense, but lately, nothing did.

"Look at me, Jane." His hands cradled her face.

She stared at him through drenched lashes.

"You're safe—I promise. Okay?" He leaned in and tried to give her a hug but she pushed him back.

"No, it's not okay. Far from okay. I want to know— why me? What makes me so special that I lived and these women didn't?" Pain echoed off the words she conveyed.

"Jane."

"That's not my name! Why can't I remember my real name?" She pounded the table with her fists while a deluge of tears and sobs choked out.

Elias couldn't watch her fall apart. Her breakdown— her anguish, tore his heart to shreds. He needed her to be strong. He stood up, lifted her out of the chair and carried her upstairs.

Jane didn't protest. She wrapped her arms around his neck and soaked his shirt with tears.

His wall of sensibility had crumbled the moment he'd heard her cry again. From the second Jane was found, his life had changed. She challenged him in a way that no woman ever had before. He'd never met someone like her, who used her strength to push past her fears and keep going.

Jane was the reason he wouldn't leave Beaver Ridge like he'd planned. The obligations of his job, to Magda and the damned farmhouse weren't enough to make him stay. But Jane, she gave him purpose and the will to fight for her. The reason to want to stay and beat back the demons in both their lives.

With each step he took, his heart pounded faster. The rush of blood through his veins charged his adrenaline. The second he reached his bedroom, there was no going back. Once inside, he closed the door with his foot and leaned back against it.

Elias kissed her wet cheek. "It will be all right. I'm here," he said, touching his forehead to hers.

She tilted up her face and kissed his lips with such gentleness. "Love me," she said and kissed him again. "Make me forget."

Those words nearly knocked the air out of his lungs. The way she pleaded with him pushed him over that line. He captured her mouth with hungry urgency.

His tongue and lips danced in a tight tango with hers. The need to have her grew stronger with every second her hands stroked his neck. Jane's fingers combed, pulled and held his hair tight. He had intended to take their dance slow, but not anymore.

Cradling her in his arms, he carried Jane to the bed and laid her down gently. The purple robe loosened and untied, spreading open to expose her flesh. She wore nothing under that robe.

Elias took in a sharp breath. His eyes traveled from Jane's face down to the dark curls nestled between her legs, memorizing every curve of her body.

The urgency for skin-to-skin contact rushed through him. Elias ripped his clothes off and slid himself between her thighs, up her body—chest to chest. He braced his weight so not to crush her, yet still connect every inch of her flesh to his.

His rigid shaft pressed against her pelvis, grinding, taunting. Her tight buds rubbed against his chest, teasing back. Elias had to touch them, taste every bit of her skin.

In a slow, lazy drag of his tongue, Elias savored his way down to her chin, to her neck and breasts. He gave them equal attention as he tasted, teased, and nipped at her pert nipples.

He wanted this ecstasy to last forever.

Jane trembled under his gentle assault. Her moans became louder as his fingers massaged her creamy flesh, then trailed down to the triangle of hair.

She was wet and hot. His fingers tested and teased, dipping deep, deeper. Jane's hips rocked against his hand. As Elias's fingers explored, his thumb played havoc with her clit. She bucked faster.

With her sweet essence coating his fingers, he sped up his thrusts. Releasing her breasts, Elias kissed his way down to her core. Spreading her thighs apart, he feasted.

His first touch was a tease, a kiss. The tip of his

tongue traced along the ridge of her. Jane whimpered his name, which spurred him to move faster, go deeper.

He ravaged her with his mouth. He stabbed her deep with his tongue, repeatedly. He licked and sucked every bit of what she had to offer. His voracious hunger kept up with the need to satisfy her. He pushed her legs farther apart. He then lifted her up to him. She slid out of the robe, exposing her body to him fully.

Elias stopped, looked at Jane and saw how her parted lips were swollen, and her delectable nipples were red and tight from his love play. He smiled and nipped the inner part of her thigh. He'd never felt the need to indulge, but it was easy to get lost in Jane. She made him forget his past, everything.

*   *   *

Jane thought she had died and gone to heaven. The ravenous way his mouth touched her body made her crave more. She didn't want him to stop.

He took her on a fast ride up, then slowed down. And then did it all again, not quite reaching her peak. She had never felt the glorious torture Elias was putting her through.

The pressure built until his wicked mouth finally let her careen over the edge. She called out his name as wave after wave of euphoria took over. She swore she was set ablaze. She bucked up faster to match his delving fingers and mouth.

Elias withdrew from her, leaving her temporarily empty. He sat up and pulled her with him. He kissed her with a fevered frenzy. Jane encouraged him to hurry, which didn't take much. He groaned as she reached down for his cock.

"I want you," Jane begged, stroking him to his balls.

He let out a growl before he reached over and grabbed a condom from his nightstand. The moment Elias rolled the rubber back to the hilt of his cock, he grabbed her close, and slid his shaft into her slowly.

"Jane, I don't think I can hold on."

"Then don't," she encouraged.

No more words were spoken. There was only the simple pleasure they shared. He lifted his hips and plunged into her again and again. Her body trembled. The friction melded her body with his. He had set her on fire.

Elias lifted her legs up over his shoulders and stroked her fast and deep, and she soared high again. Jane screamed out his name as the waves of her orgasm whipped at her senses. She came hard and swift. And so did he.

He collapsed on top of her, but Jane didn't mind his weight. The way he stayed inside, connected to her, made her feel... Whole.

Laughter bubbled up from her. She couldn't help but laugh at how wonderful her body felt, especially under him, connected to him. Jane wanted to stay that way forever.

The scent of their love play filled the air. She kissed his shoulder, tasting the saltiness on his skin. He was as intoxicating as strong whiskey. Jane was drunk from Elias loving her.

As though he read her thoughts, Elias slipped out of Jane, disposed of the condom, then laid next to her. She frowned at him but changed it to a smile once his arms wrapped around her and pulled her in. His arms were the one place she was safe.

"Why are you laughing?" Elias asked, nipping at her earlobe, stroking her arm.

"I don't know. Happy?"

"I'm glad," he said back in a lazy whisper.

She wished they could leave, forget this place, forget what had happened and start fresh. "If you had a chance to escape this place, where would you go?"

"Half Moon Bay, California. I have a place right off the beach."

Jane turned around and faced him. "Why aren't you there now?"

"It's complicated, but someday I'll be back there." Elias caressed her cheek.

"So, a beach house?" she asked, stroking his nipple. "I would have never guessed."

He grabbed her hand and kissed her fingers. "It's not a beach house. It's more like a large shack. I fell in love with the dump the moment I laid eyes on it. There's a small rotted porch where I used to sit and watch the sunset. Now, I rent it out to a buddy of mine who is enjoying the scenery."

"Sounds beautiful." Jane choked up. She turned her back on him. No crying. Self-pity wasn't going to ruin this moment.

But who was she? Where did she come from? Could she be a part of what Elias hoped for himself? Jane knew the answer to all her questions.

"Are you okay?" he whispered, and leaned in and kissed her.

She closed her eyes and tried to absorb the serenity around her. "Just tired. Tell me more about Half Moon. Is Charlie's Bar still there?"

Elias cocked his head up and turned her on her back. "How do you know about Charlie's Bar? Have you been there?"

"I don't—I think I have been there." She closed her eyes and envisioned the place. "The entire bar looks like it was made out of driftwood. By the entrance, there's a picture of Charlie in a speedo and a couple of women in tiny bathing suits posing on the beach.

"There's an outdoor area he opened to attract more business, but wasn't finished with it." Jane opened her eyes, excitement burst out of her as she continued to describe the bar Elias frequented. "I think I was there the first day he opened it. He had a huge party."

"Jane, Charlie opened up that outdoor area five years ago. Do you think we could have met then?" he asked, his mouth slightly opened, his eyes glossed with surprise.

"I don't know, but I wish I could remember." Jane smiled.

"Me too."

"Elias?"

"Jane?"

"Make love to me again," Jane purred.

Elias said nothing, but loved her as she'd asked. He loved her just as she asked. All night.

Mind and body spent, Jane fell asleep content in Elias's arms.

CHAPTER TWENTY-TWO

The hospital ran quiet at night. The third shift hospital staff members hunkered down in their usual positions. They were always told not to leave unless for rounds and patient needs.

He walked in through the bright main lobby without much notice—just like any normal day—or night. There wasn't anyone around except for a nurse sitting at the main desk filing her nails. Lucky for him, her focus was down on her fingers.

The gritty sound made him remember how he was taught to sharpen his blades.

The way his mother used to exhale a blissful hiss when he glided the honed blade along her skin. He been only five years old then, but she taught him how to hold the handle in such a way that he'd cut with a surgeon's precision. He'd given her such pleasure until she up and died on him.

Tonight was the night he'd take Jane back. It had been a week since he last saw her. The need to be with her wore him down. He'd made sure his special room was ready for her, and he now checked off the list in his head and patted his pocket to confirm he had the plastic bag with the chloroformed towel.

Hardly anyone saw him as he made his way toward the elevator. As the doors opened, he changed his mind and decided to take the back stairs instead. Avoiding the security cameras at the end of the hall, he took the stairs two flights up like he had all the time in the world. He didn't want to exert too much energy. He had to save his strength for Jane.

He nudged open the heavy metal door as quietly as possible and stepped just outside the psych wing. As he peeked around the corner, he saw the night security guard. The electronic doors behind him were still opened. He must have just made his rounds.

With the ring of keys strung on his belt, the tall man could be heard through the halls. The guard disappeared around the corner; this was his one chance to get past the door before it closed.

When the double doors started to close, he slid past the entrance and hid in the alcove near the empty nurses' desk.

The hallway was dark except for the emergency exit sign lit up at the far corner.

A janitor mopping the linoleum floor at the far end finished cleaning the floors and headed toward the exit. He ducked back into the alcove until the cleaner was gone.

As he stepped out of the shadows, he was surprise to see the redheaded nurse—who had helped Jane before—working this floor. Cherry. What a bad girl. All that make-up slathered on her face assured him that she earned the title *naughty*. He became bone hard as he studied the woman. She could be dessert, but he wasn't prepared for one more. *Maybe next time.*

She strolled back to the desk, grabbed a bag from

behind it, and headed for the exit. How odd. There was no one to watch over the patients. He was fine with that; less hassle moving Jane out of there.

Once she left, he started at the closest rooms, hurriedly searching each one. Looking for Jane was turning into a tedious task. Every room he stepped into was either empty or occupied by a crazy patient.

The last room was directly in front of the nurses' station. Jane had to be in there. He slipped into the room next to it, which was occupied by a sleeping, tied down old man. Poor bastard. Arms wrapped in bandages. If he'd had time, he'd show the old fool how to cut with precision, but there was no time for that.

He made sure he was alone in the wing, and walked into Jane's room.

He giggled with excitement as he looked at his sleeping Jane. She was covered up pretty well, even her head. He wondered if she was strapped down. Wouldn't that be his luck? How perfect. Pulling back the blanket, he found the bed... *Empty!*

No Jane. *Damn it!*

"Where are you?" he hissed out between clenched teeth before he knocked off all the pillows, and ripped the sheets off the bed. He wanted to shout out her real name, but instead he bit down on his tongue.

He had to think. Tapping his right temple with his finger as he walked out into the hallway, the truth came to him quickly.

Jane wasn't there. He'd checked every room on this wing. Jane was nowhere.

That sneaky bastard. He'd never thought Elias had it in him to use deceit. The only question was—where was Jane? Where was she hidden?

Sounds from the entrance caught his attention. The

nurse. Maybe his night wasn't for nothing. He stepped into the room next door. The clapping sound of her heels got closer, louder. He looked over at the sleeping patient

He grabbed the remote, pressed the nurse button to get her attention and waited behind the door. The moment the redhead entered the room, he reached out to cover her mouth and used his left arm as leverage around her throat. With a quick shift of his body and hands, he broke the nurse's neck. She crumpled to the floor, dead. *What a waste of a good nurse.*

He let out a hard breath. *Pity.* He'd killed her too fast. There was no enjoyment with this one. But she was no Jane.

After he shook off the disappointment, he placed the nurse's body in the bathroom, grabbed her security card and left. He used her card to swipe out of the wing, then wiped it down with his shirt and threw it in the trash can.

The closer to the exit he got, the higher his rage spun until it was nearly uncontrollable. He spat out the blood from chewing on his tongue and inner cheek. It left a red-pink stain on the cement. He didn't worry about that DNA. No one was going to think anything about it.

He got into his car and pounded on the steering wheel. "Jane, where are you? Where did that son of a bitch hide you?"

After a few more whacks at the steering wheel, he stopped and started laughing.

Oh, what a wonderful game this was turning out to be. Unbeknownst to the chief, he had added a level of excitement to this party. With Jane hidden, it made him want her more than life itself.

What better way to finish this. He'd find her, enjoy her and then the chief would be blamed for Jane's murder. Giddy as a school girl, he was satisfied with his newly woven plan.

The moment he turned the key, the radio sang out his favorite song. He blasted it as he made his way home. He belted the words as the electric guitar hissed in unison with the bass and drums. *Run to the hills, run for your lives,* reverberated off the closed windows.

As he turned down Route 41, a truck lay in a ditch with the back end sticking up. A woman on the side of the road tried to flag him down. He didn't need much encouragement. She was in a shag miniskirt dress and platform boots. *Ooh, another naughty one.*

He pulled over and slid down the passenger side window. The painted brunette had a cigarette in her mouth, and was puffing like a dragon in the cold. She leaned into the opening and gave him a wicked smile. Oh yes, she was a bad one.

She was nothing much. Her slim build could easily be handled. Though the slut wasn't Jane, she would do until then. It wasn't anything that he hadn't played with before. His blood raged, and he needed it quenched.

"Is everything all right?" The smell of alcohol wafted off her like heavy perfume.

"Yeah, man. Our truck fell into the damn ditch and we can't get the fucking thing back up. Do you have a cell I can use to call for a tow?" She was shaking and was rubbing at her bare arms.

He looked around when she said "our" but didn't see anyone else. She was too drunk. "Sorry no, but the tow place is about a mile down. Do you want a lift there?" He wasn't lying about the mile, but it wasn't the towing place. It was his place.

"You're not some fucking weirdo, are you? I won't fuck you or anything for the ride."

He laughed. "No. I won't touch you." *This one definitely needs to learn a lesson.*

"Um." She looked back toward the ditched Dodge, then back at him. She shivered. "Okay. A mile... Yeah. It's fucking cold."

"Yes, ma'am." He was polite, which always hooked the stupid ones. He unlocked the door and she got in. "Were you with someone else? You did say 'our.'" He wanted to cover his tracks. He didn't want her to be missed, not yet anyway.

"Yeah, my boyfriend—that fucking bastard left me to freeze my ass off."

"Where did he go?"

"He hoofed it to get help, but I think he went the other way."

"How long ago? We could go pick him up." He tried to make easy conversation so she would let her guard down. He knew she had something in her spangled purse —she kept her hand inside it, hiding what it was.

"Who the fuck knows. The bastard can go freeze his balls off for all I care. He has my keys. Let him walk, he fucking deserves it. But you know what I'm really pissed about?"

He put the car in drive and leaned forward on purpose and turned up the heat. "What?"

She jumped at his nearness, but quickly relaxed when his hand went down and the heat blasted. "I don't normally take rides from strangers."

"Smart. Now why are you mad?"

"Oh yeah. I'm fucking pissed because he took the fucking bottle of Jack and left me nothing. Jimmy, you're an asshole!" she yelled out.

"Jimmy?" He leaned in again and raised the heat a bit more. She didn't flinch that time.

"Yeah. Do you know him? He says he used to live around here but I think he's a fucking liar."

His brow pinched together. "What's his last name?"

She eyed him for a moment before she spoke. "Macvoy. Micaboy. Beats the fuck out of me how to say it."

"McAvoy? James McAvoy?"

"Fuck yeah, that's it. Do you know him?"

"Oh yes," he said coolly. adrenaline fueled his mind. James sure liked his women young and this one was primed for play. "What's your name, sweetheart?"

She looked at him and tightened her hands on whatever was in her purse.

"I'm James," he lied with confidence, extending his hand out to her.

"James? Just like Jimmy. Sorry for you. My name is... Nadia." She didn't take his hand.

"Well, it's nice to meet you, Nadia." He smiled and retracted his hand.

He saw her shoulders relax more as she looked out the window.

"I thought you said the tow place was a mile down," she said, shaking.

The opportunity came quick, when she looked at him. He cocked his arm back and gave her a sharp jab to the face. His fist landed perfectly across her temple. She was unconscious. "Almost," he said with a light laugh.

Someone upstairs must have listened to his prayers, because this night was getting better and better with every turn of the road.

The wheels in his head spun faster as his plan's radius enlarged. Why not blame James McAvoy for Jane's death too. With her murder tied to the deadbeat daddy and his no-good son, his activities stayed safe.

He looked over and saw the brunette twitching. She wasn't fully out, so he gripped the steering wheel with his left hand and swung with his right to her face.

Oh, what a wonderful night this had turned out to be.

CHAPTER TWENTY-THREE

"What the hell am I doing out here?" Harold Kantor uttered with chattering teeth. With his new night vision goggles strapped to his head, he was sprawled in the prickly grass.

"Shit," Harold spat. He was sleepwalking again and was in a ditch, freezing his ass off. Served him right if his feet would fall off from the damn cold. With only a T-shirt and sweats, he swore icicles hung off his balls. His head ached from the elastic band of the goggles, or was it the cold? Didn't matter. He was stranded out in the middle of fucking nowhere—half naked and freezing his ass off.

Harold tried to stand but he kept slipping further down the slope. With a few more attempts, he was able to get up to the lip of the ditch. That was when he heard the woman's voice. He turned to his right and crawled onto his belly to the edge of the road.

Still flat on his stomach, he flipped his goggles down and watched what unfolded.

Twenty feet away, he saw a young woman getting into an Impala. He didn't recognize the girl or the car. Even with his goggles, it was hard to fully see her features or get a visual on the license plates. The car took off way too fast.

As the Impala drove away, Harold stood from where he'd been laying. Then it dawned on him. He was stranded and had to walk back home, barefoot.

"Fuck," he spat and hoofed it in the opposite direction.

CHAPTER TWENTY-FOUR

"Play with me, Jane." Laughter rang out across the meadow as the little girl skipped along in her yellow sundress. She twirled about, happy as a child could be. The sun cast so much glare Jane couldn't see clearly.

"I can't." Jane tried to follow but her legs became lead weights.

"Yes, you can. We all want to play with you." The girl pointed to the meadow behind her.

"Who's 'we'?" Jane asked with trepidation. She looked out over the expanse and saw nothing but bones scattered all over. Terror caught her throat, and she could barely catch a breath.

"All of us. Come join us." The girl's smile melted away. It became distorted. Green-black splotches replaced the sun-kissed freckles on her face.

The sky darkened and the wind picked up with a razor sharpness that slashed across Jane's face. She wanted to run away but her legs were buried in the dirt.

Jane kept looking back to where the girl stood. She

tried to pull at the roots that stuck out of the ground, though her attempts were futile.

The roots reminded her of arms with long deep gashes, similar to hers. They twitched and reached for her with bony fingers. Jane tried to slap them out of her way, but they were strong—too strong for her.

She screamed as one hand after another reached out of the soil and tried to pull her under.

"Jane." She heard Elias's voice. "Wake up." She shot up with her fists flailing forward.

"Elias," she uttered in a teary gulp.

He grabbed her hands and held them together. "Jane, calm down. It's only a dream."

His soft words eased her fears. Her shallow breaths slowed and deepened with each inhale. Oh God, she was drenched with sweat.

"Hold me," she whispered.

He hugged her close. "It's all gone now."

"Water. Please?" Jane could taste mud at the back of her throat.

Elias didn't hesitate. He raced into the bathroom and returned with a full glass.

"Here. Drink it slow." He sat next to her and caressed her back.

Jane downed the contents and handed the glass back to Elias. Her palate still had that gritty taste. The smell of decay lingered in her nose.

"Thank you," she said, leaning back against the headboard.

"What were you dreaming about?" He put the glass down on the nightstand and sat next to her.

She hesitated. "The girl, Jane...and the others."

"Others? Meaning the women in the photos?"

"I don't know. I can't remember all of it, but maybe —I think so—I don't know."

Elias pulled her into his arms. "Let it go. It was only a dream. You're safe now."

Jane pulled away. "It was a nightmare, Elias. But it felt so real. She—Jane said she wanted to play with me. I dream of the same place over and over again. I know she's trying to tell me something." Jane laid her head back on his chest. The rhythm of his heart eased the anxiety.

Elias shook his head. "Jane, it's only a nightmare. Nothing more. Try to forget it."

She sat back up and faced him. "The dirt smelled of death, like dead bodies. It tried sucking me in. I choked every time I breathed it in. And those cut up arms— they were pulling me down. Bones littered the ground." She stared into his eyes. "I know in my heart it's a warning."

"About what, Jane? Don't play with ghosts?" Elias got up from the bed, grabbed his pants and yanked them up. "Sorry. That was totally uncalled for." He sat back on the edge of the bed, shoulders slumped forward, and rubbed at his temples.

"You might not want to hear it, but I know that girl is warning me." Her eyes blurred with tears. She reached over and touched his back. "Elias, I have a feeling there are more bodies around that lake."

"Not possible. We scoured the area. Hell, we swept around the perimeter of the lake and found nothing. Jane, it was only a dream."

She shook her head no. She cupped her legs to her chest and tried to hold back the tears.

"Jane, I'm sure that there aren't any more bodies around the lake."

She refused to believe him. "Please leave me alone."

Elias ignored her request and scooped her up in his

arms. He held her tight and kissed her wet cheek. He whispered in her ear, "No. I will not leave you alone."

Her skin was cold and clammy to his hot touch. She could smell the wet dirt in her hair. It made no sense if it was only a dream.

"Why is this happening to me?" Her voice sounded drowned. She wrapped her arms tighter around him.

"Listen to me, Jane. You were found next to a lake. Maybe some of your dream came from your memories. Do you think you're remembering something about your attack or the attacker?"

"I don't know." She leaned her head on his shoulders. "I don't want to think about it anymore. Just hold me." Her plea couldn't be ignored. He held her even tighter until her body melded with his.

CHAPTER TWENTY-FIVE

Elias laid there and listened to the sound of Jane's breathing as it slowed to a rhythm matching his. He molded his body to hers and waited until she relaxed more.

Glancing over at the clock—two a.m., Elias let out a quiet groan. He should've been at work over an hour ago —although he didn't care. Jane came first.

Jane turned and smiled at him. The frailty reflected in her sleepy eyes made his heart lurch. Elias leaned in and kissed her. He'd do anything to rid her dreams of the nightmares. Love her over and over until she felt safe to sleep.

He deepened the kiss, trailing his hands to the one spot that made her forget—made her shiver—made her want him.

Wetness coated his fingers. As he delved deeper into her heat, she rode against his hand while he feasted on her mouth. Elias took his time, making sure her only thought was of *him*. Her groan was all the encouragement he needed. He moved down the bed, lifted her legs over his shoulders, and plunged in with one fluid motion—sliding in and out of her sweet heat.

He hissed as her nails dug into his arms, but his quick pace never wavered. Jane was like a drug. While his fingers played havoc with her clit, he rocked her until they both cried out.

Elias collapsed on top of her but immediately turned to his side.

Mind and body spent, Elias dragged her close, molded her back to him. He absorbed the calmness she gave him. Her body was soft and hot to the touch. He kissed her shoulder, tasting the salty sweat. Perfect.

A few minutes flew by as he heard Jane's breathing even out. She fell back to sleep.

Reluctantly, he got up and slipped out of bed without waking her. But not before he turned and kissed Jane's temple—wanting another second to connect with her. Elias smiled down at her and then quietly walked out.

Elias knew his career changed the moment she was found. But the moment he slept with this woman, it wasn't all about *his life* anymore. This had never happened to him. Letting a woman into his heart—he wasn't sure how to handle it.

After he washed and dressed in the bathroom, Elias headed downstairs.

The house was dark except for the light over the sink. Peacefulness filled the whole place. *Interesting.* Peace was something never associated with the McAvoy household before. It was nice.

He stood in the kitchen and noticed everything had been put away. Magda had cleaned, the way his mother used to. A twinge of pain knocked a bit of wind out of his lungs. He swallowed the grief down.

As he made his way to the living room, a chilly wind brushed against him as though someone had run past. It was enough to make his hair stand on end. Elias turned in a circle, eyeing every corner of the room. There was nothing. Strange.

He took a few backward steps into the kitchen and turned around. In his momentum, Elias almost knocked Magda on her backside. Arm cocked back, he almost punched her.

"Elias!" she yelped and raised her hands in surrender.

"I'm sorry." Elias lowered his arm and took a step forward. "You shouldn't surprise people in the dark."

"I heard noises," Magda explained as she smoothed out her night coat. She straightened one crocheted slipper, came up and patted him on his arm, "How'd you sleep?"

"Good, for a change. But now I'm late for work."

"I'm restless." Worry was etched in the corners of her eyes. "I figured a cup of tea could soothe me back to sleep. How's Jane?" By the tilt of her head, she asked as though she knew what had occurred between him and Jane.

He cleared his throat and turned away. "Um, she's good, too—sleeping." Elias stumbled over his tongue.

"I'm not dead, or deaf, Elias. But…I don't want to see you two hurt." She touched his chest where his heart pounded fast.

"We're fine," he said and turned away from her touch.

Magda nodded, not saying another word. She went to the stove, grabbed the kettle and added water to it.

He felt the rush of blood to his cheeks. Was he blushing? That was impossible. "I'm late for work. Call my cell if anything happens. And, no venturing out."

"Okay. And if she wants to talk to you?"

"Let her." Elias kissed Magda's cheek, grabbed his coat off the chair and rushed out the back door. "Get to bed, it's late. I'll be back by—" he checked his cell, "around nine or so."

"Will do," Magda said as she saluted him with a quick smile, but he ignored her sarcasm.

Elias walked the perimeter of the house and barn with a flashlight before he headed toward his truck. Everything seemed safe.

As he leaned into his gun and holster on the seat of the truck, a weight of cold steel pressed hard against the back of his skull. He slowly raised his hands.

"Don't move unless you want your brains all over your fucking truck."

Elias's adrenaline ran high. His chest hurt from the hard erratic pounding of his heart, knowing who was behind him. "Not moving." The gun pressed even harder against his skull; the tip of the barrel digging into his scalp.

"Who the fuck are you and why are you in my house? Answer quick—I have a twitchy trigger finger."

"I own the house," Elias said, his voice flat and devoid of emotion. The stench of whisky invaded Elias's nose. James McAvoy's liquored breath still smelled the same. Bad—like rotten garbage.

"Like hell you do. Fucking turn around. Slow."

"James McAvoy, don't you recognize your own son?" Elias asked. He faced the man he once was terrified of. He had on a pair of ratty jeans, shredded Converse high tops and a yellow-pitted white T-shirt.

Old, that was all Elias saw. Once a tall, virile, intimidating man, now he was gray, much older and weary like his clothing. But Elias was no fool. His old man was unpredictable, especially now since he wasn't sure how much his father had drank.

"Boy? Is that you?" With the shotgun still pointed at Elias's face, James grabbed at his son's jacket and pulled

him closer. "Fuck. You look like her. Weak and useless."
James spat at the ground and pushed him hard, knocking
Elias back against the truck.

Though he was disgusted to admit it, Elias was the
spitting image of his father—blonde, wavy hair and eyes
as green as emeralds. In his day, James was the catch. His
mother should have thrown this fish away.

James wiped the spit from his mouth with the back
of his hand. He lowered the gun, stumbled back, and
wavered. "What are you doing in my house?" Rage
slurred his words.

"What do you want, old man?" Elias wondered where
he'd gotten the shotgun. He hoped no one was hurt or
killed in the process.

James took a step closer and aimed it at his face again.
"I should have killed you when I had the chance. You are
a worthless piece of shit, like your whore of a mother."

Elias had despised this man all his life. The lies that
he spewed about his mother made his anger escalate into
a raging storm. He wanted to beat him to the point of
death and bring him back and repeat it again and again,
like his father had done to his mother.

"What do you want, old man?" Elias repeated. He
knew he had to be quick and disarm James before he got
a shot off. But his father stood too far away for Elias to
knock the shotgun out of his hands. He needed to wait
until James got closer.

"I want what's coming to me. This house—my
money your mother stole—everything. I want it all
back." James's wobbly stance indicated his drunken state
was far worse than Elias had realized. Or was it that the
cold had gotten to him?

Either way, James shivered, losing some control of
the gun. The barrel dropped slightly as he tried to wipe

frozen snot from his nose. Elias had the advantage and took a small step forward to get a better shot at kicking the gun out of the bastard's hands.

As he took another small step forward, something caught in his peripheral vision. His mother's window curtains shifted.

Elias turned slightly and stared up at the window. Much longer than he should have, because he was smacked in the face with the butt of the gun. Pain shot from his nose and mouth—he fell back against the truck's door.

"Don't fucking move, boy."

Elias shook off the fury, spat the blood out of his mouth and growled. "Old man, you made the worst mistake coming here." He glanced quickly up at the window again then back at his father.

James's eyes had followed Elias's stare. "What the fuck you looking at?" James shivered.

"It's cold out here, isn't it?" Elias kept his attention on the gun. He'd had enough with small talk. He had to get ahold of that gun.

With one shaky hand, James wiped at his brow. "Don't you worry about me."

"There is nothing here for you. If you want to live the rest of your life in one piece, you better put down that gun."

James squinted at him and took a step closer. "Talking to me like that, boy, will get you killed." He lifted the double barrel and loosely pointed it at Elias's head. "You're dead to me anyway, like your bitch of a mother. Maybe I should have beaten some sense into you."

Elias shifted to his right to give himself better access to the gun. Kicking it out of James's hand was the only way. As he reared his foot back, he saw Jane standing right behind his father.

Jane was naked. She had a piece of firewood in her hand. Her face twisted with anger at each foul word James spoke. While loose snow swirled around her, the icy wind didn't affect her determined stance. She had the element of surprise. Jane raised the wood when James aimed the gun right at Elias's chest. With a full swing, she hit James on the side of his face, knocking the drunk to the ground, and the gun fell with him.

The gun went off as it fell. The bullet caught Elias's top left shoulder as he tried to move out of the way. The hit knocked him hard, back against the truck. Pain sliced through his shoulder like a white-hot poker. It intensified as he moved to Jane's side, but she pushed him back—wouldn't let him near her.

Jane hovered over James with the wood aimed at his head. Elias tried to coax her to drop it but she held on to it tighter. "He has no rights," she said in a sad, angry tone.

"I'll kill you, bitch!" James roared while holding onto his nose.

Jane laughed. The sound of her voice wasn't hers. "You will never touch me again." Her laughter faded and malice shaped her smile.

Elias was shocked that Jane sounded so much like his mother. Just like earlier, in the bedroom. But for the moment, he had to get the wood away from Jane, before she smacked James again, and get her out of the cold.

"Look at me, Jane," Elias said. He had to keep his tone soft or he'd rile her up more.

She turned her attention to him. Her features softened for a brief second before she returned hardened dark eyes back to James.

"Momma?" Elias whispered. A tear slipped down his

cheek. He wiped it away quickly. "Don't do this. You are not like him."

Jane's attention wasn't deterred. "You'll never touch me or my son ever again." She swung the log down on James's face, which knocked him right out. Blood seeped from his broken nose and dripped onto the graveled ground, forming a tiny puddle.

Elias's breath caught in his throat. It had happened so fast that he wasn't able to stop her from hitting his father again. She was about to take another swing when Elias finally disarmed her.

He threw the wood away, circled his good arm around Jane's waist and pulled her back from James. His shoulder stung something awful. Elias could feel the warmth of the blood coating his skin down to his pecs. But he didn't care. Jane was more important.

Jane resisted his pull but Elias's gentle words in her ears calmed her and she relaxed against him.

Once he knew Jane was okay, Elias focused on James's face, which was covered in blood. He wanted to be sure that the old man wasn't dead.

"Don't move, Jane." He took off his coat and covered her. Taking those few strides over to James, he checked for a pulse, and found it steady. He blew out a breath of relief and moved back to Jane.

Elias wrapped his arms around her. "It's going to be okay." He noticed her eyes were still dark. Her smile was gentle, but not like Jane's where it slightly cocked to one side.

She touched his cheeks and said, "We're safe now," then collapsed against him.

The weight of her body added to the spasms tormenting his wounded shoulder. Magda ran out with a blanket and covered Jane.

"Are you okay? I saw your father and went to check on Jane when I heard the shot. I called for backup."

"You what?" Elias exclaimed.

"I couldn't take the chance if James shot you dead." Magda saw Elias's bloody shirt and sobbed out a gasp. "He shot you."

"Elias?" Jane uttered. She leaned her head against his shot shoulder. He grimaced as the pain magnified.

"Get Jane inside quickly and hide her in my room," he declared. "We can't have anyone finding out she's here."

"What about your shoulder?" Magda tried to look at it, but Elias pushed her hand away.

"It's a graze, I'm fine. Get inside before she's discovered," he urged.

Magda wrapped Jane's arm around her neck and pulled her along the best she could.

Elias picked up the shotgun and placed it in the back of the truck.

"Damn it," He hissed as he checked his shoulder. The pain was getting worse and he was a bit dizzy, but he shook it off.

Once he got his second wind, he checked James's pulse again. He wasn't dead, though his nose wouldn't be the same. It was definitely broken.

As his father stirred awake, Tyson pulled up, and rushed out of the squad to Elias's side. "Holy mother."

Elias turned, light-headed, and had to take a few steps back to lean against the truck for support. The barbed pain in his shoulder was worse. The blood flow from his wound seemed to have stopped, which was a good thing.

"Take this bastard to the ER and get his face looked at and then take him to the station. I'll be there as soon as I'm patched up."

"Yes, Chief."

As Tyson pulled James up to his feet, the officer read him the Miranda. He cuffed his hands behind his back and stuffed the old man in the back seat.

After Elias gave him an okay nod, Tyson took off without any sirens or lights.

Seconds later, Tom showed up from the other direction.

"What the hell is going on here? Cindy Lee radioed saying you were shot. Let me drive you to the hospital."

"It's only a graze. But you missed James. Tyson's taking him to the hospital, then to the station."

"That mother—How do you want to proceed?" Tom asked with indignance.

"We'll call Green Bay in the morning. I'm sure James has a long list of warrants on his ass." Elias moved his shoulder to test how bad the injury was. "I'll just add attempted murder to the list."

Tom tilted his head toward the kitchen window. "Why is Magda here?"

Elias looked at his deputy. He had to come up with something plausible and noticed his mother's clothes heaped over on the stoop. "Magda is helping get rid of my mother's things, finally." He pointed to the box.

Tom eyed the box, then back to him. "Hmm. Let me drive you to the hospital."

"No. I'm good. I'll check with Magda before heading out."

Tom nodded. "Well, thank God Magda was here." He pulled off his hat and rubbed the back of his neck. "All right, since you are being stubborn about the ride— you're good, right?"

"I'm good," Elias replied evenly.

"Then I'm heading to the station. I'll meet you there.

I want to get my hands on that bastard for shooting you."

"Don't do anything, deputy. He'll get his."

"Sure thing," Tom said as he got in his squad and reversed out of the driveway, his tires spitting dirt, snow and gravel.

Elias immediately made his way inside to check on Magda and Jane.

Magda waited in the kitchen. "Did Tom see me?" Her brows creased together and she wrung her hands.

"Yes, but it's okay. He thinks you're here to help get rid of my mother's clothes."

Magda let out a heavy breath and slumped against the counter. "That's good."

"Where is she?"

"In the living room, on the sofa."

Elias walked into the room and found Jane slumped over, her hands covering her face. "Jane," he whispered. She looked up; her eyes were glazed with tears. Her pupils were large and dark, but not like before. She looked lost.

"Are you all right?" Elias asked as he sat down next to her.

"You were shot." Her lips quivered and tears streamed down her face. Her fingers touched his bloodied shirt. "I'm so sorry, Elias."

"It was a graze. I'll be fine. And you have nothing to be sorry about. You didn't shoot me." He shifted his shoulder away from her touch and wiped her tears with his thumb.

"Elias."

"It's okay. I want you to rest." He kissed her cheek. "If you need me, call me on the cell." He looked into her eyes and his heart fell. He was falling fast for this woman and he wasn't sure if it was the right thing. Not now anyway.

He kissed her forehead. "I have to go get this checked out and head to the station."

Jane wiped away the rest of her tears. She leaned up and kissed his lips. "We'll call if we need anything." Her voice was jittery.

Magda stood at the threshold of the room. "We're fine."

As Elias got up, the pain increased. Maybe it wasn't just a flesh wound after all. He gave Jane a reassuring smile, headed upstairs for a fresh shirt to change into later and left.

Elias managed to get to the hospital without passing out. As he stepped through the ER doors, Caroline spotted him and ushered him into one of the examination rooms. No wooing or insinuations about sex were made. Thank fucking God.

She closed the curtain and told him to remove his shirt.

Once he took off his shirt and sat on the gurney, he examined the hole. Caroline kept quiet while she set up the necessary items on a small table to clean Elias's wound.

For the first time, the blonde nurse focused on something other than marriage. Maybe he was wrong about her. But he wasn't going to hold his breath.

"Chief, when I heard you were shot, I got really worried," Caroline said with concern.

She pouted like a little kid. Then the sincerity in her voice switched off.

"Ooh, you shaved. I like your face this way."

"Caroline, what are you doing here?"

"The ER was shorthanded, so I volunteered. I'm all yours, Chief," she said as she snapped the gloves on her hands and sauntered over to his side and began to clean the blood off his skin.

"Get me the doctor, Caroline." He pushed her hands away.

"Sure, but not until I clean your wound. It's my job, Elias," she said with a smile.

Her pink lipstick was smeared on one of her front teeth again.

Elias let out a small chuckle until she grabbed his shoulder. He cringed as the pain intensified deep into his muscles. "What are you doing?"

"I have to clean both sides," she explained. "The bullet came in this way and out through here." Elias felt her fingers digging into his wound.

"Caroline!" Elias shouted. He glared at her.

She licked the corner of her mouth. "Does this hurt?" she asked, sounding surprised.

"Hurry up," he hissed out. The throbbing pain turned worse the moment Caroline touched it.

"I don't want to hurt you any more than necessary. So stay still." The way she cleaned the area, it was more like torture. Was it payback for not dating her?

Caroline took her time cleaning the wound in a slow circular pattern. When she dragged the wet gauze over the wound, it felt more like sandpaper than cotton.

He gritted his teeth and growled, "Are you done yet?" Elias could tolerate the intense pain, but he didn't like the way she touched him with her free hand. Her gloved nails grazed his skin, up and down his back.

Pain ripped through him as she cleaned the inside part of the wound.

"Damn it. Is that necessary?" His patience was as thin as plastic wrap.

"You don't want to get an infection, do you, Chief?" She smiled again and then dug her fingertips into both sides of the wound at the same time. "Almost done. I promise." Her smile turned into a sneer. She was enjoying herself.

"Where's the doctor? I don't have time for this shit, Caroline. Go get him now." He jerked free from her grasp.

To his surprise, she listened. While she stepped out, he gave his wound a better look. The blood was gone but the ragged hole was red. The pain seemed to ease, though there was a slight persistent burn.

Dr. Rollins walked in with Caroline right behind him. "Chief McAvoy, I heard you were in here. Let me take a look. Thanks, Caroline. That will be all." Rollins ushered her out and closed the curtain. He gave Elias a thin smile. "Sorry."

"Thanks," Elias said.

"No problem." The doctor leaned in and checked out the wound. "Well, from the looks of it, the bullet went straight through. Caroline cleaned it up quite nicely. I'll have you sutured up in no time. You will have to be careful for a few weeks. No heavy lifting of any kind or it will tear the stitching and make it bleed again."

"Understood."

As the doctor readied the needle and thread, he asked in a low tone about Jane.

"She's good. Magda is taking great care of her."

"I talked to Magda yesterday about Jane's condition. I'm still concerned about her head. Has she regained any bits of memory?"

"Very minor details. Why?" Elias asked, his tone slightly gruff. "Is there a reason why you ask?"

The doctor stumbled on his words. "No. No, I was wondering how she was doing. Purely a medical concern."

"Trust me, Doc. She is feeling much better."

"I was curious. After the episode about ghosts, I wanted to know if she is still having delusions. Or has she gotten worse? Hallucinations aren't a good thing with head trauma."

Elias paused, looked at the doctor and lied. "Not so far."

The doctor nodded. "Good. Let me know if there are any changes."

"Will do." Elias looked away from the doctor's intense stare. He wasn't about to tell him anything further. Was he wrong about him? He could very well be the one who was after Jane. But if he was, Jane would have been dead many times over. No, it couldn't be the doctor.

The doctor administered a shot of local anesthetic the pain and burn dissipated. It took ten minutes to get stitched up. Once Rollins wiped the area up, he covered Elias's wound with square gauze and taped it down.

"If anything happens to the stitches, or it starts bleeding, I want to see you right away," Rollins said and then walked out.

"All right, Doc," Elias called out. He threw the bloodied shirt into a bag as evidence and got dressed in the clean one.

Elias walked out of the ER exhausted. It was ten minutes past four in the morning and he had to go to the station and face his drunken ass father. He'd rather head home and slide into bed with Jane. But that wasn't going to happen. He would have to settle for coffee before he confronted James.

As he headed out, he saw Caroline standing by the sliding glass doors. He should have expected this.

She had a wide grin on her face. He could tell a fresh coat of lipstick had been applied. The hue was brighter than before.

"Caroline, what do you want?"

"You're hurt. And I'm here to help you. I just got off of work and thought maybe you wanted company." She went to touch his hand but he pulled it away. Caroline's brows furrowed and her lips thinned. "I know you are alone and I figured right now you need someone to tend to your needs. I'm here to lend my nursing services." She sounded sincere, but he read her like a script.

"Thanks. But no thanks." Elias walked past her.

She pulled his arm and stopped him. "But Elias, you're not understanding me. I'm going home with you. You shouldn't be alone right now. You were shot." Her serious tone conflicted with the smirk.

He knew about her sincerity. "I appreciate that you are trying to help me out. But you need to get this through your head, Caroline. I don't need you. Ever." He said it loud and clear enough for the registration desk to hear.

Elias didn't make it past the awning of the hospital before he heard the clip-clap of heels behind him. He didn't bother to look back; he knew it was Caroline.

She met up with him by his truck. Her outrage was apparent by the way her nostrils flared wide and her sneer made her ugly. Her left foot constantly tapped against the pavement.

"Elias McAvoy. I was offering to help you. Why are you such a bastard to me?"

"I've heard that before," he said with ease. He opened the door of his truck, then sat inside. He shook his head at her. "Get back inside before you freeze off some of your body parts."

Caroline gasped. "How dare you treat me this way! It's that woman, isn't it?"

"What the hell are you talking about?" He looked at Caroline while starting the vehicle.

She stepped closer to him. "Jane. She said something to you about our little talk, didn't she? I wished she'd stayed dead and buried."

If Elias's scowl could kill, Caroline would have been dead right there. He had never wanted to hit a woman until he met this nurse. She could push him to that point.

She quickly took a couple of steps back as he jumped out of the truck.

He snapped out. "If I ever hear you say that again, I'll make good on my promise and throw your ass in jail until you understand the meaning of harassment."

"You know, you're cute when you're angry." Her tone softened.

"Go away, Caroline." Elias had wasted too much energy on her already. He was halfway back in his truck when she wrapped her arms around him. Pain sliced through his shoulder when she pressed tighter.

"Elias, I love you," she cried.

He spun around, almost knocking her to her ass. "Get away from me. I don't want anything to do with you. Why can't you take that hint and stay away from me?"

"You've changed since that bitch showed up. You never acted like this before. What the hell did she do to you?"

Elias stood in front of her, tired of Caroline's shit. Arms folded across his chest, he stayed quiet so as not to goad her more. He hoped his silence would spur her to leave.

"I'll kill her myself if I ever see her around you," she yelled at him.

That was it. He grabbed her wrist and twisted her around, so her front was plastered to the vehicle. He rattled off the Miranda while she tried kicking him, but failed. He tightened his grip around her arms.

"Caroline, I warned you. Now you're going to jail."

"You have no right. Get these fucking handcuffs off me!" she screeched. "I didn't do anything wrong."

"This is twice now you have threatened a person's life."

"Please, Elias. I promise to not say a word."

"Of course not. Because anything you say can and will be used against you. You have the right to an attorney. Enough said?"

"Fuck you, Chief."

"Well, that's a start." Elias opened the back door and pushed her in. She tried to kick him again but stopped her bluster when he slammed the door on her.

Elias purposely drove around the entrance of the hospital where a few nurses stood watching the scene play out. Caroline kicked the front seat until she saw the women she worked with. She then ducked down, but kept on yelling expletives at Elias.

Her ranting didn't stop. Her screaming became louder as he dragged her out of the truck and into the station.

CHAPTER TWENTY-SIX

With all of Caroline's shrieking, Tyson, who had been nodding off at his desk, jolted awake and almost fell off his chair.

"Tyson. Where's James?" Elias asked as he held Caroline by her handcuffed wrists.

"Cell one."

"Good. Now book Caroline Weaver with the intent of bodily harm and stalking." He winked at the officer, who cracked a smile and nodded once.

Tyson cleared his throat and asked, "Should I set up the same transport to Madison?"

"Maybe." He loosened his grip on Caroline's arm and passed her off to the officer. "Behave yourself, Caroline."

Her face contorted into a snarl. "Fuck you, Eli."

"Take Miss Weaver to cell two."

Tyson had to pull her all the way to the back. Her yells turned into sobs as he closed the doors. It took only a few minutes before he emerged from the holding cells.

"What a stray cat. She tried to scratch me." Tyson

wiped his forehead with the palm of his hand. "How's your shoulder?"

"It's good. Why don't you head home? I'll process Caroline."

"Got it. Beth will be here in a couple of minutes," Tyson said as he grabbed his hat and coat.

Within minutes of Tyson's departure, there was yelling and wailing from the back. Elias opened the door a crack and heard his father telling Caroline to shut up.

Elias chuckled. How funny to know that James was getting his reward with Caroline in the cell next to his. He closed the door and sauntered into his office.

As he switched on the light, his eyes bulged. The top drawer of each cabinet was open, and the files inside them were scattered all over the floor. The paperwork that had been on his desk was ripped up and scattered like confetti all over the room. "What the hell?"

Even Henley's hunting magazines were torn to pieces. He radioed Tyson immediately. "Who was in the station when you got here?"

"No one. Why?"

"Just curious, thanks." Then he remembered about Tom. "Did Tom come in at any time?"

"He showed after, but for only a few minutes, then he took off."

"10-4." He dropped the radio on his desk and looked around. Whoever ransacked the office only went for certain drawers of the file cabinet. The other drawers were untouched. They must have been looking for something specific.

What was in this office that was so important? What was valuable enough to risk getting caught? The only thing Elias could think of were the map and photos of the unsolved cases, and he had those back home.

If Elias was right about the connection with Jane's

case and all the unsolved murders, then that damn map had to be a key that unlocked the answers. As he did a slow pace around the room, he came to the conclusion that the next logical place to look for clues was at Henley's house. But he had to do it discreetly. When? Elias wasn't sure, but right at that moment, he needed coffee to clear his head.

Elias was heading to the storage room when he noticed that the metal door that led to a narrow alleyway out back was slightly ajar. He immediately took out his gun, opened the door and carefully checked the alleyway. It was empty.

He slid his gun back into his holster and took a better look at the jam and lock. The door appeared to have been pried open with a crowbar. Bits of splintered wood from the trim lay on the ground and the metal frame was scratched up and bent inward. And the worn handle had gouges.

The intruder got in and vandalized his office... "Shit." Elias rushed to the gun case and checked for tampering, but he found it untouched.

He sighed with relief when all guns and ammunition were accounted for. There was nothing valuable in the station except for those guns. Whoever broke in had only his office in mind.

It made no sense. But lately, nothing seemed to. More things had occurred in Beaver Ridge in the past month than ever before.

Beth walked in and disrupted his thoughts. "What the heck happened here?" she asked, shaking her head.

"Someone broke in through the back door and ransacked my office. Beth, get the fingerprint kit and see if you can get something off the door and frame. I'm going to have a talk with our guests."

Beth let out a snort. "Yeah, I heard you dragged

Caroline Weaver in here. I would have loved to see that. She is such a b—"

Elias interrupted and frowned. "Beth. The kit?"

"Yes, Chief."

He had to smile as Beth turned her back to him. She was right. Caroline was a bitch.

Elias headed back to the jail cells, and heard someone vomiting. It had to come from James. He was glad that the cement block back room kept the noise mostly contained.

The air was cool and dark in the three-celled room. The long fluorescent lights overhead flickered every few minutes, which gave the light green walls the hue of pea soup. There was a creep factor about the space.

Elias walked the length of the aisle while he kept his eyes on his father and Caroline. She was sound asleep, but his father was leaning over the toilet, throwing up. The green walls had an adverse effect on drunks. It was a sobering experience for most.

"Good, you're up." Elias stood in front of the cell door. No empathy was shown for the man.

"What the fuck do you want?" James said between gags.

"I want to know if you saw or heard something odd since you've been here."

"Why would I tell you anything, pig?"

"Do you really want to start that?

"Fuck you," his father jeered.

"Off the record. Your sorry ass will see bars for a long time. But you know that isn't good enough for a piece of shit like you. If it was up to me, I'd kill you myself but not before beating you down like you did to Mom. You should feel lucky to be alive."

James's laughter echoed off the walls. "Do I really give a fuck what you say? Besides, I was defending myself when you pulled out your gun and tried to shoot me." Chunks of whatever he had eaten earlier slid down his chin and dropped to the floor.

"Do you think that'll stick, old man?"

"You think you're untouchable because you have that badge. I'd like to see how you deal without it." James gagged between words. He tried to stand but collapsed on the cot.

"You have no clue what I'm capable of. Give me a good enough reason to drag you out of your cage."

James got up again. He tried to flip the small cot on its side but failed and dropped onto the thin mattress.

"They are bolted to the floor," Elias said with a chuckle. *Idiot.*

"Boy, you don't have the balls. You're like your mother."

"Ah, but I'm also like my father." Elias smiled.

"Prove it." James shot up from the cot and crammed his face between the bars. His mouth twisted in a snarl. "No-good piece of shit. You are just like your whore of a mother."

Elias knew all James was doing was goading him, but he couldn't help it and took a step forward.

His father reached out through the bars but Elias shifted around and caught James by his arm and twisted it. "The only whore in this family is you." He yanked at his father's arm until James fell onto his knees.

With James's face contorted in pain, Elias leaned in and whispered in his father's ear, "If you ever get out of jail and come near me, I'll be there to beat you back in." He took a deep breath and released him. Elias stepped away from the cell and eyed the old man.

James quickly scooted away from the bars and kept quiet.

Sniffles caught Elias's attention and he turned toward

Caroline. She was watching him. He walked over to her cell. "Are you going to be a good girl?"

Caroline sneered and then turned away. "Kiss my ass."

"You wish." Elias shook his head and walked off without a second glance.

As he got to the doorway, James demanded to know where his girlfriend was.

"Who?" Elias turned around and asked.

"Her name is Nadia. Don't remember her last," he said, winded. "Where do you have her?"

"We don't have her anywhere. Where did you leave her?"

"I...don't know."

"Don't know or can't remember?" Elias chided. "What does she look like?"

"Long brown hair, gorgeous ass, and can suck a mean dick," James cackled.

"Pig," Caroline snapped.

James looked over at Caroline and smiled. "Awe, sweetheart, don't be jealous. You can suck me off anytime."

"You can suck your own—"

"That's enough," Elias barked. "I'll ask around." He walked out.

He went back into his office and began cleaning up the floor.

His radio chirped. "Come in, Chief."

"What's up, Tom?"

"Get to the hospital. They found a dead nurse in one of the psych rooms."

Elias's jaw clenched tight and his hands curled into fists. "I'll be right there." He dropped the balled-up papers and ran out of the station.

CHAPTER TWENTY-SEVEN

Silence filled the hospital as Elias made his way toward the elevator. Fear and worry were apparent on every nurse and doctor's face. He guessed the news had spread.

Elias stepped out of the elevator onto the third floor and noticed Tom right away. The deputy met him halfway.

"The dead nurse's name was Georgia Hammond. Her neck was broken and her body was shoved in the bathroom of room 304. There was a patient in the room, but he was heavily sedated. He didn't see or hear anything."

"Who found her?"

"First shift nurse."

"How long?" Elias asked.

"The coroner said she's been dead no more than a few hours. What the hell is going on here? Who could have done this? Elias..."

Elias had never seen Tom so emotional. "What's going on with you?" He touched the deputy's shoulder.

"I—I had a date with her this Friday," the deputy choked out. "I really liked her."

Elias scratched the back of his neck. "Sorry, man."

"I guess it wasn't meant to be." Tom walked away, wiping at his eyes.

Elias felt sorry for Tom.

Tom was always flirting around. Elias had never seen the deputy in a serious relationship. Maybe he was right —it wasn't meant to be, or just damned poor luck.

Elias turned his attention to the room where the nurse was found. Nothing seemed out of place. The bed was empty since the patient had been moved to a new room. He stuck his head in the bathroom and checked it out. Other than the body of the dead nurse, everything seemed normal.

What is normal? he thought, looking down at the dead nurse, her eyes glazed with death. He had seen this before, in Iraq. Elias hated when they died with their eyes open. It was as though they questioned why you were alive and not them.

Elias turned away and noticed the coroner coming in.

"Dr. Farley," he addressed, and stepped out of the large man's way.

"Chief."

"What do you think?" Elias asked, trying not to look at the nurse's face.

Dr. Farley bent over as best he could in the small space and checked out the body. From her wide-open eyes, to her fingers and left foot, from which she had lost her shoe.

"From a quick glance, she didn't struggle much, but I'll clean under her nails for particulates. Her neck—the C3 or C4 vertebrae was broken. Probable cause of death. I won't know for sure until I do an autopsy."

"Just let me know anything you find."

The coroner gave a nod and then returned his attention to the body. Elias wasn't doing any good standing there, watching the man work. He stepped out of the room.

Without a doubt, this was a blatant attempt to get to Jane. Elias was relieved that he'd made the right choice by removing her, but the sad part was a woman had died in her place. However, he wasn't about to let this death stab at his conscience. He stepped out of the room and saw Dr. Rollins standing by the desk.

"Find anything?" Rollins turned and asked, his tone was coated in sadness.

"Nothing so far. Dr. Farley's in there right now, looking over the body. But whoever did this was looking for Jane," Elias said in a low tone as he walked up next to him.

"I agree. So what are you going to do?"

He looked the doctor square in the eyes. "Nothing."

The doctor's forehead wrinkled tight. "Why? If Jane's in danger—I think we all are." His voice raised an octave, shaking.

Elias pulled the doctor away. "Calm yourself. I know we are all at risk, but I truly believe this bastard is only after Jane. The nurse was an accidental casualty but we still have to keep up the pretense that Jane is in the hospital."

"But the maniac who did this atrocity in my hospital knows now that Jane isn't here. What good will it do to keep up this lie? Does it take another nurse to die before you let out the truth? You have to do something else, Chief."

"I'll call in a favor and get a few extra men to patrol the hospital." Elias blew out a hard breath and rubbed the back of his neck before he spoke again. "Doc, as of right now, Jane's safe and so is everyone in the hospital."

"I will not lose another person, Chief." Dr. Rollins walked away before Elias could respond.

Concern knocked Elias in the gut. Keeping everyone in this town safe had always been his biggest priority. But Jane? Elias wasn't sure if he'd be capable of closing this case—not without someone else dying.

Elias met up with his deputy at the entrance of the room. "What do you got?"

"Nothing. I talked to the night staff at the front desk. No one saw anything out of the ordinary. I also checked the security footage and didn't see anything odd," Tom said as he lifted his hat off his head and scratched the top of his scalp.

"So, we have nothing," Elias countered.

"Nope. But whoever it was, was looking for something, or someone. Jane was in this section, wasn't she?"

Elias nodded. "Yeah, but she was moved to another wing a few hours before it happened." He wanted to tell his deputy that Jane was safe at his house; instead he kept with the lie.

"So, where is she now?"

Elias swallowed the deceit and spoke evenly. "I don't even know where she's at right now. It's safer that way." Elias didn't look at him when he spoke.

"Oh," Tom furrowed his brows slightly. "Well, at least she is safe."

"I know it's unusual but as for now, it works." Elias watched Tom wipe sweat off his brows.

"If it works, it works. I'll meet you at the station?"

Elias's stomach churned. "Okay." He trusted this man. Then why did he not want to tell him the truth?

He shook off the question and waited until the coroner left with the body. He went through the room from top to bottom even though he knew he'd find nothing.

He was right.

*   *   *

As Elias stepped out into the cold, he took in a few deep breaths and tried to let go of his guilt. Right before he got in his truck, Magda called him.

"Jane's gone," Magda said in a frantic shout.

"What do you mean she's gone?" Panic surged up and knocked the breath out of him.

"Jane isn't in the house. I searched top to bottom. I even checked the barn. My car is still parked inside it. She's outside somewhere, walking around."

His heart faltered before it began pounding hard like an erratic drummer. *Please, let her be safe.*

"When did you last see her?" Elias's fear spiked as he jumped into his truck and sped off toward the house.

"I put her to bed in your room about an hour ago. I sat there with her for a little bit. We talked about what happened. I guess I fell asleep. Then the next thing I knew, I woke up and she was gone."

Elias gripped the steering wheel tight. "What were you two talking about?"

"She asked what happened outside. Jane said she didn't remember anything, so I told her. Then she asked about Beaver Lake and how far it was from here." Elias could hear Magda softly crying. "Do you think she went there?"

"Maybe. Magda, keep an eye out. Call me if she comes back. I'll head to the lake." He snapped the phone shut and floored the gas pedal.

The idea of Jane being found by the bastard wore heavily on his heart and head. The urgency to reach her before she was seen flooded his system with anxiety. He wrenched the wheel to the left and skidded onto the road that led to the lake.

As he turned down the gravel path to the lake, Elias flashed on his high beams and craned his neck from one side to the other to see if he was able to spot Jane. He drove past the ridge line where vehicles normally parked. His truck ran over brush and small skeletal trees until the lake was fully in his view.

He saw her, kneeling by the water's edge. She faced the tall reeds, weathered pussy willows and cattails. She didn't move. Her skin was ghostly white, reflecting the headlights.

Elias jumped out of the truck and ran to Jane. He knelt down next to her.

"Jane, what are you doing here?" he asked with an expelled breath. He tried to stay calm but his pulse was so erratic, it gave him a head rush.

Elias put his shaky hand on her shoulders. Through her thin cotton nightdress, her skin was icy cold to the touch.

"Jane."

She didn't react to Elias's hard tone. It took all of a few seconds to notice her eyes. They were as black as onyx. Her body was stiff and her lips were blue. Panic trickled down his spine. He was scared for her.

He touched her cheek. "Can you hear me, Jane?" This time, he kept his voice low and even.

"Yes, Elias. I hear you." Her teeth chattered from the cold.

He moved in front of her. "Why are you out here—and how did you get out here?" He had a gentle grip on Jane's arms. He didn't want her to pass out.

"I needed to know where I was found." Jane stared off toward the edge of the lake. "I want to leave." Jane stood up and turned to him.

"Oh, Jane." He wrapped his good arm around her and guided her to the truck.

"Find him, Elias, before he kills again." Jane slumped toward him.

He tried lifting her up but almost dropped her when his sutured shoulder burned and strained under Jane's weight. He ignored the throbbing and carried her to the truck.

He laid her down in the back seat and wrapped the blanket tight around her from head to toe. Elias got into the driver's seat and sped back toward his house.

Jane remained passed out throughout the ride. Elias made sure no one was around before he carried her into the house. Magda was in the living room when he raced in. She moved out of the way to let Elias put Jane down on the couch.

He saw the distress across Magda's face. This was not the time to tell her about the nurse.

"What happened?" Magda rushed forward and touched her forehead. "She's ice cold."

"She was at the lake. I think she was—God, I can't believe I'm saying this, but I think she was possessed, again."

Her eyes became wide when he admitted possession. "There are many explanations, Elias," Magda said as she checked Jane's pulse.

"She didn't sound like herself and her eyes... Magda, you had to see them, they were black. Like before."

"Are you sure?"

"I know what I saw. And I have seen Jane this way before." Elias paced the room, rubbing the back of his neck.

"When?"

"Once at the hospital, yesterday and earlier this morning." He sat down on the overstuffed chair, then stood right back up. He couldn't sit still. "Who in their right mind would come out naked in this weather and pummel someone with a log? I think—no, I *know* she was possessed."

The bitterness of belief on his tongue made him cringe a little. He had always been a logical person, but no matter how much he didn't want to believe, he knew what he'd seen and heard.

"Elias, if that's true, then who is possessing her?"

"I don't know." He blew out a ragged breath. "I think my mother yesterday. Not sure at the hospital. But at the lake, Jane mentioned she wasn't the first. I think it's the first victim. I can't be sure. But she told me to find him before he kills again." He moved his shoulder around to loosen his cramping muscles.

"Let me see your shoulder." Magda pushed his shirt back to expose his battered skin. "You popped a few stitches. I'll fix it but you can't be lifting anything, including Jane." She scuttled out of the room and quickly returned with her medical bag.

"Elias, as much as I'm open minded about the hereafter, I'm not sure I believe that Jane was possessed. I know she has issues and maybe her head injury is causing her to sound and act differently."

He sat back in the chair. "Believe it. You know I'm the biggest skeptic. I saw her with my own eyes, Magda. Jane had to be."

"Possessed or not, I worry for her health more. She is getting paler with each passing day. Not eating much and sleeping even less. If she gets worse, it's my duty to her to bring her back to the hospital."

"I'm worried too, Miss Magda, but we cannot take her back. Her life is still in jeopardy."

Magda touched his cheek. "You're falling for her, aren't you?"

He shook his head. "I don't know," he said in a low voice.

Magda gave him a small smile. "Don't kid yourself. I see it, Elias."

He remained quiet and distant, while she checked Jane again.

It was only for a few minutes but it was too much for him to take in. "I'm leaving."

"Don't leave yet. Help me bring her upstairs. She needs the rest, then I'll sew you up."

He nodded. "I'll put her in my room."

"I don't—"

"Please don't argue with me. I promise not to bother her," Elias said. "My bed is more comfortable than the one in the other room." He wrapped Jane's arm around his good shoulder and carried her upstairs.

He laid her on the bed and covered her with the blanket. He gave her a soft kiss on her forehead.

When he came back down, Magda had her instruments ready on the kitchen table. He sat and endured her poking. She replaced the ripped stitches and covered his wound with a new gauze pad.

"Now, please take it easy," Magda advised, packing up her medical bag.

"I will try."

"You know I was serious about what I said. You're in love with Jane. Don't you feel it?"

Elias had gotten a sudden splitting headache. "I have to head back to the station right now. Call me if anything happens." He ignored what she'd said. He kissed her cheek and headed out.

Acknowledging the idea of love or that he was in love with Jane intensified his pain. He didn't want to talk about it anymore. He shot a look back at Magda before he left the house.

CHAPTER TWENTY-EIGHT

J ane woke with a jolt. Her body ached as she twisted herself around onto her back. The last thing she fully remembered was falling asleep in Elias's arms. It was wonderful, blissful. Then the next thing she vaguely recalled was water and cold. Was it a dream? It made no sense to her. She tried to put the pieces together, but her head hurt too much to think at the moment.

Staring up at the ceiling, trying to release the balled-up tension from her body, Jane rubbed at her eyes and yawned. She stretched from side to side, letting the aches in her muscles and joints work themselves out. As she turned to her side, she noticed Magda sleeping on the rocker.

With her arms folded together and head tilted to one side, she looked so peaceful, almost... Jane's panic spiked. She reached out to touch the woman's hand. Her skin was warm. Magda shifted her head to the other side.

Jane expelled a heavy breath. Relief flooded her as she sat on the edge of the bed. She let out a small laugh.

In the short time she had spent with the nurse, Jane had grown to adore the woman. Magda had become a solid part of her life, a support system from the moment she had woken up in the hospital.

Jane took a moment to let her pulse calm when she noticed all the clothes Elias had on the floor. They were placed in neat piles by the door. She then saw her feet crusted in dried dirt. Bits of brown grass stuck out between her toes.

"What the—" She brought one foot up to get a better look. "Grass?"

"You went for a walk," Magda said as she straightened herself up in the chair.

"Where? I don't remember." She wiped the dirt off with her hands. "Am I losing my mind?

"No, dear. But maybe you're being possessed. That is what Elias says."

Jane's head shot up. She wasn't sure if she heard the old woman correctly. "Say that again."

"Elias believes you were possessed."

Jane nodded. "With all of the lapses of memory and time I have, I believe him."

"How are you feeling?" Magda asked, rocking slowly.

"Sore, but good." Jane continued to pick at her feet. She paused and looked up at Magda. "Why are you looking at me like that?"

"It amazes me that you can't remember anything."

"What do you mean?"

"Elias found you by the lake," she explained with worry.

"What?" Jane dropped her foot. "When?"

"A few hours ago. That's where the mud came from," she said, staring down at Jane's feet.

"I'm going to throw up." Before Jane could move, vomit spewed forth like a small fountain. The liquid splashed all over the floor. Her legs and nightgown were covered with the slimy yellow mess.

"Oh dear. Jane, let's get you into the bathroom." Magda led her to the tub. She turned on the water and helped Jane undress.

"Wait." Jane grabbed her arm. "Where's Elias?"

"Work. But you should wash up before you call him —and I think tea will help your stomach."

Magda pulled off Jane's nightgown and dropped it in the vomit puddle. Then she led Jane to the bathroom and started the water in the tub.

Magda helped Jane into the tub. "Here's some soap and a washcloth."

The hot water rose quickly. Jane tucked her knees to her chest and wrapped her arms around her legs. "Why don't I remember anything?" she asked. She didn't want to be alone.

"I don't know," Magda said as she sat on the edge of the tub. With a warm smile, she brushed back Jane's hair. "Elias says that you were possessed by his mother and maybe someone else. He swears it, and I have never seen him swear to anything. Maybe that is why you can't remember things, it wasn't you inside here." She pointed to Jane's temples.

"Everything I've been seeing is through..." Jane choked. She took deep breaths so as not to throw up in the tub. It all made sense. All the visions and dreams. It wasn't her.

After a few minutes of silence, Magda asked, "Do you want me to help you wash? I can clean up after."

"No. Thank you. I'd like to be alone right now."

Magda nodded. "Do not get your head wet. I have dry shampoo for after." She reminded Jane before she stepped out of the room.

Jane rocked herself, sloshing the water all around the tub. "Why is this happening to me?" she cried out.

Her temples pounded like a kettledrum. Jane stuttered out a breath. She couldn't breathe through her nose. She splashed the hot water to wash away the tears. Jane wished Elias were there to hold her, to put his arm around her until the world disappeared.

She covered her face with both hands and wiped away any remnants of tears. Her whole miserable life—or what she knew of it, had been horrible. She had been beaten, buried and left for dead. She nearly got a cop killed while being naked and possessed by ghosts and she had been running around outside, exposed to the one person who wanted her dead. And for what, she had no clue.

The only real thing in her life was Elias. The strength he exuded made her stronger but...

Then it hit her. Was she falling for him? That realization smacked her like a baseball bat. She couldn't be in love with the man. Elias made Jane feel as though she had an identity, was somebody. And, she had slept with him, once—okay, twice, but it wasn't love. Maybe sleeping with Elias was a bad idea. *It can't and won't happen again.*

Jane didn't want to think about him anymore, or anything else for that matter. She sniffled back her last remnant of tears and leaned against the tub. The hot water melted away the anguish, confusion and worry she had. She closed her eyes and let the heat seep into her bones.

Less than a minute had gone by when a subtle, cool breeze swept across her face. It chilled her right away; her stomach tightened and she couldn't help but shiver. Jane sank further into the hot water to ward off the cold.

The back of her head pained her but it wasn't terrible. Someone was with her in the bathroom. Jane scrunched her eyes tighter and held her breath. *Just go away. Just go away.*

Against her better judgment, Jane opened her eyes. She exhaled slowly and saw her breath crystallize, mixing in with the warm steam of her bath.

Jane slowly sat up. Near the toilet, a dark shadow hovered. The form shifted, turning from a hazy blur into a frail woman. She was lovely. Her smile was warm and genuine. Sincerity reflected in her brown eyes. Jane was not afraid. "Barbara." She spoke in a soft whisper.

Elias's mother gifted her with another smile. There was an understanding between them. Jane saw it. A mother who loved her son so much that she came back to protect him. Jane choked up from the love she felt in Elias's mother.

Barbara extended her hand and touched Jane's head. A soft electric zap coursed through her scalp. Jane couldn't—wouldn't move. Love and appreciation flowed through her; she wanted to weep.

As fast as she appeared, with a simple nod, Barbara disappeared into thin air.

Jane choked back the sob. "You're welcome."

It was scary, but at the same time, it was the greatest feeling in the world. It was gratifying to know that she helped someone get a bit of revenge and move on. If only she could do that for herself.

She leaned back and let her arms rest on the edges of the tub. A bit of her resolve changed. She was no longer afraid, but more determined to find out what had happened to her. Hiding out in the chief's house made her realize it wasn't about her anymore. In her gut, the killer had taken other lives. Her dreams proved it.

She bet he hadn't counted on her surviving. Jane needed to break down her dreams, see the clues given to her and figure out who the girl in the yellow dress was. Deep down in her gut Jane knew the girl died a horrible death.

Her blocked memory was the key. Jane had to find a way to unlock it. All the pieces were there. All she needed to do was fit them together and decipher it. There was no doubt that the girl in the yellow dress wanted retribution, and so did Jane.

CHAPTER TWENTY-NINE

"Who cleaned the floor?" Elias growled through the doorway of his office, scratching his head.

"It was me, Chief. I didn't throw anything away. I placed all the papers in a pile and the magazines in another." Cindy Lee stood in the threshold of the storage room with a box in her shaky hands. Her timid smile quickly softened Elias's irritation.

"Sorry for shouting. It has been a long, crazy Sunday."

"I'm surprised you're here. Rest is most important after being shot. I've got the station covered, Chief. Tyson, Beth and Tom have got the rest," Cindy Lee said as though she was an expert. She jostled the large box in her arms.

Elias looked down at the neat piles. "Did you see anything odd while cleaning up?"

"No. I guess I wasn't paying much attention. I thought you'd knocked the piles down and didn't clean it up."

"Thanks, Cindy Lee." He half grinned. "Hey, what's in the box?"

"Halloween decorations. It's in a week, and I thought... You don't mind if we put up decorations, do you? Henley let us, even though he hated holidays. I also have ten bags of candy for our little visitors."

"Sounds good to me." He was so wrapped up with the case and Jane that a simple holiday like Halloween would have passed by and he wouldn't have noticed.

The dispatcher squeaked with joy. "And by the way, I like you without the scraggly beard." She smirked and walked away.

"Um, thanks." He shook his head and closed his office door.

Elias took off his jacket and hat, tossed them over to the coat rack. He stared at the two mounds for what seemed like forever before he sat down and sorted through them.

Frustration burned at him. Another life was lost and he was no closer to finding out who was behind this. His gut told him it was the same elusive man who had tried to kill Jane. That bastard seemed to be always a step ahead.

He had a sudden urge for a cigarette. That blanched tar taste coated his tongue—his mouth watered. Instead of reaching for his emergency cigarette hidden in the back of the top drawer of his desk, he snatched up a pen and popped it into his mouth and began chewing on the tip.

Think, damn it!

Then the thought hit him. The state police.

Contacting State might be the only solution to move this case forward. They had the resources Elias needed. But, if State took over, Jane would be taken away to a true safe house, out of reach of the killer, but also away from him.

However, he didn't think it would stop the murders. Jane was just one part of this twisted up situation.

And the idea of the killer being a local scared the shit out of him. It could be anyone. Someone he had known all his whole fucking life, not realizing they were a murderer.

Jane. Her name filtered through his mind like a caress.

Damn! When did he lose his balls? Over a woman. But Jane was different. Elias had to admit she had changed him. If he acted on impulse, he'd be heading home.

Instead, Elias took a handful of papers and rifled through them. He found nothing, dumped it and moved on to the next set of papers. An hour of this set his teeth on edge.

A few move hours dragged by, but he finally got through all the papers and magazines. He didn't find any additional information hidden among them.

He dropped the last small pile of papers and magazines in the garbage bag and took the bag out. Elias threw the trash in the dumpster and headed back inside.

Tyson stood just inside the doorway. "What happened to the back door?" he asked with a mouthful of donut holes. Powdered sugar rimmed his lips.

"Someone tried to break in but nothing was taken. Hey, call Sherman to get a new door in right away."

"Do you think James did it?"

"No." Elias walked back toward the holding cells.

Caroline and James were sound asleep. Elias walked up to his father's cell and stared down at the old man. He didn't know why, but at that moment something about James intrigued him. How peaceful he looked when there wasn't a bottle of Jim or Jack in his hands, or when his fists weren't swinging.

Right after James took off, Elias and his mother's lives had changed for the better. It was the only great deed that bastard did for them. Could James had ability to be a good man for his family? The answer was clear as glass. Maybe McAvoy Senior could have been a decent father and a loving husband, if it wasn't for the poison he drowned himself with.

Elias shook his head. But he had to be real with himself. Was he like his old man, or just the product of the environment he was raised in?

After the upbringing he had, Elias would never bring a child into this world and then discard it like garbage, the way James did to him.

That concept choked him. Could he be a good father? A large ball of indignation formed in the pit of his stomach as the importance to that question laid heavy on him. He feared what he was capable of being if he went for the bottle again.

Elias had enough of his own worthless appraisal and walked out.

He saw Tom standing in his office. "Where have you been?" Elias snapped while taking his chair.

"I had to finish taking a statement from one of the nurses who was friends with the victim. What the hell happened to the back door? Tyson told me it was busted." He thumbed in that direction.

"Someone decided to break into our establishment and play confetti with the papers in my office."

"Isn't the usual custom to *break out* of jail?"

Elias laughed. He walked back into his office and took a seat. "Tyson is calling Sherman to get a new door put in right away."

"So, what's missing?" Tom asked as he picked a folder off the desk and sifted through it.

"I don't know. Nothing? Henley had so much crap

piled up here and there, I never got a chance to go through it all. Anyway, I think they were looking for something in particular. Nothing in the station was touched except for my office."

Tom shook his head. "Do you know what they were looking for?" He touched his forefinger against his temple and stared at Elias.

"I really don't know. But whoever was in here might have been looking for something of Henley's. Who knows what that man hid in here. God knows, I haven't found anything worth keeping."

"That man kept everything," Tom said with a chuckle. "Or, it could be related to your Jane Doe case."

"Tom, you think this incident may be connected to Jane's case?"

"It's possible."

Doubt filtered into Elias's mind as he scoped the mess. "Well, I don't. There is nothing in here relating to Jane, except her file, which consists of nothing." The lie gnawed at his gut. Maybe he should tell his deputy what he'd discovered, but having decided not to trust anyone in this town—this county, he kept quiet about the map and pictures.

Tom nodded and then changed the subject. "How is Magda doing?"

"What?" Elias nearly forgot about the lie.

"Your mother's things?"

"She should be almost done." Elias cleared his throat. "The church will be happy to take all of my mother's clothes." He touched his shot shoulder and gave it a slight rub.

"Head home." Tom suggested. "I've got things covered here. You need to rest your shoulder."

Elias blew out a breath. "Sounds good to me." He slowed his steps as he grabbed his jacket and hat. He didn't want to look eager. "Let me know if anything comes up."

"Will do. Hey, how's Jane?"

Elias faltered on his step out. He turned around and looked at his deputy. "I guess she's fine. Dr. Rollins has her under constant care."

"You haven't been going to see her at the hospital?"

"Why this sudden interest in Jane, Deputy?" Elias's tone was a little clipped.

"I want this case to be over with as much as you, Chief. I'm hoping she might have regained some of her memory. That's all." Tom stood up and faced him. His tone was as hard as Elias's.

Elias relaxed his stiffened posture. He leaned against the frame of the doorway. The guilt had started to eat at him. "With my father here and this murder, my focus is split ten different ways. Sorry for snapping. And I'm worried how Magda will react about the nurse."

Tom's hard stare softened. "It will be hard on her."

"Yeah. I'll see you in a few," Elias said before walking out.

"Will do, Chief."

He hated when Tom called him Chief. But Elias knew he deserved his deputy's condescending attitude for his cantankerous shout out.

He gave Tom a nod and left without looking back. Elias drove home fast. His mind whirled around Jane. He couldn't wait to see her, touch her. He did his usual check around the property, but quickly. The late afternoon sun streamed into the living room where Jane and Magda sat playing cards.

He stood quietly in the doorway and watched the women. Jane had on some new clothes, his mother's. How beautiful she looked, happy and carefree. It was as though it were another normal day.

It had been a long time since his home had had serenity, contentment and laughter.

Elias's chest hurt. His heart stuttered hard against his ribcage. The certainty that he was falling in love with this woman made him lightheaded. It had happened so fast, he didn't see it coming. But Magda had.

Jane made him smile whenever she looked at him in her simple, honest way. Secretly, he loved the way she called him *Ass*, with her nose stuck up in the air, flared, and her wide eyes boring through him like an awl. He purposely didn't answer her to get a reaction out of her. He had to laugh.

But most of all he loved her for the strength she had inside her. To overcome such tragedy and still take whatever came her way in stride. But did he love her enough to keep her in his life?

Oh yeah, he did love her. That acknowledgement made him shake. Did she feel the same? What if their relationship was only a physical connection? Damn, why was he thinking like this?

Their laughter broke through his thoughts. He didn't want to break the happy flow, so Elias stepped back from view.

Now, he had to figure out how to break the news to Magda about the murdered nurse. She was in too good of a mood for him to spoil it right now. But he had to break the news to her soon. It'd be better coming from him instead of her finding out from one of her staff.

Elias stepped back into the living room.

Jane looked up from her cards and gave him a welcoming grin. Her silent greeting melted his anxiety and gave him an instant hard-on.

Elias wasn't a horn dog but he sure acted like one around her. He craved her touch the second she smiled. He had never wanted anyone as much as he wanted Jane.

Elias winked at Jane and grinned back, before he walked up next to Magda and settled down next to her.

"Oh, Elias. I didn't hear you come in," she said as she dropped down a five of hearts. "Gin."

"That's not fair." An unsexy snort came from Jane as she dropped her cards onto the table.

"Who's winning?" he asked while eyeing the run of cards displayed on Magda's side.

"Magda. She's beating the pants off me," Jane declared. She threw up her arms. "I'm done playing."

"Ahh, honey. You're not quitting on me, are you? One more game."

"Nope, I'm done. Plus the back of my head hurts."

Elias instantly straightened up. "What's wrong with your head?"

Jane laughed. "Magda took out my staples. It's sore, that's all."

"Okay," he said. His body relaxed.

Magda nudged his leg. "How's your shoulder feeling?"

"Sore but good," he said, but his eyes stayed on Jane.

"Are you hungry? Neither one of us has eaten yet. I got some potato salad and ham." Magda got up and headed to the kitchen.

"I am hungry." His voice came out in a low growl but Magda didn't reply. His answer was directed toward Jane, who blushed.

Elias cocked his head to one side and signaled her to go upstairs. She laughed, but shook her head no. He bowed his lips into a pout, a silent plea for her to agree. But she wouldn't surrender to his childish ruse.

Jane's chair scraped as she got up. "I'll help you, Magda," she said, with a cute giggle. He loved the sound of her laughter.

She skirted around the other side of the sofa to avoid his reach. Disappointment trickled in as he watched her walk away. He rubbed his face and leaned back against the couch.

What the hell was he doing? Acting like some sex crazed teenager wasn't him. He had to tell Magda about the death and here he was thinking with his dick.

More emotions bound him to Jane than simply sex, but the image of her naked under him seemed to get in the way of most everything else.

Elias sat back up and rubbed his hands almost in a prayer-like manner, then got up to tell Magda what had happened at the hospital.

As he watched the scene in the kitchen, Elias got a glimpse of what reality could have been for him if he'd grown up in a normal home. Could he still have it?

A splinter of sorrow wedged in his heart. Instead of walking away, which was his usual tactic, he stepped up and grabbed the plates out of Jane's hands and placed them on the table. "I need you two to sit for a second."

Jane slipped her hand in his and squeezed it tenderly. "Is everything all right?" She whispered so softly that the words were barely audible.

He gave a slight nod and released her hand.

"Elias, I need to check my house. And I forgot to grab the tea. We're running out," Magda stated while she pulled out the ham.

"I'll go check your house and grab your tea, but Magda, I need you to sit."

"No. I'll go— And before you start saying no, I need to be seen. And while I'm out, I'll head to the hospital and check on what's going on. You're here, so Jane will be safe."

"Miss Magda—"

"She is right," Jane interrupted, stepping up next to her, showing unity.

Elias turned off the subtleties. "I need both of you to

sit down. Please," Elias said solemnly. He pointed to the table.

"Elias, your tone is scaring me," Magda said, taking a seat.

"Please, Jane, sit."

Jane sat down next to Magda.

"Sometime early this morning, a nurse was killed."

"Oh, my lord." Magda clenched sweater to her chest. "Who was it?"

"Her name was Georgia Hammond. I think whoever is after Jane, was the one who killed her." He kneeled in front of the old woman and held her free hand. "Magda."

"Georgia? She was a sweet girl." Tears streamed down Magda's face.

"Elias, are you sure it's the same person who's after me?" Jane asked. Her voice cracked when she spoke.

"I have no doubt about it. I don't want you leaving this house—not until that bastard's found. I can't chance losing either of you."

Jane leaned over to Magda and wrapped her arms around the old woman. "I'm so sorry." Tears rimmed Jane's eyes.

Magda's brows knit, and she tightened her hold on Jane's hand. Her voice turned sharp. "Don't say that. It's not your fault that maniac killed someone." She then turned her attention to Elias. "I have to go now."

"No."

"You don't have the right to keep me here. Besides, a nurse died. I have to show. I am going, Elias." Magda refused to budge on her decision.

Elias knew it was a bad idea but he couldn't refuse her. "All right. But please, don't stay long."

Magda wiped away her tears with a tissue she pulled out of her sleeve. She stood up and grabbed her coat and purse. While she bundled herself up, Elias took out her car and warmed it up.

He walked Magda to the car and helped her in. "If you're not back in two hours, I'm coming after you. Got it?"

"Yes, yes. I'll be back as soon as I'm able—and Elias?"

"What?"

"Thank you."

Elias nodded, and closed the driver's door. He rubbed at his jaw as he watched the gray Corolla drive off. He walked back to the house, concern for her heavy weight on his mind. He shouldn't have let her go, but Magda was right. Although he didn't like it, she had to show up and keep up appearances.

As he walked into the living room, he found Jane on the couch, slouched with her hands folded around her knees, her cheeks wet and red.

"Don't cry, Jane. Magda is right. This isn't your fault." Elias sat down next to her, but kept his hands to himself.

"Are you sure about that? If it weren't for me, that woman would still be alive."

"Don't blame yourself for that bastard's actions. You are innocent in all this," he said while he reached out and brushed off her hot tears with his thumb.

She leaned into his hand. "This is so hard." Her eyes were a storm of emotions.

"I can only imagine," Elias whispered back, a strain in his chest that was hard to breathe through. He hated seeing Jane cry.

Then, like she flipped a switch, her face turned stony. "We have to talk, Elias." Jane let out a breath, stood up, wiped more wetness from her cheeks and faced him.

He was leery about what she had to say. "Okay, let's talk."

"I told you I'm twenty-six years old."

"Yes, you did tell me that," Elias replied. The late sun beamed through the window and blinded his view of her steady pacing. "Jane, sit down."

"I can't. I'll lose my nerve if I stop. Anyway, I remember a few more things. After what Magda told me about being...possessed, a few things weren't lining up. Did I tell you I have a brown Impala? Or had—not sure how old but it's not new—and we can't sleep together anymore."

The way she switched topics caught him off guard. "What?"

"I have a brown Impala."

"Not that part."

"About us sleeping together?" Jane stopped pacing and sat down next to him.

"You're right." Elias tried to stay calm, but his insides were knotted tight. "We shouldn't have slept together. It was impulsive and I crossed the line. I promise it won't happen again." The last sentence came out a little harder than he wanted it to.

Jane turned away quickly. Elias wasn't able to see her reaction.

"I'm only agreeing with you, Jane. We shouldn't have done what we did. I'm here to protect you." That was partly a lie. He didn't want to stop touching her. But the truth was, he couldn't focus on the case when his mind was consumed with her body.

"Yes," she said and turned around to face him again. "There's something else." She blew out a quick breath and continued. "Don't ask me why but I know all those pictures of those dead women are connected to me. And somehow, they are also connected to that little girl in the yellow dress.

"That girl, her name is Jane, is the key to this. I know it. I get flashes, like a movie in my head, but I wasn't sure if they were from my life or someone else's. And I saw your mother. She was the one who knocked the gun out of your father's hand. Not me. Do I sound crazy? I sound like I'm crazy."

Elias raked his fingers through his hair. So much to take in. "No, you are not crazy." *Another lie.*

"She thanked me and told me to take care of you. I know you don't believe in—" Jane got up and walked to the window, a rule she broke on many occasions.

"I do. As crazy as it may sound, I do believe you, Jane," Elias said as he got up from the chair and walked to her. He wrapped his arms around her waist, not caring if he broke his promise to not touch her again. Jane's trembling body leaned back against him. He couldn't help it and hugged her tighter. "Jane, do me a favor. When you do remember something, tell me right away. I need to know right away." His voice was gentle but he got his point across.

"All right, I will."

He turned her around and kissed her forehead. "Is my mother happy now?" His voice was slightly strangled.

Jane wrapped her arms around his neck. "Yes, she's at peace."

Elias lightly kissed her cheek. His heart pounded hard and heavy against his chest. He tightened his arms around Jane's waist and drew her in closer. "Thank you," he whispered. His forehead met hers.

CHAPTER THIRTY

J ane leaned up and kissed him with all the passion growing in her. "Make love to me, Elias."

So much emotion swam between them. High and low, like a roller coaster in full throttle. She saw the need in his eyes, but she wanted more. Her vow to never sleep with him again had flown out the door the moment her lips touched his.

Her pulse quickened. Her breasts ached for his touch. Heat pooled in her middle; it was hard for her to not rip his clothes off right there. His smile assured her that he felt the same way.

Elias picked Jane up, being careful of his shoulder, and carried her upstairs. He took the wooden steps two at a time until he reached the threshold of his bedroom door.

Cradled in his arms, Jane felt safe—protected, and loved.

He kissed her with gentleness, which swiftly changed to urgency when her feet touched the floor. His tongue danced a fast tango with hers while his hands fumbled with his buttons.

Jane was engulfed by a yearning desire, her body charged from his kiss. She was desperate to get her clothes off, and his.

She pulled at his shirt while stepping backwards into his room.

Elias took her hands and kissed each fingertip. "I. Don't. Want. To. Rush." He then looked into her eyes. "I want to take my time with you."

He released her and took a few steps back. A wicked grin played across his face. Elias unbuttoned his shirt. Jane wanted to rip the material off his body fast and devour him. When a tiny bit of skin was exposed, she took a step forward. He was taking his time, which she didn't like.

Two can play that game.

Jane stepped back until she felt the bed against her legs. She gingerly got on the mattress and kneeled before him. She undressed, one piece at a time. First her flannel shirt, then she pulled off her sweat pants, one leg at a time.

She was down to her bra and underwear. His reaction was what she wanted. His erection pushed against his faded jeans.

Elias took a sharp intake of breath as Jane unclasped her bra and released her breasts.

"Is this what you want, Chief?" He stepped forward and reached for her but Jane swatted his hand away. "Not yet."

Elias frowned. "I'm not liking this tactic." He unzipped and pulled his jeans down on his hips.

Half of his luscious cock stuck out. Her mouth watered for a taste. She was tempted to reach out and wrap her fingers around his hardness, but she stayed planted on the bed.

Instead, he surprised Jane and grabbed her around

her waist. He pulled her hips to his. Holding her ass tight, he ground her against him.

"How about that for fair play?"

Jane laughed. "Elias, I—"

"Shut up and kiss me." His lips covered hers. His hands were rough on her skin but it didn't hurt. He trailed down to her breasts, giving them equal measure. Nipping, tasting and sucking until they peaked tight and red.

"Oh Elias," Jane purred. She wrapped her arms around his neck and enjoyed the torture he was giving.

"You have no idea what you do to me, Jane." Elias leaned forward, letting her fall back onto the bed.

"Ditto," Jane hummed. She gripped his shoulders as he made his way down to her belly button.

Elias winced as she dug into his injured shoulder.

"I'm sorry." Jane said in a stifled cry. She turned her face away from his.

"No. Look at me, Jane." He commanded. But there was no anger in his tone.

Jane turned and saw his gentle smile. Her anxiety ebbed.

"I got shot because of my father. You had nothing to do with this." His gentle touch on her face soothed her conscience. "You saved my life. If it weren't for you knocking the gun out of his hands, James would've shot me in the chest."

Jane touched the square cotton pad that was taped to his shoulder. "Is it still painful?"

"It doesn't hurt," Elias said.

She knew he was lying. "Really?"

He smiled at her and then kissed her soundly. "Really."

A rush of blood to her brain made her slightly light-headed. She was falling for this man. That admission hit her like oncoming traffic. She wasn't sure how it had happened, but her heart soared whenever he looked at her with such care.

In just the short time they had spent together, it was a miracle they hadn't strangled each other. Instead of war, love had made a play and might possibly win.

*   *   *

Elias took her mouth with all the gentleness he had. Their kiss turned ravenous. Their tongues dueled, teeth clashed and their bodies entwined as the fever reignited between them. He wasn't able to get enough of her.

As his hands found her warm mounded flesh, her nipples perked tight. He grazed them between his calloused fingers, replacing them with his mouth, his tongue.

His left hand trailed down her abdomen, to her inner thigh, to the center of her wetness. Elias nudged her legs apart and caressed the inner folds of her silken flesh. He dipped his fingers inside, invading her tight core.

A sharp moan escaped Jane. He loved the way she shivered and called out his name.

While his fingers played, his mouth took advantage, tasting every inch of her skin, but he wasn't done with her yet. Elias slipped off the bed without breaking rhythm and tasted her. Licking from her clit to the very center of her heat. His tongue jabbed deep. His teeth scraped, coaxing her to give him more.

Jane almost came right off the bed. The harder she shuddered, the faster he delved.

As she shouted out his name, Elias stood up, his dick just at her entrance.

"I need you." His voice was hoarse.

"I need you," she repeated back.

Elias encouraged her to turn on all fours. He lifted her right leg and wrapped it around his waist for easier entry and slipped into her with urgency. Jane cried out his name. He ground against her as he reached for her breast, not moving his hips.

"You make me forget who I am," Elias confessed as he kissed her back.

Jane rocked back and forth. It was all the encouragement he needed. Elias pulled back almost completely and drove into her again. His hips moved in a constant rhythm.

She met him with equal speed. Her movements were unexpected, so he let her take over.

"Don't stop," he crooned, holding onto her hips and leg.

Jane's movements quickened, goading him to move as well.

He couldn't stand the torture any longer and took over. He pushed her further down to where her breasts touched the bed. He picked up her other leg and wrapped it around his waist, while holding onto her hips. He had total control of her body.

The pace he set careened them both over the edge. Elias's strength was spent. He released her legs, letting them fall gently onto the bed. He lay on top of her but then rolled onto his back.

Jane's breathing was labored, which matched his own. He reached over pulling her to him. He nestled himself tight behind her.

"Oh yeah, you do make me forget myself," he whispered in her ear and kissed it.

"You make me want to remember," she whispered back, entwining her fingers with his.

Elias was happy, until an ache suddenly weighted his chest. He recognized the fear and held Jane closer. He wasn't sure which scared him most, keeping her in his life or letting her go.

"I've done things, Jane." He was ready to confess his past. Elias wanted what they were building to start clean. She deserved to know what he had done.

"Hmm."

"Jane?" He sat up a little and looked down at her. She was asleep.

CHAPTER THIRTY-ONE

Elias's mind and body hummed from their lovemaking. Thank God Magda was gone for a while. He only had a few hours before he had to go back to work. His time alone with Jane was precious.

He got up without disturbing her and peeked out the window. The October moon was but a fingernail in the sky.

Feeling antsy, Elias got dressed and waited downstairs for Magda, who arrived twenty minutes later. After he hid her car in the barn, he came back inside to talk to her.

"Was everything all right?" he asked as he grabbed his coat and hat. "You took longer than I wanted."

"I was needed. Elias, everyone is so upset and very worried. Some are questioning if you are doing anything about their safety. I reassured them that you are."

"Thanks for controlling the panic. With the extra men patrolling, they have nothing to worry about." Elias said. "I'm heading out. Jane's asleep. And I think you need rest too."

"That's a good idea." Magda expelled a breath, before she walked off toward her bedroom.

Elias left and headed over to the lake. He really should have been heading back to the station but decided against it. All he would do there was look over the paperwork again, and he'd done that a thousand times before.

*   *   *

He shook off the built-up stress and focused on the night. It was quiet, almost eerie, as he drove down 41. The wind moving through the bare tree branches in the distance gave the appearance of an old black and white horror movie.

He slowed his truck, turning right at the stone bend. When he reached the lake, he parked the truck near the spot where Jane was found. The narrow crescent moon cast down only a sliver of light—it would make visibility hard. Therefore, Elias left his vehicle on with the headlights on high beams.

Elias grabbed his large flashlight from under the seat and made his usual walk around the area where Jane was found. The smell of tilled corn fields and lake water made him wrinkle his nose.

Without making a sound, he walked up to the hole she was pulled from.

By the water's edge, he spotted a Canada goose swimming, bobbing his head for a drink. He thought it odd, only one goose.

His back was to the truck when a soft snap echoed through the air. The single goose took off in a frantic flight. Elias shifted quickly on the balls of his feet. Gun in his hand, he spun around and made sure no one was behind him.

He could see nothing in the dark. Yet, something didn't feel right. The hairs on the back of his neck stood on end.

Elias headed toward the southern end of the lake, where the sound had come from. *Shit.* He almost face-planted, nearly dropping his gun but he righted himself. Then he stumbled over a small mound of freshly loosened soil. His bad feeling got worse.

Elias didn't want to admit it but the one night he didn't want things to happen, the son of a bitch had possibly struck again. The four-by-six pile of dirt hadn't been there a few days ago. He wished he had patrolled last night. He couldn't be sure there was a body under the dirt, but he couldn't rule it out either.

He scanned the area once more, then went back to the truck to retrieve his shovel from the back.

After propping the mag-light, Elias carefully handled the dirt. He slowly shifted the loose soil into a pile off to the side. As he dug, he also kept his eyes on the surroundings. He didn't want to be caught off guard if the perpetrator was still around.

Elias held his breath the whole time until the shovel hit something solid. He didn't wait to see what it was, Elias called over the radio for assistance.

"I have a possible 10-31 at Beaver Lake. I need both officers here quickly."

"10-4, Chief. I'm en route," Tom chirped.

"I'm fifteen minutes out," Tyson added.

"Get here quick." Elias dropped the radio and continued digging.

Little by little the mound of dirt was removed, and a hole—about a foot deep was made. Elias decided to wait for the others. When he stepped back, out of the corner of his eye, by the lake's edge, stood a person. A girl. The beams from his truck cast an eerie yellow glow around her.

Elias stood motionless with his eyes straight, not looking at her. His gut told him that it was the girl Jane was talking about. She was dressed in a yellow sundress and had long blonde hair. Just as Jane described her.

He spoke with an even tone, so not to scare her off. "Hello."

She didn't respond. His nerves were tense as a drawn bow. Elias turned his head slightly to get a better look but she was gone. "Damn it."

Why was *he* seeing her? Then a flash of realization slammed him. There was another body in the ground.

With his heart thrashing against his rib cage, he knelt down and began working quickly through the soil with his hands. Using a shovel might destroy any possible evidence and damage the victim.

The dirt was much softer and easy to remove. Another eight inches down, he found an old woolen blanket. It reminded him of an old military blanket, the ones soldiers received back in the day.

As he pulled at the corners, something heavy was stuck on it. Elias made fast work with the shovel. He dug around until an oval form emerged.

Tom's squad pulled up. The deputy rushed out and helped immediately. "Holy crap," Tom said as he helped scoop out the dirt.

Elias paused for a second, "I don't think..." The ache in his throat pained him to acknowledge that the person wasn't alive.

As they pulled more of the blanket, the ground loosened its grip and they were able to lift the blanket-wrapped mass out.

It was a woman. Her feet dangled from the blanket. She had on only one black boot.

Tom lost his grip on the blanket and accidentally let go of his side. The body partially fell out, which exposed a mangled face and arms. The deputy backed up and gagged.

Elias turned his flashlight onto the victim. The woman's long hair was tangled up around her right arm. Elias dropped his side of the blanket and covered the blood-drenched body. She had to have been dead before she was put into the ground. Her skull was smashed in and there were more pieces than he cared to see.

The woman wasn't dressed either. Her boot was her only apparel. Her free ankle had the same rope burns and slash marks on her shin and calf as Jane. He lifted the blanket and against his stomach's protest, he examined the slash marks gouged deeply onto her arms.

A thought crossed his mind. Could this be the woman his father asked about? With the string of bad crap, Elias's instincts screamed yes.

The brutality this woman suffered was much worse than the earlier victims. The bastard had destroyed the woman's face almost past the point of recognition. Was this what he wanted to do with Jane? Was this a message to Jane, or to him? It was as though he'd made this woman an example of what he was capable of. Loud and clear.

Elias had no choice but to make damn sure Jane had round-the-clock protection. He had to let his deputy know where Jane was hiding. Elias alone couldn't safeguard her. With another murder, making this victim number two—three, if he had succeeded in killing Jane, Elias had to call State in.

Tom straightened up and wiped his mouth with his sleeve. "Sorry."

"Okay?" Elias asked Tom before calling in the coroner.

The deputy took a few breaths, spit and answered. "Yeah."

Elias had never seen his deputy so shaken. Tom's reaction made him more nervous. After they blocked off the area, it took another thirty minutes for the coroner and the ambulance to arrive.

As the dead woman was being removed, Elias got a sinking feeling in his gut, and knew he had to call Magda. He pulled out his cell, looked at his deputy for a brief moment before dialing the nurse's cell phone. He moved out of earshot before pressing the green button.

"How's everything there?" he said in a whisper.

"Everything is good here. Jane's resting. Elias, you don't sound good. What happened?"

"I'll tell you later. Just checking in, talk to you later." Elias hung up before she asked further questions.

"Who were you on the phone with?" Tom walked up behind him, wiping his forehead with his sleeve. He had a roll of yellow caution tape in his hands.

"Magda. I asked how Jane is doing."

"Oh. How is she?"

"She's resting," Elias said while staring out toward the lake.

Tom let out a slight huff. "You two getting close?"

"Magda and—"

"Not Magda. Jane Doe," Tom interrupted.

Elias turned around and faced the deputy. "Just checking to make sure she's safe. That's all."

"Are you sure?" Tom had a sly grin on his ashen face.

Elias wanted to slap the smile off his face. "Get to the point, Deputy. We have a crime scene to scour." Elias took a step forward.

Tom took two steps back and raised his hands up. "Nothing. I'm only asking. What's up with you? You've been dangling on a short leash ever since Jane was found."

"I know. I can't wait until this son of a bitch is caught. Tonight proves that I need to bring someone bigger into this investigation. I'm calling State. They have more manpower to handle this."

"It's only two bodies. Sounds terrible to say that, but I don't think it's big enough for the state cops to take over. But it's your call."

Elias stared at his deputy. "I know we're in way over our heads." He watched his deputy's ashen face turn red.

"Are you sure?" Tom questioned. A hint of ire resonated in his voice.

"Damn sure. This case was way out of our league to begin with. We can't do this alone. This asshole upped the ante the moment he killed that nurse. And now, with this," Elias said, pointing at the empty shallow grave, "I can't take the chance of him getting his hands on Jane or anyone else. Not anymore."

"Well, you said yourself she's safe at the hospital. No one can get to her there."

Elias cleared his throat and rubbed at the back of his neck. "Jane isn't at the hospital."

"What?" Tom stammered out the question. "What do you mean she isn't at the hospital?"

"I moved her the night she was attacked."

"Where?"

"My house." Elias looked away again.

"Are you kidding me? This whole time, I have been patrolling the hospital grounds, walking the halls, and the damned woman wasn't even there?"

"I had to make sure the killer thought she was there. It was the only way to keep her safe."

"What was the reason for not telling any of us? Or

me. Is it trust? You don't trust me enough to tell me the truth?"

"I figured the fewer people who knew about my plan, the better. It's not like I don't trust you, I felt it would be more effective if no one knew."

"You thought you could handle this case without me." Tom's brows furrowed tight; his frown showed no appeasement.

"No. I kept it quiet because I know the killer is local. Not sure who, but hiding Jane was a tactic to protect her. That's all. Tom, I'm making the call and the state police will be taking over this case."

"So, that's it." Tom's grated voice shot up. "I guess in a few hours, this case will be out of our hands."

Every muscle in Elias's body became taut. "It's my call and I'm taking it. What's pissing you off more, Tom, that I hid Jane and didn't tell you or that State is taking over? I've never seen you act like this before."

Tom didn't say another word. He stood there in silence, lips thin and white, eyes cold. The deputy dropped the yellow caution tape and headed off toward the water. He stopped just a foot out of range of the beamed headlights. Elias only saw his statued silhouette in the dark.

Elias walked off toward his truck, giving Tom time alone, but kept looking back over his shoulder. He trusted Tom. Though with his deputy's sudden belligerence, he wasn't sure about anything at that point.

Once at the truck, Elias opened the back for the evidence gear. He looked up and watched the outline of the man he thought he knew disappear into the night. He tried to adjust his eyes to the darkness but he couldn't spot him. The knot in his gut told him to beware.

The phone rang, which made Elias jump. Magda's

cell. He flipped the phone open and answered. "What's wrong?"

"What happened? You hung up on me." Concern laced the older woman's voice.

Elias blew out a breath and hesitated. "We found another body."

"Oh, my Lord. Is she alive?"

"No. She was beaten to the point that we can't recognize her. Her face is in bad shape. I think the bastard is sending a message. I have no choice now but to call state police in."

"What does that mean, Elias?"

"That means the state police will be taking over this case and Jane will be in protective custody under them. This case is way out of our league."

"What should I tell Jane?"

"Don't say anything. I'll be home soon. I'll tell her."

Elias hung up but leaned against the truck for a little while longer. He needed to regroup his thoughts. Anger and contempt swirled in his blood for what the bastard had done to the victim, but worse, aggravation with Tom bolstered tight in his gut.

The man's rage was too quick to explain away. What was behind his anger? It made no sense to Elias.

As though the deputy had read his thoughts, he walked up to the truck. "Can I talk to you?" Tom approached Elias with hesitant steps.

Elias straightened away from the truck, but kept his eyes on the man. "Yeah."

"I'm sorry for my temper. It's my wounded pride that lashed out. I felt you didn't trust me enough to handle that secret but I understand why you did it. I probably would have done the same thing," Tom said with a partial smile.

Tom sounded sincere, but something inside Elias's gut warned him to be cautious.

"I'm glad you understand," Elias said evenly. "Why don't you start gathering what you can while I call State. I'll help you after the call."

It took all of ten minutes on the phone to get his answer.

"They'll be here by tomorrow," Elias said as he slipped on a pair of gloves.

Elias walked back toward the hole they had cordoned off.

"So who's watching Jane?" Tom asked while picking up a small soil sample.

"Magda."

"That old woman doesn't have enough muscle to protect herself. Why her?" Anger laced his question again.

"If no one knew where Jane was, then I didn't need the muscle," Elias explained. "Let's concentrate on the evidence."

Tom nodded and went back to what he was collecting. "Not sure but I think this is blood and maybe some brain matter. It's too dark to see anything clearly."

Elias quickly glanced down at his watch. Three-oh-five. "You're right. We'll wait until State arrives to facilitate what needs to be done."

"I'll stick around to look a little more," Tom said. "I'll be careful."

"All right. I'll head back to the station. I need a chat with James."

"Why?"

"I have a bad feeling this woman is his girlfriend."

Tom shook his head. "That's a shame."

"Afterwards, I'm going to the hospital. I want to know if Dr. Farley found anything on the victim. Until

State gets here, we still work this case. Be extra cautious."

"10-4." Tom saluted Elias, then hunched over the gravesite with a flashlight and a small shovel.

Elias slid into his truck, taking notice of how Tom kept looking into the hole and then spitting off to the side. He'd thought the deputy had a strong constitution, but apparently not when it came down to mangled bodies.

As Elias pulled out onto the road, he headed straight to the station. He hadn't wanted to admit it in front of Tom, but he'd also felt green when he pulled back the blanket.

His nerves were yanked tight and his chest hurt from the boulder-sized weight of an investigation going nowhere. An acrid flavor burned at the back of his throat, but he kept it down by swallowing. He hated the anxiousness crawling over his skin. A cigarette would cure the taste but not the terrible feeling coursing through his body.

Jane was the only one who took that anxiety away. When he was in her arms, it was as though all the rotten crap of his past was wiped away. Dissolved into nothing. Even his nightmares stayed at bay.

Admitting his emotions for Jane was difficult—he never imagined in his wildest dreams he'd fall fast for a woman like her. She was someone who wouldn't take his crap, but loved him, unconditionally.

The thought of not seeing her on a daily basis stabbed at his heart. But Elias couldn't—wouldn't—put Jane in danger any longer. This was for her.

If he found Jane brutally murdered, the badge he took strength in wouldn't hold back the vengeance he'd unleash.

Elias shook off that imagery and rushed into the station and headed straight to the holding cell in back.

Nearly running into the bars, Elias demanded, "What kind of shoes did your girlfriend wear?"

"How the fuck should I know. I'm a guy. If she isn't flashing lace or something see-through, then I'm not looking." James got up from the cot and pressed his face through the bars. "Why? Did you find her?" His voice shook slightly.

"Maybe. But I need to know what she was wearing."

"Beats me. Short skirt and black heels—no, boots...I think."

"We found the body of a woman but her face was smashed in. Does she have long hair?"

"Very long, and black," James said shaking his head.

"I think the victim is your friend," Elias said, leaning back against the adjacent wall.

"She's dead?" James leaned against the cell, slipping down to the floor and threw up.

"Eww." Caroline cringed.

Elias walked over to her cell and opened it. "Get out. I don't want to see your face around here again."

She nodded in quick agreement. Elias opened the door wider and she dashed out of the cell.

"Hey, what about me?" James shouted.

"State's coming. I'll leave it up to them to see if you are a suspect."

"What? I didn't kill anybody!"

Elias walked out, ignoring James's yelling.

*   *   *

Caroline raced out of the station. She wanted to claw Elias's face off for putting her in jail and leaving her there overnight, but refrained. She didn't want another night in jail, especially next to that nasty old man.

Beth offered her a ride back to the hospital, but she ignored the fat bitch. Every person in the county knew she'd been carted away from the hospital like some criminal. She wasn't going to add the humiliation of a squad car dropping her off at the entrance. She'd be a laughingstock.

"That bastard will pay for my humiliation," she mumbled. "He. Will. Pay."

The cold wind made her shiver. Caroline's teeth chattered while she checked her coat pocket for her cell phone. Laney would give her a ride. She didn't want to go back to the hospital, but her purse and keys were in her locker.

"Fuck." Caroline stamped her foot in frustration. She remembered the damn thing was in her purse.

Going back into the station to use the phone was the last thing Caroline wanted to do. The farther she got away from Elias McAvoy, the better. She had no idea what she'd seen in him anyway.

She stood by the light post and contemplated what she should do. Caroline smelled her rumpled clothes and noticed her fingernails. "No way. I broke a nail," she whined as she examined her ring finger.

After chewing off the rest of her nail, Caroline hugged herself for warmth. The icy wind had seeped through her thin coat. She stomped her feet to relieve the numbness, trying to decide what to do.

As she stepped away from the light post, Tom pulled up next to her.

"What's up, Caroline?"

"What do you want, Tom? I'm in no mood for your sweet-talking crap tonight."

"Ahh. Did Elias hurt your feelings?" Tom said in a

girly voice, pushing his bottom lip out. "So, jail didn't agree with you?"

"You are an asshole, too. All the men in this fucking town suck. Leave me alone." Caroline walked away. She was about to take a step off the curb when Tom almost hit her with the front of the squad. "Hey! Bastard, you almost hit me! What the hell is wrong with you?"

"You shouldn't swear, Caroline. Nice girls don't talk that way."

"Who said I was a nice girl?" Caroline stepped back to see Tom's big grin.

"Get in the car, Caroline. I'll drive you home."

"No way. Not when you almost ran me over. Besides, I'm going to the hospital."

"Don't lie to me. You are heading in the wrong direction. I know where you live. Come on, if you want, I'll drive you to the hospital. Get in. Your legs are going to hurt from the walk and it's too cold and dark outside."

As if on cue, the wind whooshed past her. It made Caroline shudder more. She looked at the deputy, then at the dark road ahead. Her trailer was located at the other end of town, much farther than the hospital.

"Ok," she conceded, sounding like a pouty child, and got into the squad.

She could feel the heat from the vents blowing on her cold skin. "Mmm. This feels so good." She rubbed her hands in the air stream.

"See, if people would listen to me more often, they would be a lot happier," Tom said, increasing the heat and the blower.

"Thanks, Tom, for driving me home."

"You are welcome." He put the car in gear and took off toward Caroline's trailer. "Are you warm yet?"

"Yes. Thank you," Caroline said.

Silence filled the cab space. She had never seen the

inside of a squad before. She swore Tom had every known gadget in the vehicle.

Caroline looked over and noticed Tom watching her.

"What?" she asked, rubbing her hands together.

"I was wondering, how was your overnight at the station?" He chuckled.

"That isn't funny, Tom. That bastard embarrassed me in front of my friends and co-workers. All I wanted to do was to show my love for him and he throws me in jail," she whined.

"Caroline, you have to understand that Elias is a no parking zone. He doesn't want you."

"Fuck you, Tom—

"Wait a minute." He slowed the car down. "There is no need to be hostile with me. I am only telling you the truth," Tom said with a growl.

Caroline was instantly contrite. "Sorry, Tom." She wiped away the tears and noticed the dark smudge on her fingertips. "Damn, I must look like death right now. My mascara is down to my cheekbone."

"You look fine. I know you are distraught over being thrown in jail," he said as he pulled up to her trailer. "I want what's best for you. Elias isn't the best."

"Thanks again." She leaned over and kissed his cheek. She opened the passenger door, got out and closed it right away.

"You are welcome," Tom said with a grin.

Caroline reached her trailer door, turned and watched Tom drive off. His rear lights disappeared in the dark.

The whistling of the wind through the adjacent trees and nearby cornfields made her skin crawl. She hated living next to the woods. She'd hated the country since she was a child. Too dark and eerie for her cup of tea. The city was where she wanted to be.

Caroline bent over, pulled up the welcome mat and grabbed the extra house key. With the click of the flimsy lock, she opened the door and entered the trailer.

The interior was as black as the night. She wished she had left the light on in the kitchen. Blind, she felt the paneled wall for the switch by the compact kitchen.

She flipped it on, casting a soft glow of light into the living room.

Her breath rushed out with relief and she dropped herself into the black leather loveseat. She wanted the fuck out of there and fast. For good this time.

As she leaned back and closed her eyes, the light flashed off. Panic surged up in Caroline's chest and choked her. She froze as the front door slowly opened and a dark silhouette stood in the doorway.

"What the..." Her scream pierced the cold night air.

CHAPTER THIRTY-TWO

Jane woke up and found Elias wasn't in bed. He'd gone without waking her, which left her feeling raw and slightly abandoned. She grabbed his pillow and inhaled. His scent filled her with a rush of euphoria. Her body tingled as she remembered their lovemaking.

Staying away from Elias was out of the question now. She not only craved his body, Jane yearned to talk to him. He made her whole, even without her memories.

Funny how she had hated the man and now she was afraid she'd never see him again.

Damn. She was falling hard for him but still wasn't sure it was the right thing to do. Lately, her emotions had been all over the place. Were her feelings for Elias purely physical? Or was it more? Not wanting to think about it, and unable to sleep anymore, she got dressed and headed downstairs.

She crept quietly so as not to wake Magda in the bedroom off the kitchen. With every creaky step, she stopped and listened. Poor Magda. Jane worried for her.

Jane made her way over to the picture window and cracked open the curtains. Dawn had not peeked over the horizon yet, she withdrew from the window, yawned and stretched out her arms.

Maybe a walk would clear her head, but Elias's warning stalled her from stepping outside. Besides, her head had become more sensitive the moment Magda removed the staples. Exposing her Texas-sized scar to the cold could lead to severe pain, and she'd had enough of that.

She glanced up at the wall clock; it read four thirty-five. Jane wandered around the first floor until the yearning for coffee hit her. She wasn't quite sure if she remembered how it was made. How hard could it be? Magda made it look easy.

She entered the kitchen with a new sense of purpose. As she approached the sink, a dark figure stood outside the window, looking in—a black silhouette against the black backdrop. She let out a yelp and hid beside the refrigerator, out of sight.

Jane clutched at her flannel shirt, her heart jack-hammering against her ribcage. She became slightly lightheaded and leaned against the appliance for support. With wobbly legs, and a few deep breaths to calm herself, she gathered enough nerve to peek around the corner.

No one was there.

Jane straightened up and cautiously walked toward the window. As she stepped closer to the sink, that menacing dark shadow turned out to be a straggly bush, swaying side to side in the wind.

A relieved breath escaped her lungs. She shook off her nervousness and directed her attention to the perco-lator on the counter. Jane opened the lid and took out the brown basket full of old grounds. This coffee maker must be an antique.

Jane dumped the old coffee grounds down the sink,

as she had seen Magda do countless times, and rinsed the basket. She did the same with the pot and then filled it with cold water. After finding the coffee can in one of the cabinets, she eyeballed how many scoops it needed and proceeded to add ten heaping teaspoons. Not too strong.

She plugged it in and waited. And waited. Standing there was stupid. Jane wanted to keep busy. There had to be something else to do. Looking around the room, everything was cleaned and put away.

With her arms folded across her chest, Jane thought, since she'd made coffee, why not breakfast? Breakfast for the chief. A show of appreciation for all he had done for her.

Being in the kitchen felt natural. Jane swiped the apron off the hook on the pantry door and looked in the refrigerator for possible breakfast foods.

Eggs, milk, bacon and butter were pulled out and placed on the table. She then went into the pantry and retrieved the flour and set it next to the bowl Magda used for making pancakes.

Jane stared at the items and shrugged. "How hard could it be?" She had lost her memory, but not her ability to cook.

Hope flickered in her mind that she might be a chef, or a cook of some sort.

Of course, she could only assume.

She flowed between the stove and the table with fluidity. She searched for a couple of bowls and found an old cookbook on the lower shelf in the pantry. One teaspoon of salt, another teaspoon of baking soda, a cup of flour, and stir together with some milk. Jane remembered the eggs, and cracked them into the soupy concoction. After rescuing a few shells from the batter, it looked complete.

Jane retrieved the frying pans from the oven and placed them adjacent to each other on the stovetop. She opened the bacon package and dropped the fatty slices into one pan. While the strips sizzled and popped, she poured pancake batter into the other.

Between the bacon and pancakes, she found a rhythmic system emerging. Once she finished making pancakes and stacked them on the plate, Jane glanced at the misshapen circles. She was pretty proud of her accomplishment. So what if a few stuck to the bottom of the dark heavy pan?

"Ouch." She stepped back and examined the small red welts on her left hand and arm. The splattered bacon grease did a number on her skin. But the welts weren't so bad. Especially after what she had been through, a few grease burns wouldn't deter her from her goal.

Smoke began to fill the kitchen. Jane quickly turned off the burner. She waved the haze away from her face and scooped up the last of the charred bacon strips and placed them on the plate.

Fried eggs were last on her mental list. She plopped butter into the pan. Like Magda, she took a spoon and scooped up some of the fat from the bacon and drizzled it over the melting butter.

"Six should do it." She smiled as each egg splashed into the grease. "Dang it." A few shell pieces fell into the eggs. She dragged them out with her spatula and finished the scramble.

Excitement bubbled through her. Even though she had a couple of burned fingertips and grease splatters along her arms, she'd made a meal that was fit for a king. Well, maybe for a chief of police. Nonetheless, she was very proud of what she'd cooked.

Now all she needed was for Elias to walk through that door and be surprised.

Jane sat at the table, staring down at her lovely breakfast creation and wondered when he would be home. The eggs were getting cold. Maybe she'd rushed with breakfast and should have waited until he got there.

Fifteen minutes had passed before Jane decided to clean up the kitchen. After she covered the cooked food with foil, she returned the butter and eggs to the refrigerator. She washed the pans and put them away, then wiped the grease off the counter and stove.

The coffee stopped percolating. As she was about to pour herself a cup, Elias strolled through the back door.

Jane had an overwhelming urge to run up and kiss the man. Instead, she stayed cool and gave him a smile. "Good morning." Inside, she was shaking. She was actually giddy.

*   *   *

Elias froze in the doorway for a second, staring at Jane dressed in his mother's purple flowered apron.

"Coffee?" Jane asked as she extended the filled cup.

"Thanks." He took the mug and placed it on the counter. He guessed he could wait and tell her about the victim. "You're up early. Couldn't sleep?" Elias asked as he shrugged off his jacket and draped it over the back of a chair. He took the cup and sniffed the dark brew.

"Not really. How's work?"

The normality of the moment was so surreal to him. Elias kept staring at her. His life, love and happiness were now entwined in one single woman. She made him see what he could have. But did he deserve it?

She stood there, hands fidgeting at her sides. Why was she nervous?

"Are you okay?" Jane's brows knitted when she asked.

"What—oh, I'm sorry." Elias took a sip of the coffee.

"Yeah, I'm good," he choked out. He almost spit out the awful liquid but he was quick enough to swallow it down without cringing.

"I also made breakfast," Jane gushed as she lifted the foil off the plates. "Are you hungry?

Elias didn't know how to react. "For me?"

Flat, dark discs that resembled pancakes and charred pieces of what he thought was bacon... Elias smiled at her. He feared what the third plate hid. *Please, don't let it be eggs.*

Sure enough, a yellow and white mess was revealed under the foil. He hated eggs. Though it didn't matter, he'd eat anything she made for him.

"Yes, I made it for you. And for Magda too. I wanted to show you my gratitude for keeping me safe and for using your home as a hideout. And..." she didn't finish. Her face flushed red and her smile was enchanting. Elias noticed she had dimples. How could he have missed those? They were only slight but they made her face all the more kissable.

He reached out, wrapped his arms around her waist and bent down and kissed her. "Thank you."

"Are you hungry?"

"Yes," Elias uttered with enthusiasm as his stomach protested. *How bad could it be?*

"Here's some bacon, a couple of pancakes and some scrambled eggs. They started out as sunny side up but then I broke a few of the yolks as I tried to flip them."

She plopped down four small, hard disks. Elias swore the plate clinked when they hit it. The bacon almost disintegrated on contact. But those eggs... *Yuck.* They drooled off the spoon.

"That's okay. It looks... great," he said looking over his morning meal.

"Well then, dig in." Jane poured herself a cup of coffee and sat across the table from him.

"I don't know where to start." Elias picked up the burnt bacon and sniffed it. He broke off a piece and popped it into his mouth. "Good." Hoped the char wouldn't choke him.

He took his fork and slowly scooped up a small mound of eggs and put it in his mouth. The moment the slimy, salty forkful hit his tongue, his gag reflex started. But he held it in check.

"It's good. Why aren't you having any?" Elias coughed.

"I don't like eggs. Besides, I'm not hungry anyway. I'll have the coffee." She sipped at her cup, then quickly placed it on the counter, splashing the liquid over the rim.

Her smile pinched tight at him before she gulped what was in her mouth. She shivered. "Mmm. Good coffee."

Elias had to wash down the mess in his mouth. He took a large gulp of his coffee. He almost squeezed his nose but forced himself not to. The strong flavor of the dark liquid was bitter but cleared his palate from the heinous egg taste. "You made the coffee too?" That was a stupid question.

"Yes. How is it?" She laughed. Her eyes sparkled with mischief.

"Strong. The way I like it." He cleared his throat from the sharpness of the coffee.

"Sorry. I didn't realize how bad the coffee is. And from the green hue of your face, my cooking skills are the same." She took the plate from him and placed it in the sink. "Sorry, I tried," she said, looking over her shoulder.

Elias got up from the table and wrapped his arms

around her waist. "It's much appreciated." He kissed her nose. He couldn't resist and took her mouth.

The kiss was soft and gentle. "Thanks for thinking of me."

He trailed his lips down her chin and around her jaw line. He nibbled on her neck before asking where Magda was.

"She's still sleeping. Elias. She told me about her stroke and how you stayed here for her."

"It wasn't only for her," Elias said. "I'm a..." He couldn't finish.

"I know about the alcohol. Magda explained everything to me." Jane leaned back and kissed him. Her silent approval. She then continued. "What surprises me the most about her? She has so much energy."

"I know. She needs to slow down but she doesn't listen to me. When I leave here—"

"You're planning on leaving?"

Elias released her from his arms and sat down. This was his chance to let her know what had happened—come clean about his fucked-up life. And that was the reason why he wasn't a good bet for any relationship.

"After I escaped this town, I enlisted in the army. With my ASVAB scores, the recruiter suggested MP."

"I knew that." She slid in the chair adjacent to him and took his hand. "Magda told me."

"I served six years. After I got out, I followed an army buddy to his hometown, Half Moon Bay, California. It's a beautiful place, but you know that. Well, through his connections, I was hired on at the police department. I was happy—content. I found a small place right away and started my new life." Elias took in a breath before he continued. "Almost four years ago, my partner and I got a call. Domestic disturbance. When we arrived, it was a husband beating up his wife."

Jane's hand tightened around his fingers. "Go on."

He let go of her hand and got up from the table.

"What happened?" Jane asked. Her voice shook a little.

That familiar lump lodged in his throat. It hurt to talk. "After we took the husband down, I stayed by the wife's side until the ambulance got there. She was beaten pretty bad. Broken arm, sprained ankle and a couple of cracked ribs." Elias's heart was beating faster with each word spoken. "Her name was Elise. She was twenty-two years old. I could tell from the way she acted, this wasn't the first time she'd been beaten by her husband. I don't know what it was. Maybe she reminded me of my mother. But I felt it was my job to protect her. Anyway. She was taken to the hospital and admitted for a week. I came by every day and made sure she was okay. The day she got out..." Elias couldn't finish the sentence.

"What happened to her? Elias?" Jane swiped a tear from her cheek.

He cleared his throat. "She asked me to drive her home from the hospital. It was against my better judgment for her to go back to her apartment, but she insisted. I thought she was safe, but that wasn't the case." Elias felt the wetness on his face. He was crying. He couldn't help it. It had been four years since he had spoken about it.

"What happened to her?" she repeated in a whispered sob.

"I checked out the apartment before she entered. Everything looked locked up and safe. Elise thanked me and went inside. I was heading back to my squad when I heard a crash. I ran back to her apartment and knocked on the door. She didn't answer, so I kicked the door open and saw her lying on the floor holding her face. There was broken glass around her.

"Her husband was standing on the other side of the room with a gun in his hand. It was pointed at me. Turned out he was released on bond the day before. No one had notified the station that he was out." He wiped his eyes with his palm. "It happened so fast. As I drew my gun, her husband pulled the trigger and it hit me in the shoulder. I got a shot off, but by then Elise had stood up between us. My bullet hit her chest."

Jane got up and went to him. Elias felt he wasn't deserving of her, and tried to push her away. She wasn't deterred and wrapped her arms around him and hugged him tight.

He couldn't hold it together any longer. Elias wept hard like he had when his mother died. But this time he wasn't alone. His failure as a cop and as a decent human being was now exposed. What did she think of him?

Elias held onto her tightly as he rode his own emotional roller coaster. Everything inside him hurt. He couldn't control his tears either. It took a few minutes to regain his composure. He pulled away from Jane and finished what he'd started.

"I couldn't sleep anymore, unless I was shit-faced. I drowned myself in alcohol to forget. But the look on Elise's face as she fell to the floor was burned in my memory." He walked around the table to put some distance between them. "I was put on suspension until I got some help. So I left and came here. Jane, I don't want to hurt you. I can't..."

"Elias, if you had a chance to change what happened, you'd do it, I know. You had no idea what Elise was thinking or why she got between you two. Forgive yourself. It was an accident." Jane reached out to hold him, but he stepped back.

"Jane, I need time. I can't wrap my brain around how I feel right now about you. It's hitting me too hard—too fast. I don't know if I can live up to anyone's expectations." He grabbed his jacket and charged out of the house.

"Elias," she called out to him. She tried to follow him to the truck, but he jumped in and took off before she could stop him.

CHAPTER THIRTY-THREE

Elias banged the steering wheel as he drove to the station. His heart was about to burst out of his chest. The headache, confusion, and painful memories of his past; he barely contained his growing madness.

As bad as he wanted to stay, Elias had needed to get out of that house. He was able to think more clearly away from Jane. And the look she gave him stabbed straight through his chest. He should have stayed clear of her from the start, but his heart and dick didn't obey.

Their situation was complicated to begin with; sleeping together only made it more twisted.

Damn. He needed to clear his head. Caffeine.

He stopped at the Coffee Barn and grabbed a large cup. He pulled over to the side and took a gulp. He hoped the brew would erase the burnt taste of Jane's breakfast, ease the ache in his chest and wash away the memories plaguing him.

As he took another sip, his cell phone went off.

"Chief McAvoy," he answered briskly.

"Chief, this is Dr. Farley. Do you have time to stop by the hospital? I've completed my exam on the victim."

"I'm heading your way now." He hung up and shifted into drive.

He swallowed the last bit of coffee when he pulled up to the hospital parking area. He wound his way through the hospital, down the elevator to the coroner's office.

Dr. Farley was outside of the examination room talking to an intern.

"What did you find?"

"I have to show you." As the coroner pushed the door open, Elias saw the woman's damaged body on the table, covered with a blue sheet. "How's your stomach?"

"Fine, why?"

He flipped back the sheet, which exposed the victim from head to toe.

Elias automatically stepped back as the stench of decay filled his nostrils. The sight wasn't any better. Her head was smashed in and some sort of brain matter seeped out of where her left eye once was.

"Want a minute?"

His stomach fought in protest, but he managed, "No, I'm good."

Dr. Farley eyeballed Elias before he started his explanation. "Okay. I took scrapings from under her fingernails and some hair samples, and bagged them. But this, I couldn't bag." He turned the body slightly on its side, which showed the mutilated part of her torso. "Poor girl. She was cut up with a knife, here and here." Farley pointed out.

"What kind of knife?" Elias bent slightly, to get a better look.

"Possibly a midrange hunting Bowie. But these markings..." He shook his head. "Chief, someone carved words in her skin, with a much smaller blade... Maybe a utility knife."

Elias's stomach wanted to revolt as Farley read each word out loud. "This one's for you, Chief."

Elias's jaw hurt from clenching his teeth so tight. This deranged asshole sent *him* a message. *Fuck!*

"What else?" Elias choked out.

"Her cheek. I tried to clean it up as best as possible without losing any viable evidence." He turned her head where the skull wasn't caved in. "Here," Dr. Farley pointed to two fragmented words dug into her skin.

"I can't make it out. What does it say?" Elias got closer without touching the victim.

Dr. Farley handed him a magnifying glass. "Now look."

The moment Elias peered through the glass, he sucked in a breath, and almost dropped the magnifier onto the victim's head. "Jane's next."

Elias's body drew up tight. Panic flooded his veins, and the overwhelming sense to call Jane exploded in his head.

"Anything else?" was all Elias could ask.

"Yes. I found this to be a little odd." He separated her hair, exposing her scalp. "I don't know a lot about how women dye their hair, but I think rinsing is important. The way the color was caked on her scalp isn't normal. Did you find anything like this on the Jane Doe victim?"

"I wasn't told of anything strange found on Jane's scalp. But her hair was colored black. I just assumed she did it herself before..." Jesus, why wasn't that in the details when Jane had been brought in. "Thanks, Doc. Keep this information to yourself until State comes."

"State's taking over?"

"Yes."

Elias left the morgue, headed up to the emergency room and had Dr. Rollins paged.

Rollins denied any knowledge about color on Jane's scalp. None of the notes specified any substance on Jane's scalp. But the doctor promised to call Elias as soon as the nurses who had assisted him that night were questioned.

Elias reluctantly agreed and left the hospital.

As he approached his truck, he found it keyed on both sides. "Of all the petty crap, Caroline." Elias saw her car in the parking lot and headed back into the building.

He walked up to the receptionist and demanded to speak with Caroline.

"She never made it into work. Her shift started an hour ago. Some of us assumed you still had her in jail, or somewhere else." She blurted out a quick laugh but covered her mouth.

"Did anyone call her?" he snarled.

"I did. But she isn't answering her cell or her home phone."

"She was released last night. I'll go check out her house." Elias strode off. As much as he hated Caroline, if something had happened to her...

The receptionist stopped him outside the sliding doors. "Chief, Caroline never misses work. She really is trying to save her money to get out of this town."

"Do you think she would leave town now, without telling anyone?"

"Possibly, but I doubt it."

"All right. I'm heading over to her place now. Call me if she shows up or you hear from her."

Elias headed straight to Caroline's trailer. He knew she was pissed off when he released her, but he didn't think she had it in her to take off, and not without her car.

The trailer was dark. He checked the windows and the door. They were locked. Elias peered into the small window next to the entrance and saw her cat eating out of a toppled box of cat food.

Caroline might be a crazy bitch and narcissistic, but one thing he knew she wouldn't do. Leave her cat and all her belongings. How ironic that he'd be worried for her.

Elias headed back to the station when the radio chirped. "Chief, come in."

"What's up, Cindy Lee?"

"The transport for your father is here. They're waiting in your office."

"Tell them I'll be right there. Who's on patrol?"

"Right now, it's Beth and Tom."

"All right. Radio them to keep their eyes open for Caroline Weaver. She didn't show up for work and she isn't home."

"Really?" He heard a note of surprise in Cindy Lee's voice.

"Radio them."

"10-4, Chief."

As Elias pulled up to the station, he saw the mayor getting out of his black Regal. *Damn.* He was the last person Elias wanted to see.

"A quick word with you, Chief McAvoy."

It was never a quick word when it came down to the mayor. "What is it, Mayor?"

"I heard about the other victim. I demand to know what you are doing about this. I've gotten calls since early this morning from concerned citizens. I want answers," he said, tapping his cane against the cement walkway.

"State is taking over. Once they get here, then you can have a chat with them. In the meantime, Mayor, I have work to do." Elias walked away as the old man continued grumbling on the sidewalk.

Elias didn't look back when the mayor called out his regrets for appointing him as chief.

Elias ignored the barb and went inside. He stepped into his office and closed the door.

He shook the two officers' hands, bantered a little while looking over the transfer papers and then signed them. He then graciously led them back to the cell where his father was held.

"Did you find my girlfriend and her truck?" James demanded as he took a step back from the bars.

"No. You didn't mention anything to me about a truck. What is it?"

"How the fuck should I know, I can't remember everything. It's a truck and it's gray, I think."

"A gray truck. Where did you leave it?"

"We ditched it off the... Fuck, I can't think of the road. Nadia drove it in the ditch. Stupid bitch. I wouldn't be in this mess if it weren't for her."

Elias eyed his father. "I'll make sure to look for the truck." Elias's tone was less than convincing.

"Damn it. I'm not making this up. Her name is Nadia and it's her gray truck," James shouted as the two officers stepped forward and shackled him from wrists to ankles. "I'm telling the truth."

For the first time ever, Elias actually believed what came out of his father's mouth. "I said I'll check it out."

James nodded. Then the man broke down right in front of him. "Elias, I'm—"

"Don't," Elias interrupted. "It's too late." He walked out to avoid looking at his old man.

He closed his office door and turned his back to the window. After throwing his jacket onto the coat rack, Elias needed to focus his attention on something else.

He pulled out the folder of the dead women's photos and studied each picture. Elias couldn't tell if there were any similar markings on their heads, like on the recent victim. There was so much dirt on the bodies that he couldn't distinguish slashes from dirt stains.

According to the coroners' reports, the victims had slash marks on their arms and legs. About half had battered and unrecognizable facial features. Though their deaths were caused by either loss of blood or strangulation.

Damn. The coroners. Why hadn't he thought about them before?

If he wanted any more answers, he had to call the three coroners who were involved in the old cases. As he picked up the phone, his hand paused midway. "What the hell am I doing?" He set it down and leaned back against his chair.

State was taking over this case. It'd be better to wait for them. But it could be too late by then and another victim could surface.

His hand hovered over the phone again. It wasn't like him to drop things. He had to finish this to the end. Elias had to do it for Jane.

He made his phone calls to the three coroners' offices. Two had passed on and the current coroners had no information. The third had retired and moved to Arizona. After much heated debate with his replacement, Elias managed to get a contact number for the retired doctor.

Elias immediately called and the doctor answered. *Thank fucking Christ.*

"Dr. Banner, can you remember anything about those cases?"

"At one point, we thought all the murders were done by one person. But as we tried to link the murders to each other, things weren't adding up and not all the murders were the same. Some victims were bound by their wrists and ankles, while some weren't. There were several victims that had many identical markings to confirm the connection, while others had only severe bruising. About half of the victims had their nipples removed.

"Right before I retired, a few of the later victims that were brought in with rope burns around their necks and slash marks down their arms and legs. The older deaths were much cleaner, more like a mercy killing. Whereas the later victims died more barbarically, beaten with total malice."

"Were there any odd substances you or the other coroners found on the victims?" Elias asked.

"Nothing I can remember. But a few had severe vaginal and anal tears, as though they were raped repeatedly. Their heads were also bashed in, which was the cause of their deaths. But most of them weren't touched sexually."

"Thanks, Doc—"

"Wait a sec. I remember Dr. West mentioning a couple of his victims had dark dye on their heads. At the time, I didn't bother checking the victims for hair color. Women do that all the time, I didn't think it was suspicious."

"Do you remember when that was?"

"The seventies? It's been a long time, Chief. I'm not sure exactly of the date."

"Was there any follow up with the dye by Dr. West's office?"

"Like I said, they were women. Many women dye their hair. So, I think he thought the same as I did."

"Thanks for your time, Dr. Banner."

"Good luck and I hope you catch that bastard."

Elias hung up the phone. His mind whirled with the information the doctor had given him.

He studied the pictures again, separating them into two stacks. One pile with no marring of their faces and the others beaten.

After studying each image, Elias realized all the brutalized victims were from the past twenty years, possibly a little more. In the earlier cases, which stemmed as far back as forty years, the bodies weren't beaten like the newer victims were, just like Dr. Banner had disclosed.

Then it hit him like a train wreck. There might be two killers. One older than the other—one was the master and the other was the student. That had never dawned on him. "Holy shit. There are two."

Elias made a few more phone calls to the retired police chiefs who were involved in the old cases. One of the officers had handled three different cases in a span of five years. He said that the killer left no clues. It was as though he knew every movement they made. They did have a witness, a farmer outside of town. But by the time they reached him, he'd died in a tractor accident. Was it co-incidental? Elias thought otherwise.

They went as far as putting decoys out for a month, but they weren't picked up.

With the new information and the possibility of two killers, Elias really couldn't trust a single person around him. It could be anyone. Even a cop. A chill raced down his spine.

Cops knew how to manipulate the system in their favor. They could destroy any evidence that incriminated them. Very simple.

Was he wrong with his assumption? Elias didn't want to take any chances.

He looked down at Henley's writing on the top

corner of the photos. It read "no trails." Did this mean, there was no evidence found at the scenes? Or that the killer left no evidence behind?

If the old chief had any idea who was behind those murders, he might have hidden any evidence he'd had at home. There were no other leads in the office. Elias had to go to Henley's house. But the idea of breaking and entering didn't hold well. He'd lose his badge. Elias knew getting a warrant was near impossible. No judge would approve it, not without any real probable cause or evidence—he would be asking for pigs to fly.

The house had been vacant since Henley's death. With no family to claim it, the property went into probate. Any secrets Henley had lay dormant inside. Elias had to get in there.

After popping a few Motrin, he called Magda to reassure himself that Jane was safe.

"Hello," Jane answered in a cool tone. She was mad.

He had to tread lightly. "Hey. How is everything over there?"

"Fine," she hesitated. "Magda told me the state police are taking over the case."

"I think it's the best protection for you."

"Ha. So when were you going to tell me about the murdered woman?"

"I wanted to, but—"

"No. I don't care anymore, Elias. Talk to Magda."

"Jane."

Silence.

"It's me," Magda responded.

"Please get her back on the phone."

"She went upstairs."

He rubbed the back of his neck in frustration. "Okay, listen. I want you to make sure you lock all the doors and windows. I don't care who's at the front door, don't answer it. Even if they call out your name, you and Jane stay hidden."

"Why? Elias, what's going on?"

"Just precautions." The frustration edged his voice. "I'll call you when I am on my way." Elias saw Tom and Beth coming toward the office. He hung up without hearing her response.

"Who was that?" Tom asked while he took a seat across from him.

"Officer James from Will County," he lied. "Anyway, did you find anything?" He directed the question to Beth.

"Nothing. I talked to some of her relatives but they haven't seen Caroline in almost a month," Beth explained while flipping through her notes.

"You locked up Caroline Weaver and now she ran away because you broke her heart?" Tom chuckled. "Brave man."

"She was making threats toward Jane. I had to teach her a lesson."

"Then where is she?" Tom countered, all humor gone from his face.

"I don't know," Elias hissed. "She left her car and her cat. She never showed up for work. This doesn't make sense."

"I saw her last night coming out of the station and offered her ride home, but she refused my help. So I coaxed her with my charms, and she accepted," Tom explained as he leaned back against the chair.

Elias's brows drew tight when hearing his deputy admit to seeing Caroline. "Why didn't you say something sooner?"

"I just found out from Beth that she was missing," Tom defended.

"Where did you drop her off? Did she say anything

about leaving?"

"Only that you are the scum of the earth and she hates you now for all eternity. I don't think she wants you anymore." Tom smiled.

"So where did you drop her off?" Elias repeated, eyeing his deputy.

"I dropped her off at home around—I don't remember what time," he said. "What did the Will County Police want with you?"

Elias inwardly cringed. "More unsolved murders."

Tom wouldn't let up. "Is Will County a part of this investigation now?"

"I called around to see if there was anyone fitting the latest victim's description." Elias frowned. "I got nothing. But I think the missing cases are all related. And with the new information, we can figure out who some of the victims are and possible lead to the killer."

"Who?" both officers asked in unison.

Elias explained about the gray truck in the ditch. "I'm not a hundred percent sure if the victim is her. But if it is, then we need to find the truck. It might lead us to the identity of the owner and possibly the killer."

"I can get on that right away, Chief," Beth said as she jotted things down. "Brandon Jobe might have towed it out of there, if he saw it. I'll give him a call," she offered.

"Get on that," Elias urged.

Beth nodded and left.

Tom snorted. "Sorry, but it sounds like you're reaching."

Elias turned his attention to his deputy. "It doesn't matter. We have to follow all leads. And there's more. The coroner showed me the body. There are words carved into her skin."

"What did they say?" Tom asked as he straightened up in the chair.

"Threats against Jane." Elias didn't elaborate. "We need to find that truck. I'm sure there are prints on it to determine who our victim is. And we can figure out where the killer picked her up."

Tom leaned over and saw the two piles of pictures on the desk. "What are these?" He picked up one and studied it. "Where did you find these?"

"They're crime scene photos. I found them hidden in between the pile of magazines stacked up on the filing cabinet. Henley hid them."

"What case is this?" Tom asked as he stood up to get a better look. "Is this what you're referring to as a connection to the Jane Doe case?"

"It's funny that you say that." Elias shook his head. "It doesn't matter anymore. State will be taking this case over as soon as they get here. Anyway, keep an eye out for Caroline." Elias took the photo from Tom's hand and placed it in the folder. He closed it, and casually slipped it in the top drawer of his desk. "I'm heading out."

"Me too." He gave a nod. "Elias, how is Jane doing? Is something going on between—" Tom asked as he followed Elias out of the office.

"God, no. Though, she is good." Elias kept his answer simple. Saying anything else might spur on a conversation he didn't want to touch.

Elias walked past the dispatcher, who had her nose deep in one of those gossip magazines. "Cindy Lee, notify me once State arrives."

"Yes, Chief. Oh wait, Raymond Kantor called about twenty minutes ago. He wants to talk to you. I told him you were in a meeting and will call him back as soon as you can."

"Thanks."

Elias jumped into his truck and headed out toward Raymond's. There was a gnawing twist in his gut.

Henley's house was only fifteen minutes further down the road. His stomach protested and tightened the closer he got to Raymond's house.

CHAPTER THIRTY-FOUR

E lias pulled off onto the dirt driveway that led to the single level house. He saw Raymond and Traitor playing fetch in the patchy front yard.

He parked off to the side and got out. Traitor raced over and nearly tackled him. "Hey boy, nice to see you, too." He rubbed the black Lab's head and ears.

"Glad you came," Raymond said as he walked over to Elias.

"It's been crazy. So, what's up?"

"Harold. I wanted to talk to you about him. I think he's really losing it."

"Your brother is harmless. Besides, the couple isn't pressing charges. And as for Jane, he needs to stay clear of this investigation. He will not be a part of it."

"I know that, and so does he—I think. But that's not the reason I called you over here. Ever since the morning we found that girl, he has changed. Did you know that he bought these night vision goggles to track down ghosts? Ghosts! He spent nearly his whole savings to buy those damn things," Raymond said, tossing the ball out for Traitor. "I don't know what to do with him."

"He's your brother. He's always done stupid shit like that."

"Didn't you hear me? Night vision goggles to see *ghosts*. That's fucking crazy."

"I guess, even for your brother, it's a bit off the wall, but not crazy." Elias said, looking around. "Where is he?"

"In the trailer."

"Maybe he's not sleeping enough."

"He's not, and his sleepwalking is getting worse. He hasn't done that since we were kids. He said a girl ghost is haunting him. Christ's sake, Eli, talk to him. I'm worried for him and so is Sara. You know it's bad when she worries for him. She hates his guts."

"I know that," Elias said in frustration. He wanted out of there fast. He raked at his scalp. "All right. I'll go talk to him." Elias headed toward Harold's mobile home.

Harold's place was an old dented silver Airstream camper. He'd bought it from a guy two years ago for three hundred bucks. Once he took off the wheels and wedged it up on cement blocks, the place was home.

Elias knocked twice on the holey screen door.

Harold opened the inner metal door. The smell of beer and heavy sweat seeped out from the fourteen-by-nine-foot space.

The man looked like crap. Strapped to his forehead were huge black goggles. His hair was greasy and slicked straight back. Dark bags stained his under-eyes, and the whites were bloodshot like a road map. His skin was much paler than usual.

"Harold, come out here. I want to talk to you."

"Did my brother call you over? Did he say I'm crazy and I'm seeing ghosts?" Harold's eyes twitched before looking away. He stepped out of the trailer and headed to a small cooler full of beer. He grabbed one and headed back inside.

"When was the last time you slept?" Elias asked, standing just outside of the entrance.

"It's none of your damn business, Chief," Harold spat out and closed the door.

"Harold!" Elias shouldered the door to keep it from slamming on his face. "Get your ass out here before I drag you out. And if you use that bottle on me, I swear on my mother, it will go right up your ass."

Harold flung back the door and growled. "Fine."

Elias took a seat at Harold's dingy white plastic table and chairs set. "What's going on with you?"

"Nothing," Harold yelled. He sounded more tired than gruff. "Why can't everyone just leave me alone?"

Elias's inclination was to headlock him and slap some sense into the dope, but he didn't. "What if your brother did call me. He's worried, and so am I," he said in earnest.

Harold stepped down from his cement block step and took the seat closest to the door. "What do you want?" He twisted the cap off the warm beer and chugged half of it down.

"You're sleepwalking again. Raymond said it's gotten worse to the point that Sara's worried."

"I know." Harold used his not-so-white T-shirt to wipe his nose. "Eli—this is fucking crazy—but I don't remember." He finished the beer and tossed it in the small white garbage can next to the door.

"Why did you buy night vision goggles?"

"It doesn't matter anymore." He looked at Elias with welled up eyes. He took out a cigarette and lit it. "I see her with or without those damned things."

Damn. Elias took the wafting smoke into his lungs before the gravity of what his friend said hit him. "Who's *she*?" He shifted his seat away from the trailing smoke. *Concentrate.*

"The girl Jane Doe sees," Harold whispered.

"What?"

Harold ripped the goggles off his head and dropped them on the table. "I tried to tell you that night at the hospital." He was pulling at his thinning blonde hair. "But it came out all wrong. I'm not fucking crazy, Eli. I really do see her." He took in big drags of the cigarette, almost finishing it to the quick, then flinging it into the scorched-out fire pit.

"Explain." Elias leaned back and listened. Even if his friend sounded nuts, he would keep an open mind. With everything Jane had been through, anything was possible.

With a shaky hand, Harold took out another cigarette and lit it. "That first night, after finding Jane, I drank until I got shit-faced. I wanted to get her beat-up face out of my head. I thought I was drunk to the point that I was seeing things." He took a drag, shook his head and blew out a cloudy breath. "The girl was laughing, then smiling, and then she was... Covered in blood. And some—something dark green." Harold gagged. He fell forward and dry heaved.

"Take deep breaths," Elias offered as he studied his friend.

"I'm good," Harold said, wiping his mouth on the same sleeve as he'd used for his nose. "Almost every night these past few weeks, I keep seeing this girl calling me for help. She tells me to help Christine. Who's she— who the fuck knows," he cried out and collapsed back into the chair. Harold dragged his cigarette down a third of the way before exhaling.

"Who's Christine?" Elias asked.

"Beats the hell out of me. In the beginning, the girl told me to help Jane. Now it's Christine. That girl can't make up her fucking mind."

Elias wanted to be sure it was the same girl Jane had seen, and not his friend losing his mind. "Harold, what does the girl look like?"

"She has long blonde hair and bright blue eyes—sometimes. She wears a yellow dress. Sometimes she..." he trailed off and shuddered.

"What's wrong?"

Harold looked like an addict going through withdrawal. He kept shaking.

"Sometimes she comes all melted, slimy, almost like in a horror movie. You know I hate horror films. Face all mangled, no eyes and her dress is green, like dark mold or something. I can smell the rot. It scares the shit out of me."

"What's with the night vision glasses?" Elias picked up the goggles and studied them.

"She told me to get them. I needed to see clearly, she said." He paused as though he was in a trance, took another long drag of his cigarette and then continued. "You know she told me the night before last I had to leave and drive down Route 41. She told me to leave my headlights off and use the goggles to see. But I didn't want to listen to her."

"You didn't?"

"No. But I woke up in the ditch a mile and half past Miller's Farm on Route 41. The goggles were on my head and I had no fucking shoes on. Again! Did you know I had to walk all—"

"Harold, what did you see?" Elias's heart thrashed against his ribcage.

"I was laying there when I heard a car pass by. I tried to get up but I kept slipping back down into the ditch. When I finally crawled out, I saw an older Impala pull up to a woman. She must have been thumbing it, not sure, but she got in." He took the last small drag and flicked it.

The hairs on the back of Elias's neck stood on end. A chill had gone through him when Harold had said "woman." "Did you catch the license plate?"

"Actually, I didn't see any," Harold said while scratching his head.

"Do you know what the female hitchhiker looked like?" Elias's voice turned stern.

Harold swallowed hard. "I need a drink." He got up.

Elias grabbed his arm. "Harold, listen to me. Look at me. I need to know what she looked like and what she was wearing."

"I couldn't see her face. Damn, man, let go of me," he hissed, jerking his arm out of Elias's grip. "It was too dark, even for the night goggles. But I remember she had one of those hippy purses with strings, you know the type with crap hanging off of it. She had long hair and, that's it."

"Nothing else?"

"It was pitch-black outside. Oh wait, she had on big ass shoes—the ones with fat heels. Maybe it's boots."

"Boots?" Elias asked.

"You know the ones that Sara wore at Halloween last year. The sexy black ones."

Elias became numb. "Platforms." Damn. It had to be the same woman who lay dead in the morgue.

"Yeah, those." Harold got a beer and drank it down fast. "Eli, what does this have to do with my sleep-walking?"

"Did you see the driver of the car?"

"No. The driver never got out of the car."

The bastard got a witness to his crime. "Harold, I need you to stay here. I don't want you to leave at all. Promise me." Elias got up and stared down at his friend.

"Why not? What if the girl shows again?"

"Ignore her."

Elias ignored Harold's protest, and headed back toward Raymond's house. A few minutes later, Elias returned with Raymond on his heels.

"I'm not going into the fucking loony bin. You both can go kiss my ass!" Harold rushed into his trailer.

"Harold, you're not crazy," Elias called out. "I believe you about everything."

The door swung open, and Harold stood there with tear tracks down his cheeks. "Really? And I thought I was going crazy, like Daddy. Right, Raymond?" He came out and faced the two men.

"I told you, numb nuts. We're not like him." Raymond wrapped his arm around Harold's neck and knuckled his head. "You need to listen to me."

Elias broke off the brotherly gesture. "I want you to stay with your brother, Harold. I don't want you to leave the house, no matter what. I don't want you to say a single word to anyone about what you told me. Do you understand? Your life and Jane's depend on it."

"Okay." Harold shrugged.

"Harold, he means it. You have to keep your mouth shut," Raymond growled out.

"I'm not deaf, dumb ass," Harold countered. "I won't say anything. I promise, Eli."

Elias grabbed Raymond off to the side and talked to him in a low voice. "You have to keep him from sleep-walking out of your house. Don't let him out of your sight."

Raymond nodded in silence.

With assurance from his friend, Elias strode back to his truck. He took off toward the old chief's place at the edge of the county.

Trepidation swirled in his gut. Getting caught was

the last thing he wanted, but if he found evidence, Elias would have to lie about where he found it. It was the only way to keep his badge.

Surrounded by acres of farmland, Elias spotted the white rusty mailbox at the end of the driveway leading to Henley's place. He pulled up to the dark blue two-story farmhouse and parked in the back.

He kept the vehicle idling and waited. No one had followed him. *Never be too cautious when it comes to murder.*

Elias got out of the truck and carefully took a good look around. It was a bit strange that all the drapes were closed except for one upstairs.

After checking the front door, which was locked, Elias made his way to the screened-in back porch. He hesitated at the bottom steps, knowing he was taking a great risk on only a hunch. But if Henley left clues or evidence about the killer or killers, then that was the break he needed for Jane's case.

Then again, if Elias's assumptions were wrong and he was found breaking in, he would lose his badge and any future in law enforcement was over. Jail might be his next residence.

It doesn't matter. He was doing this for Jane and that's what mattered.

The house was locked up tight, but Henley used to complain about how he had to get his back door fixed.

He jimmied the handle until it came off in two pieces and pushed the lock out.

"Two to five for this." He placed the rusty pieces on the cement step.

It was dark inside and a faint moldy odor lingered along the doorway. It burned his nostrils as he inhaled.

He grabbed for the flashlight on his belt and remembered he'd left it on the seat. Elias went back to the truck to get the light. He happened to look up and thought he saw someone standing in the upstairs window. A chill zipped down his spine, but it didn't stop him from proceeding inside. If it was a sign, then let it show him the way.

As he entered what looked like a mudroom, he called out in a whisper, "Okay, I'm here." He felt ridiculous saying it out loud. Though he had to try.

The back room was connected to a small, all-white kitchen. A faint smell of bleach lingered in the air. He poked his head into the baby blue tiled bathroom and found nothing but a clean room. Not even a toilet paper roll hung in the roll holder.

Elias stepped into the sparsely furnished living room. An odor of mildew, rot and pipe smoke filled his nose. The crime scene tape was still across the front door. The white chalk lines on the green corduroy lazy boy chair Henley had sat in when he shot himself had faded. Blood splatters and brain matter still stained the dingy gray wall behind it. Buckshot holes marked the drywall where he blew out the back of his head.

An old cabinet style television sat adjacent to the chair. The man sure didn't like change.

Wired bunny-eared antennae sat on top of a TV tray next to the chair. No photos of family or artwork adorned the walls.

There were two small bookcases that anchored each side of the small room. They were filled with books about police procedures and crime scene investigations from various states. *But where are the hunting magazines?* He expected a pile of them, just like at the station. Maybe he had them somewhere else.

Elias headed down into the basement. Everybody stored crap down there. But all he found was a furnace and hot water tank, and nothing else. Not even a box. The entire lower level looked like it was wiped clean. One could eat off the cement floor. It was too sterile— too neat for his liking. He couldn't remember exactly what the place looked like the day Henley killed himself. But he didn't remember it being quite like this.

He headed back upstairs and continued up to the second floor. Each step creaked with his weight. As he reached the top of the landing, he watched the farthest room door open on its own. It made no sound, but he knew something, or someone was telling him to check there.

After he unsnapped his gun, Elias proceeded down the hall. He checked each room along the way; they were all empty. When he reached the doorway at the end of the hall, he realized it was the room with the open curtains.

Elias stuck his head in and quickly looked around. Clean and sparse. Go figure.

There was a full-size bed, made up in a tight orderly fashion that any soldier would be proud of, and a single tall dresser. And clean white walls. That was it.

He opened every drawer and found only clothes, piled neat and tidy order. Elias went as far as checking for false bottoms, but there was nothing.

Only one place left to check. The closet. As he slowly opened the slim door, something inside shifted and caught him off guard. He jacked his gun from his holster and aimed, then whipped the door wide open and jumped back. His heart pounded against his ribcage. Whatever moved had scared the hell out of him.

As he took a cautious step forward, nothing but clothes stood before him.

"Shake it off." Elias put his gun back into his holster

and closed the door. As he turned away, the closet the door flung open so hard, the small doorknob was imbedded into the drywall.

In a flash, Elias had his gun back in his hand, aimed right at the closet. "What the fuck?"

Silence once again filled the space. Elias listened, hoping to hear something. A muted clank reverberated from the closet, then something metal hit the floor.

There were metal hangers, but they didn't move and weren't heavy enough to create the sound he heard.

He took a watchful step toward the closet but kept his gun pointed and ready. Elias reached up and pulled on the white cotton string that connected to the fluorescent light above the small space. It blinked on.

Elias split the clothes hangers in half. He checked the floor and found nothing. He put his gun away and eased his breathing. Shaking his head, he called himself an idiot. There was nothing there.

As he clicked the light off, he heard the faint sound of a woman's cry. Frozen in place, Elias leaned into the closet and listened. The crying came from behind the wall.

Elias gulped down his dread and proceeded to yank the clothes out of the space. Henley had been dead for nearly six months—no one should be in the house.

After pulling every single thing out, Elias noticed a tiny latch to the very right on the back wall of the closet. He slid the bolt and the door slowly swung open. The woman's whimper stopped instantly.

The heavy stench coming from the dark room made him gag. It smelled of death and decay. Flies flew out of the doorway, and Elias swatted them away from his face.

Fragmented rays of light filtered through the eave vents but it wasn't enough for Elias to see clearly. His gut told him to call for backup and wait. But damn it, what if someone was alive inside? No. Not with that noxious smell.

He drew his flashlight out, but for some reason it wasn't working. He slipped it back into his belt.

There had to be a light switch somewhere. Elias reached inside the doorway and felt around the frame until his fingers brushed across a light switch.

With a flip of the switch, a one-bulb light turned on. It hung in the center of the attic room, barely illuminating a long, but narrow area.

The stench was too much for Elias to bear. He went back into the bedroom and looked for something to cover his face. Grabbing one of Henley's shirts, he covered his mouth and nose and tied it behind his head. Once secured, and his gun ready, he stepped inside the dark space.

The smell hit him harder as he got closer to the middle. Elias ignored his stomach's protest and continued to look around. Even his eyes were watering from the smell. As he reached the single bulb, his flashlight turned on.

Elias directed the strong beam around him. There was a makeshift bed at the far wall, with chains strapped around the four posts. The small links had leather-spiked straps attached to them. A neck manacle and ball gag were left on the pillow.

With each step he took closer to the torture device, the pressure in his head began to build.

In the far left corner were three slender shelving units filled with items. Clothes and shoes, purses and wallets, and even jewelry were situated neatly in rows. Elias picked up a wallet and opened it. He was drawn to it because it lacked dust, compared to the rest of the items on the shelves.

Jolie Lynn Bird. Damn. This wallet belonged to the girl who went missing in Waldon County six months ago. He started looking through the other wallets. Different states, different counties—all women, young, and most likely missing.

Elias couldn't fathom what he was staring at. He had only known the man for a few years, but he never imagined Henley was a sick and twisted pervert.

He turned his light beam to the chains that hung from the ceiling. Hooks of various sizes dangled at the end of them. It made Elias ill when he noticed there was dried blood on the tips.

A small table to the right of the bed had various utensils that must have been used for cutting and slicing. There was a vaginal spreader—what a gynecologist would use, and a long corkscrewed nail. He didn't want to know what Henley did with that.

There were shriveled up pieces of skin on a small platter and what looked like dried pebbles sat in a small bowl. With another gag, Elias could only imagine those were nipples.

Vomit rose quickly. Elias's stomach protested. He couldn't hold it in any longer. He bowed over and threw up. As he wiped away the remnants of the bile from his mouth, he noticed a cage, big enough for a large dog, in the right corner of the room.

He stepped closer and noticed something crammed in the corner. The nearer he got, the sicker he felt, and tears streamed down his face.

The fly activity intensified as he approached the cage. The flashlight beam fixed on a blackened pile and the form inside it came into focus.

"Oh, Jesus," he hissed, and shot out of the room before the vomit rose up again.

Elias ran into the bathroom and threw up in the sink.

He cleared the acrid taste from the back of his throat with water and spat it out.

"Sick bastard." He pounded the sink with his palm. Elias knew what—or who was in the cage. Jolie Lynn Bird. He recognized her face from the image on the file he had received.

That was no way for anyone to die. She was curled up naked, like a caged animal. From the look of the decay, she had been dead for a while. As sick as it sounded, why didn't Henley dispose of the body before he killed himself?

And why eat the bullet? Elias didn't get it. The man had it good. There was no reason why he would kill himself. Unless... He *didn't* kill himself.

As Elias made his way outside, Jane filled his mind and took away the image of the dead woman. He envisioned her curled up in his bed with a smile that melted his heart. Elias desperately wanted to be there, holding her tight, making love to her for one last time before State took her away.

But right now, he had to worry about the body inside and the other killer. Everything Henley hid confirmed that he was one of two killers. But who was the other?

He cleared his throat with a loud cough and was about to dial State headquarters when his cell phone rang.

"Hey, where are you at?" Tom answered.

"I'm heading home for a second. What's up?"

"State called. They will be here first thing in the morning."

Elias blew out a breath. "Fine."

"Eli, what's going on?" Tom asked. "You sound out of breath."

"Nothing. I'll explain later. Right now, I have to get home." Elias hung up. But his temples pounded, his throat ached, and his nose still burned from the acrid odor.

One more day to keep what he found in Henley's home quiet. State would take over and Jane would be safe.

CHAPTER THIRTY-FIVE

J ane circled the living room, her pacing anxious. She'd tried to help Magda earlier in the basement, but she was too riled up to sort out boxes of clothes.

She wished Elias would get home and talk to her. Then she could yell at him and she'd feel better.

Her jaw hurt from grinding her teeth together. She wanted to throw something—at his head. Why didn't he tell her about the new victim? Shouldn't she be privy to that information? With the state police stepping in, Jane probably wouldn't see him again. She dreaded that the most.

Since moping wasn't doing her any good, and she was a bit stir crazy, Jane headed back downstairs.

As Jane stood at the edge of the basement doorway, a sudden wave of dizziness overcame her. She grabbed onto the door trim to steady herself, but stumbled against a small round table, knocking a tiny ballerina figurine and a picture frame of Elias and his mother onto the floor.

Jane twisted, her back to the wall, before she slid

down to the floor. Her body became dead weight. She tried to move but her limbs weren't responding. She lay there, still, eyes closed, trying to ward off the helplessness. Calling for Magda was impossible; her mouth was unresponsive.

Suddenly, she dropped into a nightmare. Someone yanked at her hair. The pain across her scalp was excruciating. Jane was being jerked down the stairs. Her spine connected to every sharp edge of the wooden steps. She tried to scream but her tongue was fat and numb. The torture her body was enduring was too much.

Jane tried to push away the evil tendrils choking her, but the darkness infiltrated—it swallowed her up. The dark, wet stench of death hit her nose hard. Sounds of women crying penetrated her ears. They were familiar and scary.

Jane knew this was another vision.

"Jane!" Pain lanced across her cheek.

The heaviness of her arms lightened and the cold that webbed her skin had dissipated. Jane blinked, and the blurry haze fogging her vision cleared.

"Oh, my dear." Magda's voice shook as she hovered over Jane. "Can you hear me?" The nurse's eyebrows creased into a deep V as she touched Jane's forehead.

Fear gripped Jane by the neck, and she wished Elias was there to hold her. But he wasn't and she had to get used to that.

Jane attempted to get up but her legs crumbled and she landed back on the floor.

"I remember something." Her throat was scratchy—parched, which made her cough.

"Hold on. Let's get you to the couch." Magda tried to lift her up but struggled. "Jane, you have to help me."

As Magda leaned down, Jane pushed against the wall

for stability. She was able to get on her feet and stumble to the couch.

"Magda, I think I remember what happened to me." Jane sat on the sofa.

"Did you see the person's face?" Magda asked as she covered her with the blanket.

Jane shook her head. "I remember it being very dark. It was hard to see anything. The smell was so putrid I couldn't breathe. Magda, I tried to escape but he caught me, and that was when he did this to me." Jane touched the back of her head. She ran her fingers along the ridge of her scar. "The rest was bits and pieces."

"I'm calling Elias. He needs to know this."

"Don't call him. He's not in charge anymore, remember?" Jane spat out, but was instantly contrite. "I'm sorry. I know we need to tell him but there is something I need to do first." Jane wiped away her tears with the tissue Magda gave her and continued. "I need your help, Magda."

"What's more important than your memory?"

"The girl."

The old woman shook her head no. "Jane, I know you want to help her move on but right now you have to help yourself. You have a killer after you."

"I am helping myself. I know she's the key or at least a connection to my case. We need to know who she is," Jane said earnestly. "She won't let me rest or move on until I find out who she is and what happened to her."

"We don't know anything about her—and why didn't you ask me about her earlier?"

"I guess... I thought I had more time. It doesn't matter now. The girl's first name is—was Jane. I know she was a local, or I think she was." Jane moved to the edge of the couch and pleaded with her. "Can we at least check out old newspaper articles at the library or even call a local who might have a good memory of those events?"

Magda sat down next to her. "I don't know about this, Jane."

"Please, Magda?"

Magda's brows knit together. Jane bit her lower lip and smiled when the nurse slowly nodded yes.

"Okay. Now I need coffee. Want some?" As Jane got up, she became lightheaded and sat back down.

"You sit. I'll make the coffee." Magda got the pot brewing, then she went straight to the phone.

"You're not calling Elias, are you?" Jane called out from the living room.

"No. But you gave me an idea of who to call," she said while she dialed a number.

Jane stood up, took a solid breath and made her way to Magda.

"Hi Francine. This is Magda Burstone. Yes, it has been a long time. ...Yes, that sounds fine. ...How about lunch next Tuesday? ...Great. ...Francine, you've been living around these parts for a long time. ...Seventy years? ...Good. ...Would you happen to remember a girl gone missing around these parts. ...Hmm, about thirty or more years ago?"

Jane was chewing on her bottom lip. The long pauses were killing her. She wanted Magda to get off the phone and tell her what this Francine was saying.

"Oh, thank you, Francine. Call me on my cell phone if you get anything." Magda hung up and looked back at Jane with a small smile. "She might have something, but she isn't sure. She'll give us a call back."

"Who's Francine?"

"Francine has worked at the Beaver Ridge Library for about fifty-five years now. If anyone knows who or what went missing in this area, she will."

"Did she recall anything when you asked her?"

"She said she remembers there was a case where an out-of-town family came to visit relatives for the summer and their daughter went missing. She couldn't recall the name, but several county sheriffs and police officers from nearby towns came and helped. They formed search parties, though they never found her."

"Do you think it might be the same girl?" Jane's stomach twisted and her temples pinched in pain.

"I don't know. But right now, you need your rest. When the police come, you'll be moved to a different location and I..."

Jane sobered. "I don't want to leave, Magda."

"Honey, I know, but it will be for the best. They can protect you better than Elias can. Right now, let's worry about getting some rest."

To be reminded that she might not see Elias for a long while made her want to cry. Maybe it was better that their short-lived love affair stopped when it did. It probably saved her any heartache in the future. They were both broken, and maybe they weren't meant to be together.

"I'm fine. My head hurts. I'll take a couple of Tylenols and I'll be good." Jane filled her cup.

"If the pain is that bad, I have those Demerol pills Dr. Rollins prescribed. Why not take a half of one? It will help ease the ache."

Jane shook her head. "They make me have nightmares. I won't take them again."

"Ok. Maybe you should—" Magda's cell phone rang. She rushed over and answered. "It's Francine."

After a brief exchange of words, Magda stayed quiet a good portion of the time, listening while she paced the kitchen. She wasn't getting off the phone fast enough for Jane.

It was a good ten minutes' wait, during which time Jane wanted to pull out her hair. Instead, she sat down at the table and focused on her empty coffee cup.

Once Magda said her goodbyes, Jane rushed to her side like an impatient child.

"Francine found a newspaper article that showed a picture of a girl in a yellow sundress. It was the same dress she went missing in that day. Her name was Jane Marie Proster and she was thirteen and a half years old. She and her family came up from Chicago to visit relatives for the week. She went missing a few days after they arrived. From what Francine says, they never found her body." Magda took another sip. "Is it her?"

"I'm almost positive. Did she say how she'd gone missing?"

"She went hiking with her cousin on their back property. The boy thought she was right behind him and by the time he realized she wasn't there, he panicked and ran back to the family." Magda wrapped both hands around her cup. "It's odd. If you and your cousin went on a hike, wouldn't you talk to each other the whole time?"

Jane had to agree with her. "Who's her cousin?"

"Francine only said his first name, Franklin."

"Can we get a copy of that article and possibly a picture?" Jane asked while she refilled her cup.

"Francine is doing that now. But you need to calm down. You're all flushed. I don't want you to pass out on me. I'll call Elias and have him pick it up."

"No. I'll tell him," she countered. "He's going to be mad but I don't care."

"Are you sure?" Magda asked.

Jane turned and watched Elias walk in. Her stomach dropped when she saw his deep frown and scolding eyes.

"What will I get mad about?" he asked with his arms folded across his chest.

Jane sat down and focused on the cup in her hand. "Nothing." Staring into his eyes would only make Jane lose her nerve and tell him the truth.

His lips thinned. "We need to talk," he insisted as he took the chair.

"Just say it." Jane gripped the cup tighter.

"Got a call from State. They will be here tomorrow."

"All right. Jane will be ready as soon as they arrive," Magda said. "What else is there?"

Elias paused. "And... I think there were two killers involved in these cases."

"What do you mean there were two?" Jane's voice was strained.

"I found further evidence that links old cases to yours."

"You know who they are, or were?" Magda asked. Jane reached out and touched the old woman's wringing hands.

"I know Henley's death wasn't an accident," he said with conviction.

"How? Elias, I'm confused. What does Henley have to do with Jane's case?" Magda's voice broke up.

"Who's Henley?" Jane swallowed hard. No one answered her. She wanted to fall apart right there as she listened to them talk about the case as though she wasn't there. She yearned for Elias to hold her. Instead, she got up from her seat and paced the kitchen.

"This might be hard to believe, but I found proof that Henley was one of the killers."

"What kind of proof?" Magda shook her head. "No way. He was a good man."

"Who's Henley?" Jane shouted. Both looked at her wide-eyed. "I'm sorry. I didn't mean to yell."

"He was the old chief of police," Elias explained.

"So he killed all those women?" Jane asked.

"Most of them." Elias paused for a moment. "I went to Henley's house and found a section of the attic where he had been torturing women. I found a decaying body inside it. I think it's the girl that went missing six months ago from Waldon. He must have put her there right before he was murdered."

Jane pressed her hands to her mouth and tried to control her tears. Pain wrenched her chest with every breath. The thought of some poor woman wasting away without anyone to help her made her sick.

An image formed in her head of a dead mutilated woman locked in a cage. Jane couldn't handle listening any longer. She needed air to clear her pain away. "I can't do this anymore." Jane raced out of the house.

Elias reached out and grabbed her, but she evaded his arms. "Jane, stop."

She wouldn't listen—couldn't listen to his words.

The cold wind gave her an icy slap, which brought back some of her senses. It felt good for a change to run, to move, to be free from that house.

As Jane rounded the bend toward the front part of the house, Tom pulled up, almost hitting her. Luckily, she saw the vehicle and tried to move out of the way. The edge of the squad car grazed the back of her leg, and made her tumble down to the gravel.

"Jane!" Elias shouted. He ran over to her and checked her legs.

"Holy crap. Elias, did I hit her?" Tom popped out of the squad.

"I'm okay, but my leg is scraped up." Jane flinched when Elias ran his hand over her skin.

Jane looked up and locked eyes on the deputy. For a split second, the world shifted and the day became night. The howl of the wind off the lake seemed more like screeches of crying women warning her to run.

A profound pain coursed through her body. Her head felt split in two. Her skin was sliced open as if the cold hard soil scraped against it like jagged fingernails.

"Jane, talk to me," Elias pleaded.

The sound of Elias's desperation was muffled by the screams of all the victims swirling around her. Trapped in a black hole, the world above her spun faster. Nausea pulled at her stomach.

"He sees you," the little girl whispered, looking down at her.

Jane's fear strangled the air out of her lungs. "Who is he?"

"Look deeper, Jane."

"Where?" Jane shouted. The girl laughed and then vanished.

Elias stood in her place. His green eyes were wide with worry. Jane tried to grab his outstretched hand but the hole got deeper by the second. She called out his name but her voice didn't carry.

As Elias tried to help her, another person walked up next to him. The man's face wasn't clear, but he seemed familiar to Jane.

The man smiled. In that instant, she knew who he was.

He was the one who'd put her in the hole.

CHAPTER THIRTY-SIX

"What the hell is she doing out here?" Tom yelled. He shuffled back a couple of steps.

"She took off on me. Magda," Elias called out while he tried shaking Jane awake. He scooped her up and then cradled her in his arms. He carried her inside the house.

"Why are you here, Tom?" Elias asked over his shoulder as he laid Jane down on the couch. Tom filed closely behind him.

Magda's skin paled as she scrambled to Jane's side. "What happened?"

"Tom hit her with the car and then she passed out."

"I only grazed her leg. But she shot out in front of me," Tom defended.

"Now why are you here, Deputy?" Elias wanted to strangle the man.

"The state police came early. Literally right after you hung up on me. They took over the entire station. And, they want to see you," Tom explained as he studied Jane.

Elias turned and faced his deputy. "I guess this is as

good a time as any. Magda, how is she? Should we take her to the hospital?"

Magda checked Jane's heart rate and breathing. After a few minutes of silence, "Everything sounds good. I'll keep watch on her," Magda said in a shaken voice.

"Okay." Elias touched Jane's cold cheeks. "I'll be back as soon as I can." Elias quickly hugged Magda. "Are you going to be all right?"

Magda nodded without a word and waved him off.

Elias walked out of the house with Tom on his heels.

"Should I stay and keep an eye on them?" Tom asked.

"No. I need you with me." Elias wanted to rip Tom's heart out for almost running over Jane.

"Elias, what *is* going on?" Tom grabbed Elias's arm to stop him from getting in the truck.

He yanked his arm away. Now more than ever, Elias couldn't trust anyone, especially his deputy. If his assumption was true, anyone in the five-county area was a suspect.

Elias opened his driver's door and leaned against it. "Everyone is a suspect, Tom. I went to Henley's house and found a hidden attic behind his closet." Elias swiped his mouth with the back of his hand, looked Tom straight in the eyes and continued. "I also found the decaying body of a woman in a cage. I think he was behind some of the old unsolved murder cases."

Tom took a couple steps back and gave him an incredulous look. "No way. As long as I've known that man, he couldn't harm a fly. I can't believe that."

"Well, you better believe it. I saw the body myself. The smell was horrific. Chains were bolted in the ceiling and floors. There was a bed with blood stains on it." Elias cleared his throat and spit out the lingering scent from his lungs.

"Wait a minute, you said 'some' murders. What do you mean by that?" Tom took another step back.

"I think there is a second killer, a partner of some sort."

"This is too incredible to think about. Are you sure?"

"Henley killed himself before Jane was taken and buried. So yes, I know there is a second killer still out there," Elias said. Since it was only an assumption about how the old chief had died, he kept that bit of information to himself.

"What about your father?"

"He was in Illinois when the incident with Jane happened. He's ruled out."

"How do you know that?"

"When the marshals picked him up, they told me he was spotted on one of the traffic cameras robbing a convenience store in Chicago. In a gray F-150."

"So, he didn't do it."

"As much as that bastard deserves to be punished, no, he has no part in this case."

"We'd better get to the station quick. I'm sure they want to hear about Henley," Tom said smoothly.

"Let's get this over with." Elias slid into his truck and glanced into his rearview mirror. He saw Tom getting into the squad and waited.

Elias wanted Tom to lead, but he wouldn't budge from his spot. So, he took off first out of the gravel drive.

He had Tom's squad in and out of his rearview mirror until he hit the edge of town.

Elias pulled up to the station and noticed plain-clothes policemen standing outside the doors. They stepped forward and met up with him on the sidewalk.

"You must be Chief McAvoy. I'm Detective Holmes

and this is Detective Jansig. State called us in," the tall blonde man addressed him as he flashed his badge.

"FBI? Why are you guys involved?

"State called us in because your case matches with several out-of-state unsolved murders."

"Out-of-state?" Elias echoed while looking around for Tom. "I'm sorry, I thought my deputy was right behind me. One second." Elias radioed Tom. "Deputy Faber, what's your 10-20?"

Tom didn't respond.

"What's your ETA, Deputy?"

A chirp came back. "Here at the light on Wells and Band. I got a flat. I'll be right there."

"10-4. Detectives, let's take this inside." Elias took a quick look down the end of the street, then led the men inside the station. He quickly told them about Henley's house and the body and his suspicions about two killers.

Both detectives were tall, but Holmes had a bulkier build than Jansig. With the three in the small office, there was barely room for one more person.

"Chief McAvoy, let's get down to brass tacks," Holmes said while he adjusted his black-rimmed glasses. "We believe you about the second killer."

"Good." Elias took his seat but kept his coat on.

Jansig took out a small notepad from his pocket and flipped through it. "We've compiled a large number of unsolved murders that have some similarities to your Jane Doe case. But there was no significant connection to conclude that there are two killers. But," he said, holding his finger up, "if there is proof, as you say in Henley's house, then we are able to connect the dots."

"There is clothing, other items and wallets with out-of-state licenses."

Jansig kept his eyes down on his pad of paper and penned everything Elias said.

"I want to go with you to Henley's."

"We will send a team to Henley's home," Holmes interrupted. "Once we get the court order to enter, then we'll see."

"Okay," Elias said. Then he got up and grabbed the pictures and diagram out of his locked drawer. He handed the folder over to Holmes. "Take a look at this."

"Is this the map?" Jansig asked, looking over the images.

"Yes." Elias pointed out where Jane and the latest victim were found. "At first, I thought it was a case Henley was working on. But after I talked to a couple of the officers that led the previous investigations, they confirmed that Henley wasn't a part of nor did he help in the cases.

"Henley's been dead for over six months. He didn't come out of his grave and grab Jane and the last victim. But after finding the woman in the cage, I'm certain Henley was one of the two killers. Whoever is after Jane is still out there."

"Jane. Meaning Jane Doe."

"Yes."

"Where is she now?"

"My place—and before you say anything else, I thought it was the safest place to hide her," he defended.

"I get it," Holmes said.

"Where did you find these?" Jansig asked while he studied the pictures.

"They were mixed in with magazines Henley had stacked up."

Jansig looked up from the photos. "How well did you know Henley?"

"I worked with the man for almost three years before his death. But he wasn't a friendly sort. Kept to his office when he was in."

"What are the numbers on the back of the pictures? Are these dates?" Holmes shuffled from picture to picture.

"I thought the same thing until I talked to the officers who ran the cases. The dates the victims were found were later. My assumption is that Henley had these photos as mementos of the victims." Elias kept watch for the door.

"Some of those victims had their nipples removed," Holmes admitted.

"I'm almost positive that the missing nipples were Henley's handiwork," Elias cleared his throat.

Both officers gave him a raised brow.

"Next to the bed in the attic was a bowl with dried looking pellets. I assume they are the nipples," Elias said. "Some may match the victim in the cage."

Jansig, who seemed to be paying attention only to the map, finally looked up. "I think you might be right, Chief. Did you realize that on this map, with all the marked places, only Beaver Ridge was untouched?" Jansig said while counting the dots. "Except for Jane Doe. I have a feeling that there are more bodies out there than this map shows."

"How do you know?" Elias asked.

"It's my job to know," Jansig replied, then handed the map to Holmes.

Elias didn't appreciate the detective's aphoristic attitude, but kept his opinion to himself.

"We need to talk to the surviving victim," Holmes stated as he tucked the map and the pictures back into the folder. "She is vital to this case."

"I'll take you to Jane."

"No. We will send one of ours. What's the address?"

"13549 Union Road. I'll have to call Magda to let her know you are coming."

"Who's Magda?" Jansig asked.

"A nurse that's taking care of Jane."

"Fine." Holmes took his cell phone out of his jacket pocket.

"Wait, I have another witness. It's not much but he saw the killer pick up a woman who resembled the latest victim."

"Is he with the Jane Doe?"

"No. He's at another location," Elias said. "44891 Route 50, off the US 41."

Holmes pushed back his glasses. "Okay, I'll have someone get him too."

"Is your deputy always this insubordinate?" Jansig asked, turning the topic to Tom.

"This is the first time." He clicked his radio on. "Deputy Faber, please respond."

"What?" Tom answered quickly.

"What's your location?"

"I just finished putting my tire back in the trunk and will be heading in."

"No. Head to the Kantors. The agents want to talk to the brothers."

There was a bit of silence before Tom answered, "10-4."

Elias stared at the two detectives, waiting.

Holmes's brow furrowed tight. "Is it wise to send the deputy?"

"It should be fine."

"Then I suggest we go get Jane Doe," Jansig said.

"I'll give them a call, so they can get ready." Elias dialed the house number.

The phone kept ringing. The old answering machine didn't pick up. Elias hung up and immediately dialed Magda's cell. It went right to voice mail. Fear spiked him hard. It stabbed at his chest as he tried the house line again. "Pick up, damn it."

"Not answering?" Jansig asked

"No. I'm heading out. Cindy Lee, radio Tyson and tell him to get to the Kantor's house and help Tom."

All three men rushed out of the station to their cars. As Elias got into his truck, Holmes slipped into the passenger side.

"Jansig will follow in our vehicle," Holmes said as he strapped on the seat belt.

Elias put the truck into reverse, skidded back and then slammed the gear into drive. He raced to the house as fast as he could.

CHAPTER THIRTY-SEVEN

J ane paced the living room, trying to sort out some of the memories bombarding her. She wished Elias was there to help. He calmed her, inside and out.

A click and a slight squeak caught her attention. She turned to see what it was. Tom stood at the front door. Her heart slammed against her chest as he took a step in.

"Shhhh." He put his finger to his lips.

Her pulse ramped up as blood hammered in her ears. She wasn't sure what to do.

"Hello, Christina," Tom whispered.

What the...

He took another step.

Jane tried to move but her legs were useless. She tried to scream, but Tom rushed forward and clamped his hand over her mouth. Jane bit his knuckle and broke free from his iron grip but he punched her head. The world spun out of focus and turned black.

*   *   *

Jane wasn't sure how long she laid in the living room. But her vision was blurry. She tried sitting up but her hands were bound behind her back and her ankles were tied together. Tom had duct taped her mouth, so yelling was out.

"Shhhh. She can't hear you anymore." Tom bent over and proceeded to drag her out of the house by her feet.

The cement steps bit into her skin, knocking the wind out of her. The gravel driveway grated along her spine through her T-shirt. Jane tightened her muscles to bear the pain, but it didn't help. She tried to fight back but Tom was too strong.

She used both legs to kick at him, but Tom swiveled and landed a punch to her stomach. The air escaped her lungs and pain radiated from everywhere.

Tom picked her up like a rag doll and threw her over his shoulder. He carried her over to a brown car and tossed her in the open trunk.

When Jane quickly looked up at Tom's smiling face, he slammed the lid down. The smell of oil and rust sparked an image. She pictured herself leaning into the trunk of a car. This car.

Jane couldn't catch her breath. Tears kept coming. Her nose filled and it became hard to breathe. She tried little by little to open her mouth, but the tape was too sticky and her tongue was too dry to moisten the edges.

She had to move—do something other than wait to die. Jane shifted her connected wrists, but he'd wrapped the duct tape around them so tight she was losing circulation in her hands. Though, this was nothing compared to what that bastard would do to her.

With the stretch of her arms, she shimmied her tied hands under her butt and finally around her legs.

Jane gently pulled the tape off her mouth and breathed in a deep breath.

There was no time to relax. She reached out and felt around for something to use as a weapon. Her fingertips scraped along the spare tire. Extending her hands further around, the twisted tape bit into her already tender skin. She needed to unravel it, and began using her mouth to remove the bindings.

The engine raced, but the car had stopped moving. Jane froze and waited. *What was he doing?*

The car bounced and lurched forward, which jostled her. She raised her head to listen. And without warning, the trunk swung open and Tom stood there with a shovel in his hand.

CHAPTER THIRTY-EIGHT

E lias pulled up in the front of the house and saw the front door partially opened. He looked over at Holmes. "No one ever uses the front door."

He and the two agents split up. Jansig headed toward the barn and Holmes made his way to the back kitchen door while Elias was ordered to stay and watch the front. Panic and fear for both Magda and Jane swirled in his gut. There was no way he was staying put.

Gun drawn, Elias walked through the front door and stepped into the living room. He found nothing out of place as he circled the room. As he stood in the threshold of the kitchen, Holmes walked in.

The agent lowered his gun. "Really?"

Elias gave him a smirk. "I'm heading down to the basement."

He walked toward the open doorway and stepped to the edge of the stairs. The light switch to the left wasn't working. Elias grabbed his flashlight and turned it on. With his gun still drawn, he descended toward the dark space.

Halfway down, the pounding of multiple footsteps

above alerted Elias that the agents were heading upstairs to the second floor.

Once Elias reached the bottom, he made his way to the string hanging from the ceiling. He pulled it and the small area filled with a soft glow. The light cast an eerie hue off the cement; shadows played off boxes and old furniture.

A soft banging caught his attention. The sound echoed from behind the water heater.

Elias listened closely. The banging turned into a whimper. His gut tightened and gnarled up. Someone was down here.

As he cautiously walked to the furnace, the crunch of glass under his feet made him stop. The second light overhead was smashed. Elias pointed his flashlight down and confirmed his suspicions. The bulb was shattered.

Another bang sounded and Elias pointed the slim beam right behind the old water tank.

Magda. Her hands and feet were bound with duct tape and her head was covered in a black fabric bag. Elias knew it was her, because of her small stature.

"Holmes! Jansig!" Elias hollered for the agents and then bent over and carefully pulled the bag off her head. "I'm here, Magda. Where's Jane?"

The same silver tape covered her mouth. Time wasn't on Elias's side and he ripped the tape off quickly. "Sorry. Magda, where's Jane?" he repeated.

"Elias," she coughed, "He took her." She tried to catch her breath.

"Who?" Elias pressed as he cut the tape from her hands and feet. "Who took her?"

"I don't know who, I didn't see his face. He caught me from behind while I was on the phone. But, when he threw me down here, I thought I heard something metallic drop." She rubbed at her arm and then her head.

"Where?" Holmes came up behind Elias.

"Who's that?" she whispered as she tried to take the rest of the tape off her wrists.

"Agent Holmes. He's from the FBI," Elias explained. "Now where did you hear the metal sound?"

"It has to be close by. Maybe, right around me and the water heater," she said, shaking.

"Chief, get her upstairs," Holmes ordered. "I'll look around."

Elias carefully picked Magda up with care and carried her upstairs to the living room couch. He then radioed for an ambulance.

"I don't need a—ouch, my arm hurts," she declared as Elias checked her cut elbow. "Who's that?" she asked as Jansig walked out from the kitchen.

"This is Agent Jansig—Magda, don't move," he said then turned to the agent. "Holmes is searching for something metal the killer might have dropped."

The detective gave him a nod, then disappeared down the stairs. Elias got a wet towel from the kitchen. He quickly folded it and placed it on her arm. "This should stop the bleeding for a bit. Stay put while I help them downstairs."

"Okay," she breathed.

Elias rushed into the pantry, grabbed a potato and a light bulb. He raced down the stairs and went straight to the electrical box and turned off the power. Right after, he took the potato and plunged it into the socket with the broken bulb, and twisted, capturing the rest of the light bulb. After he pulled the potato out, Elias replaced it with a new bulb.

In a matter of minutes, Elias had the lights back on.

While Holmes searched the area near the water

heater, Jansig poked under the old furniture. Elias checked along the furnace and noticed the evacuation drain cover was open. It must have been kicked off. He knelt down to check inside it. A glint of metal caught his eye under the furnace pipes. Just out of reach. Elias found a thin wooden slat and used it to slide the object out from its hiding place.

He called the agents over as he picked up the metal piece.

The moment his fingers touched the star, Elias knew immediately what it was. "Son of a bitch," he spat out as Jansig took the badge from his hand.

Rage took root, as Elias knew to whom it belonged. What a fool he had been.

"Whose badge is it?" Holmes asked as he shined his small flashlight on it.

"Tom Faber, my deputy," Elias snarled between his teeth. "That bastard got Jane. This whole fucking time, it was him," Elias snapped out, then took the stairs three at a time, with the agents right behind him.

When he got to the main floor, the paramedics were by Magda's side.

"Did you find what made that clanking noise?"

"Yes. A badge. Tom's badge," Elias barked. His mind and body filled with fury.

"Tom's?" Magda looked up. Confusion knitted her brows.

"Tom is the second killer. Tom took Jane and threw you down into the basement."

Magda's mouth dropped open. "That can't be," she said, shaking her head.

"Yes. It's him." Elias walked out of the house and ran to his truck. Just as he reached for the radio, Holmes and his partner reared up behind him, and Jansig got ahold of it first.

"What the hell are you doing?" Elias shouted.

"What were you planning to do? Call Tom and ask where he's at?"

"Damn straight."

"No. You calling Tom will only clue him in that we know he's the killer," Holmes explained. "There has to be a better way to find out where he's at."

One of the paramedics ran over. "Chief. Magda wants a word with you."

Elias rushed over to the ambulance. He touched the woman's hand and offered her a small smile. Inside, he couldn't quell the rage that surged through his body. "Yes, Magda?"

"Jane and I found out who that girl in the yellow dress was. Her name was Jane Proster and she was thir-teen years old. I called Francine at the library and she told me that a girl went missing in July of 1977 and the police never found her body. And Elias... She was Tom's cousin. He was there when she disappeared."

Elias couldn't breathe. His lungs ceased to work. All this time, a person he trusted was the psychopath. How did he miss that? "I don't want you to worry anymore. The agents and I are going to track down Tom and find Jane. You're going to the hospital to get yourself looked at," he said calmly, but inside, everything melted to the core.

"I'm scared for her. I should help," Magda said as she pushed away the paramedic's hand.

"No. I'll get her back. I promise." His oath scorched his tongue. Jane might be already dead and buried, or was being brutalized as he spoke. He shook off the ill thought. What good would he be to her now, if he fell apart. He prayed Jane was okay. This woman had gotten into his heart so fast, and there was no way in heaven or hell he'd lose her.

"But I might know where he took her."

Jansig stepped forward and asked where.

"From what Francine said, the girl had gone missing near Tom's grandfather's place."

"Where? Ma'am, you need to get to the point," Jansig said, slightly abrupt.

Elias glared at the agent. "Back off, Jansig." He turned his focus on Magda. "Go on."

Magda's voice shook slightly when she spoke. "From what Francine said, the property is near Beaver Lake, but not sure how far. That is all I know."

Elias leaned in and kissed the old woman's forehead. "Get her to the hospital," he said to the paramedic and helped push the gurney inside the ambulance.

"Ask her," Magda blurted out. "You've seen her yourself, I know it. Ask her to help you find Jane," Magda called out as he closed the door.

"What was that about?" Jansig asked, scratching his shaved head.

"Nothing pertaining to the case," Elias lied. From the way the agent smirked, telling him about ghosts would have landed him in a padded cell.

Once the emergency vehicle drove away, Elias turned to both agents. "We need to move fast. Tom has nothing to lose at this point and will kill Jane."

Holmes held up a finger as he spoke into his cell phone. Within a minute, he got off the phone. "Our warrant's cleared. The men went into Henley's house and found the victim in the cage. They're searching the rest of the home. There's a crew heading to the lake now, where we should be going. Jansig?"

"You are not losing me that quickly. I'm coming with you," Elias rushed out.

Elias's radio chirped. "Chief, come in."

"What, Tyson?"

"Tom hasn't showed up. Should I wait?"

He forgot about Harold.

Holmes leaned in and said, "Your officer doesn't need to know."

Elias nodded in agreement. "I want you to bring Harold to the station and keep him there. Watch him closely."

"Should I put him in a cell?" Tyson questioned.

"Only if he gets ornery," Elias replied back.

"10-4, Chief."

Elias raked his hand through his hair, and looked at the agents walking away. "I'm coming with you." His heart thrashed against his lungs as reached their side.

"Chief McAvoy. We'll take it from here."

"I can't stand here and wait." His words came out clipped and sharp. "I know this area well, you need me."

Jansig turned and faced Elias with a finger pointed to his chest. "You are going to do nothing. You are out of this, as of right now. If we need you, we'll call." The agent walked away.

Elias knew she'd be dead before they found her. As hokey as it had sounded, he had to try what Magda suggested. He had to somehow reach that little girl. Maybe the ghost knew Jane's whereabouts.

He got into his truck and headed toward Beaver Lake where he might have first seen her.

CHAPTER THIRTY-NINE

J ane woke up to a pitch-black room, pain surging through her head. The back of her skull felt pierced through. Her temples pounded. She had a hard time controlling her ragged breath.

She had no idea where she was.

As her eyes got accustomed to the dark, Jane realized she was chained to the floor, spread-eagle and naked. The cold wet concrete against her skin made her shiver. The metal cuffs around her wrists and ankles were tight and shackled to metal links in the floor. Jane jerked and twisted, but she wasn't able to move. There was little play in the cuff around her neck.

Tears flowed as she tried again to yank herself free before giving up.

The stench of decay and mildew swamped her, a putrid stink filling her nostrils, making her stomach lurch.

Then it hit her.

The smell was all too familiar. Jane knew this place. She'd been here before.

Jane closed her eyes and took a slow inhale, then

exhaled. All at once, all the missing images of her life engulfed her, filling the holes in her memory.

Her name was... Christina Brown. A slight sense of relief rose in her. However, she couldn't wrap herself around that name. *Jane* seemed more suitable. She was a CPA for Lyons Corporation in Madison. Grew up in California and took the job last year. All was good, until...

She gotten lost trying to find an easier route up to Green Bay. A flat tire in the middle of nowhere and a friendly face nearly ended her life.

Jane remembered pulling the tire out of the trunk when a cop car drove up.

Tom's smile had eased her worries immediately. He got out to help. As he'd stepped up behind her, he'd clamped a cloth-covered hand over her mouth and nose. Jane had tried to fight, but he was too strong. She'd woken up on a table, a single light bulb hanging above her.

A frenzied panic had filled her when she spotted glints of silver on the table next to her. Knives. Her instinct to survive took over. She grabbed a small knife off the table and with all the strength she was able to muster, Jane swung out and stabbed the deputy in the shoulder.

Pushing back the severe pain in her body, Jane had raced up the uneven stairs. She'd rammed into the locked screen door, broke through it and flew out of the house. But she wasn't fast enough. The deputy had grabbed her from behind. He yanked her hair and punched her face repeatedly.

She had tried to make a last-ditch effort to escape but something slammed against her skull. Spangled lights lit around her and a deep burn resonated from the back of her head.

Jane had prayed for death that night.

She remembered how she had dug herself out of her grave. The misery, pain, and pure determination she had felt when she punched through the topsoil into the bitter, icy air. She shivered.

The only thing good that had come from this atrocity was Elias. Her desperation to stay alive made her pull again at the cuffs. But it was no use.

Jane swallowed hard at the thought she might never see Elias again, which caused her more agony than thinking about what Tom had planned for her.

Her inner voice screamed to stay strong. She tried to calm her thrashing heart, one breath at a time, but she was losing the battle. Jane closed her eyes and tried to imagine Elias's gentle hands on her skin. His imaginary caress touched her face and stroked down her body. Her heart eased into a calmer rhythm.

Elias made her feel beautiful and loved. Even in a short period of time, his respect and adoration had filled her with needed strength. Jane thought of the way his green eyes bored right through her. She grabbed hold of that picture and held onto it for courage.

She fought against the sharp lash of pain around her wrists while she tried to pull off the cuffs. With every twist and turn, the metal gouged deeper into her skin. As Jane managed to slip her left hand through, a sense of relief filled her, and her determination grew.

Jane examined her wrist. Blood seeped out of the wound. Wet and sticky, she wiped the fluid onto her other wrist, working on freeing her right hand.

Her heartbeat echoed in her ears with every painful twist. Jane had her palm halfway through, when a whimper to her right caught her off guard. She paused and listened.

A soft spotlight flashed on, casting a shadow on the

wall. A towering silhouette. *It can't be the deputy.* The light flipped on and off twice more before it stayed off.

Jane's insides clenched and a large lump formed in her throat. Panic flooded through her as she shut her eyes and waited. A full minute passed as silence filled the dank space.

Another whimper—more like crying—rang through her ears. Jane looked over and studied the shadow on the wall. With a deep breath, she took a chance and whispered, "Hello?" Her voice was barely audible.

A strained moan replied.

"Who are you?" Jane asked a little louder.

There was no response. Jane took a chance and slipped her right wrist an inch out of the cuff. She almost had it. A bit more... She twisted and pulled her palm completely through.

"Are you all right?" Jane asked while she examined her neck strap, hoping to find a clasp. She tried getting up but her head only lifted off the floor a foot. Jane dropped back down.

A woman's voice broken through the silence. "C-Car..."

"Car? Is that your name?" Jane asked. She shifted her head to get a better view of the person, but she only saw part of her.

"T-T-To..." The woman barely got a syllable out when another light flipped on at the far corner. Car whined. Was that fear in her voice?

Heavy footsteps from above made Jane's throat tighten with dread. The woman's desperate cry turned louder as a door squeaked. Her sobs made Jane shudder.

She quickly adjusted the handcuffs to give a wider hole for her hands to slip through with ease and then closed her eyes. *Don't panic.*

Too late.

A wooden plank creaked. Jane's anxiety became full-on terror. The echo of footsteps got louder as they descended down the stairs. *One. Two. Three. Four. Please, God. Five. Six. Seven. Eight.* She swallowed down the fear. *Don't move!*

He might kill her now. Tears streamed down, Jane couldn't help it. *Breathe.*

With each creaky step closer, Car's cries grew louder.

Jane stopped crying and listened. With her head turned away, she was only able to hear the woman's agony.

As quickly as she began, Car stopped crying. A calm before the storm?

Jane's chest burned from her slow, shallow breaths. The sudden need to urinate jabbed at her bladder, but she kept her body still and her eyes closed while she focused on the surrounding sounds.

The soft shuffle of feet on concrete brought a prick-ling fear straight down her spine. The footsteps stopped right by her. She sensed his study of her.

Jane kept reminding herself to keep her eyes shut and her body limp. *Don't react.*

He kicked her leg. She remained still as the dead. It felt like an eternity before Jane heard movement.

"Shhh," Tom said to Car.

Jane relaxed a bit, but her ease was short-lived. Loud slapping assailed her ears. Car screamed out in pain.

Jane bit her tongue and took in the anguish Car was going through.

That bastard kept hitting her until her wails were silenced. Did he knock her out? She hoped so. Or did he beat her to death? Jane's stomach lurched.

Oh God, please let her be alive.

The shuffling got closer again. Jane held her breath. She couldn't hold it for too long and exhaled slowly. A stench of sweat and beer pillowed her face. The warmth of his rancid breath brushed her right cheek. He was very close.

The deputy caressed her gently along her jaw line. Jane cringed inwardly. His fingertips were so light that it tickled her.

His fingers trailed down her neck, along her collarbone and then between her breasts. He stroked down to her belly button and then back up to her face. Jane didn't expect gentleness. His touch made her more uncertain about her survival.

The soft gentle touch changed to a sharp jagged dig along her skin. His fingernail scored her from ear to cheek and dragged across her chin. He scratched down her neck to her left breast. He circled her taut nipple, scraping along her areola. Jane wanted to lash out, punch and kick, and get away from him.

Jane's skin was on fire. She clamped her teeth tight and forced down the pain. If he knew she was awake, would he hit her the same way as Car? Probably.

He pinched her nipple hard. The pain lanced deep, but Jane fought to keep her body from jerking.

The deputy mumbled something. "Wouldn't rush" was the only thing she was able to hear. Rush what? Her death? He released her nipple, snickered and walked off.

Jane cracked open one eye and watched him walk away. He picked up a thin strip of leather off a small table—the same small table she remembered with all the knives. He swung once at Car and rolled the strip around his hand. The man stood there, arms crossed and studied his handiwork. Bastard.

The deputy shook his head and chuckled, which caused a tremor to run through Jane's body. He turned back, dropped the leather, and headed upstairs.

She counted the creaks until he reached the eighth

step. She heard metal scraping along the cement—like nails on a chalkboard. The soft light from the single bulb turned off.

Darkness shrouded her again.

A couple of clicks and that spotlight flashed on. It pointed to where Car was flat against the wall.

Jane didn't dare move to see if Car was okay. She needed to be sure Tom wouldn't come back down. She sucked in a few deep breaths to alleviate some of the pain he'd caused her.

Once Jane felt it was safe enough to move, she freed both hands, then worked on her leather neck manacle. After she stripped off the neckband, Jane sat up and began untying her ankles. She understood immediately why he'd used twine. It burned and dug into her skin every time she moved, but she didn't give up. Once loose, she unraveled it and stood up.

Jane got her footing and carefully walked toward where Car was. She almost let out a gasp but stifled it. The woman was naked and chained in an X fashion, shackled tight from wrists to ankles. She had a dog collar around her neck that seemed too tight against her skin. She had lacerations all over her body. Her beautiful blonde hair was blotched red from her blood. The woman was beaten so badly, Jane gagged.

Jane closed her eyes, took in a deep breath and opened them again. She needed to know if Car was still alive—hoping she was.

As she took a nervous step, Jane paused. Something about the woman was familiar. The more Jane stared at her, the more familiar she looked. *Oh my God, Caroline.* The nurse she'd met in the hospital. She was no longer the tall voluptuous blonde Jane had hated.

She looked like a rag doll, beaten and cut up. Her face was slashed up, bloody, swollen, and black and blue.

Deep welts along her breasts and inner thighs were thick and puckered. They were overlapped with cuts sliced in the opposite direction. Fresh blood dripped down her leg. Guilt seeped in. No one deserved what the deputy had done. Had she looked like that when the hunters found her?

Jane reached up and checked her pulse. It was very weak. "Caroline, can you hear me?" she whispered in her bloody ear.

Caroline lifted her head slightly, exposing her face to the bright light. A calm reflected in the nurse's bloody eyes and then she dropped her chin down to her chest. Tired and weak herself, Jane leaned against the wall. She wasn't sure what to do next.

But one thing was for sure, Jane had to remove the cuffs around Caroline's wrists and ankles and get her off the wall.

She had to find something small to unlock the cuffs, and went over to the table. Luck must have been on her side, because keys to the handcuffs were sitting on the tabletop.

Just after Jane took the dog collar off Caroline's bruised and bloody neck, a chirp echoed off the walls. The loud scratchy sound made her jump out of her skin. She also dropped the keys.

Overhead, there was a small stereo speaker screwed into the low ceiling joist.

The deputy's voice blared out. "It's your turn, Christina. You won't escape me this time. I left that slut on display for you to study and learn. This is what happens to whores. Are you a whore, or are you a good girl? Remember, you're getting what you deserve. And your precious chief will never be able to find you once I'm done. I'll be down there in a little bit to show you."

Jane's throat constricted with each word that bastard

uttered. A clear image of herself in Caroline's place made her drop to the floor. Jane attempted to push the gruesome picture out of her head but with Caroline right there—vomit rose fast. She threw up all over herself.

Jane hugged her knees to her chest, put her head down and rocked in place. What was she going to do? *Where's Elias?*

Trembling out of control, Jane was suddenly shrouded in cold. An icy wind swept past her making her shudder even more. She lifted her head and exhaled a breath—it frosted the air. *Jane.*

"Jane Proster, I can feel you here with me," she whispered.

The metal cuffs on Caroline's wrists and ankles sprang open and she crumbled to the floor.

Jane launched forward and caught Caroline before she hit the cement.

Caroline's dead weight strained against Jane's small frame, but she managed to drag her away from the horrid wall.

"Thank you," Jane whispered. She hoped the girl heard her.

As Jane pulled Caroline to the other end of the basement, a string that hung from the ceiling brushed across her face. Jane pulled on it and a small light turned on. With great comfort, she found a small pile of rags and laid Caroline on them.

Jane brushed back Caroline's hair. One eye was completely swollen shut. Her other eye was staring up at her.

"I'm going to try to get us help, Caroline?" Jane touched her cheek.

Caroline lightly shook her head no. With a shaky hand, she touched a part of her abdomen where the blood seemed fresh. "He st-stabbed me."

There was so much blood on Caroline's body, Jane couldn't see the wound and the low lighting didn't help. She took one of the rags and wiped the blood away. There was a deep laceration just below her belly button. The blood seeped out every time she breathed.

Jane got up and quickly looked around the basement for something to stop the bleeding. She found duct tape on one of the shelves and used it to cover the hole.

"I'm getting us out of here. You need to hold on," Jane said as she put the last strip of tape on Caroline's stomach. She found a small blanket in the pile and covered her.

The blonde grabbed her hand. "Thank you," Caroline said in a strangled whisper.

"You're going to be okay. Elias will find us." Once Jane said the last word, Caroline closed the one eye and dropped her hand from Jane's.

Tears ran down Jane's face. She shook Caroline. "Please, Caroline, open your eyes. You can't die on me." She checked her wrist and found no pulse. "Hold on," she whispered into her ears. "Don't leave me."

But Jane knew it was too late. Caroline was dead. She took the blanket and covered Caroline's face.

Jane wiped away her tears with her forearm. *Can't feel sorry about this.* The only way to survive was to stay strong and be smart. She sucked back her fear and sorrow and took a good look around.

The one light bulb didn't give enough light to see the full basement, but Jane walked around and found nothing to use as a weapon. She looked down at the rags Caroline was lying on and realized they were clothes. Women's clothes.

Jane rummaged through the pile, found a ripped up shirt and slipped it on. The shirt barely did any good.

The hem reached her hips and there were so many holes, but at least she wasn't totally naked.

The floorboards above her began to creak. Jane heart raced faster with every footfall. She needed to get out of there before the deputy came down and pasted her in Caroline's place.

All the windows were boarded up except for the one in the far corner. She took the hanging light and pointed it in that direction. The pane was painted black and the window was very small and above the coal furnace. But Jane was willing to try anything.

Another creak from above made her heart slam against her chest. This was her only chance to escape. She took a few deep breaths before she slid behind the hot furnace.

She flattened herself against the stone foundation. Sharp edges of rock scraped at her exposed abdomen. With only an inch of space between the hot metal and her rear end, Jane felt the heat from the pipes on her skin.

She shifted slightly and accidentally touched the pipe, which made her press harder against the rough wall. A few red blotches wouldn't matter, if she was dead. The pain didn't deter her. She scraped along the wall until she stood right under the window.

She reached up and tugged at the frame. It was old and brittle from termite damage. Her luck. Jane nudged the lock handle up and pushed the window open. The cold fresh air was a welcoming feeling across her face and in her lungs. But there was no time to relax.

After seizing the window with both hands, she had to figure out a way to climb up. She had no choice but to step onto a hot pipe that jutted out of the wall. Jane wished she had wrapped her feet with the rags. Too late to go back. Rags or not, she had to get out of there fast.

She took a few encouraging breaths and stepped onto the pipe. The moment her tender sole touched the metal she wanted to jump off and scream. Jane endured the scorching pain that seared her foot and shot up through her leg.

Her burning flesh fractured her concentration, but she pressed on. After planting her arms on the outside part of the window frame, her legs hovered centimeters over the furnace. Almost there.

Jane used what little upper body strength she had left and wormed her shoulders through the opening. She had to turn partially on her side so her hips could squeeze through the window. Right before she slid her legs through, the deputy grabbed hold of her feet.

With all she had, Jane kicked and twisted, trying to free herself. However, something sharp dug deep into her burned foot. She screamed out in torment as he kept gouging at her sole.

"You're not getting away from me, bitch." Jane heard his rant through her shouts.

She turned on her belly and used her arms as leverage and kicked with all her might. Jane broke free and crawled out the window. When she tried to get up, searing pain shot through her foot, which made her collapse. Looking down at the damage, a small knife stuck out of her foot. Blood quickly pooled when she pulled it out. The bastard had cut open a part of her heel and exposed the bone.

Jane had no time to worry. She had to get up to run, but the second she got up, Jane fell to the ground instantly. Everything spun. The mix of cold and pain made her dizzy. A whisper clung in the wind; it was the girl in the yellow dress, telling her to hang on.

There were shrieks coming from inside the house. Jane attempted to get up again but fell over.

She couldn't run. Her foot was damaged and bleeding terribly. Fighting back was her only choice. Jane got on her knees and with a firm grip of the small knife, she waited for the deputy.

The world spun around her. Jane closed her eyes to help regain her focus.

A hard kick across her middle knocked out her breath. She fell forward, face first onto the ground.

She tried getting up but her body protested. Pain exploded across her face. Jane wasn't sure what hit her; she didn't see it coming.

Her vision faded in and out. Jane's eyes were playing tricks on her. At first, the girl in the yellow dress hovered over her, but then she changed. The deputy stood there naked, with a large knife in his hand.

"Help," Jane called out. Her head swam from one image to the next and back again. Nothing was clear anymore.

She tried to stay awake, but between the blinding pain and cold, Jane knew this was the end and she slipped into the dark.

CHAPTER FORTY

E lias sped to the lake and found state officers marking various areas. He couldn't ask for their help. He had to find Jane on his own. Magda said Tom's grandfather's house was near the lake. With luck he'd find it.

He backed up the truck and headed back toward his house.

His cell phone went off. "Chief McAvoy."

"Hey, Elias, it's Mike."

"Can't talk right now—"

"Wait. I completely bypassed one piece of the evidence you sent me," Mike said quickly.

"Which evidence?"

"Your ripped up card. I put it together but didn't get a chance to check for fingerprints."

"What did you find?"

"I got three fingerprints off it. Yours, Jane Doe and your deputy's."

"Thanks. Please fax your findings to my office right away."

"You're welcome. Sor—"

Elias hung up. He didn't need to hear what he already knew. When he sped back down Route 41, the familiar tightness in his throat caused him to slow down. Tom had played Elias like a fool. He repeatedly hit the steering wheel, blaming himself for not seeing the deputy as he was. A monster.

Throughout this whole ordeal, he'd wanted this damn case solved, the farm sold and his ass back in Half Moon. Now, all he wanted was to have Jane back safe and alive.

When Elias drove around the bend, the girl in the yellow dress appeared on the side of the road. She pointed in the direction opposite his house, east toward Route U. He slowed to see her, but she disappeared. The hairs on the back of his neck stood straight up.

Fear clawed at Elias's composure. He pushed the ill feeling aside, turned around and drove as fast as he could. He decided not to use the lights and siren, since he didn't want to alert Tom.

When he neared Route U, his cell phone went off.

"Chief McAvoy, this is Holmes."

Elias's body turned numb. He didn't want to hear that they had found Jane's body. "What?"

"Jansig found out your deputy has his home off of Route U. Jane Doe must be there."

"What is the address?"

"W6641 Birch Hill Road. Do you know where this property is located?"

He glanced at his watch. "Yes. I'm about five minutes away from there. It's before the Sawyer County boundary," Elias said as he pushed the gas pedal down to the floor.

"We are on our way. And you were correct about the two killers scenario. Your deputy and Chief Henley had worked together for many years. My officers found photos of them with the women they killed. Some of the victims matched the photos you found."

"They fooled everyone," Elias said in disgust.

"Your deputy's house is really clean." Holmes explained. "We are trying to get a court order to exhume Henley's body for DNA samples. We think Tom killed Henley."

"Then why dig him up? If Tom did kill him, justice is served at that end."

"McAvoy, our ETA is fifteen minutes. Don't proceed without us."

"10-4," Elias acknowledged, then hung up. There was no way in hell he was about to wait for them.

The serpentine road curved hard to the right, then left and hard right again. Elias's adrenaline had reached the boiling point. He swerved on to Birch Hill Road and didn't let up on the gas pedal until he pulled into the dirt driveway.

He grabbed the extra gun out from under his seat and tucked it in the back of his jeans. He left the truck door open and made his way along the left side of the driveway, using the tall bayberry bushes as cover.

Gun drawn, Elias made his way up to the house. As he stepped onto the dilapidated porch, he heard screams coming from the back. His heart stopped. *Jane.*

Elias raced around to the rear of the old clapboard house and saw her on the ground. Ashen and bloody. *Oh, hell.* Was she dead?

Tom, shirtless, stood over her with a Bowie knife in one hand and a gun in the other.

Jane moved. She tried getting up but fell back to the ground. Agony etched across her face, until their eyes met. She gave him a small smile. His heart jumped in reaction. *She's alive.* Adrenalin flooded him as he turned his focus back to Tom. Now he wanted the son of a bitch to pay for what he had done.

"Tom!" Elias shouted. His gun aimed dead center at Tom's chest. He wasn't taking any chances; he'd shoot to kill.

Elias held himself steady. "Deputy, I want you to drop that knife and gun," he said loudly.

The long-jagged scars all over Tom's torso gave clues to a horrific life Elias hadn't known about.

"Well, it's about fucking time you showed up, Chief. I barely contained my enthusiasm, having your whore all to myself." Tom grabbed Jane by the neck and pulled her up to his side. He took the barrel of his forty-five and scratched his bloody cheek.

"Drop it, Tom." Elias tried to stay calm.

"Okay. I'll drop my gun." Tom turned and whipped it toward the house. "See? I'm listening. Besides, the gun's empty." He licked the corner of his mouth and grinned.

"Step back from her, Tom. It's between you and me."

The deputy pointed the knife at Jane's neck. "Make me," he said in a low growl, taking the tip and nicking her skin. A small drop of blood seeped out.

"I don't want to shoot you, but I'll kill you where you stand if you mark her again," Elias countered as he took a step closer.

"You better halt your ass right there, Chief." He drew the knife to her jugular, then dragged it down to her chest, slicing open the ragged shirt Jane wore, leaving behind a red line.

With his gun trained on Tom, Elias spoke evenly. "It's too late. The state police know what you and Henley have been doing all these years. Torturing and killing innocent women."

"You have no fucking clue, Chief McAvoy. Chief. Ha! You're not fit for that title. I should have gotten that job. Then none of this bullshit would have happened. I'd be king of the world," he said, waving the knife in the air, then quickly pointing it back at Jane. "Henley was a crotchety old fool. He thought he was God. He thought he was my teacher, but I'm the one who taught him. *I'm* the God." Tom chuckled. "But I got to give him credit. He told the mayor to appoint you before I killed him. I should have done it sooner—then this wouldn't have been an issue."

"Why did you kill him? Was he going to rat you out?"

With his right arm locked around Jane, Tom lowered the knife, the point digging into his leg. "He had no right telling me what I can or cannot do. Henley got what he deserved. He turned all righteous on me. Too bad I didn't make him suffer more."

Out of the corner of Elias's eye, he saw Holmes and his men pull up and surround the house. One of the officers hid in the bush behind Tom, not twenty feet away, ready to bring him down.

Tom brought the knife up to his forehead. Blood dripped from the tip onto Jane's shoulder and chest. He swayed, then righted himself. "You know this is not my fault," Tom said low enough that only Elias and Jane heard him.

"What are you talking about?" Elias took another step closer. "You killed all those women."

"I'm not stupid. Tell those FBI fuckers to stay back or the bitch will die. I don't care." Tom had the knife to Jane's chest. She winced as he twisted the blade and the tip pierced her skin. Jane cried out in pain. "I told you, tell them to back off."

"Keep back," Elias shouted. "Tom, you said I don't know. Tell me."

Tom straightened up. Stone cold eyes directed at him. "My poor bitch of a mother ruined me. She wanted me to cut out the welts my grandfather gave her. But she made me take it too far and... she died and left me to my grandfather." He dragged the tip of the knife down Jane's arm, to her fingers and back up to her chest. "Do you know my grandfather showed me the way to right-eousness by punishment? I didn't want to learn, but I had to—endure." Tom paused to wipe the corner of his eyes with the back of his hand. "He also taught me that all women are whores. They had to be beaten to learn abstinence." Tom laughed. "I remember Grandfather would come into my mother's room. He'd fuck her, then beat her for her sins... You can't hide. I know you're there." He called back toward the bush and turned back to Elias.

"Tom, don't do this," Elias said, his finger sitting on the trigger. "We can work something out."

"Do you want to see how it feels to watch your whore be killed right in front of your eyes? I did. My grandfather taught me no mercy."

"Deputy, put down the knife and we can talk," Holmes shouted. He stepped out from behind the house. He walked up beside Elias and stopped. "Put down the knife and let Jane Doe go."

"Her name isn't Jane Doe, asshole—and I don't have nothing to say to you," Tom spat out.

"What about me, Tom?" Elias inched forward another step. "I'm here. You want the job? You can have it."

Tom's face lost all expression. "If you take another step Elias, I'll pluck her heart out." He then looked at her. "Poor Christina. She already lost a lot of blood from her foot." He shook her like a rag doll and gave her a kiss on her temples. "I can see why you keep her close. She tastes yummy."

"Christina? Is that what Jane's real name?" Elias

sighed in relief. She was paler than usual, but she was alive.

"Don't you want to know why I did this, Elias?" Tom asked in a sweet tone, a total contradiction to the evil in his eyes. The way he trailed the tip of the knife up and down Jane's skin was the opposite to his delivery.

Elias had one chance to get to Jane. Since there were many guns trained on Tom, he lowered his weapon and took a large step. "Yes, I do. But you need to put down the knife."

"Don't tell me what I need to do!" Tom pointed the knife straight at her neck.

"All right. I'm listening, but please don't hurt her," Elias said, dropping the gun.

"I did this because... I can." Tom chuckled.

"How long have you and Henley been doing this?" Holmes interrupted.

"Forever," he whispered, looking down at Jane.

Elias didn't like the way the deputy said that. He took another step closer, hoping what he said next would drag Tom's attention back to him. "I know why Henley left me in charge. He always told me in private that he didn't trust you."

Tom's head snapped up and he took a step toward Elias. "Trust? He had no clue what trust was. You want to know why I killed him? Because the bastard told me I had to stop. He said I'd get caught." Tom spat. "I shot the bastard with his own gun. And no one found out."

"Until now," Elias countered. He glanced down at Jane. Her eyes were closed.

"Until now," Tom laughed. "Do you know how many women I've had over the years? Lots and lots. From all over the world. I'm that good. I would have never gotten caught."

"Why don't you put the knife down?" Holmes asked as he sidestepped to Elias's left.

Tom ignored the officer's question. "Since it's a day of confessions, the first person I had the pleasure of killing was my cousin Jane. How ironic, ha? She was thirteen. Hardly a woman, but..." Tom shuddered and loosened his grip on Jane. He closed his eyes for only a second. "Jane whined constantly. She was visiting my grandfather. I had to teach her a lesson of obedience, like my grandfather had taught me. But you know what? I really didn't mean to kill her. I got so caught up that I couldn't help myself."

"Tom. It's over. Drop the knife," Elias said evenly. He was a few feet from them, but Jane wasn't out of danger yet.

"I can still see her, you know. She haunts me, but I don't give a fuck. She can't hurt me," Tom whispered, and then shouted, "You can't hurt me, bitch!"

"Oh yes, she can," Harold screeched as he raced out from the other side of the woods. "Jane's here for you, Tom."

Harold was knocked down by one of the officers. The rifle in his hands went off, biting off a chunk of the brittle wood siding on the colonial house. He was quickly grabbed and dragged back to safety.

Tom wrenched Jane around her middle and pulled her off her feet. The tip of the knife dug into Jane's neck. "Don't come any closer!"

"I want to take him alive," Holmes shouted at his team.

Jane's eyes popped open. Even from a distance, her eyes were as black as onyx. Her face held no emotion. Elias knew this wasn't going to end well. The little girl had taken over her body.

"Tom, you can't do this," Jane said, but her voice was different, childlike.

Tom released Jane and spun her around.

The deputy's face had turned ashen. He stumbled back from her, waving the knife between them. "You stay away from me. You're dead." Eyes wide, fear now etched around his gaping mouth. Tom tripped, almost dropping the knife, but quickly regained his balance.

Jane tilted her head. "Did you miss me, cousin?"

He shifted the knife into his other hand. He extended the point to her. "I—"

"Yes, Tommy." Jane smiled. The wind picked up like a mini tornado. Blasts of snow, dirt and decayed leaves swirled around them. "Yes, it's me, Janie," she said, taking a step closer to him.

Elias wanted to lunge forward and grab her but she stepped out of reach. Jane was still within arm's reach of Tom's knife.

"Why, Tommy?" Her voice gargled out.

"I'm sorry. Grandfather made me do it," Tom replied as he took another step back from her. He trembled. "Get away from me!"

"Tommy, why? I loved you."

Tom shook his head, shrieked and lunged toward her with the knife.

Elias swore his heart stopped. He reacted without thought. He rolled over, grabbed his gun from his waistband and shot. Right before the tip touched Jane's skin, two bullets hit Tom. One was his.

His aim was true and went straight to Tom's head, while the other was from Holmes, which hit the deputy's wrist. The knife dropped, and so did Tom.

Jane collapsed too, hitting the ground hard. Elias raced over to her side, took off his jacket and covered her with it. His voice cracked when he spoke. "You're safe now, Jane. He can't hurt you anymore."

Elias stared down at the shallow cuts along her skin. The small gashes would heal, but she'd have the inner scars for the rest of her life. He wrapped his arms around Jane and held her tight.

"Elias?"

"I'm here," Elias said. He held Jane tighter.

"I-I can't breathe."

Elias choked out a laugh. "Sorry. The paramedics will be here shortly. Just hang on." When he lifted her up and carried her to the truck, he noticed Jane's foot. "Damn." He placed her in the driver's seat, raced to the cargo box in the back and got a blanket and a towel.

He covered her up in the wool blanket and wrapped the towel tight around her foot to stop the bleeding.

A deluge of emotions overpowered Elias's controlled demeanor. There was so much to say, but not there.

"Elias." Jane's voice was weak, like her body.

"Everything is going to be all right now," Elias whispered.

"I know," she uttered, then burst into tears.

EPILOGUE

April 4th
Six months later

C hristina stood at the edge of Beaver Lake, looking out over the calm clear water. She watched the spring wind scatter the crisp leaves of last autumn over the expanse. The once yellowed grass showed heavy promise of green at the roots. Time for rebirth.

How could someone mar such a beautiful place?

She tried to ignore the small flags sticking out of the ground where the state police and FBI had found bodies. But they were too hard to forget. A slight chill ran down her spine. She could have been one of them. Christina remembered the desperation she had felt in Tom's basement—what he did to Caroline was unforgivable. He was a monster.

Her dark blonde hair whipped in her eyes; Christina controlled the strands by pushing them around her ears but she couldn't stop the tears. She'd come here to reflect, heal and say goodbye.

She sent a prayer of thanks to Jane Proster, Tom's

cousin and first victim. Without her, she might not have survived. Without her, the killings would have gone on.

Wiping her tears away, Christina vowed to never forget the people who were involved, dead and alive. Her nightmares had robbed her of her sleep at first, but day by day they had eased—with the help of Elias. He made her forget. She looked back at the truck, where he sat on top of the hood, watching her with a smile.

Christina had to laugh. In these past six months, her life had changed drastically. The sad truth was, her life began when she was found half-buried in the ground. Strange, but she couldn't imagine going back to her old life. Elias was a big part of that.

Christina couldn't imagine her life without *him*. He was the pillar she leaned on when she was about to fall. He gave her a reason to stand strong and fight back. She loved him for that.

Ripples in the water turned Christina's thoughts back to the girl in the yellow dress. They had found Jane's remains only a few feet from where she stood, along the water's edge, just past the tall reeds and cattails.

Christina took the crisp air into her lungs and walked over to where Jane's post stuck out. "I will always remember you. Thank you, Jane," she said, sniffling back the tears.

Out of the corner of her eye, she saw the little girl in her yellow sundress. She stood a few feet from her. She smiled with such tenderness, mouthed "thank you," and then disappeared.

Tears rushed down. Christina sensed happiness, closure. She laughed and cried at the same time.

Christina looked back at Elias. She could tell he was antsy to get moving. He kept adjusting his Giant's cap.

Through all this, a miracle of love had occurred. She

sent out one last prayer, turned and headed back to her future.

*   *   *

Elias slid off the hood and watched Christina walk back to him. She needed closure and so did he. During the last few months, he'd helped locate several bodies in the surrounding areas.

After the Feds excavated nearly twenty-nine bodies around Beaver Lake, calling those families that were local was the hardest thing Elias had ever done.

Most of the bones and decayed fragments were old and untraceable, but they'd been found and a proper burial was set for them.

The FBI traced back a few of the old unsolved murder cases that had common links. It went as far west as California and as far south as Florida. Over forty-five more possible murders were thought to be connected to either Henley or Tom, but without solid proof, no one knew for sure.

Going through Tom's house, they found Caroline's body. They also found shredded clothes, shoes and a few personal belongings that linked to other victims. Hundreds of boxes of black hair dye linked to the murders, too. He never understood why Tom dyed the victims' hair. Maybe the color reminded him of his mother, but Elias would never know. No one would.

It saddened him that serial killers like Tom and Henley went without notice until absolute carnage happened. Nonetheless, their killing spree was finally over. People could move on, especially him.

He'd stepped down from the chief's position and Tyson Ryan was appointed in his place. The mayor was elated with the results. Poor Tyson.

Elias helped hire three more qualified officers and then settled a few more issues that the mayor had brought up. He forewarned the new chief to keep a level head when it came to Mayor Daniels, but that might be asking too much of even a patient man.

Elias had finally sold the farmhouse. Beth and Tyson, who were expecting twins in November, bought it. The house needed new, happy memories, and he was glad to let it go for half the market value.

With encouragement from Christina, he contacted the Half Moon Police Department. He was able to get his job back with probationary measures, which was fine by him.

Magda recovered fully and her resolution to retire soon made him happy. Her decision to visit her home in Georgia came as a surprise, but Elias thought it was about time. She told him life was too short to hold onto old ghosts. It was time to live. So true, those words.

Elias was in full agreement. All he needed was his Christina.

Christina smiled as she reached the truck. He drew her in his arms and kissed her soundly. "Are you ready to go?" he asked, with another kiss.

"Yes." She smiled back and touched his cheek. "Are you?"

Without saying a word, he led her to the passenger side of the truck and opened it.

Once she got in, Elias closed her door and walked back to the driver's side. He slammed his door shut, put the truck into drive and looked over at Christina. "I'm ready now."

He turned the truck around and they never looked back.

LETTER TO THE READER

To My Readers,

I want to you thank you for reading Forgetting Jane. This was my first novel I wrote and I'm really proud of how this story developed into. I hope you fell in love with Elias and Jane, like I did. Their journey might be done here, but who knows where they might pop up elsewhere.

Please leave a review. It would greatly appreciated. It takes a village to spread the word!

Smooches,

CJ

ABOUT THE AUTHOR

CJ Warrant is an Award Winning Author for dark romantic suspense and contemporary romance that pulls at your heart, makes you shiver with fear, and hope for a happy ending. A lover of coffee, baking and family, CJ's Korean Italian heritages are a great influence in her life. Her stories stir in dark plots with addictive flawed characters you will fall in love with.

Want more of CJ's world? She would love to hear from her readers. Come join her:

www.cjwarrant.com
https://www.instagram.com/cjwarrant
https://www.twitter.com/cjwarrant
https://www.pinterest.com/cjwarrant
https://www.bookbub.com/profile/cj-warrant

Come join me on CJ's facebook group, The Coven. https://www.facebook.com/groups/167874440806362/

BOOKS BY CJ WARRANT

ROMANTIC-SUSPENSE/THRILLER

Mirror Image

Dance of the Mourning Cloak

Protecting Delaina

SAINTS-VS-SINNERS-SERIES

Deacon, book 1

CHANGE-AT-LOVE-SERIES

Four Days

One Kiss

Two of Hearts

Five Seasons of Love

Three Times Lucky

BOBA-BOOK-BABES-MYSTERIES

Pandemonium in Peoria, Book 1, Boba Book Babes Mysteries

CJ-BARLOWE-MM-ROMANCE-BOOKS

Killer Notes, Book 1, Warrior Black Series

Beyond the Stix, Book 2 , Warrior Black Series

PROTECTING DELAINA

A Dark Romantic Thriller

CHAPTER ONE

MERRICK

Under the intense August heat of the Florida sun, I lie still beneath the old mangrove roots on the west side of the property where my mark resides. My legs are partially submerged in swamp water, surrounded by an ecosystem that can swim up and bite me in the ass and suck me under until I'm primed for eating.

All of this, for a cool mil. Is it worth it? Yes... or so I thought until I saw my mark.

"The money is too good to pass up, Merrick," Joe, my handler, insisted to me a few weeks ago before I relented and accepted the job. I want to beat the shit out of him at times for picking up contracts that put my life in a precarious place. Like this fucking swamp filled with gators.

The money will be worthless to me if I'm dead.

I shove that thought aside and focus on the mobile home in my line of sight. When I first arrived on this God forsaken inlet, I thought I'd finish the job within the day. But I immediately had reservations on pulling the trigger. My gut told me to hold off. The niggling suspicion that keeps pounding louder in my head hasn't relented with each passing hour either.

Why? I simply don't know.

I have no problem taking out garbage from this world. With a single bullet from my *Katie,* a CheyTac M200 with an NXS scope, they forfeit their lives for the shitty things they've done in this world. *If* they deserve it. And normally they do. Then I slink my sorry ass back to my tiny unencumbered town in the northern part of Vermont with the easy cash in my account.

However, this mark's different. She's a woman—which I don't have an issue killing—if she deserves it. But I've been watching Delaina Wells for a full week. She's no scum of the earth like my usual marks. She has no outrageous wealth displayed. Hell, the 1985 beige Subaru Outback she drives is band-aided together with silver duct tape on the front and back bumpers. I can guarantee that vehicle has way more miles on its four-cylinder engine than most old clunkers on the road.

She parks that piece of shit at the airpark across the waterway and every day drives it to the café she works at in Everglade City. Then she takes the outboard skiff that's tied to the tiny pier to this ten-acre property, where her single-wide sits like a rusted out open sore.

Delaina's no beauty queen. And what I mean by that is there's no vanity shown in her. By clothing or jewelry, or the minimal makeup regimen she undergoes on the daily. There haven't been any extravagant shopping trips or expensive salon visits. Her light brown, curly hair is always up in a messy bun on top of her head, except when a few tendrils get free and frame her oval face. Then my fingers twitch, and I want to walk up to her and sweep them around her ears, to see if her hair feels as soft as it appears to be.

Simple is what I would call her. And breathtaking.

Her rich espresso eyes might be called hypnotic, but the smattering of freckles across the bridge of her straight nose is damn distracting.

Delaina's just shy of five-six, with long, attractive legs. Her bronzed skin is reminiscent of smooth expensive silk, which has me thinking all too much of touching her in ways I shouldn't be thinking about my mark.

I quickly bury that frisson of want deep down where no thoughts grow and remain eye contact through my scope.

The woman lives paycheck to paycheck, with barely a hundred dollars in her savings account. When I say Delaina Wells is no one special to pay attention to, more ordinary than most, I'm talking truth. She isn't the typical garbage I focus down the barrel for. Not a scumbag at all.

Then why does someone want her dead?

That question is on repeat in my head, but I come up with nothing.

I pull just a hair back when a glint of silver catches my peripheral to the left. I freeze, and slowly—very slowly, turn my head a few millimeters in that direction.

There. Against a Florida pine, I see it—or should I say, him... or her. Where hitmen are concerned, there's no discrimination on the genders.

Damn it. An overwhelming need to protect Delaina rushes at me like a three-hundred-pound linebacker. Besides, I got here first.

As to whoever is hiding in the underbrush across the way, I decide to change my tactics and see who's after my mark. With a million on the line, there's no doubt this killer is here to take out Delaina and collect the big cash prize.

Leaving my Katie on point, I silently slither deeper

into the swamp water until my nostrils skim above the waterline. I cringe at the rotten egg stench of the Everglades. But what do you expect from the combination of wet earth, decaying vegetation, and stagnant saltwater surrounding me.

Staying near the edge of the bank, I slowly creep forward but remain alert for nearby gators, cottonmouths, or eastern corals.

With my KA-BAR knife in hand, I glide silently to that side of the property. Not ten feet away, there're legs camouflaged by fabricated grasses, dirt, and pine branches. If I want to surprise this fucker, I have to be quick.

Cautiously I move closer. Five feet away now. I'm about to leap out of the water when Delaina's loud skiff chuffs up to the small rickety dock that is on its last pillar.

Shit. She's home early.

I have to take down this hitter before he reacts and pulls the trigger, and Delaina ends up with a bullet in her head.

A slight shift disturbs a pine branch that's stacked on top of the human mound. Before Delaina reaches the mobile home, I don't hesitate and launch at the sneaky fucker. But the assassin knew where I was, too, and quickly twists his upper torso, pointing the 9 mm right at my face.

I swiftly knock the guy's Ruger out of his hold, slice at his wrist and immediately turn him on his back. He grunts in pain while trying to wrestle out of my grasp, but I draw my knife under his chin, barely cutting into the flesh next to his jugular.

With my knees locking down his arms, blood pooling from his lacerated wrist, I lean in and put a finger to my lips to tell him to stay quiet.

I take this moment to memorize his pocked face. Bald, a bit on the rangy side. His light blue eyes are cold, calculating, and emotionless. Like mine.

He doesn't move, not even his eyes, which are trained on my face and boring through me like honed ice picks. Considering his Winchester Magnum is pointed toward Delaina's place, the implication of who this man is and why he's here rings true to my earlier scenario. He's here to take out *my* mark.

The sound of keys rattling perks my ears, but my eyes remain coldly faceted on the killer under me. Then the front door of Delaina's trailer slams shut. It must not be a good day for her either.

Knowing I'm in the clear, I lean in almost nose to nose and demand, "Who the fuck are you?" Nothing but chill comes off his silent demeanor. So, I repeat myself, as I tuck the knife tighter against his neck until a thin line of blood forms on the blade's edge. "Who the fuck are you?"

"Why are you on my mark?" he counters evenly, as though we're having a casual conversation.

"Last time, buddy." I know this is a useless question, but I have to try. "Who hired you to be on *my* mark?"

"You know how this game goes, Merrick Gentry. Now, either kill me or get the fuck off of me."

How in the hell does he know my name?

I know I've made a name in this business, but no one knows my face... Until now.

I don't go sharing my shit worldwide. So this is a problem.

I study his face a bit more. There's a slight sheen of perspiration across his furrowed brows. In his steady gaze there's a knowing that he's a dead man, no matter what he says. Hell, I wouldn't either if I was in his shoes. But I'm better than him.

I tighten my hold on the knife, the edge of the blade cutting deeper into his flesh. "How do you know me?" I emphasize with open hostility.

A smirk mixed with pain shadow across his face. "Everyone knows who you are now, Merrick. And as for your previous question, I'm here for the same reason as you are. One. Million. Dollars."

His words have my body locking even tighter than Aunt Winnie's pickle jar.

"Everyone knows who I am." What, the, fuck?

It's dawning on me that someone has two hitters for one slip of a woman. Why?

Now there's no way I'm killing Delaina Wells—not until I get to the bottom of this shit.

For a second, my mind drifts and the asshole takes advantage. His right arm slips free from under my left knee, and the sneaky bastard slams a small dagger he pulled out of nowhere and the short blade cuts into the outer edge of my thigh. The knife might be small, but it's lethal and sharp.

Thankfully, it didn't hit my Femoral Artery, which this asshole was aiming for.

I snap my teeth closed and quietly hiss, "Fuck." Blood seeps through my slashed cargos, but I can't worry about it right now.

I bite back a growl as he pulls the blade out and tries to jab at my face, but I don't hesitate and slice my fat blade across his throat. He lets out a strangled gasp as blood gushes out of his carotid. My hand covers his gaping mouth as he gurgles out his last breath. The blue of his eyes loses its intensity and the panic fades into stillness.

Fuck. Fuckity-fuck!

I didn't want to kill him just yet. I have more questions about who hired him and what he meant by everyone knowing who I am now. But he left me with no choice.

This isn't what I expected today. But in this line of work, one has to anticipate the unexpected. Even with another hitman coming at you.

I take in a heavy breath and release it, centering myself before digging into the killer's pockets.

Finding a receipt time-stamped seven-ten yesterday morning from the restaurant where Delaina works, my gut twists at the idea that he knew I was already here. Honestly, I'm surprised he didn't take me out firsthand before aiming his barrel at Delaina. His loss.

There's a hiss and a splash behind me. I turn, eyeing movements in the water. I quickly check the rest of the dead man's pockets, finding nothing else—not even a wallet. Then I pull his lifeless body into the water.

"Gator bait," I say with a smile.

Once the body is submerged, I ease back to my place under the mangrove tree. After checking my wound, I dry the area and superglue the small one-inch gash. Then I turn my attention back to the trailer, but this time I keep my legs out of the water.

With solid ground under me, I hear loud crashes coming from inside the trailer. I'm instantly on alert. Looking through the scope, the dirty, screened windows show nothing but closed blinds.

Right then, Delaina stumbles out of the trailer with a bottle of tequila in hand and plops her shapely ass down on the small wooden porch and starts bawling. I see her lips moving with soundless words. Between the tears falling from her eyes and the agony across her—bruised face?

"Now where the fuck did you get those bruises?" I whisper, knowing her face was unmarred when she left this morning.

She continues talking and crying to herself, having a full blown argument with no one. My heart speeds up and my gut knots at seeing her distressed. There's no fucking way I can ever put a bullet in her. She is one of the innocents I promised myself a long time ago I would never kill, for any amount of money.

After a guttural scream, Delaina guzzles back what's left of the alcohol in the bottle and then chucks the glass container against the rusted metal shed before stalking back inside and slamming the door.

In the week I've been observing her, not once did she show any rage or displeasure. Until today.

Someone has put those bruises on Delaina's face and has her so angry that she turns to alcohol. I want to know who. And I want to know now.

There's only one person who can give me those answers. I pull out my phone and call Joe.

This is his deal. Joe should be able to scratch up more information about Delaina's life and why she's so important that someone wants her dead, and hires two hitmen. Who could have laid their hand on her? And how did the other hitman know who I am?

"Job done already?" Joe briskly answers the phone, surprise edging his voice.

"Did you send another hitter to my mark?" Silence. "Joe? Do I need to track you down and put the hurt on your sorry ass?"

"No—"

"Don't fucking lie to me, asshole," I warn, turning toward the waters and watching a white egret take flight and lands on the nearby sandy shore. The bird has a tranquil bearing, which reminds me of Delaina. But underneath the wild beauty surrounding her, there lies danger. And I'm one of them.

"I'm not. Why would I do a stupid thing like that?" Joe admits with a hesitation.

"Because I took one out not ten minutes ago," I say with clenched teeth. "He also said that everyone knows who I am. What the fuck does that mean, Joe? What did you get me into?"

A rush of clicks echoes from the other end of the phone. "Hold on—Shit. Did the hitter actually say that?"

"Yes," I spit out.

"Okay—okay. Give me a second." He mumbles through the clicks and clacks, while I impatiently lay there under the shade, but my eyes trained on the now-quiet trailer.

After a several long minutes, my tolerance is worn so thin, it's clear as glass. "Well?"

"The client that took out the contract hired three more hitters. The latest one just five minutes ago."

What the fuck? Three? Four including me.

"How's this possible?" I utter, more to myself than to Joe.

"Whoever wants her dead has to be desperate," Joe says with more clicks on his end. "But the job is done, right?"

I snort. "No."

"What? Why?"

"Did you get any leads why my name is out there?" I growl out, completely ignoring his question.

"No, not yet. But, dude, what are you waiting for? Finish the contract." There's a hint of desperation in his voice, which isn't like Joe at all. Granted, there have been times that he's opened his mouth before thinking, but that's due to over imbibing in too much caffeine. Or he hasn't slept for more than two days. But I don't think this is one of those times.

"Something is off," I finally admit, glancing down at the screen.

"Shit, Merrick. This isn't the time to think. Tell me she'll be dead by the end of today and we could walk away with the million."

The greedy motherfucker.

"I want to know what's so important about this girl, and who in Delaina Wells's life would put their hands on her. I also want the name on who's spreading my name and face around. Got me, Joe?" I demand with rising annoyance, ignoring his whiny plea.

He expels a hitched breath. "Fine," he drags out. "If there's more to this girl, I'll find it."

Joe's the best damn hacker around. That's one reason why he's my handler, aside from a few other qualities about the money-grubbing bastard.

"I want everything as soon as you get it. Understand?" I glance back at the trailer. "Look into the property, too. It bumps up against the Everglades. It might be worth something, if someone thinks it's worth killing for."

"Nothing's different from what I emailed you last week."

"I don't want a fucking recap, Joe. Give me something new," I growl into the phone.

"You're not going to kill her, are you?" A curbed irritation settles in his tone.

"Joe," I bark, but it's too late, the asshole hung up. I glare down at my phone before tucking it back into my pocket. I hate it when he hangs up on me. It's a pet peeve I can't stand, and Joe does it all the fucking time. On purpose.

I don't give two shits if Joe's pissed off. Money isn't as important to me as it is to him. I don't kill the innocent, and this mark is innocent. I can feel it down to my bones that I'm right.

As for Delaina's basic background, which is basic and easy to remember. Her stepfather, Brent Miller, owns three car dealerships. One in Sarasota, another in Miami, and one in Orlando. And her stepbrother, Mark is the sales manager for the Orlando branch. There is no blood family living.

She's alone.

But there's more than meets the eye with Delaina Wells. And if I'm going to find out, I will need to get close to her. With a million up for grabs, my concern at this point is the other hitmen coming for her. Tomorrow, with Treg's help, I will uncover who my mark really is.

www.ingramcontent.com/pod-product-compliance
Lightning Source LLC
Chambersburg PA
CBHW071737110726
47908CB00006B/1619